SPIRIT WARRIOR MAIDEN'S PATH

Tracey Love

Spirit Warrior: Maiden's Path

First printing edition, 2023.
ISBN# 979-8-9893693-0-0

Cover art by Yosbe Design.

Dedication

To my mom, Laurel, who showed me the magic that exists in stories. Who taught me the importance of please and thank you, that a promise is sacred, that saying I'm sorry means changed behavior, and that it's the simple things in life that are the best. Although you're in spirit now, you always believed with your whole heart that I'd accomplish this goal. I promised you long ago that I would dedicate my first book to you someday, but I know you wouldn't mind sharing the honor with the daughter-in-law that you adored so much.

To my sweet wife, my love, and my best friend, Michelle, who has stood by me patiently and in genuine faith as I have worked to step into the reality of the last name I chose for myself and now share with you. Who has shared so many adventures with me, reminded me about the magic found in nature, and taught me all about the power of hope.

I dedicate this book to you, Mom and Michelle, two of the best friends and greatest forms of support I have ever known, two of the people who've encouraged me to be myself and live my truth. Thank you for everything! I love you both!

Gratitude Pages

Kristy, my soul Sistah. The first person to help me understand soul family. Thank you for knowing my soul and helping me know it more myself. For listening to my stories, both real and fictional - my sweet dreams and beautiful nightmares. And for being dark and magical with me, despite our humanity.

Dusty, my forever friend. Thank you for being my first best friend and first sister. For sharing precious childhood memories and continuing to grow and make memories with me through every season of life. For being the first person that I could share secrets with and being here when it matters most. And for making me an Auntie to my beautiful nieces, Alyssa and Emma.

Gramma (Margeurite). Thank you for being the first to help me begin to understand and embrace my light and magic. Although you've been in spirit for so long, your quiet, gentle wisdom continues to give me a foundation for going much deeper than the human experience.

Kim and Dan, my dear friends and sponsors. Thank you for the time we spend being weird and genuine together and for your generosity. The support you've given me, not only financially but through your sincere belief in me, has been invaluable. Artists wouldn't succeed without this kind of support.

Jennifer, my friend, business partner, alpha reader, and spiritual counsel. Thank you for wearing all those hats, being salty with me, and reminding me how darkness and light can play together so nicely.

Amber, my Anam Kara (soul friend). Thank you for being among the first people to be excited about and supportive of my Spirit Warrior series and for helping me create the series' name and logo. For reminding me what the light feels like. For all the spiritual lessons, even the painful and difficult ones. Maybe, most importantly, for challenging me to become a stronger feminist and kinder human being.

Jess, my friend and fellow author. Thank you for the hours spent talking about characters and storylines, for inspiring me to go deep in ways I never knew I could, and for introducing me to the fun additions to my series, like character art, playlists, and mood boards. And for introducing me to your badass character, Rio; I can't wait to hold your books in my hand.

Craig, my friend who's more like a brother. Thank you for making me believe that I was smart enough to go to college – you had no idea what you started.

Sam, my sis. Thank you for your support, inspiration, and friendship and for being my official photographer, someone who can capture my spirit in such a genuine way.

Vicki and Lori, my mentors. Thank you for helping me establish my early foundation of feminism and social justice. I wouldn't have known how to tell this story the same way without your early guidance.

To my spiritual community, especially Deana and Pam. Thank you for walking this journey of growth with me so that I might better understand how to tell my stories in the name of collective and generational healing.

To the compassionate therapists who've helped me heal, Barb, Li, and Stephanie.

To the cats who have shared their lives with me, especially Kitty, Sunshine, Jasper, Thea, Jazmine, Maggie, Willow, and Storm. Thank you for your wisdom and kitty vibes.

Emily, my book coach. Thank you for pushing me out of my comfort zone and helping me see how to draw out the most important parts of my story more deeply to make them shine. For helping me understand how to take the leap to begin book coaching.

Yosbe Design, my cover artist. Thank you for getting my vibe from the start and working with me to ensure my story was so beautifully represented on my cover.

To the other people who see themselves depicted as characters in this book. Thank you for changing my soul in your own special way.

Honestly, my gratitude is endless. I keep a piece of everyone I've met with me as a lesson and reflection of my journey and myself. Thank you to the fellow storytellers, poets, and artists, especially Jody and George; living your passion helps others do so, too. To all my friends and family who've loved me and believed in me, my donors, reviewers, and promoters. To my soulful readers. Thank you for going on this journey with me. Finally, to the Spirit Warriors out there. Thank you for bravely choosing to heal and refusing to let the world destroy your divine energy. The Generational and Collective Healing Movements needs each and every one of you.

A note on trigger warnings:

As a trauma survivor, it is importance to me to be sensitive to the pain of others. As a Spirit Warrior, my movement and message would be incomplete if I failed to remind you that exposure to triggers is also an opportunity for healing. When we avoid our triggers forever, we also avoid healing. You are the ultimate authority and expert of yourself, so trust your gut; only you have a say in if, when, and how you heal. Stories act as windows and mirrors – windows that look in on others' lives and mirrors in which we see ourselves. If you see yourself in the mirror as you read my story, may you find the courage to choose healing, whatever that looks like for you.

Trigger warnings:

While no explicit details are present, childhood sexual abuse is part of the main character's story. Racism, xenophobia, homophobia, biphobia, fatphobia, body image issues, and internalized phobias, as well as mention of a hate crime, are present in the story, and a homophobic slur is used. The use of alcohol and marijuana are present in the story. Mental health issues, self-harm, and suicidal ideation are mentioned, although self-harm is not depicted in a scene.

CHAPTER ONE

It wasn't as if she wanted to live in a cabin deep in the forest summoning woodland creatures, but Susan had certainly imagined something far more magical than working retail at Barnes and Noble. Still, shelving fresh titles with that new-book smell always made her feel better, no matter how bad her day had been. She clacked them as hard as she could against the back of the shelf today, finding it difficult to fight her crabby mood. The store had been hectic, and familiar thoughts of escape filled her head, not just from Barnes and Noble but nearly every part of her mundane life.

She stood back and released a breath as she saw the end result, a row of rainbow spines on the Pride Month display, all in perfect order. Books gave her something that therapy never had. They let her escape the world and offered her a mirror that allowed her to see herself more clearly. She looked around the store at the people milling about and shook her head; how the hell had she ended up in Worcester, Massachusetts? As much as she loved books, working retail would never bring her joy. There were far more adventurous possibilities out there than the confines of this little world she was living in at the moment. At the same time, she recognized the irony; she'd gotten exactly what she'd asked for: a life surrounded by books. Maybe she needed to be a little more specific when she lit a candle and asked the universe for what she wanted.

From the time she was very young, she'd been perplexed about how the world worked, especially about people and the things they did. She couldn't remember a time when she hadn't dreamt of escape. Even starting kindergarten had felt like a ridiculous concept. It made no sense why she should go to a noisy place where everything scared her. She had her mom and gramma at home to keep her safe, and the outdoors offered her all the adventure she could ever dream of. But now, at twenty-three, a recent graduate of the Worcester State College class of 1997, nothing was different. If anything, the feelings just seemed to intensify as she got older.

She'd played the game. Earned the college degree with the plan of living a better life with more security than her mom or gramma had known. But she still couldn't say what the English degree had done for her other than the value of the learning itself. The vast worldview, which the small-town life she'd lived never could've provided, was still something, but the degree certainly hadn't delivered the security or happiness that the world had led her to believe it would. And it was naïve to think that college could have ever given her direction; only her soul could provide that. But here she was, locked into a full-time retail job where she had to interact with people just so she could pay off her student loans and pay rent. So much for adventure.

"Excuse me, could you tell me where I could find the poetry section? I could swear it used to be right there."

Susan looked up, locking eyes with the woman who'd just spoken to her. As if her weakness for a woman with dreadlocks wasn't enough, the wide, beaming smile drew Susan in even more. Heart thumping, she attempted to speak without letting her awkward nature come spilling out.

"Oh, yeah. We just did some rearranging..." She paused, looking away. Although her gaydar was spiking, she resisted the urge to add that the changes had been to make room for the Pride Month displays. You had to play it safe in a world filled with hate. "...we have people all confused." She fidgeted, making sure to pull her dark green polo shirt down over her gut.

"Good, it's not just me." The woman smiled, a single dimple emerging.

"Come on, I'll show you where we hid the poetry." Susan smiled back, pleased with herself for getting the thought out without tripping on her words.

"Well, at least there's one perk," the woman said, smirking.

Susan looked at her, puzzled.

"I have a beautiful woman to escort me to the poetry. Get to talk to you for a few minutes."

Susan felt her cheeks flush. People had always told her that her every feeling showed in her hazel green eyes, so she turned away to hide the shyness mixed with giddy pleasure that ran through her. It took great focus to remember where she was headed. Was this gorgeous woman actually flirting, or was she just charming? Susan had made that painful mistake before.

"I've seen you here a few times and wanted to talk to you," the woman said.

In awe, Susan turned to look at her, meeting her deep brown eyes for a quick moment and then willing herself to speak. "Me?"

The woman laughed. "Yes, you. You're the manager here, right?"

"Assistant manager," Susan replied.

"Well, I have seen you doing your thing here. I know you're good at what you do. This is more than just a job to you."

"Thanks. I love it most days. Just being with the books..." Susan smiled but shifted her eyes down to the floor. What a book nerd.

"I know a lot of things. I'm Tamika, by the way."

"I'm Susan."

Neither of them seemed to notice that they'd stopped walking and had arrived at the poetry section.

"Well, Susan, I can tell that you like books more than you like people, but you have a good heart. I can tell that you can be serious if you have to be, but you prefer to let go, to be a little more...free."

"Wow. That's just plain witchcraft. Are you sure you aren't looking for a book on improving your psychic work?" Susan laughed, feeling herself soften a bit and allowing herself to meet Tamika's eyes again.

"Oh, I own a few *magical* books." Tamika winked.

Susan's stomach fluttered. "Are you looking for something specific here?" Susan asked, waving her hand over the poetry section.

"Yeah, I'm looking for Bell Hooks' *Ain't I a Woman*," Tamika replied.

"No fucking way!" Susan's mouth fell open, and she put her hand on her chest, fully giving in to the book nerd.

Tamika laughed. "Somehow, I'm not surprised that this title excites you."

She was so smooth. Although Susan loved words, getting things out of her mouth the same way that she felt them was not her strong suit. She was far more eloquent on paper.

"I actually read it in my freshman year in college for a feminist lit class, and it's just so...it's a favorite now," Susan said, speaking with her hands and emitting a little sigh.

"No kidding. That's why *I* need the book. I'm starting that class next week at Worcester State."

"That's where I took it. Who are you taking it with?" Susan asked.

"Fox," Tamika replied.

"Yup, that's who I had." Susan shook her head slowly.

"Uh oh."

"Oh no; she's great. Passionate about what she teaches..."

"I like passionate." Tamika interrupted her.

Susan stumbled to finish her thought. "Ugh...but she's picky and weird about exams. If you get a B, she'll return it to you with feedback and won't let you quit until it's an A."

"Yikes. Good to know. With an accelerated summer course, *that* should be fun," Tamika said.

Susan smiled and thought about offering to help but decided that would be weird.

"So, you go to Worcester State, too?" Tamika asked.

"Actually, I graduated a few weeks ago. I earned my Associate's from Q.C.C., then transferred to Worcester State," Susan replied.

"Oh, that's amazing! Congratulations!"

"Thanks."

"I'll be done next May. This class will count as my last elective, and then, I'll just have my clinical rotation next year. Nursing," Tamika explained.

As Susan bent down to look at the bottom shelf, her long, brown ponytail fell forward, obscuring her view. She flipped the frizzy mess backward, thumbing through the shelf. She stood up to face Tamika again when she realized why she couldn't find the title she was looking for.

"About the book...I have some bad news. I just remembered I just reordered it last week. We only stock two copies of that title; we must have sold both."

"How long will it take to come in? Summer classes are just *so* fast-paced, and it's the first one on the reading list."

"Ugh, they really are. It will probably take another four or five days."

Tamika sighed.

"They didn't have any at the campus bookstore?"

"No. They sold out, too. Said they'd order more, but there's just not a lot of time."

"Hey! Listen...I don't want this to sound...I mean, I *have* the book. You could borrow it." She shrugged, and her stomach dropped as soon as she'd said it.

"Aww. That's so sweet. Really?"

She giggled and nodded. Tamika's wide smile made Susan feel like she might liquify right there on the carpet.

"Are you around tonight? I could take you to dinner or something to say thank you. We could celebrate your graduation."

Was she for real? "Oh, wow, thanks. Sure! I get off at six."

"Probably be a few hours later," Tamika replied with a grin.

"Oh. Umm...I mean, whatever works for you is fine," Susan said, confused.

"No, I was...never mind." Still wearing the grin, Tamika brushed Susan's hand with a fingertip.

Susan could feel her arm shake a little with the touch and hoped it didn't show.

"Any place special you like?" Tamika asked.

After Tamika's touch, Susan struggled to find words; she'd never felt anything like it. "Umm...uhh...do you like Chinese?"

"Love it," Tamika replied.

"How about Nancy Chang's? Right across from Tatnuck Bookseller," Susan suggested.

"Great choice. Do you want to just meet me there right after you leave here?" Tamika asked.

"That works for me, but...I'm here until six," Susan said, confused. Hadn't Tamika said it would be a few hours later?

"I'll see you then."

They stood silent for a minute. Susan looked at the shelves, unsure what to say now.

"I'm glad they didn't have the book. I'll see you in a few hours, Susan," Tamika said cooly with a single, firm nod, shining that smile again.

Hearing her name come out of Tamika's mouth left Susan breathless, so she was relieved she didn't have to speak.

Every minute of the last three hours and twenty-seven minutes of her shift dragged, but she forgot all about the bad mood she'd been in just minutes before. At first, she remembered every detail of the conversation with excitement. Tamika had definitely been flirty, hadn't she?

Eventually, the excitement turned to doubt and overthinking.

She'd sworn when Tamika had told her which book she was looking for. She never swore in front of customers. Maybe Tamika hadn't been flirty at all; she might be that way with everyone. She'd probably read too much into the things that Tamika had said. Maybe there wasn't the kind of connection she thought she felt between them. Maybe Tamika just needed the book. As it got closer to six, the doubt and overthinking turned into full-on dread. What could she even say to this strong, beautiful woman? Susan just knew she'd make a fool of herself somehow.

She tried to calm herself as she drove to the restaurant, telling herself it was just one dinner. Memories of previous dates that had turned out badly ran through her head. Was this even a date? She was guilty of making just about anything romantic when a woman drove her wild. She tried to drown out the thoughts with the radio but found herself unable to focus on driving, so she had to contend with the silence instead.

"Just chill out, Susan," she said aloud to herself.

Tamika spotted her and waved as Susan pulled in. She parked and fidgeted a little before getting out of the car, wishing she'd had time to change, even if she would've just thrown on her favorite jeans and a cute tee shirt. The khakis and polo shirt had been fine in the store, but now she felt frumpy. At least Tamika hadn't changed, either. She looked adorable in her hot pink and purple striped shirt and her ripped black jeans. Pulling her own shirt down over her belly as she got out of the car, Susan waved at Tamika across the parking lot. Tamika wasn't thin, but taking notice of her perfect curves, Susan was very aware of her size.

Tamika's bright smile flashed across the lot as she leaned against her seemingly brand-new, white Dodge Charger.

"How was the rest of your shift?" Tamika asked.

She never knew how to talk to people that way. To ask them about themselves without sounding strange.

"It was pretty good," she said simply, refusing to say that it had been torture waiting for this moment.

Susan felt more at ease once they were seated at a quiet table in the back.

"So, what kind of girl are you?" Tamika asked her, looking serious.

"Umm..." Susan just laughed, trying to think of something clever.

"Are you a scorpion bowl kind of girl? Because I think we should share a scorpion bowl."

"Oh, yeah. Sounds great," Susan said, relieved.

"Did I scare you?" Tamika asked gently.

"Naw." Susan waved her hand.

But they both knew that was bullshit.

"So, what was your major?"

"English and Women's Studies."

"So, you've probably read *all* the books I have to read for class," Tamika said, looking intrigued.

"Shit. The book." Susan put her hand over her eyes and shook her head. "I forgot to swing over to my place and grab the book."

Tamika reached over and touched her hand. Susan liked this about her. She needed touch to communicate. "Susan, I can see that I'm going to have to tell you straight out...I was hoping you would invite me back to your apartment later, anyway."

Susan felt her hand shake under Tamika's and withheld the nervous laughter that was rising up in her throat.

"Happy Friday, ladies. Here are some menus. Can I get you any drinks to start?" The waitress asked.

Tamika yanked her hand away. Though she was hungry for more of Tamika's touch, Susan was almost relieved that the waitress had interrupted them; sometimes, she didn't know what to do with herself when she felt the kind of intensity that Tamika's touch delivered.

"We'd like to share a scorpion bowl," Tamika said.

The waitress looked them both over. "Can I see some ID?"

Once satisfied, the waitress hurried away to retrieve their drink.

"What about you? What are you studying?" Susan had thought that one up when the waitress was still there.

"Nursing." Tamika shrugged.

"Oh right, you told me that. Sorry. You don't look too thrilled about it."

"I don't know. I mean, it's fine, I guess. No, as long as I get to work with children eventually, it's good. I just got to the point where I had to choose something. Right now, it's about getting out into the workforce and making some money. My degree will end up taking me six years to complete, so I'm just ready to be done."

Susan nodded, although she never could have chosen her major that way. She knew that was also probably why she was only an assistant manager at Barnes and Noble; what could you really do with an English degree if you didn't want to teach? But she couldn't imagine spending four years studying something she wasn't completely passionate about. English was the only major she ever considered. And when she had taken her first Women's Studies class, she knew instantly that she would double major.

"You sound like you have a five-year plan." Susan smiled, making air quotes.

"Oh, I absolutely do."

As Tamika's face grew more serious, Susan was even more attracted to her.

"I'm going to get a good job, save some money, buy a house, and have a few children...and a wife, of course. All by the time I'm thirty."

"Wow."

"Does that scare you?" Tamika asked again.

"No. I mean, it kind of impresses me, actually. I'm really not that good at being a grown-up." Susan laughed.

"That's okay." Tamika smiled.

As they ate, Susan discovered that Tamika was five years older than her, had grown up right there in Worcester, and had a younger brother, MJ. While Susan herself had been an only child raised by a single mother, Tamika had come from a conventional two-parent household. They both enjoyed live music, movies, and the beach and hated small talk. Tamika hinted that she, too, had a fondness for the darker, magical side of life, but still, Susan decided she would hold off on using the word Witch to describe herself; not everyone understood what that really meant.

As the waitress cleared their plates, Susan's stomach fluttered again. They'd talked so easily over their dinner that she'd forgotten she was on a date at all.

"So, I can give you directions to my place in case you lose me on the way. I warn you; my apartment is...well, it's nothing special. And it's probably a mess. It's kind of around the Webster Square area." Her run-down place suited her just fine, but she was always afraid it would scare women away.

"What's the address?" Tamika asked.

"One-fourteen Lyman Street. Do you know where the Old Swedish Cemetery is?"

"Oh yeah, I know just where that is." Tamika nodded.

"Well, the cemetery is basically my back yard. It was kind of a perk for me."

Grateful for little traffic, Susan flew home, hoping to tidy up before Tamika arrived, but Tamika was already parked on the street waiting in her car.

Tamika didn't seem to notice the broken banister up to her second-floor apartment or the peeling linoleum that looked like it had been there before either of them was born.

"Like I said, it's kind of a mess. Sorry," Susan said as she cleared some mail and books from the kitchen table.

"I don't care. Really," Tamika assured her.

"Wanna just hang out in the living room? I don't really have a lot of company, but I could put some music on."

"Sounds nice. I just want to spend some time with *you*. Could you point me in the direction of the bathroom first, though?" Tamika asked.

"Sure. It's kind of a weird setup. You have to go through my bedroom to get to it." Susan felt her face get hot as she let Tamika into the bedroom; it felt rather intimate. "It's the left door, not the right. Don't pee in my closet."

Shit. She'd managed to make it about two hours before saying anything truly dorky, but thankfully, Tamika just laughed and didn't look at her like she was a total freak.

Susan spotted Emily on the futon and went over to give the cat a quick scratch on both sides of her chin. "How's my little old lady tonight?" She cooed and leaned in closer, whispering, "I think I might have met someone special."

Emily jumped down and weaved in and out of Susan's legs, leaving black fur all over her khakis, before going to sniff at the bathroom door to investigate their guest.

She was devastated when she spotted her doll on the side table and her underwear on the bed, waiting to be put away. Susan snuck in quietly, hiding the doll in the nightstand drawer first. But Tamika came out just as she was reaching for the underwear.

"Susan, you're fine." Tamika laughed.

Still, she couldn't leave them there, so she picked them up and shoved them in her dresser.

Emily weaved around Tamika's legs, but Tamika didn't seem to notice.

"Groovy wallpaper." Tamika smirked, eyeing the giant orange, brown, and yellow flowers.

"Thanks. I'm kind of in love with it."

While the rest of the place was nothing special, with every wall covered in dull tan paint, when she had first spotted the bedroom wallpaper, still in pristine condition from the seventies, she knew she wanted the apartment.

"No, really. I love it," Tamika assured as if she knew Susan had been wondering whether she'd been teasing. "It's very hippie. Very you. Speaking of which...I assume you toke?" Tamika asked as she held her fingers up to her ample lips. And suddenly, Susan couldn't help but think about kissing them.

"Yeah. I mean, not often, but if it's around, I will. Sounds fun." She gestured to the tie-dyed futon. *Sounds fun? What kind of dorky thing was that to say?* "What kind of music do you like?" She asked, hoping to cover up the absurd thing that had just come out of her mouth.

"Almost anything; I love music. Well, not really anything, I guess. I don't like metal. Or opera. Mary J. Blige is probably my favorite lately, but basically, I just love powerful women singers. What's in your CD player?" Tamika pointed.

"I think the same three CDs have been in there forever. Or the same three singers, anyway. Melissa Etheridge, the Indigo Girls, and Tracy Chapman, most likely. Pretty stereotypical lesbian." Susan laughed.

"Nothing wrong with that; I happen to have a thing for lesbians." Tamika winked and cupped Susan's cheek in her palm, slowly rubbing her thumb along her chin. "Who are some of your other favorites?"

"Umm, Catie Curtis, Chris Williamson..." Susan could barely speak after Tamika's touch.

"I don't know them. I love Tracy Chapman, though; she's one of my favorites, and of course, Melissa Etheridge is a major powerhouse, too. Push shuffle, and let's see..." Tamika sat down and lit the joint.

It took Susan by surprise when a familiar dance song began to play.

"Remind you of someone?" Tamika asked, holding out the joint to her.

Susan sat stiffly on the edge of the futon, took a small puff, and willed herself not to cough; it had been a while.

Susan nodded. "How'd you know?"

Tamika shrugged. "I thought that was nostalgia I saw in your beautiful eyes."

"Ex-roommate. Ex-friend, I guess." She shrugged. "Reminds me of our club days. This must be his CD."

"He?" Tamika asked.

"Yeah, Michael and I were living together for like a year before I moved here," Susan explained.

"Just a roommate, though?" Tamika eyed her.

"Oh God, yes. He and I are both as gay as they come." Susan laughed.

"Good. I'm not into bisexual girls. Too messy." Tamika held a hand up in emphasis.

They passed the joint back and forth a few more times and talked about music and people they knew from Amen, the gay club downtown.

"Oh my God, I love this song." Tamika leaned into the back of the futon, kicked her sneakers off, and moved to the club beat.

Susan let herself get lost in Tamika's movements, enjoying the curve of her abundant breasts and the way her face showed her emotion.

"So, what else do you like to read?" Susan asked when the song ended, and Tamika sat down again.

Tamika smiled at her as if it were a funny question.

"What?" Susan asked.

Tamika tilted her chin sideways and eyed her. "I don't know. I like you. I can tell you're deep. I like to read the dark stuff lately. I doubt I read as much as you, from the looks of all these bookshelves. My absolute favorite is *Beloved.* It's dark, but wow does Sula find her power."

Susan let out a dreamy sigh. "Beautiful book. I love Toni Morrison."

"It's so...deep. That's the only way to describe it really," Tamika said.

Every time she used the word, she spoke it like poetry.

Susan was suddenly aware that she was still leaning in close to Tamika. "I think I could use another toke," she said, surprised as it came out of her mouth.

Tamika chuckled and lit the joint again, holding it to Susan's lips.

"Go ahead. I got you," Tamika said.

And it felt like Tamika had her. Her lips brushed Tamika's fingers lightly as she took a pull.

"I like the dark stuff, too," Susan said.

"I know." Tamika nodded and paused, then slowly unbuttoned and removed her striped, button-up shirt, revealing the curve of her perfect breasts beneath her tank top.

Susan felt her heart beat faster. Once she realized that Tamika had taken off her shirt to reveal the tattoo on her bicep, she leaned in to get a better look. She admired the grayscale ink, a detailed scorpion, with the constellation to match its name hanging from its tail.

Without thinking, she reached out to touch Tamika's arm but stopped herself as her fingers hovered just far enough above her skin that she could feel her heat. She started to pull her hand back, but Tamika gently pushed it down.

"No. Go ahead, touch me."

Closing her eyes, Susan ran her fingers over it as if she could feel it.

When she opened her eyes again and pulled her hand away, Tamika was smirking at her. Her dimple was adorable, and she looked so sexy in the tank top. Susan desperately wanted to touch her again but didn't have a reason to.

"You like it, huh?"

Susan nodded and felt her face flush.

"Well, good. I'm all Scorpio, that's for sure."

"It's gorgeous," Susan said. She wanted to add that *she* was gorgeous but didn't.

"So, what about you? What else do *you* like to read? You know, besides the dark stuff?"

"Books about strong women. I used to love fantasy, but actually, lately, I've been into the classics. Grapes of Wrath. To Kill a Mockingbird," she replied.

"Strong women. Absolutely! That's another thing. I can tell you're strong."

Susan just nodded and sat back, playing with the collar on her work polo.

"You've had to be strong," Tamika added.

Susan looked over at her and met her deep brown eyes that were much more serious now.

"Yeah," she replied with a shrug.

"It's okay. You don't have to get into anything."

"No. It's not that. I *have* had to be strong. Been through some really tough shit. I just think that's true for all of us. It's hard to be human."

"True."

They talked throughout the night, sharing more about themselves. Even after the music stopped, the moments of silence weren't uncomfortable. It felt easy to be with her, and that wasn't something she could say about many people.

"I'm going to get my new *Ultimate Dance Party* CD from the car," Tamika said, disappearing out the door.

Susan let out a long exhale as she listened to the car door, followed by Tamika bouncing back up the stairs.

"We're going to dance," Tamika said, smiling as she pointed at Susan and put the CD in.

Susan didn't reply. She hated dancing, but she was just stoned enough that she might get over it.

She wagged her finger. "You aren't telling me White girl can't dance. You get that butt up."

They laughed as Tamika held her hand out to pull Susan up from the futon.

As she let herself absorb the rhythm, she closed her eyes and moved her arms slowly at first and then with more fervor until her hips caught up and joined in. Lost in the music, she lasted half a song without wondering what she looked like to Tamika. She was met with Tamika's beaming smile when she opened her eyes.

"I knew you had it in you."

Tamika took Susan by both hips and danced against her, making Susan breathless.

"See, you just have to let go, girl."

They danced to a few more songs, then grabbed some munchies and plopped themselves on the floor. Susan pushed shuffle again for some variety. Tamika browsed through the books on her living room shelf, examining some curiously and questioning Susan about others. Susan savored the moment; she could talk about books forever.

"I don't think I remember the last time I had such a good time." Susan laughed, spraying cheese puffs out of her mouth.

Tamika either didn't notice or didn't care. "Aww. I'm having a great time, too."

Emily sauntered in with a loud meow and set herself on the floor in front of them. Susan patted her head as she purred.

"This is Emily."

"She's beautiful," Tamika replied, but didn't pay the cat much attention.

Turning down the radio, Susan leaned closer to Tamika and asked, "Can we smoke some more?"

"Of course. Go ahead." Tamika motioned to the joint on the coffee table.

After a slight hesitation and a look from Tamika, Susan leaned back, retrieved the joint and lighter from the coffee table, then handed it to Tamika.

"Light it for me?" She tipped her head down a little. She'd never been very good at flirting.

Tamika grinned and reached up. "Sure."

Susan watched her beautiful mouth envelop the joint and take a pull as the flame connected with the paper, and she heard the sizzle. Tamika scooted her butt closer to Susan's and held the joint to Susan's lips. Susan inhaled slowly, then pulled away with quivering lips.

Tamika leaned back, made sure the joint was out, and laid it on the coffee table.

"Are you scared of me?" Tamika asked as she sat back up.

Susan tried to speak, but nothing came out as she fidgeted with her ponytail.

"You are!"

"I'm...well, maybe a little, yeah. But....

Tamika let out a kind laugh and rubbed Susan's hand.

"But what? Come on, finish that sentence."

"But I like women who scare me a little."

"Ahh, well, good." She nodded. "Why, though? Why do I scare

you, I mean?"

Susan shrugged.

"I know you're sensitive. I'm safe, you know. I mean, I won't hurt you if that's what you're thinking."

Susan wasn't about to say what she was thinking; everyone hurts you, eventually.

"It's not that I don't feel safe with you. It's...it scares me that I *do* feel safe with you. I mean, we just met."

"I see."

"You do?" Susan asked.

Tamika nodded. "I think I do. You feel vulnerable."

"Hmm. Yeah. I guess that's exactly it," Susan replied in awe. How could she love words so much but often couldn't find the right one to express what she felt?

"Well, vulnerable can be a good thing. It doesn't have to be scary."

Tamika touched her hand again. Susan looked up and locked eyes with her for a second, then looked away. With her other hand, Tamika lifted Susan's chin until they were eye to eye again.

"Can I kiss you?" She asked softly. No one had ever asked if they could kiss her before; they'd just done it.

She wanted to scream yes but kept herself in check and nodded slightly instead, feeling Tamika's fingers still under her chin as she leaned into her. Tamika kissed her gently with closed lips at first. They both let the contact linger. Susan let herself soften into the embrace as Tamika put her other arm around her waist.

Breathless, Susan invited Tamika deeper into the kiss. She'd forgotten what this kind of desire had felt like. In fact, she wasn't sure she had ever wanted so badly. It felt just like hunger. Need.

They became lost in one another. When Susan felt Tamika's hand slide under her shirt, her mind went straight to her fat rolls. She pulled away, regretting it instantly.

"Are you okay?" Tamika pulled her hand back, held Susan by both shoulders, and wore a look of concern.

Susan nodded.

"Are you sure? We can stop. We don't have to..."

Susan shook her head. "No, I...I'm just...a little self-conscious, I guess. I'm sorry, I feel dumb now."

"Aww. No, please don't. I already see all of you. I like what I see. I want all of you. I mean it, though; we don't have to do anything."

Susan had been unaware of the music for a little while, but they exchanged flirty smirks when Melissa Etheridge began to belt out the chorus to, *I Really Like You.*

"Isn't it eerie sometimes how music can be more powerful than a psychic reading? It's a kind of magical, how intuitive it is."

Susan nodded, not daring to breathe.

"Susan, you are *so* beautiful."

As she heard her name on Tamika's lips, the fear seemed to slip away. She wrapped one arm around Tamika's back, pulling her closer. "Trust me, I want to," she said with a wildness she didn't know she had in her.

She felt herself tremble when Tamika's hand touched her skin again. Tamika leaned back, and their eyes met. Gently, Tamika took off Susan's shirt, and then her bra, revealing Susan's tattoos, one on each collarbone.

"This one is stunning. It's so you," Tamika said, kissing the outline of an open book with a bookmark hanging from its pages, a single drop of bright red blood dripping from one tassel.

Tamika kissed the tribal sun on the opposite collar bone; Susan lay back, breathy and blissful, inviting the intensity.

"I want to see your hair down. Can I...?" She reached for Susan's ponytail.

The way Tamika sought consent with each move was something special. Susan nodded, and Tamika gently unwound the elastic, then pulled Susan's wavy, brown hair over her shoulders.

"You're a Goddess." Tamika stood up and reached her hand to pull Susan up with her. "Come on, you deserve better than the floor."

Susan sat on the edge of the bed and pulled Tamika close to her. They lay back, wrapped up in one another's kisses. Susan was convinced that she could die that very moment and be satisfied that she'd known true ecstasy. Tamika took off her tank top and bra, lowering herself, their breasts meeting, which Susan believed to be the most wonderful feeling in the entire universe, until finally, they both lay completely naked together, so intertwined that it was unclear where one ended and the other began. While discovering one another's bodies, Susan found that Tamika was right; vulnerability didn't have to be scary at all. With everything in her exposed, she let Tamika make love to her and reciprocated, feeling free as they shared hands, mouths, skin, and souls. Nothing but that moment existed.

CHAPTER TWO

After slipping some clothes on, retrieving their leftovers from the fridge, and talking for hours, Susan and Tamika made love again, finally falling asleep in one another's arms.

After only a couple hours of sleep, Susan woke and glanced at the clock out of habit, although she almost didn't need to. It was always in the three o'clock hour that she was summoned awake. Sure enough, it was exactly eleven past. Although these nights of broken sleep left her exhausted the next day, it wasn't as if she had many options; lying there staring at the ceiling only drove her crazy.

She rose quietly; Emily was staring at her from the foot of the bed, and when she let out a single shrill meow, Susan hushed her. The cat scurried off, as if leading her somewhere. When Susan crept along on the warm, wooden living room floor, Emily jumped up onto the windowsill and stared out instead of approaching her for a cuddle as Susan had expected her to.

Of course, Susan thought to herself, peering down into the cemetery below.

She patted Emily's head in gratitude and went to her messy altar. It was covered with a fine layer of dust from neglect. She always intended to practice more but got a little lazy sometimes. If only she could be as diligent about her craft as she had with her academics. She would refresh her altar soon, maybe adorn it with fresh summer flowers and forest trinkets, but for now, she could revive herself in the cemetery. She reached past the Gaia statue that always stood in the center, no matter how she had the altar configured, and instinctively chose a pink chime candle from the colorful row. She didn't overthink it, but pink felt right for romance.

On her way out the door, she grabbed a lighter off the counter and then quietly tiptoed down the stairs, through the small yard, and into the cemetery's edge. She could hear the traffic, even at this hour, but almost didn't notice as she entered her own little world.

Although Susan had known many other Witches to talk about intricate spells, she was a much more modest Witch, an everyday Witch, and she was proud of it. Binding spells. Mirror spells. Money spells. None of those felt genuine or personal. In fact, they seemed flashy and dependent on a lot of material things that she found unnecessary. All she needed to carry out a ritual was a tiny flame and to feel her feet on the Earth.

Besides the many rituals she'd carried out in which she'd appealed to the Greek Goddess, Persephone, to free her from the pain of her past, Susan simply addressed Gaia most of the time. Her rituals were usually a combination of things she'd learned from her gramma and her mom. She'd taken the reverence and faith from her gramma; although they'd lay there at night when she was little singing classic spiritual songs like *This Little Light of Mine*, which didn't resonate with her now, the feeling was the same: a sense of being connected to something bigger than herself. When she added that with the simple yet profound life rules her mom had instilled in her, to always say please and thank you and mean it, Susan knew the words she spoke to the universe were powerful. And she had no doubt that the universe was listening. Silently responding to her.

She stood beside her favorite gravestone; the last name had long since worn away, with only illegible portions of letters somewhere in the middle of where the last name had once been, so the stone simply read Miranda. Even the inscription had been degraded; beloved was the only word she could make out. She couldn't say why, but this grave had drawn her in right away, the first time she stepped foot into the cemetery. It was even visible from the window beside her desk in her living room.

She wiggled her feet in the warm grass, letting it poke in

between her toes, and flicked the metal wheel on the lighter, grateful that there was not even a hint of a breeze. The wick on the pink candle absorbed the flame, and Susan closed her eyes. *Thank you for bringing this strong but tender woman into my life. Please bless us with many years together and help us grow together and create something beautiful.* She took in a few breaths and stood still, satisfied with her appeal to the universe, certain that the sun, moon, and stars were all in her corner. And Miranda, of course, whoever she was.

She stood there for a few more minutes, gazing out at the rest of the headstones and the mostly darkened windows of the other houses she could see between the trees, then let the sliver of moonlight lead her back to her door.

When Susan opened her eyes the next day, the way that the sun was poking through the edge of the curtain and shining on the tree of life tapestry told her that it must be closer to afternoon than it was to morning. Tamika wasn't in bed with her. She lay there for a few minutes, replaying the previous night with a smile. Never before would she have believed that two people could truly make love the first night they'd met, but that was exactly what they had done. It had been soulful. What if she was wrong, though? What if Tamika hadn't felt the same? She could have used a line on her. Maybe she'd woken up and left. A rock settled in her stomach; Susan closed her eyes again.

"Good morning, beautiful. I thought I heard you stirring." Tamika came in, sat on the edge of the bed, and kissed her on the head.

"Morning." Susan smiled.

"You okay?" Tamika asked, smoothing Susan's tousled hair.

She nodded. "Just happy you're here."

If she said she'd been worried that Tamika had left, she would seem insecure, maybe even pathetic. If she gushed too much about how happy she was about last night, she could come off as too intense. Clingy. She wasn't stupid; even if they'd had a perfect night, it didn't mean Tamika wanted anything serious. But she was sick of living like that, constantly worried about saying the wrong thing. Living a half-lie instead of her whole truth. She'd done it with all the other women. She'd done it with almost *everyone* she ever claimed to be close to.

She took a deep breath; fuck it!

"What?" The way that Tamika tipped her chin at her when she tried to get her to open up was incredibly sexy.

"This might be too much, but I feel like this is it. You. Us."

"It isn't too much at all. I feel the same way. When you know, you know."

"It's kind of fuckin' crazy, though, isn't it?" Susan laughed.

Tamika shrugged. "Love makes you crazy. There are worse things. You want to know something else? I knew before you did. I knew when I first saw you at Barnes and Noble."

Love? Had Tamika just said love? Susan could feel her heart speed up as she broke eye contact.

"Was *that* too much?" Tamika bit her bottom lip.

Susan shook her head.

"Come on, let's make brunch together." Tamika offered her hand, pulling Susan from the bed and taking her into a long embrace.

Susan was very aware of her morning breath and hoped it wouldn't be the thing that would ruin the perfectly romantic moment. But Tamika didn't try to kiss her; thank the Goddess! Susan never could understand the movies that showed couples waking up and making out. Morning was for hugs.

As Tamika found her way around the simple kitchen, Susan noticed her every move. The way she didn't seem to mind the cupboard door hanging on just one hinge. How she hummed as she put the bagels into the toaster. The way her adorable butt filled out her rainbow boxers.

Susan threw a few slices of precooked bacon into the microwave and put the kettle on the burner.

"Want a cup of tea? I think I should have some instant coffee, too." She always kept a jar around for the rare occasion when her mother visited.

"Coffee would be great," Tamika replied.

"Do you like scrambled?" Susan asked, holding up the egg carton.

"Scrambled is good. Even better if you have some cheese to throw in them."

Susan replied with what she could feel was an overly goofy smile and shook her head a little.

"What?" Tamika asked.

"Nothing. I know it's silly. It's just scrambled eggs and cheese, but it's a family favorite. Kind of special... My gramma used to make them for me, and, I don't know, there was just something about the way they tasted different when she made them. After she died, my mom and I would experiment with them, and we never could get them to taste like hers, but they were still one of our favorites."

"It's not silly. Family is comfort. I love that you value family. That's important to me." Tamika continued to hum away as she slathered cream cheese on the bagels. "Better get some exercise after eating such a heavy breakfast. Carbs really weigh me down sometimes."

Susan nodded. "It doesn't feel too hot out there yet. I can show you around my cemetery. I don't get out and walk as much as I should, but when I do, that's where I go."

"We could do that, too." Tamika smirked.

Susan felt herself blush as she realized that wasn't the kind of exercise Tamika had been referring to.

"Bagels are all set. How about I take the drinks in, put on some music, and we have brunch picnic-style in here?" Tamika asked, motioning to the living room.

Susan nodded. "Eggs are almost done. I'll bring the rest."

Tamika had spread the throw from the futon on the floor. Emily kept watch from the corner, eyeing Tamika.

"I don't think I've had a living room picnic since I was nine." Susan laughed.

"Oh yeah?" Tamika asked.

"Yeah. My mom and I lived with my grandparents for a few years..." She paused. Being vulnerable was one thing, but with a nightmarish history like hers, she was always careful not to scare people away by diving into her survivor story before they really knew her. "And when we moved into our own apartment, we had no furniture for a few weeks. Nothing except one bed. But I had no idea we were poor; I was thrilled to have lots of picnics." Shit, had even that been too much?

"Times like that can make you appreciate things more," Tamika said.

"Totally," Susan agreed.

Tracy Chapman crooned *Revolution*.

"There goes the psychic CD player again. You bring those witchy vibes to everything in this place."

Tamika had used the word Witch before Susan had to. Too often, women would think her décor was eccentric and even show interest in her modest altar with its mini cauldron and Goddess statues, but once she uttered the word Witch, everything changed. It usually went one of two ways; either they would think it was cute that she imagined herself to be like Samantha on Bewitched, or the deep-rooted Christian society had gotten to them and there was a part of them that thought she was going to hell. Either way, it usually ended badly. So, it was a relief to hear the word come out of

Tamika's mouth.

"Psychic CD player. I like that. The Goddess of music speaks." Susan laughed.

"You were telling me about how the scrambled eggs held a family connection for you. Another one of Tracy Chapman's songs is like that for me."

"Which one?" Susan asked.

"*Across the Lines.*"

She could see the rawness in Tamika's eyes; she made vulnerable look as beautiful as a rainy sky, the passion of the storm balancing out the weight of the rain.

"My family has spent a lifetime trying not to become a Black stereotype, and that song is all about the lines that are drawn between Black and White."

Hearing that made Susan want to either lay down and cry or go over and hold Tamika for eternity, but instead, she found the strength to meet Tamika's eyes and listen.

"Both of my parents are professors. My dad teaches engineering at WPI, and my mom teaches drama and dance at BU. My brother and I went to private school. We grew up on Salisbury Street, for God's sake, but none of that was enough. Our parents drilled it into our heads that we had to be more careful than White children not to do anything that might risk being seen as trouble. Well, to be honest, it was mostly my mother. Dad was too busy having quiet affairs, which he hid pretty well from the rest of the world. But none of us were stupid. But with mom.... Well, it was like we could never even make one misstep because then we'd be *that* Black family, you know?"

"Wow. That's..." What could she even say to that?

"As the older sibling, I think she was hardest on me. And God, I really hated her for a long time. I managed to stay in line until the day I graduated from high school, but then...well, I went my own way." Tamika smirked devilishly.

"You have a little rebel in you, too, hmm?" Susan replied.

"I was planning my escape my whole senior year, all the while making them think I was going to college the way they wanted me to. I had the grades to go just about anywhere I wanted. Was accepted to five really great schools. In mom's wildest dreams, I would go to BU. She loves that place. But instead, the day after my graduation, I told them I changed my mind. But I never really planned to go. I'm not proud of how I did it, but I just had to be free. I had to figure out how to be me."

Susan nodded, and Tamika continued.

"I certainly wasn't about to come out to them on top of everything else. Not at that point. I moved in with my girlfriend, Zoe, but people just knew us as best friends. It was a pretty terrible neighborhood. King Street. That, getting dreadlocks, and not going to college was quite enough to devastate my mom."

"Yikes. Well, your mom must be happy you're in college now."

Tamika shrugged. "Yeah. She just thinks I could have done better. Better than Worcester State. Better than nursing."

"And what happened with Zoe?"

"We just fizzled out, I guess. After we broke up, I got certified as a nurse's aide and got my own place here in the city. Nothing special, but it wasn't King Street. Saved for a few years, then finally enrolled in college. I've had to work pretty much full-time as I've done classes, which is why it's taking me so long to finish. My parents agreed that I made my choices and would have to make my own way after the way I dropped the bomb about not going after high school and just left."

"But what did you mean about the song? You said *Across the Lines* was a family connection thing for you."

"Well, Tracy Chapman helped me understand my mom with that song. Helped me see her. I mean, I had listened to Tracy since

I was in high school. And, of course, I had everything figured out back then. I knew that my mom was over the top with the way she raised us. She was ridiculous to think that we could be put in a *Black box*, so to speak. Not with the way *we* lived. But then, a couple of years after I left home, I was able to hear that song differently. Here I was, living in a terrible neighborhood, and my parents were still on Salisbury Street with my brother, worrying about things I was sure they were being ridiculous about. But, one night, there was some commotion in the neighborhood. A report of someone suspicious prowling in back yards or something. I don't really know. So, the police canvassed the neighborhood quickly, asking all the residents some pretty basic stuff, I guess. But when they got to our house, they were there for hours, questioning my brother. I'll never forget when MJ called me that night; from the sound of his voice, I thought someone died. And then I finally got it. It doesn't matter if you're wealthy or not. The point is that people see you differently, and you do have to work ten times as hard to be seen for who you are. Just like it could take cops an hour to take a distress call from King Street seriously, they lean more heavily on a Black family when something goes wrong on Salisbury Street. So, I'm thankful that it helped me see where my mom was coming from. Some people never see their mothers like that. Or at least not until they're much older."

Susan could feel the tears in her eyes as she spoke. "It's awful that this is still the reality. But, it's true...about your mom. People tend to see them as their moms but not as people. I think it's a really important part of the feminist experience to be able to see them as women."

"Well said."

"That's amazing that you've put yourself through school like that," Susan said.

"Had no choice. My parents were right. I made my choices.

And I'll never be sorry. But, you gotta do what you gotta do. When you know what you want, you have to be determined to get it. You want to be healthy; you prioritize exercise. You want a good job; you find a way to go to college." She paused. "You want a wife to start a family with...you work up the courage to talk to that soulful woman at the bookstore."

Susan finished her last bite of eggs, got up, and sat beside Tamika.

"So, you're out to your family now?"

Tamika nodded. "My mom is pretty artsy, so she was okay. I think she already knew on some level, anyway. She was far more concerned about college than that. My brother doesn't care. But my dad...it took a few years. Even now, it's hard for him to swallow. Gay isn't an easy thing for Black folks to accept. It's a whole thing. But he hasn't said much about it since the Thanksgiving when I asked him point-blank how he could be so hypocritical to say I was shaming the family when he was the one who'd had affairs. Now, we just don't say much to one another at all, and it works." Tamika paused. "What about your dad? You said your mom was a single mom. But is your dad in your life?"

Susan nodded and tried to stifle a gulp; how had she not seen the question coming?

Tamika turned and looked into her eyes, reminding her of what she'd said last night. Being vulnerable didn't have to be scary. In this case, it was, but she knew she should do it anyway. Tamika had just shared so much with her; it was only fair to take this opportunity to return that trust.

"No. He umm, *abused* me and my baby sister, Molly. Half-sister. His daughter. Haven't seen either of them since I was eight. He went to prison, and Molly's mom moved away with her." She looked down at her hands, one gripped on each thigh. The right words never really came when she had to tell someone about being a survivor. While being specific was far too intense, being vague left room for questions that sometimes made her cringe. Sometimes, people never looked at her the same way again. But the way Tamika reached over, loosened her gripped hand from her leg, and held it tenderly, told Susan that she'd said enough to make Tamika understand and that Tamika still saw her.

"I knew you'd had to be strong, but..."

"Like I said, we've all had to," Susan replied.

It didn't take long for Susan to decide that what she knew about Tamika was all she needed to know. She had both a dark side and a romantic side. She even made vulnerability feel safe. And, with a set of plans for the future, Susan could tell she was a strong woman. Most importantly, they were in the same place at the same time. That never happened to her with women. What more was there to know? They were in love.

* * * * *

Before she knew it, June had flown by, and the muggy weather that New England always delivered in July had settled in. Tamika had finished her accelerated summer course and had spent very little time at her own apartment since she and Susan had met.

For Susan, waking up in Tamika's arms was the best feeling; it quickly became her reason for wanting to exist. To start every day out with the one you loved was the point of living.

Today, Susan woke up far before the sun and couldn't fall back to sleep. Sleep had always been one of her favorite escapes from the world, but every now and then, she'd wake up at some ridiculous hour and know in her bones that sleep wasn't coming again. On those days, her mind just wouldn't stop; she was convinced that there was something important she was meant to be doing. Something that was calling to her. Sometimes, it was as if she was trying to live in multiple different worlds at once. She swore that these times usually fell right around the full moon, but it sounded crazy, even to her, and she rarely bothered to check to see if her suspicions were right.

She could barely make sense of all the thoughts running through her head as she stared into the dark. It felt as if her whole body was buzzing. She glanced at the clock; it was three-thirty-three. Despite the hour, she felt drawn to her desk. She rolled over slowly, then rose from bed, trying not to wake Tamika.

She sat in the hard desk chair and stared at the stack of dusty term papers and books. She missed school. She missed learning and writing. She was proud of what she'd accomplished, but she felt sad, too. What had it all been for? It was the classes themselves that had enhanced her life, not the degree, and now, that phase of her life was over. If it was over, maybe she needed all the remnants out of her sight.

She leaned over and reached for an empty printer-paper box, smiling when she saw Emily staring back up at her from inside. When they locked eyes, Emily rose, nudging her face into Susan's hand. Susan petted her for a moment but was determined to remove all the old memories from her desk, so she placed her hand under the cat's rump and urged her out. After a short, stubborn protest, refusing to budge, Emily let out a dramatic huff, hopped out, and sauntered away.

Yes, placing every college paper she'd ever written in the box felt right. She had to move on; she was in a new chapter of her life and didn't need these reminders staring at her every day. Besides, it looked messy. After finding the lid under the futon, she quietly put the box in the living room closet, satisfied with her efforts.

She flipped through some of the English textbooks that sat on her desk, dried clover and dandelions falling from the pages. The same textbooks that had once felt so powerful to her but now felt so empty. What did it matter if she knew what a comma splice or a dangling modifier was? She gathered the dried flowers on a little pile in the corner of her desk and put the textbooks in stacks on the uncomfortable purple armchair she never used; she would need more printer boxes from work to store them away. Maybe she would resell them...even as the thought crossed her mind, she knew she probably couldn't part with most of them.

The novels were different; she could never pack those away. The textbooks were teachers, but the novels were friends. Still taking care not to wake Tamika, she plopped down on the floor in front of the only shelf that had space. Placing the novels lovingly on her favorite bookcase was so different from stocking shelves at work; when she handled her own books, it felt as though she were sitting with a thousand ancestors. She imagined the writers who sat in dark, cold corners creating their stories and the lives that each story had touched.

After the desk's surface had been decluttered, Susan's mind felt somewhat clearer, too. Sitting in her chair, she stared out at the cemetery as Emily jumped up on her lap and purred away. They both sat there in a trance for a while, and Susan felt a sense of peace, as if she was healing from whatever had been vexing her mind. The kitty vibes did it to her every time.

The hum of the fridge whirred a little louder, pulling Susan from her zone and sending Emily bolting for the kitchen, racing through the living room a few times as if high on cat nip, then finally landing on the back of the desk, staring down at Susan.

"Weirdo." Susan laughed.

Susan opened the middle desk drawer; rifling through things was one of her favorite pastimes when she couldn't sleep. But this time, there wasn't much to rifle through. She remembered that it was around the time that she was writing out holiday cards last year that she had reserved this drawer for cards, stationery, and pens. At Beltane, she'd bought the feather pen and wax seal kit to send her latest letter to Fiona. Had it really been nearly two months since she'd written to her? She was an awful friend.

She'd been thinking about Fiona and meaning to write to her ever since Tamika had come into her life, but there hadn't been any time. Since meeting, they'd been together almost every moment they weren't working or in class.

It felt like a lifetime ago that she had met Fiona.

She'd come out to her mom and her closest friends right after high school, only to find out that the revelation was more of a surprise to her than it was to them. Despite the freedom of being out and the acceptance of her loved ones, coming out hadn't changed her life in quite the way she imagined; not having any queer friends was lonely. With a yearlong break in between high school and college, she had to admit that her solitary housekeeping job and spending most of her free time holed up in her bedroom with a book didn't give her much of a chance to meet anyone, but that was something she had expected to change once she was in college.

Her first year in college made her both utterly lost and free. Freedom could do that, though; like a tree with weak roots, it was free to sway but lacked solid grounding. The city was such a different world than Ware had been, which was a good thing. She'd always craved a more diverse perspective than small-town life had offered. But still, although she'd attended the Women's Center at the community college from time to time, she hadn't made any real connections yet. It still seemed that, no matter where she went, she didn't fit. Even in an open-minded city, it didn't always feel safe to be an out lesbian.

She spent long afternoons in the college library, letting books keep her company as she always had. It was there that she'd spotted the flyer for the pen pal program, and it kept calling to her. When she spotted the LGBT category on the list, she decided to give it a shot.

She'd been the one to write the first letter on the cat silhouette stationery she'd bought just for the occasion. She could still remember the freedom of being fully herself without having to worry about the response from the other end. Although it had been nearly two years since she'd come out, after all the years of not having the words to express who she was, it still felt good to come out over and over.

Right away, they clicked. What she hadn't managed to find with in-person interaction, even in the city or college, she'd found with someone from a place in Canada that she'd never even heard of: Newfoundland. In fact, the first time she read the name of the place, she mistook it for the Netherlands. She'd always been awful at geography. Maybe she was an old-fashioned, hopeless romantic, but she'd been convinced that finding Fiona had saved her from the solitude that had become a little too comfortable.

She dug the first letter Fiona had ever written to her out of the drawer and reread it, in awe that four years had passed since they'd first begun writing. As she unfolded the letter, Emily jumped down and ran off into the bedroom, but Susan barely noticed.

May 1, 1993

Hey Susan. I was glad to get your letter, although I don't even remember signing up for the pen pal program you mentioned. But I'm glad I did if it means finding you. I already feel a connection with you. Probably because of our shared love of nature especially animals. I get the feeling you're a dark soul like me. I spend a lot of time exploring the woods. It's great to just go out there and lose my mind.

Never liked talking about myself much. I find it easier to ask about other people. I'm 18 and I live with my boyfriend, Will in a crappy apartment in a small community not far from the communities where we grew up. We met when we were fourteen. I don't work right now, but I'm looking for a job. Kind of. I guess we have to pay the bills, but I really just want to go out in the woods and never come back. I don't know what else to say. What else is there to say? I feel like I'm just a creature trying to pretend to be human.

Anyway, tell me more about you. You said you came out not too long ago. Good for you. We shouldn't really have to. We should be able to just BE. But society is fucked. People love labels, but I just AM. I fall in love with souls. Do you get a lot of shit about being a lesbian? What do you enjoy doing besides being out in nature? Guess I'm not great with words. Maybe not the best trait in a pen pal, but I hope to hear from you again.

Fiona

She must have read that letter a dozen times over the years. Two dozen, maybe. Though brief, that first letter had captivated Susan right away. When she held the letter, written on Fiona's coffee-stained stationary with the llamas, she felt an energy she couldn't explain, as if Fiona was there in the same room as her. Fiona was familiar to her in a way that could only suggest that she must have spent another lifetime with her before. Every letter had been like that. Her mother had teased her about having a foreign girlfriend every time she got a letter in the mail from Fiona or mailed one out. But it wasn't like that with Fiona. Not exactly. It was more if that was possible.

They'd both moved a couple of times since they'd first begun writing, and every time, even if it wasn't right away, they eventually found one another again. While Susan could sometimes be known to write twelve-page letters, Fiona's were one or two pages at most, sometimes even just a postcard. But with Fiona, it was never what she said that made her feel connected; it was something else. Not only the familiarity but an intimacy that went beyond what they could tell one another through words. She knew more about Fiona than Fiona shared about herself.

She wrote to Fiona the most during the summer that she stayed with Steph and Michael. That summer had been so hot. Although she didn't officially live there, she might as well have. Madly in love with Steph, constantly arguing with Michael, and meeting their never-ending parade of lovers, Susan had never felt so alone in her life, and it helped her to know that someone was still left to listen and understand. Although she wasn't wordy, Fiona's replies always included such wisdom and compassion, as if she were an ancient soul who just lived her entire life meditating on a blanket.

She looked through her stationery collection, pulled out a few sheets, and began to scratch out the latest adventure in her life, spilling her soul to Fiona once again. She felt more comfortable with her than she had felt with anyone in her life. She could tell her anything and was never afraid that Fiona would think she was crazy. Her psychology classes in college made her question whether or not that level of comfort was only accessible to her with someone she had distance from. Someone she didn't have to look in the eye. Someone she didn't have to be a messy, imperfect human being in front of the way she had with her mom and her oldest friend, DJ, or any of her girlfriends. Even now, as much as she already loved Tamika, she could see that there were things she held back from her that she would share with Fiona in a heartbeat.

July 3, 1997

Dear Fiona,

I'm in love! It's completely crazy because we JUST met a couple of weeks ago. But I know you always understand my craziness. Her name is Tamika. We met while I was at work. I always knew books brought magic into your life, but

When she heard Tamika stirring, she quickly stuffed the letter back into the drawer.

"Morning." Susan smiled.

"Good morning, Beautiful. What are you doing out here? How long have you been up?"

Susan shrugged. "Been up a while. Couldn't sleep."

"Are you cleaning at this hour?" Tamika laughed, looking at the cleared desktop.

"A little. I was mostly just staring out there. Emily joined me...we were enjoying the view." Feeling like she needed to say more, she blabbered on when she was hiding something, but Tamika didn't know that about her yet. She wasn't sure why she felt the need to hide it at all.

"My little Witch," Tamika said with a smirk.

"Want some breakfast?" Her heart beating rapidly, Susan got up and left the room.

"Sure."

She began to prepare eggs and toast, and Tamika came behind her, nuzzling her neck.

They still enjoyed every brunch and breakfast picnic-style. When they were done, Tamika asked, "Do you realize this weekend is Fourth of July weekend, and we actually both have it off, but we haven't made any plans?"

"Do you usually do something special?" Susan asked.

"Well, my family was always in Martha's Vineyard all summer, so we'd see fireworks from the boat. Went on a beach trip with friends once or twice. But it's our first summer together. We should do something," Tamika replied.

"The beach sounds great to me," Susan replied.

"Which beach you want to go to?"

"I don't know. Anything but Hampton Beach." Susan curled her lip.

"You ever been to P-town?" Tamika asked.

"Yeah, Michael and I used to go every year." Of course, she didn't add that her most unforgettable trip there included Steph, too. Tamika didn't like it much when she brought up her exes and rarely talked about her own past relationships. While Susan and

Steph never really dated, something told her that Tamika might sense the feelings went deeper and feel threatened if she were to bring up Step's name.

"That could be fun. Let's do that!" Tamika beamed.

"Do you mean a day trip or spending a night or two? It's expensive to stay there, and it's probably kind of last-minute to find any vacancies."

"I'd love to stay the weekend. I've been too, but only with friends. I think it will be a different experience as a couple," Tamika said.

"It would be awesome." Susan leaned in and kissed her lightly.

"Let's just pack and go. We'll find a place to stay. Could even be in a nearby town; I don't care."

"Ok!" Susan gushed.

Tamika moved over, held Susan close to her, and began to rub her thigh. "We better pack before we get distracted." Tamika smirked, pulling away. "Be plenty of time for that when we get there."

Susan pulled on some shorts and a tee shirt, hauled her duffel bag out of the messy closet, and started throwing things in while Tamika got dressed.

"Lazy girl," Susan said as she saw Emily still curled up in her cat bed in the corner of the bedroom. When she didn't move as Susan tapped the bed with her toes, Susan dropped her bag and froze.

"She's dead." Susan gasped, feeling all the blood draining from her face and pointing at Emily. The cat looked the same as she always did. She could just as easily have been sleeping, but Susan could feel it; only Emily's body was lying there.

"What? No."

Tamika bent down and ruffled the cat's black fur, and when she still didn't move, lay a hand on her head. When Susan could see definitively that there was no life in her, she turned her head away and began to sob, feeling as if her physical body might actually break apart.

Tamika stood up and held her tightly as she shook.

"That's my baby. She's my best friend."

"Shhh. I know. She went peacefully, though. We can forget all about this at the beach."

Tamika walked her over to the bed and sat her down, then sat beside her, still holding her. When Susan felt she had no tears left, she lay down and stared at the giant flowers on the wall. Even they couldn't bring her comfort. Her world was never going to be the same without Emily. Tamika cuddled up behind her on the bed and spooned her until she spoke.

"I have to call my mom."

"I'm here with you, Babe," Tamika replied.

"I need my mom."

Tamika got up and hurried out of the room. Susan couldn't remember where the receiver was, but before she could hit the find button on the base, the phone rang from her nightstand drawer.

She knew it was her mother before she picked it up; the air around her felt the same as it had as a child when her mom had laid cold washcloths on her head until she fell asleep.

"Hello?"

The sound of her mom's voice made her start to sob again, but getting out one distorted word at a time, she told her mother about Emily.

"Honey, I'm so sorry. You loved that cat like no one else could have from the moment you laid eyes on her."

"I did. I do. As soon as she stole that brownie from my hand, I knew she was supposed to be with me." She sniffed. She could see Tamika sitting on the futon, staring straight ahead and bouncing one leg.

"I still have to...to do something with her. Bring her to her vet,

I guess."

"I know it's awful, Honey, but this is the last thing you get to do for her. You know I don't like driving in the city, but if you need me, I'll come and go with you."

"Thank you, but...I'm not alone, thank Gaia."

"Oh, God, don't tell me Michael moved in. I do miss him; I love that boy, but he doesn't make a good roommate."

"No, no, I have a girlfriend."

"Shut up. And I'm only hearing about it now? You don't tell your mother these things?"

She felt a small laugh escape. She loved how they could always laugh, no matter how bad the situation. "Well, it's kind of new...I..."

"I'm just giving you shit. You know I'm happy for you. You go and do what you need to for Emily. I'm glad you have someone to be with you. What's her name?"

"Tamika."

"Well, I'm glad Tamika is there with you, but you call me if you need me. I love you. So much!"

"Love you too, mom. Thank you..." She was lucky to have a mother who knew when her daughter needed her most.

Although her heart ached, she had to find the strength to do this one last thing for Emily.

Tamika was still in the same position on the futon, and even when Susan walked into the room, she wouldn't look up.

"I...I need to bring her to the vet. They'll take care of her body."

Tamika sprung up and wrapped Susan in a hug. "I'll drive," Tamika whispered in her ear.

"I don't know what to do first. I mean, I'm just..."

"Listen, do you...*do you* still think we should go on the trip? I mean, I think it would be good for you."

Susan nodded. "I think so. I really don't want to be here right now. I just don't know if I need to call the vet first or..." She paused and closed her eyes, trying to patch her scraps of thoughts together. "No, I don't think I need to. They know us; I think we should just go."

"What can I do?"

"I still need to get some things together. Could you...bring her down to the car for me? I can't..."

Tamika paused and glanced toward the bedroom door where Emily's body lay.

She nodded. "I can do that. Just grab enough for a couple of nights, and I'll take care of her."

Tamika gently picked up the cat bed with both hands, cradling it into her chest. As she walked away, Susan let the tears roll down her face. She wished Tamika had learned to love Emily that way while she had been alive. In her dreams, the love of her life was supposed to become best friends with the cat, too. The fact that sometimes tenderness and love weren't possible until after death had to be one of the most painful things in life. Maybe it was just that Tamika wasn't as comfortable with dark things as she thought she was; Susan supposed she could understand that.

The veterinary staff showed such compassion when they took Emily from her that, beneath the grief, Susan could almost feel something beautiful about the moment, too. They'd offered to let her sit with Emily in an exam room. To say goodbye. But she'd said goodbye at home and didn't want to remember Emily this way, with the changes her body had already gone through. So, she handed her over right there in the empty reception area, bed and all, then stood there staring at the closed door after the vet tech had taken Emily away for the final time. She shook her head no when the vet tech rubbed her back and asked if she wanted to keep the bed.

She couldn't move.

Tamika had sat in what seemed to be the furthest possible

chair, looking down the whole time. Susan wished she would come hold her and let her cry. That she would do something magical that would help her break the trance she seemed to be in. But instead, she had to find the strength in herself to move herself from this place. It was sad to think how, sometimes, strangers knew how to treat you in ways that your loved ones didn't.

As Tamika drove to her apartment, Susan tried to talk to her. "I'm sorry if that whole thing made you uncomfortable. I mean, you seemed so..." Susan wanted to say cold.

"No, it's fine. I'm just not an animal person. I guess I can't really understand that bond."

"Oh." It felt like the wrong answer. She realized that she was hoping to be comforted somehow. Hoping that Tamika would be tender with her. But instead, what little she said felt like a kick in the gut. Not an animal person?

Susan waited in the car while Tamika went in to get her things for the trip. She could finally break down and cry, even if it was only for a few minutes. Her red eyes would give her away, though, so she'd just have to pretend she was asleep afterward.

Feigning sleep turned to actual sleep, and by the time she woke up, they were halfway to the tip of Cape Cod.

"Did the sleep feel good, Babe?" Tamika asked, putting a hand on her arm. There it was, the tenderness she had needed. She breathed in the touch like both her flesh and soul had been gasping for it.

"Yeah, I guess I needed it."

"Emotional stuff really takes a lot out of you."

I really should call DJ, too, at some point. Emily was DJ's best cat buddy. And that is saying a lot because she's a dog person. DJ practically lived with us some summers, so Emily was like her cat, too, in a way. And, I mean, she helped me bring her home that first day..."

"Sure, Babe. You can call her from the hotel. We should probably keep going to make sure we don't hit traffic."

Susan nodded and began to tell Tamika the story of how Emily came to her.

"Emily just walked into the rec center like she owned the place one day when DJ and I were at Girl Scouts. We were nine, I think. And I know it sounds weird, but from that first moment, I was convinced that she was Emily Dickinson reincarnated in cat form. That's how she got her name. My gramma had just died a few months before, so I needed that cat as much as she needed me. Gramma used to read Emily Dickinson's poetry to me..."

Susan looked over at Tamika, who had no reaction. She was pretty sure she hadn't been listening at all.

Tamika must have felt her look; she turned her head and patted Susan's leg. "You ok?"

Susan just shrugged, hurt. "Maybe I'll sleep some more."

Tamika sang along to the radio while Susan thought about Tamika's comment. Not an animal person. Even if she could wrap her head around the fact that the love of her life said she wasn't an animal person, it was more than that. It shouldn't have been about whether Tamika was fond of animals or not; she should have cared enough about Susan to comfort her. The rock in her gut was one she'd known too often before. She wanted to escape. Suddenly craving the comfort of familiarity, she felt a heaviness in her gut about spending the weekend away from home. She wanted to lay in her bed and get lost in some fictional universe. The dread didn't make sense to her, and she'd never risk hurting Tamika by saying she wanted to turn around and go home. Lying her head back, sleep was the only reprieve from her own mind.

CHAPTER THREE

Susan awoke to see the worst traffic she'd ever experienced on the Bourne Bridge. They were never going to find a room in P-Town.

"Have a good rest?" Tamika asked.

Susan nodded but teared up, remembering Emily was gone.

Tamika put her hand on Susan's arm without a word.

As the DJ stopped his chatter and a song began to play, Tamika smiled at her. "See? Works with the radio, too. Psychic radio. Bob Marley and the three little birds are telling you something. Everything always turns out alright in the end."

"Three little birds?" Susan asked, confused.

Tamika nodded. "*Three Little Birds* is the song's title, even though everyone thinks the chorus is the title."

"Oh! That's what I always thought it was, too."

"Psychic radio," Susan said. She couldn't help but smile, though her heart was breaking.

Nearly an hour later, they approached Commercial Street. As usual, it was so busy with foot traffic that it took almost ten minutes to get from one end to the other. She was happy they'd arrived; she needed to stop thinking about Emily, just for a little while.

Susan discreetly wiped her eyes, put her sunglasses on, and smiled.

After driving through the narrow streets several times and looping back around to the main road, they finally found a spot at the pier.

Tamika got out and stretched. Susan just stared out into the ocean for a minute before getting out and scanning the parking lot with a smile when she got out. Seeing men holding hands and dogs in rainbow bandanas made her feel a kind of freedom she had known in very few places on this Earth.

"I think I need to get something to eat," Susan said.

"What do you want to eat?"

"Might be easiest to just go to the Lobster Pot. They have burgers and stuff, too. Not just seafood. We could sit out on the deck."

"Sounds good," Tamika agreed.

"It's only right there." Susan laughed and pointed at the giant, red sign across the lot.

"Maybe we can find a place to stay first, so we don't have to worry about it later," Tamika suggested.

"That could take hours, Babe. I haven't eaten all day."

"That's true. Let's get some food in you. We'll find a place to stay later," Tamika agreed.

But Susan didn't respond, because when she glanced across the street, she saw Michael. He spotted her, too. Neither of them moved for a moment, but Michael made a move. He floated across the street, holding one hand in the air with a lit cigarette between his fingers.

"Well, look who it is!" He said in his sing-song voice.

"Hey." Susan reached in for a hug, instantly feeling a silent apology between them. "This is Tamika. Tamika, this is Michael," she said after they pulled away.

"Well, Helllloo." Michael tipped his head, looking down past his sunglasses at Tamika. He turned to Susan with a jut of his chin, crushed his cigarette onto the ground, and put his hands on his hips. "So...?"

"Yes, Tamika is my girlfriend. And good thing, because if she wasn't, this might be awkward." Susan laughed.

"Well, you ladies look very happy. You're adorable together. I'm happy for you," he cooed.

"Thanks." Susan wasn't sure how to read him. It seemed more like he *wanted* to be happy for her, but he really wasn't.

"Well, I came with just me, myself, and I. I said fuck it; I don't need a man to spend the Fourth of July weekend in P-town. Just like I don't need a best friend." He wagged his chin with his last words.

It had taken him all of two minutes to make a dig; that was Michael.

"Besides, maybe I'll find me a hottie here this weekend," Michael added, tapping his round belly. "There have to be a few guys who like a little meat on their man's bones."

Susan could tell that he had already started drinking. He'd probably only had a couple since he was still feigning politeness.

"Anyway, where are you guys headed? Want some company? I'm kind of a mess, but whatever." He ran his hands through his short, black hair.

Did he hate her, or did he want to spend the day with them? She couldn't understand how it could be both.

Susan hesitated. "We, like, *just* got here. I need to eat."

"I'm starving. Where are you going? The Lobster Pot?" Michael asked.

Susan smiled and nodded as she glanced at Tamika, unable to read her as she stared at Michael as if she was trying to assess him. Did she mind if Michael came along?

"Sure, come with us," Susan said, finally. What was she supposed to say? From what she could tell, Tamika didn't care, and Michael would be dramatic if she told him they wanted to be alone.

Throughout lunch, it seemed that Tamika and Michael were getting along well. Of course, Michael had already gushed about how much he loved her at least four times. Michael loved everyone until he hated them.

When Michael asked, Susan told him how they'd met. He had his second rum and coke delivered to the table before the waitress cleared their appetizer plates and was loudly oozing about every detail Susan shared.

"I could just sit here all day. Brings back memories, doesn't it?"

It had been two summers since they'd been there; going to P-town for the Fourth of July had been their favorite annual tradition. Some of their best memories together had been made here. Michael had his faults, but she still missed him sometimes.

"So, don't you want to know if I have found the love of my life too?" Michael asked.

Susan laughed. "Have you?"

"Well, I thought I did. His name is James. But we broke up a few weeks ago. So, I just quit my job last week and decided that this summer is all about doing what makes me happy. Told them bye-bye, bitches." He held up his drink to clink glasses. "You don't have drinks? It's an afternoon for drinking," he shrieked, waving the waitress over.

"Actually, we are going to have to..." Tamika started. But the waitress was already standing beside their table.

Susan was relieved that Tamika was taking charge in order to get them out of there. She wondered how long it would take for Tamika to dislike him. If they left now, she wouldn't have to worry about it. At least for now—it was a tiny town, and they were sure to bump into one another again.

"Oh, no. No excuses. You can have one drink with me while you wait for your lunch. Come on, Baby Doll."

It was never just one drink with Michael. But, as usual, he wasn't taking no for an answer.

"You're on vacation. What do you drink?" Michael turned to Susan. "What does your girlfriend drink, Suzie?"

"We really have to go find a hotel. We just wanted to grab a quick lunch," Susan said.

"Here in town?" Micheal asked.

"That or Eastham," Susan replied.

"Oh, Honey, you should know better. Everything is booked. In Eastham, too, I've heard. But you know what, this is perfect. We're going to have a wicked weekend. I have the penthouse at Crowne Point, bitches! Stay with me!"

"Do you ladies want drinks?" The waitress tapped her foot on the worn, wooden floor but smirked at Michael.

"Oh, yes; they do, Doll." He stood up. "And I want another one too." He pointed to his not-yet-empty glass.

"Sorry, we aren't allowed to serve more than one drink at a time," the waitress replied.

"Well, Jenny," He said, fingering her nametag with one hand and reaching in his back pocket with the other, then waving his credit card. "Maybe you can just start a tab for us, and I'll make sure to thank you later. I'll have this one gone by the time you get back, I promise. I wouldn't want a doll like you to get in trouble."

The waitress nodded, grabbed his card, and turned to Susan and Tamika again.

"I'll take a spiced rum and OJ, please," Susan said.

"I'll have a Bud Light," Tamika added.

The waitress nodded and walked away.

"This weekend is on Mastercard," Michael said as he exhaled a puff of smoke. "You're going to stay with me then, right?"

Susan glanced at Tamika. It wouldn't be the romantic weekend she had in mind if they stayed with him, but saying no wouldn't end well, especially since he was drinking. He wasn't above attracting attention to get his way, especially since he knew that was one of the things that Susan hated the most.

Tamika gave Susan a look that said she approved. "Sure. Thank you. We really appreciate it," Susan said, finally. There was one thing about Michael; he could always be counted on for a fun time, as long as he didn't get mean.

He clapped his hands theatrically and swallowed the last of his drink. "This is going to be awesome, ladies. I'm so excited!"

"I really need this weekend. Emily died this morning," Susan uttered with a catch in her throat.

Michael covered his mouth, but Susan could see him working to suppress a smirk. Although she knew it was just his way with nervous energy, she hated it when he did this.

"Oh, Honey, I'm so sorry. You poor thing." He got up and came around to her side of the table, wrapping her in a hug from behind.

She let him comfort her but fought tears. "She went in her sleep. I'm grateful for that. And I'm here now. I need to just be here now." Fiona always reminded her to live in the moment.

Tamika reached over and rubbed her arm.

"I'm so sorry, Suzie." He pulled away and gave her a peck on the cheek.

"Thanks. I'm okay. T was with me," Susan said.

"T?" Tamika asked, raising her voice.

Susan laughed. "You're my T. My sweet T."

"It's not funny. And, No. No, I'm not. I'm Black, but I'm not some gangster. Don't call me T. It's Tamika."

"I didn't mean..."

"I don't care what you meant. It's Tamika. I need some air." She stood up, shoved her chair aside, and walked out.

Susan couldn't believe they were having their first argument in front of Michael. Would it be one of those days where he was rooting for her to fail or where he'd defend her? She could never quite tell with him.

"Oh, shit," he replied. He was more interested in ordering another drink. "Girl, you need to be drunk with me. I think we all just need to get drunk. Suck this one down. I'm getting you another one." He jabbed his finger at the glass.

Susan just shook her head with a sigh, grabbed the glass, and sucked down the rest of her spiced rum and orange juice." She preferred pot to alcohol, but with so much stigma attached to pot, alcohol was easier.

Tamika didn't come back for forty-five minutes. At first, Susan kept looking at the door and couldn't focus enough to listen to Michael talking.

"Don't worry. She's *going to* come back. I can already tell that she adores you, Suzie. And if she doesn't, fuck her. I'll take care of you." He reached across the table and pinched her cheek, which made her smile.

After her second drink was gone, she stopped looking at the door, ordered a third, and listened while Michael told her all about what their mutual friends had been up to.

"After James and I broke up, I got back with Mateo for a little while, but I haven't heard from him in a while now, so who knows? Could be in California again for all I know."

"California?" Susan asked.

"Yeah, remember? He has a man down there. I don't know what they have going on, but he spent last winter there." Michael shrugged and lit a cigarette. "Oh, and...Steph is single again," he added.

"Oh?"

"I didn't know if I should even mention her. I know you're with Tamika now."

"No, no. It's okay. I'll always love Steph, obviously. I just want her to be happy. That was all I ever wanted, even if she couldn't find that kind of happiness with me. I want to hear about her." But Susan saw Tamika approaching the table. "Um, actually..." She gave Michael a wide-eyed look across the table and shook her head slightly.

Michael nodded. "So, yeah, you would not believe the fight I got into with Troy the night of the glitter party. God, he was sorry that he disrespected me," he said, snapping his fingers.

Tamika leaned in and kissed Susan on the head, giving her shoulders a squeeze. "Sorry," she whispered and took her seat, scooting closer to Susan and laying a hand on her thigh.

"I think I got really tired and moody from that drive. I should've stopped and rested." She mouthed sorry again and then turned to Michael. "And I'm sorry I probably left you with an awful first impression of me."

Michael shook his head and waved a hand at her. "Oh, Honey, you're just fine. I mean, I won't let you go treating my Suzie like shit or anything, don't get me wrong." He smiled, shaking his finger. "But, Honey, I'm a gay man; I know about mood swings. And you lesbians...well, we're all a piece of work. I'll forgive you if you order another drink." He was already motioning the waitress over and drinking the last drop of his fourth drink.

Tamika nodded and ordered another Bud Light.

Two hours later, they were all drunk, and Tamika said she needed to get up and move. Although Tamika offered to chip in, Michael insisted it was all on him.

"So, I take it Tamika's the jealous type?" Micheal asked the moment Tamika walked away to use the bathroom before they left.

"Kind of," Susan slurred with a shrug.

"Does she know about..." Michael asked, pointing to Susan's chest.

Susan shook her head. "Goddess, no!"

"So, you haven't...? How long have you two been together?"

"No, we have. We've been together just a little over a month." Susan laughed. "I got the tattoo covered up months ago."

"Awww." Michael put his hand over his heart. "That must have been so hard, Suze. I'm sorry. Let me see."

Susan pulled her shirt collar down to expose a fiery, black tribal sun.

"It's really beautiful. It feels like...well, it feels like Steph. It looks like her, you know?"

Susan swallowed hard and nodded. "It really does. So, she's still with me."

"So, Tamika doesn't even know about Steph?" Michael asked.

"Know what? We were never even together." Susan replied.

"Well, if you're still...."

"I'm with Tamika now. And I love her. That's all that matters," Susan insisted.

"Okay. If you say so." He held one hand up in defeat and shook his head. "There she is. Let's go."

"What time is it?" Michael asked once the three of them stood on the sidewalk, breathing in the salt air.

"Just after three," Tamika said, glancing at her watch.

"Wanna just go crash at the penthouse for a while, then go out tonight? Do you want to go to the beach? Or...we can just walk around and shop or whatever. You tell me," Michael said.

Susan wanted to punch him in the face, sometimes, when he acted like the nice guy. He only did it until people liked him. Once they did, he had a way of making everything about him. But she was drunk and didn't care as much right now.

"I really need to just move for a while. Get some exercise," Tamika replied.

Susan and Michael showed Tamika some of their favorite things in town. The Pilgrim Monument, wire art sculptures, the rainbow stairs that were one of the best photo ops in town, and Susan's personal favorite, the hippie stores, Shop Therapy and Spank the Monkey. Tamika bought matching tee shirts for her and Susan that said, I got to hold my girlfriend's hand in P-town and picked one out for Michael that said, Queen and had a rainbow crown in the center.

After a couple hours of window shopping and walking, everyone was tired.

"I'd like to go get our stuff from the car. Maybe freshen up," Tamika said.

"Sure, Doll. I could use a rest. Let's get your things and go to the penthouse," Michael replied.

They didn't arrive at the Crown and Anchor for another hour. As they were walking back to the car, Michael saw several people he knew, and they stopped to talk to each of them. The gay community was small, and she knew some of them, too, but wasn't prepared to be quite so social. Susan could tell that Tamika was getting annoyed, and she was too, although at least she was used to it. He invited every one of them back to the hotel with them. Susan was grateful when they all said they had other plans. Just as Susan thought they were in the clear, she spotted *her*.

Steph was sitting under a café umbrella not two hundred feet from where they stood, and she had spotted Susan, too. Susan didn't move as she felt the color drain from her face. What was supposed to be a romantic weekend was turning into a reunion that she hadn't signed up for. She wished the ground would open up, although she was convinced she was already in hell.

It was always so good to see Steph. Her blond spikes and sleeved arms still caused a flutter in Susan's belly. But that was the problem; she didn't want Tamika to pick up on it, so she had to snap out of it.

Making an effort not to seem too eager to say hello, she waited for someone else to move. Steph stood up, waving furiously at them.

Michael moved toward Steph, and Susan followed. It would be even more telling and awkward if she acted like it was a big deal.

"You guys!!" Steph bubbled, putting one strong arm around Susan and the other around Michael, almost knocking her own glasses off in the process. She held them there for a minute, rocking the three of them back and forth in her excitement.

"So, so good to see you," Steph said when she released them.

"You too," Susan replied.

"It's like old times," Michael added.

But it wasn't. Not really.

"Steph, this is Tamika. Tamika, Steph," Susan said, putting her hand around Tamika's waist.

"Nice to meet you, Tamika." Steph held out a firm hand.

"Likewise," Tamika replied as they shook hands.

Luckily, it was just Steph's nature to connect with people. She chattered on with Michael about a beach party she planned to go to that evening and asked Tamika about herself.

Michael suggested they all go to the beach party together, obviously not thinking of how awkward that could be, and Steph talked to Tamika about the city of Worcester.

"It's such a small world. I forget that there are actually still queer people from *Woostah* that I don't know." Steph laughed. "I mean, I think half of the people from the club are here."

Susan was grateful that their chatter gave her a moment to catch her breath and realize that this didn't have to be a disaster as long as Michael didn't say something to embarrass her.

"So, you all know one another from the club?" Tamika asked.

Susan swallowed hard. She could feel Michael's stare boring into her, and she refused to make eye contact with him. He knew she hated being on display; did he want her to be uncomfortable? To fumble as she introduced the woman she was once madly in love with to her new girlfriend?

"You know...I think we actually met at SWAGLY first," Steph answered.

"I told you about Steph. Remember, I stayed with her and Michael before I moved out of my mom's place..." Susan said coolly, although it was a complete lie. She knew she'd never mentioned Steph to Tamika because what would she have said? Even if it had been an unrequited love, it had been profound. She'd even stayed single for a year and a half because she had no interest in anyone else.

Tamika shrugged and nodded, not seeming to think much of it.

Hearing her name called from across the street, Steph craned her head to spot the source.

"Listen, I have to get back to the friends I came with, but I would absolutely love it if you guys joined us at the beach party tonight. Or, if not, tomorrow somewhere...are you staying the whole weekend?"

"What do you think, ladies?" Michael asked, looking at Susan and Tamika.

Susan hesitated. "I..."

"No pressure. We'd just love to have you. They're a bunch of really great people," Steph said, turning to Susan with an assuring look. She had always remembered how shy Susan could be with new people and went out of her way to make her feel comfortable.

"Well, we're staying at the Crown and Anchor. Penthouse. If we don't see you tonight, come to the lobby and have the front desk give us a call tomorrow," Michael said.

Steph nodded, giving Michael a hug first, then Tamika. "Especially nice to meet you."

She hugged Susan last, squeezing her shoulder, and whispered, "I'm *so* happy for you." She pulled away and locked eyes with Susan for just a second, adjusting her glasses with one finger. With a distinctly sad smile, she walked away to rejoin her other friends.

"Can we go to the hotel *like now*? I have to pee," Susan said, making up an excuse to walk swiftly down Commercial Street, not looking back to see if Tamika or Michael were with her. She bumped arms with a few people in the crowded, cobblestone street as she charged forth and didn't stop until she reached the hotel. She just needed a minute. The depth of that final look from Steph had been the icing on the cake. Yes, she was in love with Tamika now, but she would always love Steph, too. It was just how her soul was constructed. The whole damn thing had just been too intense, and she needed to be alone in her head for two minutes.

Looking back over her shoulder, she could see Tamika and Michael making their way slowly, deep in conversation. She hoped Michael didn't reveal too much; he usually only did that kind of thing when he was really drunk, and he'd already sobered up some.

When she reached the hotel, she leaned against the stone wall and crossed her arms, disgusted with herself when she felt herself tearing up. She only had about a minute, so there was no time for this bullshit. She sniffed hard to quell the tears and smiled at Tamika and Michael as they walked up. Remembering her cover story, she feigned a pee-pee dance.

"Come on, slow pokes. I have to go."

"Well, there's a bathroom in the lobby, silly," Michael said. "Go!"

Susan hurried up the stairs and disappeared into the lobby bathroom. When she got out, Michael was talking pretty to the man at the desk, and Tamika was waiting outside the bathroom door.

"Better?" Tamika smirked. Her face didn't indicate that Michael had said anything to her on the walk to the hotel that might have revealed more about Steph than Susan wanted her to know.

Susan nodded, relieved.

Once they were upstairs, Susan was in awe as she took in the luxurious main room. Michael had, indeed, rented the penthouse. When he'd mentioned the penthouse earlier, she'd assumed he'd been exaggerating a little, and she couldn't care less. It had never taken fancy things to impress her. That was Michael's thing. Having any room at the Crown and Anchor was expensive enough. She had just assumed he had a room with a balcony that he was calling the penthouse, but he had the most expensive option in the hotel.

"As many times as we've been by here, I've never even seen the inside of this place. How the hell did you afford this?" Susan asked.

"Susan," Tamika scolded her.

But Susan just shrugged. "We always talk about money; we were best friends. He doesn't care." She instantly regretted her choice of words, but luckily, Michael overlooked the fact that she'd spoken about their closeness in the past tense.

Michael laughed. "No. I don't care. I told you this whole weekend is on MasterCard. There's food and drinks in the fridge. If you want anything, help yourselves. Here, let me show you your room." He led them down the hallway and opened the door to an extravagant room with a king-sized bed. The soft, luxury bedding did impress her; comfort was vital.

As she collapsed onto the plush loveseat, Susan shook her head. "You always said you were going to book this place someday."

"We've made some of our best memories here in P-town, Suzie, even when we had to stay in shitholes," Michael replied, sitting on Susan's lap and wrapping one arm around her.

As Tamika stood in the bedroom doorway, Susan could see her entire body tense up. "Suzie?"

"Yeah, she's always been my little Suzie Q," he said, planting a kiss on Susan's cheek.

"She's not yours," Tamika seethed. Susan had never seen such anger in Tamika's eyes.

"Babe, he didn't mean it that way," Susan insisted, feeling frozen to her seat.

"*Were* you two a thing at one point?" Tamika asked but didn't give time for a reply. Backing up, she waved her arms and carried on, raising her voice a little more with each thing that flew from her mouth. "You said you were only friends. I told you I don't do messy bisexual girls. This thing we have is not going to work if you lie to me, Susan." It seemed as if she could barely catch her breath to get it out.

"What? Honey, just stop. Suzie was my best friend. I'm strictly dickly," Michael said, standing up.

"You..." Tamika pointed at him.

"Excuse me?" Michael replied, hands on his hips. "Please, Bitch. Do you actually think we're lovers? I don't even have anything to say to that stupidity. But I'll tell you, you seem a little con-troll-ing to me. Susan won't put up with that shit for long. She's a raging feminist. And she might be nice, but luckily, I'm not. So, if I see you thinking you can control her or hurt her in any way, you'll be sorry we ever met." He stepped forward, putting his face right into Tamika's, and with the angry look in Tamika's eyes, Susan was convinced that things were about to get physical.

"Oh Goddess, just stop." Susan tried to drag Michael out of the room by both hands, but he was stronger than she was.

"No, I won't stop. If she has a fucking problem..." Michael continued.

"I don't have a problem." Tamika backed up a few steps and put her hands up as she shook her head. The anger was gone from her eyes, but Susan couldn't be sure what she was seeing in them now. Fear? Defeat? As much as she wanted to talk to Tamika, getting Michael to settle down took precedence. Luckily, he calmed down more quickly than usual, probably because Tamika had backed off.

"Michael threw his arms up, "Well, I'm glad *that* foolishness is over. I'm fine now. Just figure out what the fuck her problem is," Michael said, flying into the kitchen. Susan could hear him preparing another drink, which meant that he would calm down quickly.

"I told you. I don't. Do. Drama. You know what my father put our family through." Tamika said quietly.

Susan couldn't understand why Tamika had lost her mind over her friendship with Michael, especially when, if there was anyone to be jealous of, it was Steph. She'd managed to upset Tamika again. Just like she had at the Lobster Pot. Though she feared that a touch or a word would make things worse, she still had to do something quickly to reassure Tamika.

She took Tamika softly by the shoulders, looked into her eyes, and kissed her. Tamika seemed to melt in her arms as they backed up slowly and sat on the bed, still deep in their kiss.

"And trust me, I'm all lesbian. And I'm so fucking in love with you," Susan whispered in Tamika's ear.

Tamika softened even more, nuzzling into Susan's neck. "I'm sorry."

Strolling back through the hallway, drink in hand, Michael glanced in with a smirk, "I'll just shut the door for you lovers."

Neither looked up but held each other close, both breathy. With shivers running through her, Susan welcomed another kiss. Although Tamika was always passionate, there was something different about this kiss. Susan leaned more deeply into Tamika, and Tamika held her without a word. They stayed like this for a few minutes before Susan let herself get lost in it, and before she knew it, they were making love. Thrilled with passion, Susan couldn't muffle her screams as they ground their hips, and she welcomed the intensity of the make-up sex. Afterward, when they were lying in one another's arms, Susan couldn't help but think that, although the sex might have been amazing, nothing was resolved.

"We should talk about..."

Tamika cut her off, putting her fingers to Susan's lips, then slowly tracing the outside of her mouth. "Shhh. No talking."

After they made love again, Tamika fell asleep first. Before Susan drifted off, too, she lay there thinking she should probably be happy right now as she lay in Tamika's arms. So why did she feel sad and lonely instead?

*****

When she woke up, Tamika wasn't in bed beside her. Susan sat up and searched the sheets for her hair tie. She could hear Tamika and Michael talking from the kitchen. She threw her hair up in a messy ponytail and joined them.

"Hey guys," Susan said, eyeing them both cautiously.

"Morning, Sunshine," Michael sang back.

Tamika stepped forward to give Susan a kiss. "We're good. We're friends now."

Michael put one arm around Tamika's shoulder. "We figured it out. I'm a Scorpio, he's a Leo." Tamika smirked.

"Hey, *I'm* a Leo." Susan retorted.

"Yeah, but we get to channel all that passion through sex," Tamika replied.

They all laughed together, and Susan tried not to overthink what was probably meant to be a lighthearted moment, but something didn't sit right with her about Tamika's last remark.

"I think I have a nap hangover. You mind if I get a shower to freshen up?" Tamika asked.

"Not at all, Doll. Go right ahead. I mean it, my suite is your suite. Just meet us up on the rooftop when you're done."

"Thanks. Sounds good."

"Want a drink?" Michael asked Susan as Tamika walked away.

"Naw. I'm more hungry. As usual," Susan replied.

"There's deli in the fridge. I could eat. Let me take it all up with us. Here, take this and grab the cooler, too. It's right there," Michael said, putting a bag of ice in her arms and pointing to the corner.

Arms full, they ascended the stairs to the rooftop.

"I love it up here," Susan remarked as she filled the cooler with ice. "It's so relaxing," she said, taking in the birds against the clear sky.

"I hope you both got to...relax," he added with a laugh.

Susan nodded and felt herself blush.

"Yikes, I thought I was bitchy. Girlfriend needed to chill," he said, bugging his eyes out.

"Yeah. She's...I don't know."

"I'm just saying, if she's jealous of *me*, I can see why you didn't want me to mention Steph," Michael continued.

Susan held her finger up to her lips and looked at the stairs. "Shhh."

"Oh, calm down. She's in the shower."

"I know. I'm paranoid," Susan replied.

"No. I don't think you are. She's fucking jealous. I know she and I are good now, and I'm not saying I don't like her, but still...she's something else. You don't need any bullshit, Susan. Not after Robin and Cathy."

"Oh, Goddess, she's nothing like them."

"I'm not saying she is, but you deserve the best after them," Michael insisted.

"This is the first time I have seen her like this." With Tamika's family background, Susan understood why Tamika might get jealous easily, but she wasn't going to share the details with Michael.

"Has she met anyone else? DJ? Your mom?" Michael asked.

Susan shook her head as she put together a turkey and Swiss sandwich.

"She hasn't met Mamma?"

"It's only been a month. I don't even bother telling anyone anymore until I'm sure there's something to tell. Cathy and Robin were the only real relationships I ever had, you know, that was more than just a few dates, and you know how those turned out."

Michael leaned in and patted her on the arm. "Oh, please. You're so far in, Suze."

"I know I am." She sighed and bowed her head in defeat.

"But if she finds out about your feelings for Steph and you haven't told her, don't you think that will be a bigger mess?"

Susan was always shocked when he made such a profound point. He was generally so focused on fun and drama that these things didn't come out of his mouth often. But he knew her well, so when they did come out of his mouth, he was always right.

"But there's nothing to tell, Michael. You know that. There never fucking was anything to tell. She and I aren't even...friends anymore. I mean, we don't hang out or anything. I have a different life."

"Mmm hmm. Okay. I'm just saying...you know the gay community is small. You just never know what will come out, and then, it will look like there was a reason to hide it."

"I'm not really worried. I don't really see anyone anymore. Go anywhere. It's not like our club days," Susan assured him.

"Okay. Your choice. But you know...we might not be best friends anymore, but I will still tear her apart if she hurts you, Suzie."

Susan smiled. "I know. Thanks. I miss you, you know."

"I miss you too. I miss us." He took a drag from his cigarette and blinked back a few tears. "But whatever."

"Thanks for inviting us to stay with you."

"I'm thrilled you're here. I mean, yeah, we had our fights, but you know I love you, Suzie. And I'm happy you have someone...but I mean it, she better not hurt you."

"I'm sorry...about James. I can tell you love him."

"Whatever. I have the captain," he said, holding up his drink.

Susan stood up and looked down over the bustling street in the front, then at the people playing volleyball on the sand in the back.

She was happy to be away from the crowds.

Michael stood beside her as she gazed into the waves, ate her sandwich, and told her all about his whirlwind romance with James. Susan felt the hurt in her chest as she listened to how he had messed up another relationship and, ultimately, broken his own heart because of his insecurity. Of course, she could never tell him that.

"I'm sorry. Sounds like this was recent. I can still feel...." She choked back tears.

He stood and pulled her up into a hug. "I love you," he said through tears of his own.

Feeling Michael's pain didn't erase the struggle between them but made it possible for her to reach past it.

When Susan heard Tamika stirring around downstairs, she pulled away from Michael.

"Oh, wow, it's great up here," Tamika remarked when she reached the top.

Michael nodded, "You can pick out all the hotties." He leaned over to get a closer look. "I want to go down there and kiss that boy and that boy, but eww, not that boy."

"You feel better, Baby?" Susan asked, snuggling into Tamika..

"So much better. Whoa, is it really past six?" Tamika asked, looking at her watch.

"Yup, which means we better think about how we plan to party tonight," Michael replied.

After discovering that Tamika had never seen a drag show, Michael knew exactly where they were going that evening. As they exited the hotel, he shared his plan.

"The Pied Piper," Michael declared, holding his cigarette with one pinky in the air.

"What?" Tamika chuckled.

"Shenanigans. That's where we should see the drag show.

They're the best. And they have food, too. You know we'll get hungry again."

"We've had some real fun there, haven't we, Suzie?" He smirked.

"Yeah," she replied simply, trying to downplay the flutter of emotion. It was where Steph had kissed her, and she knew that was exactly what Michael was referring to. She could see Tamika looking at her out of the corner of her eye. Michael wasn't exactly subtle. She looked straight ahead, turning onto Bradford Street, hoping Michael wouldn't continue and Tamika would let it go.

"Well, let's go then. I, for one, look fabulous, and you're lesbians, so you don't even have to."

"Gee, thanks." He always had a way of making her feel like a troll with a hump on her back.

When they reached the Pied Piper, Susan could see that it was packed. She hated this part of travel and adventure. Crowds exhausted her.

"I have to check, but I think we might be full, guys," the waiter said from behind his sidewalk stand as he fidgeted with his collar.

"Nooo!" Michael squealed and put his arm around Tamika. "Honey, do you know that this cute little lesbian here has never ever seen a drag show? Isn't that just like the saddest thing you've ever heard? You know that this is the best of the best, so we just have to get her in here to see these beautiful boys. Can you check? For me? I could make it worth your while." Michael shot a bright smile at him.

The host laughed and shifted his feet a few times as if he was still deciding whether he wanted to check. "W...w...well, I'll look." He stammered and tipped his head down.

They could see the host talking to an older woman whose authority made it clear that she was the manager.

"My friend, Andy, here got you folks a good table. Right this way," the woman said as she approached.

"Thank you, Andy." Michael threw the host a kiss. Andy raised his hand with a slight wave but returned to his post on the sidewalk.

"I'm Barb. Show starts in about a half hour. Can I get some drinks started for you until your waitress can make it over here?"

Each of them ordered a drink. Susan didn't drink often, but it felt like the kind of day that called for being drunk twice.

The first half of the drag show was one of the best drag performances that Susan had ever seen. She could tell Tamika was enjoying herself, too. After making his way on stage and singing along to Ru Paul's *Cover Girl* like he did every time, Michael crashed back into his seat to recover. When the dancers took a break, he stood up, wobbled a bit, then recovered and let out a roaring laugh.

"I'm drunk," Michael slurred.

"You don't say." Susan smiled, pretty drunk herself.

"Hey, that makes three of us. You're right; this *is* awesome." Tamika stood up and hugged Michael, which made Susan happy. Even if the images of a blissful foursome who got along perfectly hadn't materialized, she would enjoy the fact that two people she loved had connected a little.

"I'll be back. I want to make sure Andy is still here," Michael said, smoothing both his shirt and his hair as he walked away.

"Oh, Goddess." Susan shook her head.

She and Tamika were so drunk that they made out right at the table. Tamika was usually much more reserved about public displays of affection, so it felt freeing to Susan to be able to let go. Susan wasn't afraid to be romantic in front of others, but she didn't usually make out with women in the middle of a restaurant, either.

The exhilaration made her feel even more drunk. So many thoughts raced through her mind. If just one person from the gay crowd back home could see her now. She was tired of being thought of as the sweet little friend who couldn't find love. The awkward, fat girl. Like Michael said, the gay community was small. So, as much as Susan loved Tamika and enjoyed making out with her, anyway, she kissed with a little extra fervor when she thought about someone from home seeing her like this.

"Are we ready for some more fun?" A skinny boy in a pink dress shrieked into the microphone. The crowd cheered. "As a special treat for the ladies who love the ladies, we have Ms. Max in the house tonight. If you're not familiar with this delicious treat, check out her solo rock performance tomorrow night right here at the Pied Piper. She's not quite butch, and she's certainly not femme, but she's one hundred percent badass. Give it up for Ms. Max!"

An androgynous woman in tight, black pants and a black suitcoat with the arms torn off and a red sports bra underneath took the microphone, needing only to speak a few words to charm the ladies.

"How are my fellow Sapphists tonight? Ready to rock?" Ms. Max called out.

The women oozed with love for her, screaming and groaning at her sultry voice.

"Well, it looks like I better not make you wait any longer, or I'm going to have to call the firewomen because these chicks are hot!"

The crowd laughed and screamed more, and Ms. Max belted out Joan Jett's *Cherry Bomb*. During breaks in the lyrics, she moved her hips and blew flirty kisses to some of the wilder women in the crowd, finally peeling off her suitcoat after her final note.

"That's...wow!" Tamika smirked, seemingly unable to find the words for the performance.

It was twelve-thirty when the show ended, and Michael still hadn't returned to the table. As they waited for their final bill,

Susan looked around and watched waitresses clear off tables.

"He does this. Just disappears," Susan explained.

Tamika shrugged. "No big deal. I can pay for this. It's a small place. We'll find him."

"The bill is going to be huge," Susan said, wincing.

"That's okay. This weekend is on Mastercard for us, too." Tamika winked.

After the crowd dwindled, they strolled down the street holding hands in perfect silence. It was funny how the most romantic moments can come when you least expected it. The air was warm without much humidity, and the smell of the ocean still hung in the air. Colorful flyers from the various shows in town were carried along the cobblestone by the breeze. The crowd thinned a little more, and when they could hear one another speaking again, Tamika suggested they get ice cream.

"I doubt there is an ice cream place open at this hour," Susan said.

Tamika pointed across the street.

"Well, I never say no to ice cream."

They strolled along with their cones, eventually ending up at the pier. Susan was happy but tired. It had been a really long day. Her stomach dropped when she realized she remembered that not only was Emily dead, but she'd never called DJ to let her know what had happened. She hadn't even thought of Emily in hours. What a terrible person she was to be having so much fun at a time like this.

"What's the matter?" Tamika asked.

"Oh, nothing. Just tired, I guess," Susan replied. Almost no one ever really understood when she tried to explain what was going through her head.

"You sure? You seem off all of a sudden," Tamika pressed.

"Naw, I'm sure." Susan lied, surprised that Tamika had been able to read her. "Should we see if we can find Michael?"

"Yeah, probably." Tamika laughed. "Any idea where we should look?"

"Not really. I mean, he usually just wanders around with people when he disappears."

"Isn't there a hook-up spot?" Tamika asked.

"Oh, he wouldn't be there. It's called the Dick Dock." Susan wrinkled her nose. "He's a big flirt, but he's really not like that. Let's just walk around; I bet we'll run into him."

They walked for another hour, checked back at the Pied Piper, and sat on the bench near the town hall. When it started to drizzle, Tamika let out a sigh.

"We could try to go back to the hotel," Tamika suggested.

"They won't let us into the room," Susan replied.

"This really sucks. Maybe they'll check if he's in the room. Went back without us, maybe? He was pretty drunk."

"I really don't think he's there, but we can try."

As light drizzle suddenly turned to pouring rain, uproarious laughter rang through the nearly empty street. Susan knew his drunk laugh all too well. She looked up and saw Michael stumbling onto the small patch of lawn in front of the courthouse. He landed on his knees first, laughing so hard that he tried to get up but gave up and sat on his ass instead. The lawn was quickly becoming soaked as he sat there and broke into a belly laugh. At least no one would be able to tell if Michael pissed his pants like he usually did when he was this plastered.

Susan rolled her eyes but got up and went to him without stopping to see if Tamika was with her. By the time she reached him, he'd stopped laughing, and she could tell from the look in his eyes that if she didn't get him up now, he would pass out. In times like this, she didn't miss him at all. It had been exhausting trying to make sure he got home safely nearly every week.

Tamika appeared on his other side, and together, they helped him to his feet.

"Come on. Let's go back to the room," Susan urged, trying to pull him up.

Her flip-flopped feet were getting soaked as they splashed through the puddles.

"He was sweet, that Andy, but not really my type. We had some drinks at his place down the way. Messed around a little, but nothing big. I mean, I don't know if it was big. Suzie, you know it wasn't like that," Michael slurred.

Susan nodded. He liked to play a part sometimes, but he wasn't promiscuous. He had always been looking for true love, the same as she had been.

*****

Luckily, Saturday was far better than their first day there, exactly the kind of relaxing, drama-free day Susan liked. They packed some lunch and snacks and spent the entire day at Herring Cove Beach. So many of Susan's best memories had been made seaside. When she was younger, her mom would take her and DJ to Rye Beach in New Hampshire, where they would exhaust themselves in the waves. It seemed that the times she and Michael had spent on this very beach dreaming about finding true love were almost as long ago as the childhood memories were. Today, she was on the same beach with her love. Even if she hadn't stopped thinking about Steph this whole weekend and half-hoped she'd run into her one more time, Tamika was her love. Besides, couldn't someone have more than one love? Wasn't love infinite?

"Where were you just now?" Tamika hit her in the arm playfully.

"Just thinking how happy I am."

"Oh yeah? What has you so happy?" Tamika smirked.

Susan blushed, and her lips quivered through a smile, but she didn't reply. Tamika rolled over from her towel to Susan's and kissed her lightly.

"If I make you so happy, what do you say we move in together?"

"What? Really?" Susan beamed.

"I want you for life." Tamika nodded with a serious expression.

She'd waited so long to hear someone declare their eternal love for her like Tamika had just done. Although Susan's first reaction was elation, a bolt of fear ran through her. She knew Tamika loved her but hadn't seen this coming. Despite the fear, she knew the choice had already been made. When you loved someone, you jumped in headfirst.

Susan opened her mouth, eyes filling with tears, but nothing came out.

"I'll take that as a yes," Tamika whispered.

"Yes." Susan smiled.

"Yes, to what? Sounds serious," Michael whispered, sticking his face in between them.

"Tamika just asked me to move in together."

"Oh. My. God. If you two are not just the cutest little things." He held his chest as he spoke. "We have to celebrate."

"Oh Goddess, I can't celebrate like we did last night. I'm tired." Susan laughed.

"No? Party pooper. You always were a little old lady."

Compared to him, it was true. Her mother always said she was born an old soul. Michael always said it to her like it was a bad thing, but she was rather proud to be a simple girl. It wasn't like she couldn't have fun sometimes, but a few days a year like the one they'd had last night was more than enough for her. Most nights, she'd rather be at home with a book and her cat.

After agreeing to laze around on the rooftop deck with a pizza, they headed back to the hotel. Susan was thrilled to be in her pajamas by seven. Despite the heat, she was chilly after her day in the sun, and it felt extra good to have Tamika's arms around her. It wasn't until Michael's sixth drink that he became obnoxious. Susan looked at her watch and smiled. It was exactly midnight. It was like he was turning into a creature of the night.

But when he proclaimed that he was going down to see who he could meet, she resisted her old urges to make sure he didn't get into trouble and welcomed the opportunity to make love to Tamika again until they fell asleep in one another's arms.

"Tamika told me that she has never seen a lighthouse, so that is the first thing on the itinerary today," Michael announced on the morning of their last day in P-town.

After grabbing breakfast sandwiches, Tamika drove them all to Race Point. The way all three of them sang along to the music in the car felt like the essence of summer vacation, but Susan was still relieved that she and Tamika would be leaving today. Everything seemed good between everyone, and she just wanted it to stay that way. Besides, vacation was fun, but she was always quite ready to get back to her life after an adventure. This time around, she felt it even more; she was about to begin a whole new chapter.

The look on Tamika's face when she saw the lighthouse come into view was what it was all about. Sharing your favorite things with someone you loved allowed you to see it again as it was the first time.

They walked along the beach and took goofy pictures, and Susan found a few seashells for her altar. When Michael threw the frisbee to Tamika, Susan plopped herself down on the moist sand about twenty feet from the surf and thought about writing in the sand but couldn't decide what to write. The rhythmic hiss of the seafoam put Susan in a different place. She could swear she left her body in these moments, a feeling that came with such great peace. Did she have to disappear into a different world to find that kind of peace?

She wasn't sure how long she'd been sitting there when she could hear Tamika telling Michael they'd have to start driving back home soon. Her heart was full, but something was tugging in her chest. The weekend was ending. For her, there was always a little bit of pain in beautiful moments.

CHAPTER FOUR

After a sentimental goodbye with Michael, Susan agreed to renew their friendship. But she already knew that she probably wouldn't follow through. If Tamika didn't like drama, Michael certainly couldn't be a frequent part of their lives, even if Tamika had been the one to cause the drama this time. He always found a way to conjure it up somehow, and she'd never wanted anything as much as she wanted this love with Tamika. Besides, as fun as the weekend was, it felt like she had been living her old life. She was ready to start her new life.

Susan and Tamika made the three-hour drive home without stopping. On the drive, Susan tried to get Tamika to talk about the incidents with Michael at the hotel, but she got next to nothing from Tamika.

"It's in the past now. We already worked it out," was all Tamika said when Susan first brought it up. It was obvious that Tamika was referring to the fact that they'd had such passionate sex after the blowup. Maybe that was the famed make-up sex that Susan has always heard about. But, for her, that hadn't truly resolved the issue. She needed communication.

Susan talked and talked, explaining her perspective. She hated being misunderstood. "You *did* seem jealous. Michael's gay. I'm a lesbian. But most importantly, I'm loyal when I am in love. I'm not a cheater. I love you, Tamika."

"I already told you. It's because of what my father did to our family. I know I'm a little messed up from it," Tamika replied.

She would wait between bouts of rambling, hoping Tamika would say more. The silence was worse than fighting. With silence, the awful possibilities ran through her head, unchecked.

"I mean, you scared me. You were so... I just can't...you can't just snap like that." She understood Tamika's reasoning but needed to make it clear that she couldn't handle the drama any more than Tamika could.

She sensed that the more she talked, the more she pissed Tamika off, although that was still just an assumption. Tamika hadn't looked over at her or changed her expression.

Tamika only repeated herself every now and then, "It's in the past. Everything is fine."

She decided to drop it when, after a gap of silence, she tried one last time. "I mean, I love you. I love you so fucking much. I just need us to be able to..."

"I said it's in the past. Leave it there," Tamika spat.

So, she left it. She would have to love Tamika enough to understand her and learn not to piss her off.

Things moved fast when they got back from vacation. Although Susan had doubts after how she and Tamika had gotten along on the trip, this was what she'd been waiting for her whole life. She would be crazy to back down because of fear. Fully immersing herself in love was just who she was.

When they weren't at work or school, they spent nearly every moment making love, looking for a new place, or packing.

One day, while Tamika was in class, Susan assessed what still needed to be done. It was too hot to do much, but she wanted to accomplish something. Setting her fan on the nightstand pointed toward her bedroom closet, she plopped herself down, moved some old clothes aside, and dug all the way to the back, retrieving the giant blue tote that held her memorabilia.

She liked to joke that she was such a packrat that this was her alternative to a scrapbook, and even named it Big Blue. It held an array of sentimental things, from cards her gramma had given her when she was little to sticker books, paper crafts she had done with her mom, yearbooks, friendship bracelets from DJ, and trinkets that reminded her of lost loves, including a label from the wine she drank the first time she'd made love to a woman.

As she unsnapped the lid, Cocoa lay right on top. Susan reached out and touched the rag doll's worn-out face, then pulled her out and reminisced. Along with her books, Cocoa had always been one of Susan's greatest comforts, and she'd only been demoted from sitting on her nightstand to the tote when Tamika had started spending every night at her place.

Her gramma and her mother, Alice, had given her the doll when she was five. Alice and Susan had recently left Susan's father and moved in with Alice's parents. Susan had to leave most of her toys behind, and although there were a few at her grandparent's house, they wanted her to have something special. They set the brown paper bag down on her gramma's kitchen table just a few days after they'd moved in. She could remember squirming in the kitchen chair; it was always hard to stay still when the puffy cushions came untied.

"Is it a kitty?" Susan asked, excited. She didn't understand when Alice began to cry.

"No, no, we can't have a kitty here, either. I'm sorry. But we think you'll like this a lot."

Still rattled by the sound of the three paper bags they'd managed to bring with them the night they'd left, Susan was afraid to touch it. Alice had held two heavy bags, one under each arm, as she tried to help Susan down the stairs in the dark. Susan carried the third bag; it was lighter than the others, but she still struggled to hold it, and Alice had to hush her several times when the paper bag started crinkling. Susan looked over her shoulder into the living room with the disgusting green carpet, hoping they'd never see her father again. She'd heard her mother talking to her aunts often enough, and she agreed; she hoped he'd finally drank so much that he would never wake up.

"I'm sorry," Susan uttered. She hated seeing her mother cry.

She looked down at her hands. Alice had told her over and over that they could not have a cat as long as they lived with her father, and Susan didn't need to ask why. He got violent when he'd been drinking. If he was capable of smacking Alice around, there was no telling what he might do to a pet.

"Open it," Her gramma whispered, putting her arm around Alice.

"I'm okay," Alice assured her, wiping away her tears and gently pushing the bag across the table closer to Susan.

Susan opened it gingerly. She stood up, looked down into the bag, and scooped up the rag doll with the flowered blue dress, giving her a giant hug. "Thank you."

"You like her?" Her mother asked.

"I love her," Susan answered, burying her face into the doll for a moment. When she looked up to see the faces of her mother and gramma, she could still see sadness in her mother's eyes.

"I can snuggle her just like a kitty. I'll name her Cocoa because she's brown and makes me feel snuggly and warm."

Her mother smiled; everything was okay.

It felt like a lifetime ago. She couldn't believe she was about to enter a new season of her life with Tamika now.

As Susan reached to set Cocoa on the bed safely so she could continue to reminisce with the other contents, she bumped the fan and heard something blow out of Big Blue. She looked around, and it took her a moment to spot the photo that had landed next to her bureau. She crawled over to retrieve it, but when she saw the image, she was surprised to see a picture of her gramma that she had never seen before.

"Where did this come from?" She asked, looking beside her and, for some reason, expecting to see Emily standing there. She had always stood right there with her when she did these little projects, watching her every move. Her heart fell as she realized her friend wasn't there in body. It was shocking, really, because, as she had spoken to the air, it felt as if Emily had been listening. Susan could almost see her head cocked sideways as she had always done when Susan rambled. A bit shaken by the revelation, Susan forced herself to focus on the picture.

When she picked it up, it felt as if a memory flitted through her chest like a bumblebee in clover, but she was certain she had never laid eyes on the photo. She had memorized every picture in Alice's single photo album, and this wasn't one of them. From the look of it, the picture had to be taken before Susan was even born. The glasses her gramma wore were definitely a style from the fifties or sixties, and her hair was still brown, not gray. She searched her mind, trying to understand the sense of familiarity that washed over her. She recognized the dress, pink with little yellow flowers, though it hadn't existed in dress form long before she was born. It was clearly the dress whose fabric was now nestled in between other squares in the doll blanket that her mother had made for Cocoa years ago, which, no doubt, was somewhere in the tote as well. Maybe it was just seeing her gramma's kitchen. That place had felt like home in a way no other place ever had. But it felt like more than that, not just the sentimentality she usually felt while she reminisced over a photo. It felt like her gramma was trying to tell her something. Like she might jump right out of the picture and speak to her. Of course, she knew that was silly. But, sensible or not, the feeling stayed with her throughout the day, and she continued to search for answers, not only about where the picture had come from but what her gramma might have said to her at this important time in her life if she had been here to do so. Was there something her gramma wanted her to know as she moved out of the little apartment she loved to move in with Tamika?

By the time August arrived, everything was packed. Tamika had finished her summer courses, and she and Susan were exhausted in the best possible way. Susan had indulged in rereading every story and poem, not only to guide Tamika through writing her papers but to enjoy the perspective shift about each familiar title and savor the new ones. Susan was in awe that the humid nights in which they'd lay side by side, books in hand, were already behind them.

With her final elective behind her, all Tamika could talk about was her upcoming clinical rotation. As tiring as the summer had been, she knew it was nothing compared to the intensity of five different specialties. She would finally get a true sense of what it was like to apply the concepts she'd learned to real, live people. But, to Susan, she didn't seem the least bit scared of the challenging and fast-paced year ahead of her; she was even committed to returning to the gym once the summer was over. The way Tamika charged forth with a fearless power she couldn't relate to kept Susan in constant awe and admiration of her lover. Susan especially loved the way Tamika's eyes lit up when she talked about the pediatric rotation, always being swept back to their first date, where she'd seen the same look in Tamika's eyes as she talked about working with children and being a mother. Tamika's only concern was balancing it all: a new relationship, a move, and her rotation. But Susan assured her that, together, they would get through it.

Both apartments were bare, making it hard to accomplish day-to-day things. Susan had always hated transitions, and this was no exception. She just wanted to be at their new place and start their life together. With stacks of boxes all around, Susan always found an excuse not to be home. It just didn't feel like home anymore. But it did give her the perfect opportunity to make a plan and whisk Tamika away. Since she was finally convinced that this was happening, it was time to introduce her love to her mother and her childhood best friend, DJ. It was an important milestone for her; although she'd had a handful of girlfriends throughout college, her mother and DJ had never met any of them. None of the relationships had ever lasted long enough. DJ agreed to meet them at her mother's.

"You're such a good sport," Susan said to Tamika as they pulled up to Alice's apartment.

"Why?"

"I would rather die than meet that many people at once."

Tamika laughed. "I don't mind. I'm happy; this is a big moment."

Susan squeezed her hand, took a breath, and they got out of the car. She was probably more nervous than Tamika was.

The neighborhood was so different than the one she'd grown up in. Although they'd been on public assistance, no one would have known it. Sure, they'd had to live humbly, but Alice had found them an apartment in a sweet, quiet, family neighborhood mainly consisting of single-family homes. Susan hadn't known how lucky she was to have lived on that quiet little street until her mother had remarried last year and moved to an area that was anything but sweet. She couldn't imagine how her quiet, tidy mother had ever been okay living in a place like this. But she supposed that was precisely what love did to you sometimes, made you do things that, five years earlier, no one could ever convince you you'd actually do.

The August air wreaked of trash from the overspilling barrels on the sidewalk. Alice waved down at them from the third floor as she hung the wash. Susan waved back and weaved in and out of half-naked children covered in colorful popsicle drippings as she traipsed up the stairs. A chicken bone littered the final flight, making Susan want to gag.

"Hi, Honey." Alice wrapped her arms around her daughter, then leaned in to give Tamika one too. "Tamika, it's so nice to finally meet you."

Seeing her mom greet her girlfriend with such genuine warmth touched Susan. It wasn't that Alice wasn't kind, but she wasn't bubbly or overly friendly either. It hadn't been lost on Susan that she was like her mother in this way. You had to be guarded in a world like this.

"Welcome to our palace," Alice joked, motioning toward the neighborhood chaos.

Tamika waved her hand. "Trust me, I've seen worse. Home is in there, not out here," she said, pointing to the apartment door.

She was smooth, even with her mother, and Susan fell in love with her a little more. Susan could see Alice relax, knowing Tamika didn't equate her character with her neighborhood.

"Let's get a drink. I have a pot of coffee on, or I made some yummy iced tea," Alice said and held the screen door open for them. "Just don't let Simba out."

Still dreading introducing Tamika to Ed, Susan took a deep breath and walked inside.

Ed was rushing around the kitchen, seemingly looking for something.

"Honey." Alice summoned him with one word.

"Oh, I'm sorry, I'm sorry. Here I am, running around like a chicken with my head cut off. Tamika!" Ed stopped and held out his hand to Tamika. As Tamika reached for it, he pulled her into a hug instead. Susan wanted to die, but Tamika didn't seem to mind.

"I usually have far better hospitality, I swear. I went to Johnson and Wales, you know. I love to cook for people..." He prattled on.

"Ed is taking your stepsisters shopping, and he's running late..." Alice interrupted.

Relief washed over Susan; today had just gotten ninety percent easier than she thought.

"Where is my...."

"It's all in the bathroom, Dear." Alice gritted her teeth.

"What would I do without you?" Ed pecked her on the cheek.

"It was nice to meet you, and I promise I'll be a much better host next time. But if I don't get in the shower now, my girls may disown me," Ed said.

"Don't worry, really. It was nice to meet you, too." Tamika smiled.

"Hey, DJ's still coming, right?" Alice asked.

Susan nodded. "You know she's always late," Susan replied.

Alice laughed and nodded emphatically.

Alice puttered around the kitchen for a few minutes, getting glasses and plates, and asked Susan how work had been. She always loved hearing about Susan's bookstore adventures.

Alice stopped in her tracks as she held the sugar bowl. "Shit. I can't believe I forgot to pick up cream before he left. I need my coffee. He's going to kill me if I ask him to bring some back and make him even later."

"Why don't I go pick some up for you?" Tamika offered.

"Oh my gosh, you don't have to do that," Alice replied.

"I want to," Tamika insisted, holding up her keys. "I'll just be a few minutes," she assured Alice and headed down the stairs.

Susan could tell that Tamika had wanted to kiss her instead of only squeezing her arm before she left. Showing affection for her girlfriends wasn't something Tamika was able to do in front of her own family.

"That man." Alice sighed, shaking her head in the direction of the bathroom door. I told him about ten times to put that goddamn paper down and get his ass in the shower, but no... I'm glad he's going out with his girls, and I get to have the day with *my* girls for a change."

Hearing her mom call all three of them her girls made Susan feel grateful that Alice already included Tamika as part of the family.

The bathroom door popped open, and Ed reemerged.

"Speak of the devil." Alice chuckled.

"You two talking shit about me?" He joked and gave Susan a lingering hug. "Didn't really get to say hello to you earlier."

"I was just saying how much I would miss you today." Alice smirked.

"Oh, you can't wait to get rid of me."

Susan took a seat at the table, relieved that he'd let go of her to wrap his arms around Alice. She had to admit that he and her mother looked sweet together. His short, stocky build, prematurely white hair, and comical demeanor reminded Susan of a funny little gnome. With the loving way he looked at Alice, it was as if his height was intentionally designed so he could look right into her eyes. And his eyes showed his weary soul, so although Susan struggled to like him sometimes, those eyes always seemed to bring her back to a place where she could find compassion for him. Besides, how could she not have a softness for someone who so obviously adored Alice? After her father and some of the assholes Alice had dated, Susan was happy that Alice was finally loved the way she deserved to be.

"So, it's nice to finally meet your brown sugar," Ed said, laughing proudly at himself.

Susan snapped her head up and glared at him.

"Her name is Tamika." She remained calm even though she wanted to tear his face off. What the fuck was wrong with people? She tried to be a loving soul, but when people said stupid shit like that, she couldn't find anything but rage inside her. Sometimes, she was even convinced she could be a powerful Witch if she were willing to go to the dark side, but it wasn't her style. Although she may have been more comfortable with darker things in life than some and fantasized about killing people to avenge the underdog, she knew those were just thoughts. She wasn't truly a dark Witch, but sometimes she wished she was.

"I know. I was just being funny.

She raised her voice. "Well, that's not funny. That's racist."

Instead of saying anything else, she got up and walked out to the porch for fresh air. Nature always calmed her, even if there seemed to be precious little of it in her mother's neighborhood.

She could hear Ed and Alice saying goodbye and didn't turn around as his footsteps faded down the stairs.

"Susan, he's not racist," Alice said evenly as she stood beside her on the porch.

She loved her mother so much, and she loved seeing Alice happy. She had to find a way to make her relationship with Ed better than the one she'd had with her mom's last boyfriend. But Ed didn't make it easy.

"He wasn't trying to be...I don't know. I think you're being a little sensitive. Ed's just a goof," Alice said quietly.

"I am sensitive about *that stuff*. I don't think that's a bad thing," Susan replied, not looking at her mom. "You're the one who taught me everyone is the same. Grampa was like that, for fuck's sake, and you hated it."

"Ed is *not* like Grampa," her mother snapped, lighting a cigarette.

Susan could tell by her mother's tone that she'd hit a nerve with the implication.

"I didn't mean...I just don't like that. He can't say things like that. How do you think Tamika will feel if he talks like that around her?"

"Well, I don't think he's stupid enough to say something like that in front of her, Susan."

"Well, how does he think it makes me feel, then? I love her. If he wouldn't say it in front of her, he shouldn't say it around me either. Or at all, for that matter. It's racist, whether you know it or not. And I know I can't change the way he thinks, but he needs to think about what he's saying."

"Yes, I know, I know. We are just the ignorant, old parents, and everything we say sounds like an insult to the educated college woman," Alice said, shaking her head.

Tears welled up in Susan's eyes. Glad that she was still facing away from Alice, she sniffed hard to stop the tears. Her mother knew better than anyone that her biggest fear was being considered a snob, and now she was suggesting exactly that.

"He's not my parent." She turned around to face her mother. "And it's not about being a college girl. I'm a feminist. You know that. I can't just let people go around saying ignorant shit and letting it go, not when it's about seeing other human beings. You don't have to wear a white robe or burn a cross on your lawn to be racist; it's about seeing people differently. Stereotyping."

"So, tell me...

She held her hand and stomped her foot. "No. I'm not done. You've always let me stand up for what I believe, so I want you to hear me."

"Okay."

"This is the same shit we have been fighting for since the first wave. You know, when Gramma was born, and women couldn't vote. And in the second wave. When you were born and didn't have the right to birth control, divorce, or abortion. This time, it just happens to be about race. Sure, maybe the majority of people have stopped using the N-word like Grampa did, but there are other forms of racism that go much deeper. And, like I said, I'm not just going to stand around and let it go. You know that." She shook her hand as she spoke. Even if she had gone off on a tangent and used some references that probably weren't familiar to her mom, she let out a long breath, satisfied that she'd said her piece.

Alice nodded. "You were never afraid to speak up about this stuff. So, tell me what was so bad about what he said." There was tenderness in her voice now as she spoke.

"It's...it's not even so much what he said. It's just that every time he talks about Tamika, he has to mention something about her being Black. She's a person. She's not just a color."

"I don't know." Alice shook her head and shrugged.

There was no use. Susan turned again and watched the stray cat poking around the trash cans, which were spilling over onto the ground. Tamika drove up, sending the cat running.

"I'll talk to him," Alice whispered, putting her hand on Susan's shoulder.

They headed inside for coffee and tea now that Tamika had gotten cream. Susan was still a little tense and hoped Tamika couldn't sense it.

"Simba! You know you're not allowed up there." Alice wagged her finger at the gigantic tiger cat that stood in the center of the kitchen table as if it were his very own throne.

"Aww, don't scold him, Mom," Susan said, scooping the cat into her arms and breathing him in to relax.

"This girl and her cats. I hope you're a cat person," Alice said, turning to Tamika.

"Not really. I didn't grow up with animals."

Susan did her best to ignore Tamika's response, getting lost in Simba's purr, but it cut through her every time she heard Tamika say it.

A knock at the door startled Simba, who jumped out of Susan's arms, drawing blood.

"Come in, Honey," Alice called as DJ's blond hair popped into view through the screen.

"Ouch! Simba, you're such a wild man sometimes." Alice shook her head and let DJ in, giving her a hug.

"Ehh, this is nothing. Remember the time I..."

"Broke up the feral cat fight? How could we forget?" DJ

finished her sentence.

"Yeah, she's always been a little crazy when it comes to cats," Alice added.

"Well, what was I going to do, let them kill one another?" Susan asked.

Just like that, Susan forgot about the tension; she was happy DJ was here.

Alice went into the bathroom and returned with a band-aid and some antibiotic ointment, and Susan placated her mother, covering the scratch.

"DJ, this is Tamika, obviously." Susan smiled.

"Hi. Nice to meet you. Finally." DJ said, turning to Susan with a smirk.

"You guys keep saying, *finally*. It's been like two months." Susan laughed.

"Still. I mean, you're moving in together. She's like, *the one*, right?" Alice nudged Susan with an elbow, playfully and purposefully embarrassing her in front of Tamika.

"You guys suck," Susan replied with a blush.

"Oh, come on, Babe, it's not like it was a secret." Tamika put an arm around her for a quick second.

"Well, come on, who wants snacks?" Alice asked, moving around the kitchen and grabbing boxes of crackers and plates.

"Need any help, mom?" DJ asked, bouncing over to the other side of the table to help clear the piles of folded laundry and toys so they would have some space.

Hell, some things never changed. DJ had always been the good kid, so helpful and intuitive. It was crazy that Susan had always been jealous of DJ, but she always half-wondered if her mother wouldn't rather have a sweet daughter like DJ than a salty one like her.

"I love your haircut, Mom. Sassy. The red is amazing," DJ said to Alice.

"You've seen it this color, haven't you? It was red at my wedding," Alice replied.

"Yeah. It's still amazing. Maybe it comes out more because of the layers." DJ said, fluffing Alice's hair.

"Mmm, that smells good," Susan said as the smell of marijuana wafted in the screen door.

Tamika turned her head, looking at Susan wide-eyed now.

"What? Is someone making hot wings again?" Alice asked.

Susan and DJ exchanged glances, and both doubled over laughing as they leaned into one another to keep from falling off their chairs. Tamika looked on, smirking at the family antics.

"Okay, why are you laughing at your mother this time?" Alice asked, her hand on her hips.

DJ and Susan had always teased her that she'd been gullible, and she never denied it. She knew how lucky she was that they were genuinely good girls when they were growing up, or they really could have gotten away with a lot.

"Mom, it's pot." Susan managed to stop laughing long enough to fill her in.

"Oh. I can't smell anything. And it smells *good* to you?" Alice asked.

"So good." Susan slowly breathed in, closed her eyes, and shook her head with delight.

"Susan Rose!" Alice shook her head and clicked her tongue, feigning disapproval.

Tamika was still looking at Susan, wide-eyed in disbelief.

"Oh, she's a cool mom." Susan laughed, noticing Tamika's expression.

DJ nodded in agreement.

"I didn't know you smoked that shit, you little hippie." Alice laughed, smacking Susan on the arm.

They nibbled on crackers and cheese and chips and dip. DJ and Alice got to know Tamika by asking about her family and the nursing program. Susan forgot that she'd been nervous about this day at all. Other than the many stories that DJ and Alice had to share, it wasn't as if Tamika was new to the family at all.

"Well, that went well," Susan said on the ride home. She decided not to tell Tamika what happened with Ed. His ignorant, racist *brown sugar* comment would just hurt her. It had to be hard enough being the only person of color meeting a bunch of White strangers.

"Did you think it would go badly?" Tamika asked.

"Well, no. I mean, I would have been more at ease from the start if I knew Ed wasn't going to be there. There's something I don't like about that guy."

"Yeah, I know you've mentioned that. Couldn't really get a feel for him in that short time. But your mom and DJ are great. I'm kind of in awe, actually."

"Why?" Susan laughed.

"It's special. What you have with them. Not everyone has such a longstanding best friend. Or a mom who is a friend, too. And even fewer people are lucky enough to have them love *one another*, too. You all have this little history together. I'm lucky to get my parents and brother in the same room once a year, and even then, we're so formal with one another."

Hearing the pain in Tamika's voice, she reached over and rubbed her leg.

"I mean, I could never have that with my mom," Tamika insisted.

"Never say never," Susan replied.

"No, trust me, Jocelyn Bradley is all mom. She could never find it in her to be a friend to her children. And that's not all bad. I know you have to protect your children. All I know is I do not want to turn into my mother."

"What do you mean?" Susan asked.

"You know, so worried all the time that you can't let your children enjoy life."

"But you said you got it. I mean, remember Tracy Chapman. *Across the Lines*."

"Oh, I do get it. She just wants the world to see us. Wants us to have it all. But I don't think the way she went about it is the only way. It's the only way *she* could pull parenthood off. She did her best with what she had, and I don't hold any grudges about it. I know we all do the best we can with what we understand. With the way we see the world. I also believe that you can give your children all the important things in the world, make sure they are seen for who they are and treated fairly, and not suck out their soul as you do it."

"You want to make sure they get the magic too. Get to be children."

"Exactly. Why do you think I want to do motherhood with *you*?" Tamika asked.

"Aww, Babe."

"I mean it. You're different."

"Everyone worries about becoming their moms."

"Not you. Not with what you two have. You can be yourself with her."

"You're right. I'm free to be myself with her. But that doesn't mean I don't worry about falling into the same traps as she has," Susan replied.

"How so?"

"Well, look at the place she lives in. You have no idea how not-her that is. The noisy, disgusting neighborhood. It's trashy, and she's not. She hates it there and is not a big fan of having four stepdaughters to help raise either. No, let me be more specific. She's not a big fan of the way Ed is such a child himself that he can't parent them. She settled. I don't want to settle. I refuse."

"So, we agree; we're not going to become our mothers." Tamika looked over with a mix of seriousness and determination in her eyes.

Susan wondered how she'd gotten this lucky. This woman had big, powerful dreams, and she'd made it very clear that those dreams wouldn't be complete without Susan.

She went to bed that night with a new sense of content. Before, it had been as if she needed more to convince her that this was real. She hoped that, maybe now, that feeling would fade away. Everything was coming together. Now, all they needed was a new apartment.

While Susan wasn't ready yet, she knew the time would come when she would want to get another cat. So, when they looked at rentals, she made it clear that they needed to choose a place where that would be possible. Tamika's was far more focused on features like a modern kitchen and central air, so she began to look at complexes. Susan had never been a fan of those places. Not only were there too many people, but they were expensive. She couldn't imagine how they'd afford that while Tamika was still in school. It would be tight with Tamika's car payment and her own student loans.

Even though their budget would be more difficult to manage than when they each lived separately, they chose a townhouse in a nicer area of the city. Tamika was in love with it; it had the shiny, new appliances and the central air she wanted, and had a gym, which was really important to her. Susan wasn't as thrilled. The complex looked so cookie-cutter, with four sections of attached buildings, that, in her opinion, were really just glorified apartments that lacked character. Other than a slightly different shade of tan, they were identical in every way, right down to the small patch of mulched squares beside each entryway. She wished there was a private outdoor space. She didn't need much. Just something simple like the tiny yard leading to the cemetery like her current place had. A place where she could feel like a Witch. But she did like the skylights that would allow her to see the moon, and at least the place allowed cats.

It seemed like everyone else around her was growing up; she tried to convince herself she should want some of those better things in life, too. DJ had always been far more responsible than she was, and now Tamika was driven too, which convinced her that it was her who was behind. DJ was busy with her career as a special education teacher, with an extra job on the side, as she and her husband, Matt, planned for the kind of conventional life that she had never seen herself living. Now, Tamika was talking about a house and children, too. Was something wrong with her? All she wanted to do was learn, be witchy, and have a few adventures. She wanted out of the ordinary life everyone else seemed to be working so hard to attain. Clearly, she would have to adjust her vision now that she was building a life with Tamika. But how could she do that and still hold onto the things that made her soul sing? Although she'd never exactly been into spells or any of the typical things people expected from Witches, there was something powerful about having a solitary space where she could connect with nature. Even from her altar indoors, how could she light a candle and commune with the moon when she looked out her window and saw a dozen neighbors living their lives? Having neighbors simply wasn't conducive to her vision.

Sure, she wanted some sort of everyday life, like someone to love and a home, but it had to be magical. It could not be as mundane as going to work, bringing children to dance class or soccer, and cooking supper every night. There was something bigger than all of that. Most times, it felt as if all the power she thought she'd found in herself during her college years never had a chance to be put to use. While college had given her a community that helped her flourish, the message that everyone needed to complete their degree and live an all-American life felt like it went against everything she was. Everything she could be if society wasn't trying to shape her into something she wasn't.

At this point, signing a one-year lease in a place she wasn't thrilled about just meant she would have no choice but to focus on her career, if she could even call it that. It was no time to throw away what little pieces of adulthood she'd managed to attain. There would be a time for magical stuff later. This was just for now. Since her own dreams were so hazy anyway, it made sense to focus on making the love of her life happy.

CHAPTER FIVE

They moved into the townhouse on September first. It was a hot, sticky day, and as Susan lugged the last of the boxes from the U-Haul, she was happy to have the central AC to compete with the blazing heat that streamed through the skylights. Maybe some things *were* worth paying a little extra for, even if she wasn't as enthusiastic as Tamika was about the ugly, contemporary light fixtures or the stainless-steel appliances that were far too complex to operate, in Susan's opinion. Sometimes, she wondered how Tamika had ever settled for her; Tamika deserved all those good things in life, even if Susan found it difficult to live in that world. She'd just been that girl who'd been happy to live in a crappy apartment that overlooked the cemetery. The girl who'd spent a lot of time daydreaming about adventure and reading about mystical things, talking to her cat, and writing letters to a friend she had never met.

Susan dropped the last box and let herself fall onto the floor with a long sigh.

"It's a good feeling, isn't it? To be home?" Tamika asked with a sweet smile.

She nodded. She knew settling into a place took some time, but she wasn't feeling it yet. Cozy spaces had always made a place feel homey to her; here, the living room, kitchen, and dining area were all one wide-open, echoey space. How was someone supposed to figure out where to put furniture with such a shortage of walls? She wasn't sure how it could ever feel like home, but she wouldn't say that to Tamika. Why couldn't she just be happy?

"I think we're just going to have to leave the mattress right there tonight." Susan pointed and laughed.

"Won't take long to set up," Tamika replied.

"But we stuck the platform against the wall behind all the

boxes, and I have no idea where we put the hardware."

"Oh well." Tamika shrugged. "Tomorrow, then. It will be kind of fun. This is exactly how it's supposed to feel on your first night. Sleeping on the floor. Eating out of the pizza box. Besides, we do like living room picnics. I even know where my CD player is."

"True." Just like that, something in her shifted. Tamika was right; there would never be another first night here, so why not enjoy the excitement?

After sharing a pizza, Tamika jumped in the shower while Susan rifled through things to find their essentials. She located the garbage bag with their first-night essentials, brought Tamika a towel, and stretched a fresh sheet onto the mattress.

Susan could see how happy Tamika was when she came out wrapped in her towel, and she looked extra sexy with her dreadlocks up in a pile on top of her head. She had a specific smile that always brought Susan back to the day they met, and every time she was swept back to that place, everything felt okay again.

"I haven't found the duffel bag with the clothes yet." Susan laughed.

"Naked can be fun." Tamika winked and fell onto the mattress.

"I can't believe this is my life," Susan said to her.

"What do you mean?" Tamika asked with a chuckle.

"I don't know. This. You. I mean...I used to just dream about these things. Being a college graduate. Starting a life with my love."

"An amazing townhouse?"

That had never been part of her vision, but she was building a life with Tamika, so she'd need to adjust.

"I don't know. Change has always been hard for me. It's exhausting, even when it's good."

"I think you just have to get used to letting yourself be happy."

"Maybe. I guess it just feels too good to be true sometimes."

"I know what you mean," Tamika replied.

"You do?" Susan asked.

"Of course I do, Babe. I knew you would be the second mother of my babies the first time I saw you, but I worry that I'll go and mess it all up now that I have it. I think everyone goes through these things. But what we have here is real, Babe." She paused and pointed across the room toward the CD player that sat atop the island. "Listen. She knows..."

Susan shook her head in awe and looked at Tamika as she listened to the dreamy lyrics about the high of a new life.

"Who is that?" Susan asked.

Tamika gasped dramatically and clutched her chest. "You don't know Nina Simone's *Feeling Good*."

"I've heard the song, but I didn't know who it was," Susan replied.

"Psychic CD player," they said in unison.

"Got enough energy left to let me rock your world?" Tamika smiled, teasing the edges of her towel open to give Susan a peek.

"I'm sure a shower will revive me," Susan replied, biting her lip.

After they made love, they were lying in one another's arms, and Susan wondered if everything she was experiencing was what happiness felt like. Her emotions had been all over the place today. Maybe feeling nothing would be easier, but she was certain she would never know what that felt like.

"It's so exciting to think about all the adventures we have ahead of us," Susan said.

Tamika nodded.

"Remember we talked about taking a whole summer to travel while we are young? Maybe we should try to save like crazy and do something like that next summer."

"I doubt we would be able to save enough in that time. Not with me still working at the nursing home and in school for the next ten months. Things are going to be tight, Babe."

Susan nodded. "Maybe the following summer, then."

"It's fun to think about, but I won't be able to just up and leave my job for a whole summer."

"You just take a leave or quit and come back and get a new job. People do it all the time."

"Who? Burnouts, maybe. No, if we want a house and children, we need to be focused on our careers right now. I'm too dedicated to indulge in those things. If we stay focused, we'll have amazing family vacations when we have children."

There she went again, being immature. Of course, Tamika was right.

"You have to understand, Susan, that if I'm going to become a powerful Black woman. An independent Black woman who starts a family by the time I'm thirty, I don't have the luxury of messing around. You have no idea what it's like...." She held a hand up, which Susan had learned was a signal that the conversation was over.

Tamika had said the same thing to her a few times already. That Susan had no idea what it was like. She meant that Susan had no idea what it was like to be Black. Obviously, Tamika was right. But it hurt sometimes that Tamika seemed to be so dead-set on Susan not understanding that she shut her down. Still, she realized that you could never fully understand something until you'd been through it. Like DJ would never understand what it was like to be discriminated against as a lesbian. Just like Tamika would never understand the sexual abuse Susan had gone through as a child or what it was like to be the small-town fat girl who was bullied pretty much her whole life.

Maybe the problem wasn't so much that they thought differently or that there were parts of one another neither understood yet, but the fact that when they had these conversations, it felt as if there was so little room for discussion.

Tamika had decided their journey, and Susan didn't want to rock the boat and risk losing what she did have. Love itself was enough, and being an adult was about making due in imperfect situations.

Blue again, she wondered why it was so hard to hold onto that feeling of happiness.

*****

Although she had agreed to unpack whenever she wasn't working, like Tamika had been, to get the new place in shape, today she didn't have it in her. Two solid weeks of this had exhausted her, and it wasn't much closer to feeling the least bit homey. With the couch positioned at an odd angle in the middle of the giant space and the tall granite island, it felt more like a city café than a home. She'd made an attempt, digging through boxes to find décor that might help some, but upon opening the third box, she found her stationery collection and letters and postcards from Fiona. Just underneath the top layer lay the wrinkled note she'd begun writing to Fiona on the day Emily had died. She picked it up and held it to her chest, tears streaming down her face for a few minutes. She wasn't even sure what she was crying about, exactly. Emily's death? All the changes? Her exhaustion? Her fears? Maybe it was all of that combined. She needed to get it all out; she had to let Fiona know about all the changes in her life before everything kept building up.

It was beautiful outside, and she needed to take the day to be with her feelings. After showering and throwing on some clean clothes, she put the letter she had started into her backpack and some additional empty sheets of stationery, hit the Dunkin Donuts' drive-through for a breakfast sandwich, and planted herself at Greenhill Park for the day.

August 15, 1997

Dear Fiona,

I'm so sorry I haven't written since Beltane. I started to write back in July but never finished it because that was the day that Emily died. Thankfully, she went in her sleep, but it felt like a piece of my soul was ripped out. I know it sounds dramatic, but I'm just a completely different person since she is gone – I almost don't know who I am without her.

I graduated in May, and I'm still at Barnes and Noble. Don't plan to leave anytime soon, even though I hate working with people. Remember how I have always insisted that books were the answer to everything? Well, in June, I was at work stocking books and met the woman of my dreams. Her name is Tamika. She came in looking for a book, but it wasn't in stock, so I offered to lend her mine, and, well...we have been together ever since that night. I'm so fucking in love with her, Fiona! It was just this instant thing between us.

Like typical lesbians, we are living together already. We just moved into a new place last week. Wanted to get a picture of us in front of the U-Haul, but I forgot to NOT pack the camera.

Like I told Tamika, sometimes it's like this is all too good to be true. As usual with me, I am having a hard time adjusting to it all. Between having Tamika and not having Emily, sometimes it feels like I am living a whole new life, and I don't quite know how yet. The new place is just ok. It's a townhouse, which is a little like a condo. Every building and feature is identical, which makes it feel a little cult-like. Kind of fancy for my taste, too, but Tamika loves it. She's all in. She wants a house and children with me. Maybe I just don't know how to let things be good, but...I don't know. I mean, I am living the life I have always dreamed of, but something is off, and I don't really know what.

How are you and Will doing? Tell me what's new. One thing I am determined to do with this new me, this new life, is write to you more often. I hope you know I think of you often, even if I don't write as much as I think of you. Fuck, I would have to quit my job to do that. I know this one is short for me, but I had to let you know that, apparently, I'm living in a whole new realm.

Love, Susan

As she stared up at the clouds, she questioned why she was hiding Fiona from Tamika. Tamika had a jealous side, but she'd been secretive even before seeing that. Was she in love with Fiona? Their connection would suggest as much. Maybe she just wanted something she didn't have to share with anyone. Whatever it was, the longer she waited to tell Tamika about Fiona, the more it would seem like there was something to hide.

It was just before Samhain when she received a reply from Fiona. Sent on a postcard with a Raven, it was her shortest and weirdest yet.

October 3, 1997

Hey Susan,

Me and Will are doing fine. Nuttin much to tell from Newfoundland. Life is kind of blah. Same old shit. You still worry too much. Write when you can – just be

Do what makes you happy and live in the moment, but never ignore your gut. I didn't like the energy I felt when I held the last letter you sent. Always trust your own self. Happy Samhain!

Love, Fiona

Susan held the postcard, staring. Just like Fiona had said, she felt its energy. It was always like there was an electric current ran through the letters and postcards Susan received from her. Fiona knew too much sometimes. She hadn't even delved fully into how unhappy she was at times, worrying about the new life with Tamika, yet Fiona had been able to read beyond what she said. Susan both loved it and hated it. Loved that someone knew her so well but hated being so fully exposed without a say when she was so used to hiding herself from the entire world. Clearly, their communication was about so much more than words, which made her uncomfortable sometimes because words were her thing. It helped some, knowing that Fiona felt it, too. She stared at the Raven on the postcard and felt words coming from her mouth before her brain could register them.

"That's going to be my daughter's name," she said out loud.

It wasn't something she'd decided in that moment or had just figured out. It was as if she'd known it all her life and was just stating it aloud for the first time. She had always known she would have a daughter, and now she knew she would have the child with Tamika. A child named Raven.

Tamika poked her head around the corner. "Do I hear you talking about having babies in here?"

"What?" Susan laughed.

"What's going to be your daughter's name?"

"Raven."

She almost held the postcard up but shoved it under her leg instead. How could she explain that a woman she hadn't told her about had delivered a psychic message about their lives?

"I love it, you dark, dark girl," Tamika replied, kissing her hard on the mouth. "We are going to have lots of babies together."

Susan wasn't so sure about that. In fact, in the same way she knew her daughter would be named Raven and that Tamika would be her birth mother, she knew that Raven would be the only child that either of them ever had.

Spacing out for a moment, Susan could picture the child, who looked to be about three years old. The child was dark and beautiful and appeared in a field that Susan had played when she'd been younger. As Susan stood at the opposite end of the field, the child began to cry and run toward Susan with outstretched hands, desperate to get to her. The child's crying got louder. Something was very wrong, and it felt as though Susan could not get to her quickly enough.

Her body jolted in real time as panic rose in her chest.

"Are you okay?" Tamika shook her gently. "What was that? God, Babe, I thought you were having a seizure or something. You scared me."

"I'm fine," she replied, mystified by the experience she'd just had. What had that been about? Was she crazy?

"No, like, your eyes were all...weird, and you jumped...like, really jumped hard. Are you sure you're okay?"

"I have a headache. Hope it's not turning into another migraine," she lied, using her recent migraines to her advantage.

"Make a doctor's appointment. I don't like this," Tamika insisted with a scowl.

Susan nodded but never made the appointment. She didn't need a doctor; what she needed was to talk to Fiona again.

* * * * *

Susan had pictured what all of the firsts would look like with the love of her life. First date. First kiss. But the reality of their first Thanksgiving together was turning out to be disappointing. As a nurse's aide, Tamika had to work every other weekend and holiday. While Susan knew that she should be grateful that it would mean Tamika would have Christmas off, she was miserable knowing that it might always be this way with Tamika's nursing career. It just wasn't the kind of life she pictured for herself. Tamika wanted children so badly, but she was prepared to miss out on Christmas morning? Would Susan just be stuck at home by herself caring for a baby on New Year's Eve instead of ringing in the new year by making love to Tamika?

Alice had offered to serve the meal as supper instead of lunch so Tamika could join them, but since Tamika's family had invited them for dessert after her shift, Susan enjoyed a quiet lunch with her mom and Ed.

After the three of them ate too much, Ed fell asleep on the couch watching old movies, and Susan and Alice giggled about anything and everything as they cleaned up. Most of her best memories were when it was just the two of them together. She'd been thinking more about what Tamika said after she'd first met Alice. How lucky she was to have a mom who was also her friend.

As emotional as she was thinking about it, Susan kept it to herself as she did more and more as she got older. Alice wasn't quite as nostalgic as she was, and sometimes Susan felt silly saying these things aloud. It was enough to just be together.

"Now what? I know I need more time before I can fit dessert," Alice said.

"Me too. But oh, I can't wait to sink my teeth into those magic cookie bars."

Alice gave a dramatic little gasp and covered her mouth. She held one finger up to her lips. "Shhh, I have an idea."

She opened the door to her bedroom, rummaged around in a bureau drawer, and came back out smiling like a mischievous child. She held two coloring books in one hand and waved them quietly at Susan. In the other, she had the big box of Crayolas, and Susan could feel her face light up.

"Oh. My. Goddess. I haven't had the 64 pack in forever," Susan said.

"Shhh. Alice giggled and craned her head around the corner to see that Ed was still asleep. "These were supposed to be for Christmas. I have been having way too much fun shopping."

"Does it have a sharpener too?" Susan whispered.

Alice turned the box around and showed her that it did.

"I think I might be just as excited to look at the color names as I am about coloring."

"Me too! I wish they'd have the contest again."

Scrutinizing the color names was something they'd done since

Susan was little. First, Alice taught Susan her colors with the basic pack. As Susan got older, the boxes grew bigger and bigger until it became a tradition for her to get the sixty-four-pack every year for Christmas. She and Alice went from discussing primary red to analyzing why Crayola chose each shade's name.

"Ugh, God, I want a coffee, but I can't even fit that," Alice said, sitting at the table and lighting a cigarette.

Susan broke the seal on the Crayola box and breathed in the new crayon smell.

"Cornflower blue," they both said and laughed. It was always the first one they checked.

"How did that ever start, anyway? I mean, how did we become so obsessed with cornflower blue, specifically?" Susan asked.

"Our old kitchen wallpaper..."

"Ohh, right." Susan nodded.

She had to have been about thirteen. They'd held up each shade of blue crayon and ruled out the others until they decided that the flowers in the wallpaper were closest to cornflower blue. It led them to decide that it was a ridiculous name for the shade since cornflowers were more of a purply blue than Crayola suggested.

"Still bugs me to this day."

"Me too," Susan agreed.

After they were done examining the names of the other shades, Alice handed Susan her coloring book.

"I picked this one out for you. Ed wanted to get you one with lots of rainbows and unicorns and crap, but I knew it had to be the cats. We have been talking a lot about how happy we are that we have an adult daughter who still likes to color and stuff."

Choosing to ignore the comment about her being *their* daughter, Susan flipped through the cat coloring book and oohed and aahed. She certainly didn't want or need a father.

"I knew it would make you smile. You and your cats. I'm actually really surprised you don't have another one. I know you can't replace Emily, but...there are others out there who need your love, you know."

A part of her wanted to complain to her mother about Tamika's unwillingness to have a cat, but she didn't want to make Tamika seem cold or controlling.

As Susan headed back toward home, she was filled with dread about meeting Tamika's family. She and Tamika had agreed to meet back at the townhouse, and the closer she got, the more frazzled her nerves were. She thought about the times she had bailed before to avoid something she was afraid of. Still ashamed of the way she had escaped in the middle of the night after a date with Robin without so much as a word or the times she never showed up at places that she'd agreed to be, she knew she couldn't do that to Tamika. However, she desperately wanted to turn her car around and go back to the safety of her own mom. No, she was just going to have to face this one.

Tamika was waiting for her in the parking lot, and once they started toward Salisbury Street, she knew she only had about ten minutes to compose herself. In her head, she recited a few normal-sounding things that she might say to them, determined not to make a fool of herself.

She promised herself she wouldn't tell Tamika how nervous she was, although she was sure her total silence on the drive together gave her away. She had driven down Salisbury Street a hundred times over the years, but today, as she looked at the wealthy neighborhood, she saw it differently. The double-wide sidewalks, separated by strips of tree-lined lawns. The houses, many of which she would call mansions, stared back at her, making her question how she could ever hide just how common she was compared to the Bradley family.

She could feel her heart speed up when Tamika flicked on her blinker and turned into the driveway of the massive stucco house. It wasn't quite a mansion, like some of the houses she'd imagined, but the tall, white columns, the numerous eaves, and the stately dormers made her sure that there was no way she could ever relate to these people. Their perfectly manicured lawn with multiple levels of stonewalls and seasonal flowers and the tall, pointy trees between their home and the next stood in sharp contrast to any place she'd ever lived. In fact, she was pretty sure she'd never stepped foot in a place like this.

But Tamika's parents did make her feel a little more at ease when they met them at the door. They seemed friendly enough, especially Jocelyn. After introductions and coats being shed and hung, Tamika's mother disappeared into the kitchen while her father led them to the dining room, asking Tamika about her rotation as they walked down the extensive hallway that echoed just a little each time they stepped. And, at that moment, Susan wasn't sure what she'd been so nervous about. Places like that had always left Susan feeling empty. How could anyone feel at home in a place that replaced comfort with a cold perfection that suggested it was all for show? Maybe she had been too hasty in judging, but at least she felt more at ease now. Things like the expensive art on the walls and the working fireplaces didn't make them all that different after all. People always hid behind the material world; it was part of the human experience.

While fancy things had never impressed her, seeing the house that Tamika had grown up in did offer rich insight. Maybe for the first time, she could understand why Tamika had set her sights on the townhouse and why being a homeowner was at the heart of her dream. Perspective was everything; when you'd only ever know living in a home, that was often the only way you could picture your own family.

"We were hoping to wait for MJ to join us for dessert, but do you want a glass of wine?" Jocelyn asked, practically gliding across the room to the wine rack. Her tall, muscular frame screamed of a dancer, and Susan could picture her on stage, with her braided bun topping off the ballerina motif perfectly.

Susan nodded. She hated wine but didn't want to be rude.

"Do you prefer white or red?" Jocelyn asked.

She *preferred* spiced rum and orange juice.

"A sweet red. I think she'll like one of the dessert wines," Tamika replied.

Susan shot her a look of gratitude across the table, and Marcus rose and sent classical music through the speakers. Susan could understand how a person could see their own family so differently than an outsider did, but still, could Tamika not see how lucky she was to come from a cultured, educated family? Having grown up in a small town with a meek, stay-at-home mother, one of the only things Susan had ever wanted from her own family was that culture and broader perspective that the Bradleys exuded.

Tamika's parents drew her out easily by talking about some nonfiction titles that Susan was excited to discuss. She couldn't always hold her own socially, but when it came to books, she nearly forgot her awkwardness altogether. When the subject changed from books to Susan's professional aspirations, she'd finished a second glass of wine, which had mellowed her quite a bit. Tamika was right; the sweet red, as she had called it, was delicious. She was going to have to find out more about this thing called dessert wine.

"So, Susan. Tamika tells us that your degree is in English." Marcus had a gruff voice and graying hair and looked the part of a professor with his sweater vest and wire glasses.

Susan nodded. "Double major, actually. English and Women's Studies."

"Mmm hmm. Mmm hmm. Women's Studies. Right."

With a buzz from the wine, Susan resisted the urge to flip Marcus off as he made no effort to hide the fact that he held her second major in lower esteem. She decided that it was fitting, seeing as he was a serial cheater, something he did *not* look the part of.

"And have you thought about furthering your studies? In English, I mean. Teaching, perhaps?"

"Oh, Goddess, I could never teach," she replied.

"And why not?" Marcus asked, scrunching his eyebrows.

"Oh, I'm better with ideas than people, really."

"Ideas," Marcus repeated, nodding. "So, research perhaps."

"Something like that." Susan shrugged dispassionately.

"I could not agree more, Dear." Jocelyn smiled at her, not just with her mouth but with her eyes, too. It was the same as Tamika's smile, which made it even easier for Susan to like Jocelyn.

"When I am dancing, I am free. Was free. If ideas are your passion, you follow that...however you have to. Not all of us want to be in a stuffy classroom. Some of us just have no choice as we age. Those who can no longer do, teach, I'm told." Jocelyn shrugged and sipped her wine.

Susan struggled to understand why Tamika had such issues with her mother.

"That must be MJ," Jocelyn said as she heard the front door open. Susan watched as Jocelyn made her way to the hall and wrapped her son in a warm hug. Towering over his mother, he made Jocelyn look even tinier. After hanging his coat, MJ adjusted his tie, smoothed his perfectly clean-cut hair, and joined the rest of them in the dining room.

"Son," Marcus said, standing to greet his son with a firm handshake.

Susan always found it odd when family members shook hands instead of hugged.

"Long flight?" Jocelyn asked as she set out fancy cakes and pies.

"Not bad at all. The drive from Boston actually felt longer. I'm sorry I was delayed," MJ replied.

"MJ, this is Susan. Susan, MJ," Tamika made introductions but didn't get up.

Susan and MJ shook hands, and he sat in the empty seat next to his father, politely waiting for a piece of pumpkin pie.

"It's good to see you, bro. How's academia?" Tamika asked, nudging her brother.

MJ hesitated, taking another bite of pie before answering. He nodded cooly as he replied, seeming to consider every word carefully. "You know. It's what I expected, for the most part, I guess. Working toward tenure can be heavy sometimes, though."

"But you're up to the task," Marcus piped in.

"We weren't sure what you liked, and we rarely have company," Jocelyn explained, pointing at the numerous elaborate desserts.

"Besides, seeing Tamika itself is a special occasion these days," Marcus added.

Susan could tell it was a dig at Tamika, but Tamika was as smooth as always and gave it right back to him.

"And I'm just so glad to be here, Dad." She smiled, looking him in the eye.

It was obvious that she was being sarcastic but hid it so well with her sweet tone that no one could have called her out on it.

"It's nice to have the whole family here. I had to make it to meet Susan. I'm happy to see my sister head over heels in love," MJ said quietly, making eye contact with Tamika.

Tamika smirked and glanced at her father, who looked uncomfortable at the mention of his daughter's relationship.

"What would you like, Susan?" Jocelyn asked, breaking the tension.

"A small piece of cheesecake, please," she replied, mindful to be more conservative about her portion than usual.

"So, what *have* you considered regarding your studies, Susan?" Marcus asked, bringing up the topic again.

"Well, I've thought about a master's in library science," Susan replied.

"And what would you *do* with that?" He looked down over his glasses at her as he took a bite of chocolate cake.

"Well, I think she would work at a library, Marcus," Jocelyn piped in, shooting him a look to back off.

"Well, I am interested," he retorted.

"You know, it's something I used to consider, but I don't think it's quite right for me."

"Libraries are important, but they can be stuffy," MJ interjected.

"Exactly!" Susan became animated as she pointed at MJ. "I don't know...I picture doing something even more...old-fashioned, I guess," she explained, still talking with her hands.

"I don't understand," Marcus said.

"Maybe studying theory?" Jocelyn asked.

Susan reached for the right words. "No. More like a village Witch who shares wisdom with the community in an organic way." Shit, those hadn't been quite the right words at all, and the shocked scowl on Marcus' face confirmed it.

"I...I see," Marcus stammered.

MJ let out a booming laugh. "I'm not going to lie. That sounds cool as shit. You should really ought to play D and D with me and my buddies..."

"Really, with the language, MJ?" Marcus sounded flustered.

Susan could see Tamika stifle a laugh. She'd told Susan that she, herself, liked to ruffle her father's feathers a little, but Susan hadn't even intended to.

Maybe she had found the exact right words after all. Still

grateful for the courage that the dessert wine had given her, she decided that she liked this version of herself. The one who just didn't give a fuck and spoke her truth.

"So?" Tamika asked on the way home.

"It wasn't as bad as I thought. Your mom is nice. Seems more...down to earth than you made her out to be."

"She can be. Just not always with me. Like I said, she just expects a lot more from her own children than she does from the rest of the world." Tamika paused. "And my father? That was fun, huh?"

Susan smirked, basking in pride with how well she'd handled herself. "I guess I held my own." It wouldn't be her first run-in with a man who'd been brainwashed by the Western world, and it wouldn't be her last. In a way, he reminded her a lot of Ed. Susan didn't feel the need to add that what bothered her most about Marcus was that he appeared so put-together that few would have guessed he had women on the side. She may have even had more respect for someone who outwardly seemed like that type of asshole, but there was something about a man who worked so hard to hide it that got under her skin.

"You certainly did, Babe. I have to say, that was pretty awesome."

"I was surprised by MJ. He seems...."

"What? More like my parents than I am, right?"

"No, that's not it. It's like he's trying to live between two very different worlds. Like he's trying like hell to be a successful professional, but he's not doing it for himself. I was actually pretty disappointed that he left before I got to hear more about Dungeons and Dragons. I've always wanted to play."

"Really?" Tamika asked, surprised.

Susan nodded.

"Yeah, I guess I can see that. He used to be off in his own world with all that stuff. Comic books, strange movies, D and D. We were much closer then. But then he got his act together, which made my dad super happy because it meant that at least he could have one child to be proud of."

CHAPTER SIX

As much as she wanted to look forward to Christmas with her mom, Susan dreaded it all. Worried that Ed would pull his shit and say something ignorant and feeling overwhelmed by how to act around her four stepsisters had her on edge. Then again, with a full house, maybe Ed would be less likely to say anything stupid. Still, she worried about Christmas so much that she just wished it were over with already.

Despite her difficulty getting into the holiday spirit, at least the season offered her the opportunity to tell Tamika about Fiona. As they sat at the island together, making out cards, she tried to be casual about it as she scrawled out Fiona's envelope, trying to make it look just like all the rest in the pile. When she finished addressing it, she pushed it close enough to Tamika that she had to notice it. She held her breath as Tamika picked up the card and asked who Fiona was. She was being ridiculous. They had only been together for five months; it wasn't as if Fiona's name was the only one Tamika hadn't heard yet. After all, she hadn't told Tamika about every cousin or friend from high school. So why was she making such a big deal out of this?

Still, her voice shook as she told Tamika about her pen pal, concerned about how jealous and possessive she had seen her girlfriend get in the past. All the hidden letters came to mind, and an odd sense of guilt washed over her. It was a surprise when Tamika didn't seem to think much of it. Maybe a pen pal from another country didn't feel as threatening to her as someone she'd had to see Susan with in the flesh. But it seemed ironic to Susan because her connection with Fiona was far more profound than it had ever been with any ex, maybe more profound than with any human being.

She was glad it was behind her, so why was she still so shaky?

They'd finished making out the cards and snuggled up on the couch together, but even as she was in Tamika's arms, she couldn't relax. She reached for something to say to hide her nerves.

"I can't believe the holidays are here."

"Yeah, I hear they come every year, Babe," Tamika teased.

"I know, but this is our first Christmas together. We've been working so hard that I haven't even come up for air. I guess the holidays just snuck up on me."

Tamika nodded. "You're right. It *is* our first Christmas together. That's something special."

Susan adored her as she lounged happily in her PJs and flipped through the television channels, possibly more content than Susan had ever seen her. Maybe Susan still hadn't fallen in love with the place, but Tamika was happy here, which counted for something.

She wondered how Tamika found that sense of contentedness, not just with their home but in general. Making an attempt to love some of the things Tamika loved about the townhouse might help. It certainly wasn't an awful place, even if it wasn't exactly the home of her dreams. Maybe she could be more patient and learn how to use the dozens of buttons on the stove instead of bitching about it. Turn the television off and enjoy gazing through the skylights and massive windows instead of grumbling about the way the noise carried in what Tamika called an open-concept space.

She just had to learn to let things go. If she could just stop her mind from swirling about the Fiona thing; it was nothing, anyway. Worrying about Christmas with Ed and her new stepsisters had to stop, too; she needed to let things play out instead of thinking about the possibilities of what might go wrong. She just had to shift her focus to improve the holidays for both of them and knew just how to do it.

"You know what would be fun? If we went and got our own Christmas tree this year. With these high ceilings, we can get a great, big one."

Tamika sat up, and her dimples emerged. Susan knew she'd said just the right thing. Tamika loved Christmas, and it was something that they could both be on board with.

"I'm surprised you'd want to do that."

"Why? We'll go buy a saw, pick it out, and cut it down ourselves. We *are* lesbians. It's probably mandatory." She chuckled.

Tamika leaned in closer, wrapped her arms around Susan, and gave her a tender kiss on the lips.

"No, I'm surprised you want to cut down a tree. Being a Witch and all, I just thought you wouldn't be into it."

"I love old-fashioned traditions. We'll just plant a tree for Arbor Day." She shrugged.

She snuggled into her shoulder and closed her eyes for a few moments, breathing in the feeling. There was a certain way that Tamika held her sometimes that made her feel loved. "Then we can come home and have hot cocoa and snuggle."

"And hang the mistletoe," Tamika whispered as she kissed her neck. Although Susan liked the affection, she knew that this meant Tamika probably wanted sex. Why did it always have to end up with sex? Couldn't they have a sweet night without getting naked? Maybe something was wrong with her if she didn't want it as much as Tamika did. After all, they'd only been together for six months. Wasn't she supposed to want to do it all the time like Tamika did?

Susan pulled back a little and kissed Tamika on the cheek. "I'm tired." She plopped down on the couch and grabbed the remote.

"Ouch. Rejected," Tamika said with a wince.

"Aww, no, I'm just tired, Babe."

"Okay." Tamika sighed.

It was only a sigh, but it was all it took to turn a good night into a terrible one in seconds. Susan wanted to scream. She wanted to blurt out everything on her mind but didn't know how to get it out without breaking down and crying like a big baby. Maybe she should have a higher sex drive, but sometimes she needed to know that she was more to Tamika than just a body. And it didn't help that Tamika seemed to think sex was the answer to resolving most of their arguments. It made Susan want it even less because it felt as if it was more important to Tamika than closeness or communication.

She wanted to share deeper things. Sometimes, she wasn't in the mood because she still had issues with her size, and her emotions were no less complex. She couldn't express thoughts and feelings that she couldn't even quite sort out or explain in her own mind, and when she'd tried to find the words in the past, it had always ended badly. There were just times that she couldn't let herself have the vulnerability it took to let someone make love to her, and she knew a lot of it probably had to do with the sexual abuse that she'd experienced as a child, even though she didn't dwell on it. But when she offered this explanation, Tamika had gone on about how she must not be a good lover if Susan didn't want sex. How she didn't make Susan feel safe. And eventually, Tamika ended up telling Susan that she just needed to let go of her past. Susan didn't want it to get to that again, so she decided that saying nothing was best.

Having felt rejected, Tamika would freeze her out for at least a few hours, and it broke Susan's heart that what had been a perfect, sweet moment had been ruined. It killed her that Tamika tended to shut her out when she needed love the most. Maybe she just should have given in to sex.

She could already feel the tension in Tamika's arms and couldn't stand being held when the anger was so palpable. She stretched and scooted away from Tamika so it wouldn't seem too obvious that she needed to escape. Then, she got up without making eye contact, feeling like she didn't belong in her own home.

"I'm going to read for a little while," Susan mumbled and disappeared into the bedroom. She looked around; she missed her old bedroom with the hippie flowers. This one felt so sterile with the same cream color that was on every wall of the townhouse and the dull décor that Tamika informed her offered clean lines, whatever that meant. Other than her little altar in the corner, which admittedly looked out of place, the skylight was her only solace.

Sometimes, it made her feel lonesome to sit by herself with her pain when her love was in the next room. Usually, she just turned to books. Even as a child, it was where she had escaped, but tonight, she didn't even have the energy to read. After staring up at the black sky for a few minutes, she flipped on the television and let something play in the background while writing to Fiona.

December 12, 1997

Dear Fiona,

Being human is stupid. I swear it's all some cosmic joke. I vowed I'd never be like everyone else, but here I am, turning into a cliche. When I'm not at work, nothing really excites me lately. I can't practice my witchy stuff because of the fancy-ass place we live in. I miss the place by the cemetery every day. I mean, sure, I still have an indoor altar, but I feel so much more connected when I go outside, and Gaia knows that wouldn't go over well with some of the uptight people who live here. I truly can't stand our neighbors. It's ironic – Tamika loves this place, and it is so fucking "white American" that it makes me sick. Since she loves it so much, I keep asking myself what I must be missing.

Between work and school, Tamika and I barely see one another some weeks, and I am stuck here with no cat and no yard to do witchy stuff, constantly wondering what the fuck to do with myself. She works as much as she can because it's so expensive to live here, but it never makes sense to me how you'd want to live somewhere that costs so much that you have to work more and so you hardly ever get to enjoy the place you're working so hard to pay for. Having a relationship is so much harder than I thought it would be. I love her so much. I just never thought it would be so much work to live with someone else and "get" each other.

I met most of Tamika's family at Thanksgiving. It was fine, but I'm secretly relieved that she's not close with her family because you know how awkward I can be and how much I hate being around people.

Tamika and I are going to my mom's for Christmas. I want to be excited, but all the stepsisters will be there, and Ed is an ignorant fuck. He made a mildly racist comment a few months ago, and I let him know. Now, because I spoke up, he and my mom swear HE'S not a racist; apparently, I'M just a snob...even if they don't use that word. So, I can't stop worrying about Christmas.

How was your Thanksgiving? Wait, I always forget that Canadian Thanksgiving is in October. Must be weird to have Thanksgiving and Halloween in the same month. What are you guys doing for Christmas? Are you still working at the grocery store? I know you couldn't stand it the last time you mentioned it.

Is this really how people live? They just settle for jobs that make them miserable? I know we have to pay the bills and all, but there has to be something better. I don't even necessarily mean me. I like Barnes and Noble enough. I mean, I'm still surrounded by books, even though I hate working with people. But it's not what I thought I would be doing. There's really no passion there. I just thought my life would be different. Guess we all think that, and then, as my mom says – life sucks, then you die. Being human is overrated; let's be mermaids instead. I don't even know what I'm saying anymore. Getting delirious and falling asleep.

Love, Susan

She popped the letter into an envelope, stuffed it in her nightstand, and fell asleep to reruns of her favorite show of all time,

Little House on the Prairie. There was always a story to get lost in when she didn't like the chapter that her life was in.

When Tamika woke her up the next morning, it was like nothing had happened. Obviously, it had been the better choice for Susan not to blurt out everything she was thinking and feeling because now it was behind them. In fact, Tamika looked like a kid as she rolled over in bed and shook Susan's arm excitedly, saying that Susan had gotten her all excited about Christmas and she wanted to go shopping. She even revealed that she'd just gotten a new credit card in the mail last week that Susan hadn't known anything about. Even though Susan was a little annoyed by this information at first, she couldn't squash Tamika's excitement, especially since she was so eager to spoil Susan's family. Tamika seemed to have mixed feelings about the fact that her parents and brother were going away for Christmas, and she and Susan hadn't been invited. But she also confessed that she was honestly more excited about spending Christmas with Susan's family, especially since there would be children there. Christmas wasn't Christmas without children, Tamika said.

As they shopped, all Tamika could talk about was children. Not just Susan's stepsisters, as they sought out the perfect gifts for each of them, but the children they would have someday. As much as Susan had always wanted a daughter, it worried her when Tamika talked about motherhood, and the thought of multiple children was utterly overwhelming. So many things made her nervous about the prospect of becoming a mom. They were still in their twenties, although Tamika was close to turning 30 and was talking about cryobanks and sperm donors more and more. Susan could still barely figure out how to care for herself in some ways. Sometimes, their values differed, too, which worried her most. Susan tried not to judge Tamika, but Tamika could be awfully focused on material things sometimes. That fact was particularly evident today as Tamika went a little crazy with spending, and Susan had to do her best to rein her in. Trying to do the math as they shopped, she was pretty sure they'd managed to use half of Tamika's new fifteen-hundred-dollar credit card.

But still, it had been a wonderful day shopping with Tamika, and that side of Tamika was rather sweet and adorable, too. It was understandable how Tamika could get caught up in it all as they walked the mall sipping their hot chocolate, enjoying the Christmas carols and all the bright bows and boxes. Maybe Christmas really was magical, not because of the material things, though. But the day had offered Susan a different kind of gift: the opportunity to see her and Tamika in a new light. Since she was being the sensible one for once and Tamika was almost out of control, Susan was beginning to see the potential. Maybe they could balance one another. There was time to keep growing together as they worked toward being moms. It wasn't like they were having children any time soon.

* * * * *

Tamika had to work at the nursing home from seven to seven on Christmas Eve, but there was no room for Susan to complain when she would have her love on Christmas day. Besides, even though she constantly missed Tamika, she tried her best not to make it more difficult by making her feel guilty that they saw each other so little. It was hard enough on Tamika, with thirty-hour clinical rotations and picking up a few shifts at the nursing home to make ends meet. She still didn't know how Tamika pulled it off; she could never work nearly fifty hours a week and maintain her sanity.

Having completed one of her rotations already, in medical-surgical, Tamika was onto her second, psychiatric nursing. She came home nearly every day telling Susan how certain she was that it would be her least favorite out of all of them, explaining that it came much more naturally to her to help people heal their bodies. Healing people's minds was far too complex, and psychiatric issues came with a deeper level of pain than any physical injury possibly could. Now, she was just happy that the psychiatric rotation was coming to an end, and she would have a week off for the holidays before starting her third in internal medicine.

With Tamika so rarely home, Susan felt responsible for taking care of as much as she could to ensure the household ran smoothly. Adapting to be somewhat domestic, especially in the uncomfortable townhouse, didn't always come easily to her. In her last apartment, she had no one else to answer to. Except for making sure the litter box was always clean for Emily, she was free to be a bit of a disorganized slob. Though the transition was a struggle, at the same time, it gave her a sense of purpose, especially at the holidays when she was excited to make everyone happy.

She sat on the floor for hours, relishing in wrapping gifts, making every package look beautiful with bows and coordinating tags. Afterward, the Christmas music kept her company as she baked, ate too much cookie dough, and indulged in looking at the many fliers she'd been collecting from local shelters and the ASPCA to see the cats available for adoption. She envisioned Tamika handing her a stocking with a kitten in it but knew it was a long shot despite the numerous hints she'd dropped. After making the house spotless, she ordered Chinese food for delivery and waited for Tamika to come home, eager to snuggle.

She only realized how tired she was when she fell onto the couch. Shutting the Christmas music off, she welcomed the silence for five minutes before the phone rang. She could see that it was DJ; she had to pick up.

"Hello." She tried to muster the energy to be perky like DJ always was.

"Hellooo. Happy Christmas Eve," DJ chirped.

"Happy Christmas Eve," Susan replied. She had always been in awe of DJ's energy and cheeriness. Sometimes, it even annoyed her. Life wasn't a fucking Hallmark card.

"Did you accomplish everything you wanted to today?" DJ asked.

"Yeah, just about finished everything, and the Chinese food arrived a few minutes ago, so I can finally rest. Tamika should be home soon. What about you?" Susan inquired.

"It was so great, Suze. We got a puppy! I say puppy, but he's a big boy already. They think he's about nine months old. He's a chocolate lab, and we named him Teddy because he is such a teddy bear. I am *so* in love," DJ prattled on.

As a rule, Susan prided herself on not being a jealous person, but she couldn't fight this. Hearing about DJ's new puppy was hard to swallow when getting a kitten was all she'd been able to think about.

"Awww. I can't wait to see him." Full of guilt about her jealousy, Susan sucked it up and let DJ have her moment. How could she not? She could practically hear the smile on DJ's face.

"Suze, he's just got the cutest nose – it's like a lighter shade of brown, and he's just got the puppy fuzz, and...he's so sweet. I think I really understand puppy love for the first time in my life," DJ said.

Susan began to take the takeout containers from the paper bag. Fumbling and barely managing to hold the phone with her chin, one bowl of duck sauce fell to the floor, and the sticky mess quickly spread.

"Oh, shit. One minute, Deej," Susan said.

But DJ kept talking. "DJ, DJ, hold on, okay?" She tried again.

But DJ still didn't hear her. Finally, the phone slipped out from under Susan's chin and fell to the floor.

"One second Deej...I dropped you," Susan called toward the phone as she saved the second container of duck sauce, a must-have for Tamika.

Oblivious, DJ was still talking.

When she finally picked the phone up again, DJ's voice was softer, but Susan didn't think much of it. "...you know? I mean, this isn't the baby we had hoped for, but I love our life, and this little guy does make us feel more like a family."

"I'm so happy for you," Susan replied, although she was a little lost.

"Thanks," DJ said with a hint of sadness in her voice.

"I just spilled a giant container of duck sauce on my freshly mopped floor. I better go. But I can't wait to meet the pup," Susan said.

"Okay."

"I hope you have a wonderful day tomorrow with your parents," Susan said.

"Thanks. I'll call you tomorrow, though, silly. If I don't catch you at home, I will call Mom's," DJ replied.

"Okay. Talk to you tomorrow. I love you," Susan said.

"Love you too."

She hung up the phone and, as she cleaned up her mess, thought about DJ's tone when Susan had picked the phone back up. Taking a moment to think about what she'd missed, Susan determined that DJ must have been talking about how she and Matt had hoped to have a baby by Christmas or at least to be pregnant. If there was one thing that Susan could say about her oldest friend, it was that DJ always pushed through the sadness and found the joy. Now, she felt terrible that she'd rushed DJ off the phone, but she heard Tamika's keys in the lock just as she considered calling her back. Playfully, Tamika peeked one eye around the door with a big grin, then rushed in and took Susan into a hug. She breathed in the smell of winter cold from Tamika's scarf as she held her close.

Something gnawed away at Susan all through supper. She couldn't shake the sadness, even as they snuggled onto the couch for a movie, and it was arguably the perfect Christmas Eve. And what was worse, she couldn't place the reason for it. She knew she should feel joy. There was clearly something wrong with her. It wasn't only tonight; the entire season had always made her feel this way. As much as she loved gift-giving and the family traditions, she was always more excited for January second to come, signaling that the holidays were officially over.

"I'm so excited to share this movie with you. It was my favorite as a teenager," Tamika said, pointing the remote at the DVD player.

"What's it called again?" Susan asked.

"The Kid Who Loved Christmas. It was weird. When I first saw it, it had never occurred to me that none of the Christmas movies really had Black people," Tamika explained.

Susan rubbed Tamika's hand and felt another layer of sadness pile on top of all the others. Sometimes, the sadness of someone you loved was heavier than your own.

The movie was both sweet and sad, but Susan spent most of the time in her head instead of in the movie. She was worried about tomorrow. Maybe that's what was bothering her most. When the movie was over, Tamika let the credits roll and cleaned up the last of the dishes from supper as Susan nodded off, then returned and nudged Susan to come to bed.

Susan's sleep was restless and broken. She saw the clock just after one, acknowledged it was Christmas, and lay awake for over an hour, wondering if other people truly had a sense of joy with the season. She fell asleep again, but only briefly, seeing the clock again at three forty-five. She thought about DJ this time, knowing she was someone who was able to find the light the holidays offered. She thought about the new puppy and replayed something DJ had said on the phone. She'd said something that she was only now processing. She'd said that the puppy hadn't been the baby she wanted. Damn. She should have been more sensitive to DJ. She and Matt had been trying to get pregnant for a while now. As each year passed, they dreamed of having a new baby by the following Christmas, but they hadn't had any luck. She felt awful that she hadn't heard DJ when she was sharing something so painful, all because of spilled duck sauce. She was a terrible friend. It was her last thought before she drifted off again.

She awoke again at four-thirty. This time, something had woken her. A thump. She managed a smile, thinking maybe there were reindeer on her roof, but the fleeting delight was quickly replaced with dread.

She had played out all the scenarios of how Christmas might be ruined; almost all of them included Ed saying something ignorant. He always did, after all. She could feel a pressure in her throat, and like the other times she'd woken up in a panic or with the weight of sadness, she wanted to wake Tamika up. She wanted to ask Tamika to hold her while she cried but knew she couldn't burden her with these things every time they arose. Tamika had to deal with bigotry all her life in a way that Susan could be sensitive to but never fully understand. She didn't need to put this on her, too. No, whatever this nonsense was, it was *her* pain to bear.

She felt Tamika roll over and get up, but she didn't move, willing the sadness away and making room for the day ahead of them.

"It's snowing!"

When she heard Tamika at the window, she couldn't stop the tears. She felt herself well up and snuggled her face into the pillow. Pretending she was more asleep than she was would buy her a few minutes to compose herself. Tamika got back in bed and wrapped herself around Susan from behind. She moved Susan's hair aside and nuzzled her neck.

"It's snowing," Tamika whispered in Susan's ear again.

Susan sniffed the tears. "Mmm." Hoping it wasn't too obvious that she'd been crying a little, Susan turned over and faced Tamika, blinking as if she was just waking up. Tamika leaned in and gave her a soft kiss on the mouth, then nuzzled her neck again.

Physically, Susan was turned on, but her emotions weighed her down. It was a weird contradiction, and she didn't know what to do with it. Again, she wanted to blurt everything out to Tamika, let Tamika hold her, and make love to her. Tamika reached under the covers, slid her hand past Susan's waistband, and caressed Susan's hip. She'd only ruin this sweet moment for Tamika if she started bawling and sniveling now, so she pulled Tamika closer and let her body ask for more. After a few failed attempts, she finally managed to get out of her head as Tamika undressed her. She let herself enjoy Tamika's hands on her breasts, pulled off Tamika's sweatshirt, and reveled in the feeling of touching skin. Christmas morning lovemaking was something her romantic little heart had always wanted, but it didn't make her feel quite like she thought it would.

As she showered, she ran it through her mind. It had been what anyone would call perfect, but she still felt sad. She had to just put the questions out of her head. The questions about what the fuck was wrong with her. It was Christmas day, and the people she loved deserved a much stronger version of her than the pathetic mess she was in her head. She felt better as she put on her green flannel straight out of the dryer. It would be a good day. She was determined to make it perfect for Tamika and her mom, the two women she loved the most.

After the presents were packed in the car and they were on their way, the dread made her stomach heavy again. Of course, she wanted to be with her mom on Christmas, but the new stepfamily was a little much for her. Tamika turned on the radio and turned up the Christmas songs. It felt like an overwhelming addition to

Susan's already noisy mind, but she turned and smiled at Tamika, letting her enjoy the moment.

Her mom excitedly greeted them at the door, and the warmth of her hug cut right through Susan's tension. The bustle of all the girls and Ed gathering around threatened to turn her overwhelm into near panic, but she said quick hellos and escaped to the living room to put the gifts she was holding under the tree.

She spotted Simba right away, sitting under the tree himself. She practically dropped the presents to pet him. Plopping down on the floor beside him, she let his purring soothe her. Her mother poked her head around the corner from the kitchen.

"You okay?" Alice asked.

Susan nodded. "Just soaking up some kitty vibes."

Her mom scrunched one eyebrow but smiled. "Okay."

"Alice, come here. Look at this bullshit," Ed called her back into the room. "The little asshole burnt the toast. This is the shit that gets me pissed."

"Again, Julie?" Shannon mocked.

The family's voices blended together, and by the time Susan managed to talk herself into parting from Simba and rejoining the family, everyone was laughing about Julie's burnt toast. But Susan didn't like the way they spoke to the girls sometimes.

"Some of us have eaten, and some of us haven't, so it's a little crazy here," Alice reported.

"What about you ladies? Have you eaten?" Ed asked, wrapping one arm across Susan's shoulders from the back and leaning in too close like he always did.

"I've been up for hours, so I ate, but I could eat again," Susan replied.

"Atta girl," Ed said, rubbing her belly. Susan backed up and asked Alice if she could help with anything.

"You can make your punch. Been thinking about that all week,"

Alice replied.

"I can help," Julie offered.

Susan smiled, but Alice shut her down. "No way, you'll just make a mess. You showed us how much of a slob you are with those toast crumbs."

"Mom." Susan felt bad for the kid. She remembered how it felt to be called a slob when she'd just been a kid.

"Just go in your room, for Christ's sake," Ed grumbled.

Nicki piped in. "Come on, Julie, I need help with something anyway." She was always hovering around, waiting to be the one to intervene when tension arose.

"Hannah, did you feed Simba?" Ed shouted across the apartment.

"No, I was going to, but then Susan and Tamika came, and you asked us to..." Hannah started.

"Well, do it now, then," Ed snapped.

Her mom and Ed tried their best, and it couldn't be easy with four girls in a small apartment.

Shannon walked by, shaking her head. "You wonder why I smoke weed."

Tamika smirked, but Susan was mortified, mostly because she knew if her mom or Ed heard it, there would only be more tension. But it seemed that no one else heard her.

Susan began to make the punch, Alice made coffee, and Tamika talked with Ed in the living room.

"You want anything to eat?" Susan popped her head in and asked Tamika after she was finished making the punch.

"No, one breakfast is enough for me," Tamika replied, curling her lip.

Susan shot her a look and walked away. She wanted to tell her to fuck off. It was Christmas, and she would eat what she damn well pleased. Besides, it was almost noon, and they'd eaten at six that morning. She didn't know why Tamika had to be such a bitch about what she ate sometimes.

Despite her earlier comment, Shannon seemed to be the least bothered by the moodiness. She sat at the kitchen table with Alice and Susan and grabbed a fresh cinnamon roll.

"So, I can go out tomorrow, right?" She asked Alice.

Alice sipped her coffee and rolled her eyes. "We really haven't gotten that far yet, Shannon; it's Christmas."

"I'll ask Dad," Shannon said.

"I'm asking you to wait," Alice said calmly, although Susan could sense her frustration.

"Why?" Shannon clicked her tongue.

"Shannon, do I have to spell it out? It's Christmas. It's a family day. And in case you haven't noticed, your father isn't in the best mood as it is. Might actually benefit you if you wait, not to mention thinking about the rest of us."

Shannon shrugged, grabbed a second roll, and returned to her room to join Hannah.

"I swear, he loves his girls so much, but he's always in a mood when they're here," Alice said.

Susan smiled sadly at Alice as Ed came walking in. "Okay, if everyone has eaten, it's time to decide who's playing Santa this year? "He held out the Santa hat with the two white braids hanging down from the sides. Susan was relieved to see his playful side had come out.

"I think you'd look best with the hat, personally," Alice replied.

"Yeah, Dad, then we can both have braids," Julie piped in, running into the kitchen.

"Well, okay. If no one else wants to..." He put the hat on and paraded around being silly. He went to one bedroom door, then the next, knocking and using a ridiculous voice to tell all the girls it was time for presents.

Laughter, smiles, and lots of wrapping paper filled the tiny living room as they opened gifts. Much like Susan had grown up, her stepsisters had always known what being from a low-income family was like. But that only meant that she shared something else in common with them; people who didn't have a lot tended to be grateful for everything they got. Alice explained that the girls had already opened their gifts from her and Ed before Susan and Tamika arrived since they'd woken up at the crack of dawn. Tamika was right. Seeing their faces light up when they opened the gifts she and Tamika had so conscientiously chosen for each of them made her happy. After the girls opened their gifts, Susan asked them to each pose separately for a picture so she could make a photo collage of this special day.

Being goofy, Hannah suggested they each do something silly with their gifts. Saving herself for last, Hannah carefully posed each of her sisters to create a specific mood. While seeing the girls act silly made Susan smile, at the same time, she noted that watching them carry on so theatrically sometimes made her a bit shy.

With Hannah's direction, Nicki had put on the Red Sox baseball hat and tee and even went into her bedroom to get her bat.

"No, don't stand that way, Dork," Hannah said, modeling how she wanted Nicki to stand.

Standing in front of the tree, with her long, brown ponytail hanging over her shoulder, Nicki posed as if she were determined to hit a home run, trying not to laugh as she did.

Next, Julie dragged the worn coffee table over in front of the tree and put her brand-new keyboard gingerly on top. She sat on the floor behind the coffee table and positioned her hands above the keys.

"Wait. Something is missing. Shannon, let her borrow your sunglasses," Hannah ordered.

Shannon returned with her pink glitter sunglasses, and they all burst out laughing. Susan snapped several pictures as Julie tried to maintain her composure and make it look like she was rocking out.

"I'm next," Shannon announced, tossing her dyed-black hair over her shoulder after she slipped her new Tupac sweatshirt over her head. "You guys don't even know how perfect this is, seriously. It's my favorite Tupac quote."

"That was all me. I saw it in the window of Spencer Gifts, and it screamed Shannon," Tamika replied. She leaned into Susan with a whisper, "Didn't I tell you to trust your Black girlfriend on this one?"

Shannon stood on the coffee table in front of the tree, trying to look like a gangster, half crouched down and throwing the camera a peace symbol and tough expression.

"You're ridiculous. You stink. You should have gotten coal in your stocking." Nicki snorted at her unsuccessful attempts to get Shannon to break her pose.

"Okay, Hannah, what about you?" Susan asked.

"Oh, I know exactly what I want to do. Backdrops and poses are my thing. Move the coffee table back," Hannah instructed her sisters, who quickly obliged.

Hannah then proceeded to throw every couch cushion and bed pillow on the floor in front of the tree and pulled the Santa hat with the braids from her father's head and his reading glasses from his face. Tucking her mass of dark blond hair into the hat as she put it on, she dropped onto her belly in front of the tree, holding one of her new Harry Potter books open. Ed's glasses fell down the bridge of her nose as she pretended to be deep in the story.

Susan snapped a few more pictures and was excited to see her mom's and Ed's faces when they saw their gifts. Although Tamika insisted that children made Christmas special, Susan loved seeing the child come out in an adult, too.

Knowing her mother wasn't fond of posing, Susan snuck some

candid pictures as they opened their gifts. While Ed was elated when he opened the DVD player and classic movies that she and Tamika had picked out for him in an effort to help him bring his massive video collection into the twenty-first century, it was Alice's expression that she'd most been waiting to see. Alice ripped open the paper of the giant box, revealing the rocking chair with gliding ottoman that she'd had her eye on since Susan was a teenager. Alice's eyes met Susan's; both held back tears. Every year since Susan could remember, Alice had talked about saving up and getting herself the chair, especially so she could snuggle in and ease her achy feet in the winter. But every year, she spent the money on Susan at Christmas, instead, just as Susan knew she had done for her stepsisters that year.

"I love it," Alice said simply, with a single nod and teary eyes.

Susan knew it wasn't so much about the chair itself. Not only had she remembered this thing that her mother had wanted for so many years, but it was more about how she'd made her mom feel spoiled when Alice was so used to putting everyone else first.

The adults retreated to the kitchen, leaving the girls as the girls to create a ruckus as they enjoyed their new things. The shyness she'd had only minutes ago at seeing her stepsisters carrying on foolishly was replaced with a new tenderness. The world had made her a little uptight, reluctant to emote her own magic at times. And she was probably a little reluctant to get attached to them after losing her half-sister, Molly, from her life at such a young age. But now, her stepsisters reminded her how necessary magic was.

Something else occurred to her, too. That deep sadness she'd had this morning, the same one she'd had every Christmas when she was fourteen, was because there were no children in her house. It didn't make sense to her then. It was not as if she had siblings who had grown up by that time. It had always been just her. But now, watching her stepsisters, she realized what she had felt that day ten years ago. It wasn't that there were no children; it was that *she* was no longer a child. Tamika was right; Christmas wasn't the same without the magic of childhood.

She smirked to herself with this realization, feeling as if she'd just grown up a little bit in that moment, and Tamika caught her expression.

"What?" Tamika nudged her with an elbow.

"You're right. Christmas is better with children," Susan said, turning to her love.

Tamika smiled and kissed her on the cheek. "We're going to be great moms."

"Maybe. But I still say that if anyone gets *our* daughter a musical instrument like you insisted on getting Julie, I'll kill 'em," she said, pointing a finger playfully at Tamika.

Tamika beamed her signature dimpled smile back at Susan. "God, I love it when I hear you talk about our daughter. Gives me shivers."

Susan knew how badly Tamika wanted children, and she was trying to catch up and want it as much as she did. Maybe she was getting there. They sat there for a long time, watching the girls and exchanging glances that held shared dreams of their future together.

Eventually, Alice directed everyone to clean up and put at least some of their new things away. Ed retreated to the bedroom for a nap, and the girls shrieked and laughed as they played with their gifts, which left Alice, Tamika, and Susan to talk around the kitchen table.

"I think it's time for that punch. Get the sherbet," Alice whispered as if it was a secret.

Susan leaned in and whispered back, "I'm going to spike mine."

"With what, you lush?" Alice asked with a laugh.

"Spiced rum, of course." Susan smirked, getting the bottle from her backpack and the sherbet from the freezer.

"You still drinking that shit?" Alice asked.

"Yeah, well, when I do drink. I don't drink like my club days. Only on special occasions."

"So, Thursday isn't a special occasion anymore?" Alice teased.

Susan stuck out her tongue.

"She was always a little wild," Alice said, turning to Tamika.

"That's not true. Well, not in high school." Susan laughed.

"True. But in college...."

"Oh yeah? Tell me about *that*." Tamika's dimpled emerged.

"I've told you about my club days with Michael."

Tamika waved a hand at her. "I wasn't asking you," she teased.

"Oh, she'd come home at four in the morning sometimes. She and Michael would just be giggling away. She would be talking about some cute chick she met." She paused and winked at Susan, then continued. "She wasn't really that bad; it was just so different from how she was in high school. But it's even nicer to see *this* new version of her...you know, since she met you."

Alice patted Susan's hand and smiled at Tamika.

"Aww." Tamika got up and hugged Susan from behind. "Well, I kind of like her too. I can't wait to have this with her." She motioned to all the girls.

"Oh, you can have them *now*," Alice joked, puffing on a cigarette.

In these moments, Susan could almost picture life like Tamika did. The children. The house. The traditional life. The warmth of Tamika's arms around her and the pride on her mother's face convinced her that she could be genuinely happy with that life.

Susan sipped on her cup of punch; the taste of the spiced rum brought her back to those club days. She didn't miss them, but sometimes she did miss the Susan she was then. Instead of worrying about everything, she'd just begun feeling powerful and free.

"Okay, let me try it." Alice reached for her punch and took a swig. "Ooh! That's pretty damn good. It's...spicy."

"Yeah, Mom, it's *spiced* rum," Susan teased.

"Shut up." She took another more generous sip before handing the cup back to Susan and pushing her cup over, "Give me a little. Just a little!"

"I'm still in awe of your relationship." Tamika smiled. "I'd give anything to be friends with my mom the way you two are friends."

It was true; it had always been true. The way their lives had played out had made them just as much friends as it did mother and daughter.

Tamika joined the girls in the living room. Susan could hear her chattering away with them and was in awe of how she could talk to them and relate to them in a way that she hadn't yet discovered. Tamika flipped through Hannah's new book, asking if she had heard of the title, taste-tested candy with Nicki, and asked Julie if she would play something for her on the keyboard after Ed woke up. Later, she talked about Tupac with Shannon, which led to a more lengthy discussion about music and celebrities. Maybe she would learn from Tamika, but it concerned her that she wasn't all that good with children. She was awkward with them, never knowing quite what to say. Wondering what others thought of her when she talked to them was the worst.

"She's good with them." Alice tapped her on the arm as if reading her mind.

Susan nodded.

"She wants a family, huh?"

"Oh, yes."

Alice looked at her, an unasked question on her face.

Susan shrugged.

"You used to want babies," Alice said.

"I used to want a bunch. But for a while now, I've known that I really only want one. One daughter. So I can recreate what you and I have. But I'm barely able to figure out how to take care of myself sometimes, so I don't know if it's the best idea."

"You'll figure it out. You have plenty of time."

"Hope so." Susan laughed it off, but it scared her more than she was willing to let on. Alice had no idea there wasn't as much time as she assumed. Susan knew she didn't have long before Tamika was serious about having a child. From the beginning, she'd been very clear that she wanted one by the time she was thirty, and she would turn thirty in November.

"Look at this. I had two sips of yours, and this one isn't even half gone yet, and I'm spinny." Alice giggled as Tamika walked back into the room.

"Spinny?" Tamika laughed.

"Yeah, spinny," Alice replied, swirling her head from side to side.

"Lightweight." Susan laughed.

"Hey, did you ever teach Tamika how to look at the Christmas lights?"

Susan laughed. "Nope. Not yet."

"Come here, come here, sit right here, and we'll show you." She turned her chair around, pulled a second one over, and motioned for Susan to line hers up with theirs so all three were facing the tree in the living room.

Tamika sat down and stared straight ahead.

"Okay, now you have to squint just right. Like this." Alice narrowed her eyes, adjusting a few times. "Not too much, or you can't really see them. Just enough so they all sort of blur, and all you can see is colorful blobs."

Susan didn't squint at first but watched Tamika get into the moment, waiting for her to see the magical image she'd known since she was little.

"When it was just Susan and I, I used to have her sit back on the couch and do this and tell me where we needed more blue, where we had too much red, where there were gaps," Alice explained.

Susan heard Tamika gasp; she'd found the magic. Susan saw the smile and awe spread across her beautiful face and saw Alice's smile beside her. This was all she really needed—these two. She turned her head and joined them in squinting, finally finding that light the season was supposed to be about.

"They *are* perfect," Tamika said.

"I know," Alice replied smugly.

"What *are* you guys doing?" Shannon boomed as she thudded into the kitchen.

All three of them laughed. They certainly must have looked ridiculous sitting there. Alice got up and showed Shannon what she'd just shown Tamika. The others came in with curiosity. Tamika grabbed Julie and plopped her on her lap, showing her how to squint. Susan gave up her seat; Hannah and Nicki were small enough to share. The oohs and aahs made this moment better than opening gifts. It felt so much like when she was young, those real, unplanned moments that she could never forget. Maybe having a family of her own wouldn't be so scary after all if simple moments like this brought her so much joy.

She remembered what it was like to see Tamika's face when she saw a lighthouse for the first time, and now, watching everyone squint at the Christmas lights. If those things had been so powerful, she had to imagine that watching her own child experience new things would be profound.

CHAPTER SEVEN

"Hey, we've been here six months," Susan said to Tamika as they snuggled in bed, watching the drifts of snow through the moonlight. It was the third blizzard in two weeks, and Susan loved every minute of it. There was something joyous about being trapped inside with the love of your life during a blizzard. The bedroom felt a little more personalized since she'd hung the tapestry that her mother had gotten her, depicting the wheel of the year. These simple moments made everything worthwhile. It wasn't so bad that they decided not to travel next summer. That they'd miss Lillith Fair. Again. *This* was happiness.

"Have we?"

"Yeah, it's March first." Susan swallowed hard. She always got a headache when she tried to figure out how to bring something up to Tamika.

"Wow, that flew."

"It did. It'll be spring in a few weeks."

"Well, thank God. That means only a few more months of clinical rotations, and then maybe we can have a real life together," Tamika replied.

"Totally. I spend an awful lot of time missing you," Susan said, rubbing Tamika's arm softly.

"Aww. Me too, Babe. Me too. It will be nice to have a forty-hour workweek like a normal person."

It relieved Susan to hear her say that. Although Tamika's drive was one of the things she found most attractive, Susan also worried that she wouldn't be able to slow down and have the life she envisioned. But maybe nights spent cuddling at home and trips were in her future after all.

"I mean, I'm ecstatic to finish with OB and finally get to the pediatric rotation, so I'm not rushing it or anything, but I feel like I haven't even gotten a chance to enjoy this place I wanted so much."

No shit, Susan thought to herself. It always pissed her off when Tamika suddenly arrived at a point she'd been trying for so long to make, but she knew she had to let it go.

"So, yeah...I want another cat." There. She'd gotten it out.

Tamika laughed and shook her head a little, trying to follow. "Wait, what? How did you get from us being here for six months to *that*?"

Susan shrugged. "It's just time. I'm ready."

"You're silly. I love you, you weirdo." She cupped Susan's cheek in her palm.

"Someone at work had kittens. Well, their cat did." Susan snorted. "After Emily, I didn't want it to be like I was just replacing her. But honestly, I just can't live without a cat anymore. A Witch needs a cat. I just...need that energy, you know? Those kitty vibes."

Tamika shook her head. "Kitty vibes?" Tamika scrunched her eyebrows as she looked at Susan.

"Yeah, kitty vibes. You know. That energy you get when you hold them right up to your chest...that vibration is magic."

Tamika cut her off. "No. I really don't get it. Sorry, Babe."

Susan sighed. "We talked about this when we moved in here. You had all the cool amenities you wanted, and it was a place where I could get a cat when I was ready. It was the only thing I asked. And I'm ready."

Tamika curled her lip. "Kittens destroy things. We have such a nice place. *This* is it, what we have here...*this* is what we want. You don't want to go and mess with perfection."

"They can. But this is just material stuff. I'll get a scratching post for every room. Kitten-proof everything. I need a little fuzzy love muffin to snuggle."

"You really are adorable." Tamika smiled at her. "They're just so... I don't want an animal messing this place up. We work so hard to have all of this. Maybe when we get a house and have a basement or something where a kitten could go wild, and we wouldn't have to worry about our practically brand-new living room set." With that, she rose from bed to use the bathroom.

Susan threw both middle fingers up at Tamika as she left the room. Who the fuck was she to tell Susan, *maybe* in that tone when she paid to live here too?

"Besides, I'll be your snuggle muffin or whatever you called it." Tamika's lingering kiss made it clear that she wanted sex.

Susan hated it when she tried to make things go away by having sex. But they'd had too many arguments when Susan said she wasn't in the mood, so it felt easier to let it happen, even when she felt disconnected.

As Tamika kissed up her neck and down her shoulders, the thought that maybe she shouldn't be with her at all if it was always going to be this way made her sick to her stomach. It was crazy. Where the hell did that thought even come from? Of course, she wanted to be with Tamika; she was in love with her. It was just one little disagreement, not even an argument. She was just being dramatic again.

As she watched the snow drift down through the skylight, she told herself she needed to let go and give in to Tamika's advances. She needed to get out of her own head again. But as she tried to be in her body, she felt lonely. How had she felt so joyous just moments ago and such despair now? The crescent moon stared back at her, reminding her that she would never really be alone, but it seemed of little comfort. Managing to quiet the noise and experience the physical sensations instead, she felt Tamika's skin on hers, soft and wanting. She switched her gaze from the skylight and looked into Tamika's eyes, giving herself over to her.

Over the next few days, Susan knew she would need to try a different approach if she was going to get her way about a kitten.

But what? Nothing she said seemed to be enough to get Tamika to take her seriously. To get her to understand that having a cat was not just a want; it was a need. At some point, she would have to realize that Susan wouldn't back down about this.

One evening, when Tamika was working second shift, it finally came to her. Maybe she wasn't much for stereotypical spells, but her experiences with the Women's Spirituality group at the community college had taught her how much power simple chants and rituals could hold. The ritual they'd done for the Winter Solstice still stood out in her mind. As they sang *Weave and Spin*, over and over together as they stood in a circle and threw a ball of yarn to one another every which way, eventually making a web that encompassed the entire room, each woman silently set an intent about something they would call forth into their lives. Susan had simply set the intention to meet someone to love. Afterward, they rounded the ceremony out by writing one thing on a piece of paper they wished to banish from their lives. They placed the paper in a golden bowl of water and watched it dissolve slowly as they shared food and drink over the course of the day. It would free up space in their lives for the things they wished to call forth. She had scribbled out the words, *low self-esteem and fear*, knowing that both held her back from putting herself out there most of the time.

The collective energy had thrummed through the room that day and stayed with her into the following week, which was when she met Fiona, one of the most transformative moments of her life. Although it wasn't quite what she'd expected when she'd asked for a new love to enter her life, Fiona turned out to be someone who had made her understand connection on a whole new level. If she had succeeded at summoning a woman like Fiona, surely, she could call forth a cat.

Once the solution hit her, she took action. Racing into the bedroom, she pulled Big Blue from the closet, and although she tried to handle some of the older items carefully, she unloaded things in a flurry until she spotted what she was looking for: her Bast incense burner. The grand Egyptian cat Goddess stood overlooking a long resin trough designed for incense. At the other end, a small hole for a chime candle; hieroglyphics covered the length of the trough. Although it no longer sat on her simple bedroom altar, it was one of her favorite pieces. Her mother had picked it up for her at a yard sale when she'd first come out of the broom closet in college. Although Tamika insisted it didn't go with the décor in their bedroom, Susan envisioned the day when she would have an entire space for her magical décor. Maybe a basement or an attic. Maybe she would even have an entire wall devoted to an Egyptian motif, although since she'd first imagined that space, she'd added so many areas of interest, such as Celtic culture. The number of walls she might need to attain her vision seemed to be forever growing.

She pulled Bast from Big Blue, grabbed a single black chime candle, a bundle of sage, and matches from the storage space underneath her altar, and dashed outside, not even considering her shorts, tank top, and bare feet. Once her skin hit the air, she gave it a second thought, but luckily, it was a relatively warm March. This wouldn't take but a few minutes anyway.

The parking lot was quiet, which wasn't surprising since it was nearly eleven. But still. There was no wind. No cars on the move from the busy city street. Nothing.

She didn't think as she made her way across the lot to the visitor section, which had only one car parked in it. She could feel herself smiling as she walked past the swings along the line of trees. Small adventures soothed her soul when all she'd known lately was the feeling of the indoors. The sideline of trees ended, and she spotted a picnic table on a square of lawn she'd never noticed before. The table was a little disheveled, but it was much more private than the tables on the patio in back, and it was somewhat hidden by a few trees while not so concealed that she couldn't still see the sliver of moon shining down.

After swinging her legs over the bench, she set Bast down, placed the candle in the hole, and put the sage in the trough. She closed her eyes and took a breath, enjoying the space for a moment. Not only was she about to conjure up what she wanted to bring forth, but she was here now. She was doing this. She was sitting in her power. While she'd spent plenty of time missing magic since she'd moved to the stuffy townhouse, she hadn't known how badly she needed this until she sat here under the open sky. She barely noticed the goosebumps that covered her skin. Leaning into the magic even more, she focused on the intentions she wanted to put out into the universe. It was simple, really; she wanted a cat. So, she opened her eyes and swiped the match. She lit the sage first, then swiped a second match and lit the candle. Her belly did a little flip as she opened her mouth to speak her intentions aloud.

"Goddess Bast. Universe. Gaia. Thank you for...well, everything. But especially a home that allows cats. Every Witch needs a little black cat, and so I humbly ask for the perfect circumstances to allow this magical little beast to be a part of my life. May she have as much sass and grace as the majestic Bast herself. I promise to care for her for life." She managed to get the last words out before her invocation was interrupted.

"*What* is going on here?"

Startled, Susan knocked the candle over, and the flame blew out. She looked up and came face to face with the on-site property manager.

"Oh, nothing, I, I..." What could she even say right now, and why was what the fuck was he even doing here at this time of night?

"Miss Sibley, right?" The property manager asked.

Susan nodded, feeling like she was about five years old.

"Whatever *this* is cannot happen here. This...Pagan worship, or whatever you call it." He shook his head and motioned to the items on the table as he spat the words. She could tell he was trying to remain professional, but the hate in his eyes pierced through her.

She wanted to ask why the fuck not. He never seemed to enforce the complex rules about noise and public consumption when the college boys were kind enough to share their music with the rest of the residents as they got drunk and puked all over the lawn. And he certainly hadn't called anyone out about large numbers of people or religious events when the family in 7B had donned their gaudy crosses and Jesus streamers all over the patio after their child's precious Christening. But if there was one thing she had learned, it was when to lay low and shut her mouth.

"The complex rules also clearly state there are to be no open flames in public areas, so... This *will* result in a warning. I won't ask you to come to the office with me at this time, considering the hour, but you will find the warning in your box next week, and upper management will be notified. There cannot be a second offense of this nature."

Susan felt as if she couldn't move or she might rip him limb from limb. She wanted to rip his pretty blue eyes from his blond skull. But it was one of the many times that she had to remind herself she wasn't that kind of Witch. Sometimes, she wished she were.

"Come on. I'll escort you back," the property manager ordered.

"Seriously?" She would lose it if she didn't walk away, so she stood up, grabbed her things, and stormed away. But she could feel that he was right behind her anyway.

"Miss Sibley...?" He called after her.

She ignored him, making it to the front walkway. She would have made it inside and lost him if it weren't for Tamika, who pulled up at that very moment, causing Susan to freeze in her tracks.

Tamika quickly got out of the car. "What's going on?" She asked with a look of concern and confusion.

Briefly, all three of them stood on the walkway in silence, but Susan couldn't just stand there, so she yanked open the door and stomped up the stairs and into the safety of their home. She could hear the manager's voice and then Tamika's. A minute later, Tamika came in, wide-eyed, and threw her keys down on the island.

"What the hell, Susan?"

"I know. What an asshole! I'd like to take that little WASP prick and..." She yelled.

"Shh. Don't you think you've caused enough issues already, for God's sake?"

She couldn't register what Tamika was saying. "What?"

"What made you...what were you thinking? That was... Are you crazy?"

"What?" She couldn't find words as she felt the tears starting.

"Susan, we could get evicted. That kind of thing isn't just something you can....be on display with. I can't even believe you. I don't know what to say to you right now."

As Tamika disappeared down the hall shaking her head, Susan could just stand there and cry as she shook and held the Bast statue to her chest. If one truth had always existed in her fiery, Leo soul, it was nothing was more important in the world than loyalty, and Tamika had just betrayed her. Tamika hadn't even asked her about her side. The woman who claimed to love her had formed an opinion based on the account of a practical stranger. Even if the manager had told Tamika that she'd been dancing naked around a bonfire and holding a skull, Tamika was supposed to be her partner. She should have had her back, and she hadn't.

The following day, Tamika told Susan it was behind them like she always did. She had quickly calmed down after reading that the complex only resorted to eviction after three warnings and a formal meeting. While Tamika hadn't used the word directly, she insinuated that she'd forgiven Susan, but Susan wasn't ready to say the same about Tamika's betrayal.

Her mind spun in a million directions. She could leave. While Tamika was at work tomorrow, she could pack some of her things and stay with...who would she stay with? Both her mother and DJ would be willing to help her somehow, of course, but she would never let them know things were less than perfect.

"Choose wisely."

She heard the words as she was lying in bed that night. They'd come from within in her mind, not from within the room, but still, she looked around as if she might spot their origin. But it almost wasn't hearing at all. It was more of a knowing, really. With the words, an image flashed through her mind. A brown-skinned baby in a yellow sun dress toddling toward her. And there was an instant familiarity. It was her daughter. Raven. Was she crazy?

She quickly got into bed and got under the covers, feeling panic rising in her chest as she tried to figure out what had just happened. She'd gone through some therapy when she was a teenager and again in her early twenties, but surely a therapist would tell her she was crazy if she shared this. Anyone would. She would have to just get through whatever this was. Alone. Like she always did.

Although her breathing finally calmed and she was able to get a little sleep, it was anything but restful. She spent the whole day thinking about the message and the vision through an exhausted fog, and the next few days brought much of the same. She had made mistakes with two separate orders at work this week because her mind was so consumed by not only whether or not she was crazy but also by what the words themselves had meant.

Choose wisely. What did it mean? She'd heard her own voice echo around in her own head before. Sometimes even her mom's or DJ'S. She assumed that was how everyone's head was. But this voice was different somehow. It was familiar, yet she couldn't place it. Other members of her family, including her magical gramma, had a sixth sense, but was that really what this was? How could she know?

She just couldn't stop churning it around in her mind. Tamika's betrayal. Leaving. The strange occurrence. Maybe she and Tamika *weren't* working. Maybe it hadn't been such a crazy thought after all if they wanted different things. Had different values. It stood to reason that if she had afforded to live alone before, even with her student loans, she could do it again. But what did the message mean? What about the vision?

Every time she let her mind swirl around with such thoughts, she arrived back at the same place. She loved Tamika. And that was always her answer. Even on the nights she lay there thinking about finding her own place, it always came back to love. She was a loyal Leo, and she wasn't one to walk away from love. She wasn't sure some days if it was a virtue or a downfall, but it always came down to love for her.

Susan's nightmares had returned, too, lasting for weeks. She hadn't had them since high school. Back then, it was always a dream about her running through a forest or, sometimes, a dark outdoor landscape that she couldn't quite make out. She always woke up feeling like Little Red Riding Hood, still in flight from something. More specifically, someone.

Some of these dreams were like that, too. But some were different. Now, many took place in a school she had attended. Her middle school, her high school, even the college. She wasn't really sure if they even qualified as nightmares. There was no blood and gore. She was never harmed in any way. But they disturbed her. The feeling of fear that she had in the dreams often lasted with her even after she woke. In the dreams, she was always late for a class or had missed a class. Exhaustion made her feel heavier and heavier as she rushed through empty hallways and parking lots, trying to locate elevators and rooms that she never found. Classes she never attended. Sometimes, unable to find her car, she stood alone, looking around, seemingly unable to move.

Racing thoughts and the uncomfortable thump of her heartbeat kept her awake for hours every night, and she wasn't sure what was worse anymore, her waking thoughts or the nightmares. It had become so bad that her last thought most nights before she drifted off to sleep was the hope that she might die in her sleep and not have to deal with this exhaustion.

Why did everything have to be piling up on her all at once? In addition to her obsession with the incident and the nightmares, her boss, Claire, had given her more responsibility at work and urged Susan to utilize some of the concepts she'd learned in the management training program last year. She was trying, at least so she could have something to report back, but it was often difficult to figure out how to use the things she'd learned. The management concepts made sense, but the application was a different story.

Claire had everything all laid out; scheduling, inventory, and ordering were all mundane and routine for the most part. She'd been trying harder to focus on profit and loss and understand projections, but it was a struggle. Her brain just didn't seem to work that way. Words and ideas were her strengths, not numbers and business.

Although Claire always encouraged her to be innovative and bring up suggestions for change, Susan struggled to trust her own ideas. At least she was good at marketing because it allowed her to be somewhat creative. And she certainly didn't like directing people. She had a good relationship with the employees but could be timid with them at times and was constantly annoyed when they were challenging.

So, she continued to focus on the books. She understood books. As she wandered around the store, thankful that at least it was Friday, she tried to recall what she'd learned about product placement and inventory but couldn't focus no matter how hard she tried. Instead, she grabbed a stationery set from the shelf with a majestic panther on the corner of each sheet, pulled the pencil from behind her ear, and plopped herself into a quiet chair.

March 16, 1998

Dear Fiona,

I'm kind of losing it over here. Like, more than my usual crazy. It's such a long story, but basically, I was doing a ritual in the back yard and got "caught" by management. They cited me for breaking some stupid fucking rule. It felt like Salem all over again. Tamika didn't back me up. She flipped out on me. So, I was laying there afterward thinking that maybe I can't do it...be with her. And the most fucked up thing happened. I heard someone say, "choose wisely," almost as if someone was standing right beside me. It wasn't the same as normal sound, though. It was like it was a message, but it was more like it was coming from inside me. And right after that, I had a vision...I know it sounds beyond crazy, but I saw my daughter. Our daughter. Mine and Tamika's. I saw Raven.

She stopped, pen still in hand. Choose wisely. It was so clear now. She'd been thinking about leaving Tamika when she'd heard it. After seeing the image of her beautiful daughter, it was suddenly clear that the message meant she should stay. She just had to hold on. Love was hard work, but it was worth it. And there was so much to look forward to, especially a daughter. She felt air in her chest for the first time that week and let the pen drop as she relaxed her whole body.

"Hey Susan, I'm off. Dawn took over the register. I wanted to ask you one last time. I think I might have someone interested, but I wanted to make sure you didn't want her," Sanjana said out of nowhere.

"Huh?" Susan asked, startled.

"The little black kitten."

"Oh..."

Sanjana had asked her three times since her discussion with Tamika, and it was getting harder and harder not to blow up at her and tell her to leave it alone. After the incident with the property manager, she knew she had no room to push Tamika about anything. Susan just wished Sanjana would take no for an answer. It wouldn't be fair to the kitten to be in a place where it wasn't wanted by both of them. There were days she thought she might just say yes and worry about pissing Tamika off later. But she never did. Not much was worth Tamika's wrath.

"No. But thank you for checking." She tried to answer stoically, although she wanted to cry. Although she'd daydreamed about the little black fluff ball, Susan knew she had to let her go. She could go to the home she was meant to, and Susan could live her life again.

"Okay. Sure. I was convinced she was yours."

She paused. "Hey, I wanted to tell you. I heard Claire and Paula talking earlier. They didn't know I was there behind the history section." She laughed.

"About what?" Susan was mildly interested in what her boss and the district manager had said that could be worth hearing. Although she hated gossip, it hadn't taken her long to learn how to play the necessary games at work. Having alliances and knowing what was going on was essential, and she and Sanjana always looked out for one another.

"Claire is leaving."

"What? Are you sure? What did she say?"

"She literally stood there and gave Paula her notice, Susan. I think Paula almost died, I swear. He had no idea what to do, but Claire mentioned you. I couldn't hear much more after that because a customer needed help, but I heard her say your name."

Susan opened her mouth to speak, but nothing came out. She shook her head with wide eyes.

"Susan, you have to go for Claire's position."

"Me?!" She practically shouted.

"Yes, you. My God, you're so oblivious, woman. Clearly, Claire's been training you for this on purpose. She must have known it was coming."

Sanjana didn't have much more to say about it, but now she had planted the seed in Susan's mind. She had never considered being a store manager and only taken the assistant manager position for the pay increase. It never felt much different than shift manage to her, anyway. Not really. Sure, Claire showed her the basics of how to do the schedule and had her help with inventory and talking to vendors, but still. She wasn't good at it.

When she was in high school, she pictured herself working alone in some dimly lit basement with musty books, certain the answers to the entire universe were within those stacks. This was such a disappointing alternative to her fantasy.

She tried to get it all out of her head and return to her letter; maybe nothing would come of it anyway.

But both Claire and Paula were waiting for her when she arrived the next morning. She did her best to make it look like it was all a surprise to her, and in a way, it was because she honestly never expected them to offer her the position, but that's exactly what they did. They told her that she would have to go through the motions of interviewing to satisfy corporate but that if she wanted it, the position was hers. It took every ounce of strength in her to maintain a professional stance and ask them if she could have twenty-four hours to think about it and talk to her partner, but they were more than happy to give her the time she needed.

Just as she'd expected, Tamika wanted her to take the job

despite her feelings about being stuck.

If she said yes to the store manager position, would she just keep giving up on her dreams, even if they weren't exactly clear yet? Sure, maybe she had to accept that she didn't live in a world where she could be a spiritual scribe or ancient historian, but surely there were opportunities other than retail.

"You can do both. You can take the manager's position now and still have those other things later. It's not either or."

"I guess."

"Babe, remember, house and children. That is what we are working toward. Stay focused. This is *perfect* timing." Susan knew how badly Tamika wanted those things, and a part of her wanted that, too, some days, although most of the time, she was too afraid of the responsibility to feel the same excitement that Tamika did.

She always mentioned the house and the children but seemed to ignore everything Susan wanted. Travel. A career she was passionate about. They never talked about those things. Hell, she couldn't even get a goddamn cat, never mind something as adventurous as going on a camping trip to Lilith Fair or traveling the country in an RV.

A week later, as Susan sat in the interview for a position she didn't want, she felt as if someone was plucking a piece of her soul out. Maybe she was too dramatic. Felt too much. But, if her soul were made of feathers, they'd been plucked out one by one over the years, some in large chunks. On these days, she felt as if it was only the raw, balding underbelly of her soul even existed anymore. She'd had these moments before. The way she had felt when she'd slept with a boy once in high school. The way she felt when a friend had lied to her face, and she knew it, even if she had no evidence. The feeling that something just wasn't right. But she had to grow up. This was just what growing up felt like. She was just a spoiled brat who wanted to live in her own world. This was it, that cosmic joke she'd mentioned to Fiona. It was the universe testing her, the terrible cycle of capitalism; they offered you more money, and while you told yourself you didn't really have to stay anywhere you didn't want to, once you started earning more, it was less likely you could break free and be that wild soul she was meant to be.

She accepted the job on a Friday afternoon in late March. Between Tamika's job and nursing rotations, they wouldn't see one another until Monday night. Susan hated it all; she couldn't believe this was her life.

CHAPTER EIGHT

One morning in April, Susan woke up and immediately called DJ to inform her that she had an 811. It was their code; it wasn't an emergency, but it was serious enough that they had to drop everything, unless the other party was dying. They didn't use it often and had never let one another down since they'd devised the system in their senior year of high school.

Although she struggled to ask for support when she needed it, she just couldn't be alone all weekend. She hadn't said much, but they never needed to.

Two hours later, DJ was at her door. In stark contrast to DJ, who had a fresh, layered haircut and sported an adorable floral jumper that showed off her cute figure, Susan felt frumpy in her jeans and tee shirt.

"What's up?" DJ asked with a look of concern when Susan answered the door, her backpack already slung over her shoulder.

Susan shook her head. She didn't want to dive right in. "I just want to get out of here. I just need a day with you."

"Okay, well, let's go." DJ always gave Susan time to open up. "What do you want to do today?" DJ asked in a cheery voice as Susan hopped into her Jeep.

"I don't know. I think I'm still half asleep," Susan replied.

"Did you sleep in again?"

Was she judging her for being lazy?

"Seems to be my norm again. On days off, anyway. Tamika is hardly ever here. I've only been able to read in the middle of the night, so I'm not getting to sleep until three some nights." She didn't mention the nightmares or the strange occurrence and wasn't sure how to explain the incident in the back yard. They were things that DJ would never understand; she would just think Susan was crazy.

"Is Tamika working today?" DJ asked.

"Tamika is always working. And we've had some issues...everything is okay now, mostly, but I don't know."

"Aww. I'm sorry."

"Yeah. Sometimes, I feel like I might as well be single again," Susan said.

"You know, you said something like that last week on the phone," DJ replied.

"Said what?"

"That you wished you were single again."

"I never said that."

"Okay, well, that you might as well be single again or something. It was when you told me how Tamika never seems to care about what you want and is only focused on her own goals."

"Oh, well, I didn't mean...I want to be with her. It's just...I don't know." There was so much that was just so hard to share. The thought of going into the details about the back yard and Tamika's betrayal exhausted her.

"I just see you're not happy lately," DJ said.

Susan clicked her tongue. "People aren't always overjoyed every minute. Doesn't mean they're not happy. Doesn't mean they don't love their partner."

"Of course, you love her. Trust me, I know it's hard. Matt and I only have Sundays together. And even then, he's just so tired. These years where you're just working toward sometimes bigger and better..." DJ trailed off.

She should have known DJ couldn't understand. Bigger and better? She simply didn't buy into the notion that sacrificing today meant a happy future. It seemed to her that the present was more important.

"...these times will test you," DJ finally finished her thought.

When Susan looked over at DJ, she saw that her expression

matched the pain in her voice. That pain she tried to mask with her eternal cheeriness. That pain that she too often missed in her oldest friend because she was so involved in her own.

Susan reached over and put a hand on DJ's arm. "What's going on?"

DJ drew in a long breath. "It's been a rough couple of months. I had a miscarriage."

"Oh my Goddess, what? No. When?!"

"It was early December."

"Why didn't you tell me?" Susan asked.

DJ shrugged, "It's just not the kind of thing I wanted to tell you over the phone."

It all made sense when she remembered the sadness that had crept into DJ's voice on Christmas Eve.

Susan thought about how selfish she had been. She'd been so inside of herself that she had abandoned DJ during what was probably one of the hardest things she had ever been through.

"I'm so fucking sorry, Deej." Susan could feel herself tearing up, so she paused. "I can't imagine...I..."

DJ smiled softly. She always gave Susan grace when she lapsed back into isolation, one of her oldest coping mechanisms. DJ shook her head.

"Don't. Seriously. If you cry, I'll cry, and I'm driving. Here, I think we need this song," DJ said, pushing play on the CD player and turning up the volume.

"I didn't know you liked Fleetwood Mac," Susan remarked as she heard *Landslide* begin to play. Sometimes, they were so different that she needed a reminder of the things they had in common. Although she was especially drawn to their witchy tune, *Rhiannon*, if you considered both songs, it was clear that their focus was how the divine intersects with the human experience. DJ was just trying to figure out how to be human and grow, the same as she was.

"This is one of my favorite songs. Keeps me going when things get hard. I've been cleared to try again, and Matt and I are getting help from fertility doctors. God will tell us when the time is right. It's all going to be fine. We just have to rise above," DJ said after the song was over.

Eternally in awe of the positivity DJ exuded, Susan couldn't find the words to respond.

"And hey, at least Tamika is almost done, right? Just a couple more months?" DJ continued.

It took Susan by surprise, but she just nodded. It felt wrong to talk about herself after the bomb that DJ had just dropped, but DJ had made it clear she wanted it that way.

"And how is work going?"

She would just have to trust that DJ genuinely preferred that they turn the conversation back to her.

"Fine. I got promoted to manager," Susan replied.

"What? That's great!" DJ bubbled.

Susan shrugged. "I guess."

"No, you earned this. You love that place; this was bound to happen. And it means more money, right?"

She certainly didn't want to sell her soul for money.

"We need to celebrate, Susan. I mean it. You should be proud of this milestone."

But it was hard to be proud of something you didn't really want. Something you felt you settled for. But, in a way, DJ was right. She had worked there since her sophomore year of college, and she'd grown in so many ways since she started. It might not be her dream job, but it was still something.

"Maybe you're right."

"Of course I am," DJ teased. "So, how should we celebrate?"

"I want to get a tattoo." She didn't even know it was going to come out of her mouth.

She laughed. "Okay. That wasn't what I had in mind, but...are you serious?"

Susan nodded. "Yup," she answered, determined. "Here's the thing; you're right. I *am* sick of some of the shit that has been going on with Tamika, but I don't really want to talk about it. Every couple has issues. That's just part of life. But I *will* tell you that one thing that pisses me off the most, and that is she doesn't seem to give a shit that I want a cat. I need a cat. And I have told her this multiple times. I guess she thinks I am just going to forget about it or change my mind." She had no intention of sharing the deeper stuff, like how Tamika used sex to get past their issues, but she could open up about the cat.

"Oh, no. Can this even work out for the two of you if she isn't a cat person? I mean...I honestly can't even believe you've been without one this long. After Emily, I assumed you were taking time to grieve, but after a while, it was pretty obvious it was about Tamika."

She knew that DJ had always liked it better when she was single. Even if Susan was lonely, she always got the feeling that it was more convenient for DJ if she didn't have anyone else vying for her time.

"We'll figure it out."

"So, wait, what does this have to do with getting a tattoo? I'm confused."

"I know, I was going off on a tangent again. I want a cat tattoo. I think it will make a statement."

"What kind of statement are you looking to make?" DJ laughed.

"Well, my statement to the world is that I love cats. But I think it will show Tamika a few things, too."

DJ was stopped at a traffic light. She looked over at her briefly, arching her eyebrows.

"I don't know—it'll tell her how passionate I am about cats. How connected I am to them. How I need them in my life. How fucking serious I am."

"If she hasn't understood all of that already, I'm not sure a tattoo will get through to her. She should know all of that about you by now, Susan."

Susan clicked her tongue.

"Well, if nothing else, it will remind her that I am not one to back down."

"So, where is this place?" DJ asked.

"Take a right at the third light, up there by Price Chopper," Susan replied.

When they arrived, Susan took her wavy, brown hair out of her ponytail and attempted to put it back up more neatly. As she twisted the elastic one final time, it snapped.

"Shit. Do you have a hair tie?"

"I have this." DJ removed a pink scrunchie from her gear shift and handed it to Susan.

"You're kidding, right?"

DJ just shrugged. "Sorry. It's all I have."

"It's just not me," she said, handing it back.

"Why are you fixing yourself up to go in the tattoo place anyway? Does Steph work here or something?" She forgot just how transparent she was to her oldest friend. DJ knew that after she threw her hair up in a ponytail each morning, she didn't usually think much about her appearance.

"No." Susan chuckled.

"Well, I guess I just associate Steph with tattoos," DJ replied.

Susan tipped her head and looked at DJ sideways. "Funny, Bitch."

"What? No, not because of that," DJ said, pointing to Susan's collarbone. "I mean because *she* has a lot of tattoos. She looks like someone who might work at a shop."

Susan stared at DJ, dumbfounded. She was so small town.

"Leaving my hair down is better than wearing a pink scrunchie," Susan said and got out of the car.

They walked into the shop to see two people behind the counter. Susan tried to act cool but was excited to see that Lucy, a friend from her clubbing days, was working.

"Hi ladies, how can we help you?" The man smiled.

Shit. She didn't want him. She wanted Lucy, even though she barely knew the woman. They had an ex in common and had flirted innocently at the club, but Susan felt at ease with her because she had an easygoing energy. DJ wandered around and looked at the flash on the walls.

"Oh, hey, Susan! Nice to see you," Lucy said. "I'll take care of her, Joe. She's my girl."

In a panic, she questioned whether it was wrong that she felt a flutter when Lucy had referred to her that way. Lucy's purple hair, piercings, and ink made her pretty badass, and back in her club days, Susan had looked at her through starry eyes. But now, it almost felt like she was being unfaithful to Tamika. Maybe it was terrible that she wanted to come to this studio because she knew Lucy would be there. She was being ridiculous. It was on her bucket list to get tattooed by a woman, and today felt like the day to check it off the list.

"I want to get a tattoo. I mean, obviously." She laughed. "Am I crazy to think I could get a walk-in on a Saturday?" Susan asked quietly. She didn't want DJ to hear her being awkward, even though she'd witnessed it since the day they'd met.

"Nope, it's your lucky day. We had two people call to reschedule. You got me, or you got Joe. What do you want to get?"

"A tribal cat," Susan answered.

"Well, then, I'm your girl."

Susan blushed for no other reason than the fact that women were enchanting, and she knew it probably showed.

"Where do you want to get it?" Lucy asked.

Susan lifted up her shirt sleeve, carefully exposing her upper arm but not wanting to reveal too much flab.

DJ walked over to the counter. "I saw a few cats on the wall. A few of them were tribal."

"Is this your girlfriend?" Lucy asked.

"Oh, no." Susan laughed at the idea of she and DJ as a couple. "This is my oldest friend DJ. We're more like sisters," she babbled on.

"I'm Lucy. I know Susan from the club." She extended her hand. She wondered what DJ really thought of her little world sometimes. The city. Her friends that didn't look like everyone had looked in the town where they'd grown up together. She couldn't even really figure out how DJ felt about her being a lesbian sometimes. It was another reason she didn't get too deep about her relationship with Tamika; some days, it felt like DJ would never see them as a real couple because they were two women. Maybe DJ was the all-American girl who married her high school sweetheart, but she couldn't expect everyone's relationship to be like hers and Matt's.

"Hey..." Lucy stared at her intensely for a moment. "I knew something was different. It's your hair. You let it grow?"

"No, I just usually have it up," Susan replied, shocked that Lucy had noticed.

"Ahh, well, you have absolutely gorgeous hair, Susan." She leaned forward and ran both her hands gently through her wavy hair. Susan appreciated her boldness. She liked women who got close or stared into your eyes an extra second longer than most people did. She liked people who weren't afraid to be intimate.

Susan refused to make eye contact with DJ while this was happening. She knew if she did, she would blush. Maybe even start cracking up.

"Anyway..." Lucy continued. I honestly wouldn't recommend any of the cats from the flash. I bet I have a pretty good idea of what you'd like. Let me go back and sketch something out. I'll be back in a few." She smiled and held up one finger before disappearing into a back room. She poked her head out a second later. "You're free to join me to see my process, or you could wait here."

"Wait out here with me; I might want to get one too. Help me find something," DJ urged.

"Yeah, right." Susan laughed.

"I'm serious," DJ replied, hands on hips.

"Okay, then. Be right back," Lucy said, disappearing again.

"What was that? Was she flirting?"

"What? No. She's just touchy. Girls touch each other's hair all the time." Susan laughed.

"Yeah, but she's a lesbian, right?" DJ asked.

Susan shrugged. "She's probably bi."

"Oh, how can you tell?"

"I dunno. It's hard to explain. It's a vibe," Susan replied.

"Gaydar?"

Susan nodded and smiled.

"So, you were kidding about the tattoo?" Susan said, changing the subject.

"No. Why? You don't think I would get a tattoo?" DJ asked.

Susan shrugged. "I don't know."

"You're getting a cat. I should get a dog. Teddy. Maybe just a little one. Wouldn't that be cute?"

"You *are* serious!" Susan smiled.

"Why would you think I wouldn't get a tattoo?" DJ asked.

"I don't know. Tattoos just don't feel like your thing."

"Whatever." DJ chuckled. "Anyway, is Lucy the reason you wanted to come here?"

"Shut up! I swear if she hears you, I'll kick your ass," Susan said playfully.

DJ smirked and tousled her own blond hair dramatically. "You were primping for Lucy," she whispered, returning to the original subject.

"Primping?" Susan laughed.

"I know. I've never used that word before in my life. I think that's mom's word, actually," DJ said.

"I think your right. It is."

Susan smacked DJ hard in the arm when she saw Lucy emerging from the back.

"What do you think of this?" Lucy walked over and held out a sheet of paper.

It was perfect. It was a tribal cat looking over its shoulder. Inside the body, the black shapes and lines, which got smaller near the face, made the cat look ancient and powerful.

Susan clapped her hands over her mouth for a moment, then said, "Holy shit. That's awesome. It's perfect."

"Yeah? Any changes?" Lucy asked, mindlessly playing with her lip ring with her tongue.

"No. Honestly, it's exactly the kind of thing I had in mind. It looks...Egyptian."

"That was my inspiration, actually. I was thinking of Bast."

"Yes!" Susan nodded, thinking about her backyard invocation and realizing that she should have been a little more specific with the words she'd spoken. Still, she was in awe of how the universe had delivered what she'd asked for.

"See, do I know you, or do I know you?" Lucy winked.

DJ was talking to the other tattoo artist at one of the flash walls. Was she seriously considering getting a tattoo? A part of her was still convinced that DJ was teasing her. She and DJ had been friends for so long that it wasn't every day that they could shock one another.

Spotting Susan's smirk, DJ held up her page of flash as she approached.

"I'm getting this one," DJ announced, pointing to a dainty dog silhouette.

"Oh my gosh, that is so you. So sweet."

DJ glanced at the sketch Susan held. "That's perfect for you."

"Right?!"

"I'll go prep. Come on over when you're ready," Lucy said.

The other side of the shop was set up like a hair salon. There were three different sections for three artists to work. Each of the spaces represented the artist's personality so well. While Joe's had monster trucks and pictures of his sons plastered all over his wall, Lucy's wall was a busy collage of all things purple, just like her hair.

Behind a beaded curtain was a small room for people who wanted more privacy. Susan wished she could have had the back room. She was prepared to take her entire arm out to get the tattoo. But she wasn't thrilled about doing it here, not only with DJ and another artist, but where any customer could come in and see her exposed.

"Ready when you are," Lucy called from her spot.

It was too late now. After the initial self-consciousness she felt over her exposed arm, Susan relaxed as they all chatted about anything and everything.

As DJ pulled away that day, Susan decided that it had been one of the most memorable afternoons they'd had in a long time. She considered that maybe while she was always so busy worrying that DJ was judging her and pigeonholing her, she was guilty of the same thing. The irony. She could be a really shitty friend sometimes.

Susan hadn't thought much about how or when to tell Tamika about the tattoo, but now that she was home and it was done, it was all she could think about. Given how tight their budget was, it wasn't exactly the most frugal choice. They hadn't had sex in a couple weeks, but they still saw one another's bodies. Instead of wearing a tank top after her shower like usual, she would have to throw on a tee shirt. She'd have to choose just the right moment to tell her.

"I made supper. Spaghetti and meatballs," Susan announced when Tamika walked in.

"Any salad?" Tamika asked.

Susan sighed. "No. Sorry, I didn't think of that. I'll try to remember to add that next time I make this. I held off on the garlic bread to cut down on the carbs." No matter how hard she tried, it never felt like she could do anything right.

Although they were back to normal, Susan was discouraged. They didn't have that many meals together at the island, and when they did, it always seemed like they didn't have much to talk about besides work. Tamika never had time to read anymore, so they didn't discuss books. Because she had been so consumed by thinking about the message she had heard and couldn't share, there was very little to say. It was a lonely feeling.

Tamika finished her meal, put her plate on the counter, and grabbed the stack of mail that neither of them had gotten to in days. She sorted through junk mail, opened bills, and made several organized piles.

"What's this one?" Susan asked, pointing to the sheet on top of the bill pile.

"Medical bill. From my visit last month."

"That's ridiculous," Susan remarked, chewing her last bite of meatball. "In fact, what's really fucking ridiculous is that we are paying twice as much for medical because we can't get married.

Pisses me off."

"Married?" Tamika smiled.

"Yeah. Legally married."

"You would want to if we could?" Tamika asked.

"Of course. You really have to ask me that? I love you." And despite the week they'd had, despite the loneliness, it was true. She couldn't even understand herself sometimes.

Tamika shrugged. "I don't know. I know *grown-up* things scare you." She smiled gently and made air quotes.

Susan could feel the old Tamika shining through. The gentle Tamika who made her feel loved just by the looks she'd given her. The Tamika she had no doubts about.

"Well, to me, this isn't about being a grownup. It's about love," Susan said.

Susan saw tears fill Tamika's eyes. It surprised her. Neither of them cried that much, and when she did, she rarely did it in front of Tamika. It usually took a lot. It was something they still had in common. But seeing Tamika tear up made her follow suit.

"Babe. Of course, I would marry you. I can't believe that wasn't a given." Susan got up and wrapped her arms around Tamika. "We've talked about this."

"Not in a long time. Lately, I have been thinking that you maybe want to bail." She felt guilty, thinking Tamika had been able to read her as she had played with the idea of leaving.

"Aww, no. I love you," Susan lied. Telling Tamika that she had doubts would be too painful for her to hear. Besides, she was over that. Why ruin such a sweet moment? She would never leave; it just wasn't who she was.

"Well, maybe we have to talk about this again real soon." Tamika kissed Susan softly on the mouth and held her face with one hand. "I'm sorry I've been crabby."

"I'm an asshole sometimes too. Being a lesbian is a lot of work."

Tamika laughed and nodded. "We're both so emotional."

Susan wasn't sure if she agreed with that assessment, but it wasn't worth arguing about. She let Tamika kiss her again.

"Wait, I do have something to tell you, though. I did something...a little crazy."

Tamika tensed up a little but didn't pull away. She looked into Susan's eyes.

"I want to marry you someday, but I can't live without a cat. I keep telling you that, and I feel like you're not hearing me. So..."

Instead of finishing her thought, she quickly lifted her left sleeve before she lost the nerve.

Tamika stared at her bicep without expression.

Susan could feel her heart thumping, and it took every ounce of self-control to give Tamika a minute instead of rambling on nervously.

"It's sexy as hell." Tamika smirked and pulled Susan into a passionate kiss that made.

Susan felt herself tremble. She didn't normally like to sweep tension under the rug with sex. But she hadn't let herself open up to Tamika these days, to give herself to her fully, sexually or otherwise. And maybe Tamika had felt it. They both needed this.

So, she let Tamika back her up slowly while still kissing her, lead her down the hallway, and push her onto the bed. She just needed to let go. She had to tell herself that mentally a few times as Tamika rubbed her back and kissed her neck. And eventually, Susan found it. That vulnerable place she'd let herself be in when she and Tamika were first falling in love. That deep sense of trust and near-total openness. Letting her head fall back, she let her body relax and enjoyed Tamika's touch in a way she hadn't let herself in a while. She thought of nothing but the energy from their blended souls and the intensity of the sensations in her body.

Tamika peeled Susan's shirt off as quickly as she could between breathy kisses. She moved Tamika's hand to her crotch, signaling she couldn't wait. Tamika indulged her, sliding her pants and underwear off and giving her thighs slow, gentle kisses, then dragged her lips over Susan's right hip. Susan gasped, which made Tamika nibble her thigh a little. Susan lay back and surrendered to Tamika's lovemaking.

After making love to Susan, Tamika crawled up and spooned her. "It's a just-for-you night," Tamika whispered.

Susan felt both contentedness and a longing to make love to Tamika in return, but she just lay there and enjoyed the bliss. Tamika hadn't initiated a just-for-her night in a while, and maybe Susan needed to let her take care of her. Both fell in and out of a light sleep and lay that way for a couple of hours before staggering to change into pajamas and find sleep.

When Susan woke up the next morning, she could smell breakfast cooking. Tamika hadn't remembered in a long time. It was a thing they used to do each time they had a just-for- you night; they extended it to the morning. Susan liked to call it the lesbian version of queen for a day, which made Tamika laugh every time.

"Bacon and scrambled eggs sound good, Babe?" Tamika asked, blowing her a kiss as she walked into the kitchen.

"Sounds delicious." She gave Tamika a quick hug from behind, poured herself a glass of orange juice, and sat in the kitchen chair by the window. She watched the birds for a few minutes and enjoyed the smell of the food cooking; it was the smell of home.

Shifting her focus away from the birds, she looked around at the kitchen floor, scanning the whole room before realizing she was looking for Emily.

That was weird. With grief, there were moments of forgetting someone was gone. She had done it all through fifth grade after her gramma had died. But she hadn't done it in a long time with Emily. This had felt different, though. It almost felt as if Emily had been there as she was watching the birds. It was the way the air felt around her when she was with Emily, so she had forgotten that she was gone and looked for her. There must have been some glitch in her brain. These were the kinds of things that she couldn't share with anyone. Almost anyone. She could always tell Fiona.

The sound of Tamika getting out the plates brought her back. She wanted to be happy about what she had in that moment, but her mind could only focus on one thought: the conversation from last night wasn't over.

"You okay?" Tamika asked her, putting a plate of bacon down on the island.

Susan shrugged.

"What's wrong?" Tamika pulled a chair up and sat facing Susan, holding her hands.

"We had such a nice night, and it's so sweet that you even thought to revive our tradition and make breakfast. I don't want to ruin a good thing, but I just don't feel like we really talked about what I brought up last night. The cat. And we need to," she said firmly. She wasn't going to cry.

"Okay," Tamika replied with a nod.

"I know that we've talked about it already. And I know why you don't want one. But it's just not an option for me. Having cats is part of who I am. Like you wanting children. You knew I was a Witch when you met me, and I thought that was one of the things you loved about me. This Witch needs a cat. But it's turned into more than that. I really can't be myself here at all. This place doesn't feel like home. I can't even go out and light a candle or feel comfortable playing Goddess music out there and being with nature. And I am willing to deal with all of it if it's temporary. I think I could deal with the other shit a lot easier if I just had a cat. Just being in their energy kind of connects me with that other realm."

She sniffled, feeling like the tears forming in her eyes could lead to sobs at any moment. But she had to get it all out first. "I thought we shared some of that...darkness, I guess. It just feels like lately, you don't like any of the stuff that makes me who I am." She barely got the words out before she broke down crying.

"Shhhh." Tamika held her and rocked her until her sobs turned back into sniffles.

Susan removed her hands from her face and looked at Tamika, who was smiling gently at her.

"I'm sorry. I didn't know it was this bad. The rotation has been a lot, and I think we need to connect more. Last night, when you said you had something to tell me, do you know what I thought? Tamika asked.

Susan shook her head.

"I thought it was something really bad. Like you cheated on me."

"What?" Susan shook her head in disbelief. "Goddess, no. I would never..."

Susan had never seen her look so sad.

"I *have* been shutting you down about the cat. And I've been moody, so I thought... Like I said, I thought you were bailing." Tamika shrugged.

"I love you, Tamika." She said, remembering how cheating had affected her family.

"Just trust me, *all of this stuff* is temporary. The cat. You having the space you need to be witchy." Tamika smirked. "Once we get a house and...let's just say next year is going to change our lives."

Maybe Tamika wasn't giving her anything concrete, but Susan felt heard, and that was a start.

CHAPTER NINE

Susan shook her head in disbelief at the beauty of the pride colors as they exited the subway station at Copley Square. The rainbow balloons and flags looked especially vibrant today as the sun shined down. It was unfortunate to have so many churches amongst the backdrop, too; New England, with its puritanical roots, hadn't always been a safe place for her people. There was a dark history of both queer and witchy folk feeling the need to hide themselves because of religious dogma, and despite the modern-day pride festival, that history couldn't be erased. It still played out in so many ways daily as people struggled to be accepted for who they were. Susan thought back to the night of the ritual in her own back yard, how she'd been shamed, and wondered if she would ever truly feel free. But she had to focus on the good.

"It's just the perfect day for Pride."

"I agree, Babe," Tamika replied, tipping her sunglasses down to look at her.

That look got her every time. She pulled Tamika over to her by the hips and kissed her as people walked by them. She wished she could always feel the way she did on Pride Day. Tamika grabbed her hand, and they began to walk along, enjoying the feeling that only pride could bring.

Seeing the four people protesting on the median was almost comical. Their fear and hate were no match for the love and excitement of thousands of pride-goers. She couldn't help but feel sad that she lived in a world where she had to wonder if one of the protestors had a gun. A world where there were people out there who wanted to kill others just because of who they loved. But nothing would shake her today.

"I have this gut feeling," Susan said, putting her hand on her abdomen. "A knowing. Today is going to be one of the best days of our lives."

Tamika shook her head and smirked.

"What? Are you laughing at my gut feeling? They're usually right, you know."

"No, no. I'm not doubting that gut feeling. I am in awe of it. It's kind of spooky, Babe. You are absolutely right. It is going to be one of the best days of our lives."

Tamika had been surprisingly upbeat since she'd graduated last month, and Susan was grateful for the change.

"Want to try to find the start of the parade route?" Susan asked.

Tamika nodded and asked, "This way?"

"You're asking me? I have no idea."

"You used to come to Boston a lot when you were in college, didn't you?" Tamika asked.

"Some."

"You've been to Boston Pride a few times, though."

"Yeah, but you know I have no sense of direction." Susan shrugged.

"You're adorable." Tamika smirked.

They stood on the steps of a bank and watched people bustle around, affixing unruly streamers to floats and hugging one another.

"Ten minutes, people," a beautiful man in a lime green dress said into a microphone. He held up five wiggling fingers to the crowd and danced around a little, blowing kisses with his other hand.

"Good timing." Tamika smiled.

Susan nodded. "Just enough time to catch our breath before it starts." While she enjoyed events such as these, all the bustle could overwhelm her at times, too. She was glad she had a few minutes to acclimate herself before they had to walk again.

Tamika reached down and held her hand as the parade began

to move past them. Pride groups from colleges all around the state walked past full of energy and smiles, a symbol of hope for a more open-minded future. Children with two moms and two dads waved and walked their dogs as they wore colorful rainbow clothing and bandanas. Nightclub floats full of lights and dancing people rolled past every so often, playing music that inspired the onlookers to dance, too. But her favorite part of the parade had to be the giant float that carried the word love, made from an array of colorful flowers. That's what pride was about to her, something as simple yet profound as love.

As the large groups passed, the onlookers joined the tail of the parade, and they all marched toward Boston Common. Seeing the colorful, winding line of people ahead of her, all marching together for love and freedom, always made her tear up, and today was no exception. Holding Tamika's hand and feeling a sense of safety they rarely knew was bittersweet for her. She should be able to feel this way every day.

When they reached Boston Common, there was someone on the stage speaking.

"We are so happy to see all of your happy faces today. We have so many great speakers and music for you. The sun is shining. Who is just ecstatic to be in Boston celebrating pride today?"

The crowd cheered a little. Susan just smiled and took it in.

"Come on. I know you can do better than that. Who is happy to be in Boston celebrating pride today?"

"Come on, Babe." Tamika nudged Susan with her elbow.

A louder cheer arose from the crowd; Susan joined in this time.

"That's more like it! But this is Boston. Boston! I know we have a *wicked lot* more energy than I am hearing from you. This time, shout it from the rooftops so even Connecticut can hear how proud we are."

A collective roar filled the air. Susan screamed so loud it hurt her throat, but it felt good to let loose.

"There you go." Tamika smiled at her.

It struck Susan as funny that Tamika was trying to get her to loosen up when it often felt like it was the other way around.

The MC gave the microphone over to the mayor.

"I'm so happy to live in Massachusetts," she said to Tamika, leaning in as they listened to the mayor's speech about equality and diversity.

Tamika squeezed her hand and smiled.

After a few more speakers, the first musical performers came on. The trill of the gay men's acapella chorus filled the air. Except for some whispers and the excited shrieks of a few toddlers, the crowd was silent as they listened to their version of *Somewhere Over the Rainbow*.

Susan's feet started to ache as they stood there through the end of their act and began to watch a comedic skit. She couldn't help but laugh at the overexaggerated stereotypes of the characters on stage, but the pain in her feet made it difficult to enjoy. She just wanted to sit down.

As much as she hated it when Tamika bugged her about her health and the way she ate, Susan knew she had a point. Being on her feet and physical activity wouldn't be so difficult if she wasn't nearly two-hundred-fifty pounds. And if she was in this much pain in her twenties, it would surely just get worse. Yes, she would have to do something different if she wanted a lifetime full of adventure. Maybe this was the time she would stick with it.

"Babe, I have to pee. I'll be back in a few," Tamika said.

"Where? I have to go, too."

"I'm just going to use the porta-potty we passed."

Susan wrinkled her nose and shook her head. "Yuck. I'll just go later."

Tamika smiled at her and kissed her before she walked away.

She tried to ignore her throbbing feet and enjoy herself. She was a people watcher, just like her mom. Over the years, she had determined that if you stood and watched long enough, you were bound to see some sort of reunion at every Pride. You wouldn't necessarily know it by staring at the crowd that day, but the gay community was small. It always made Susan feel good when she saw people running into one another unexpectedly. Whether you were from a small town in Western Mass. or almost any city in the state, you were bound to run into someone you knew from the pride community when you came to the Boston Pride parade.

As if she thought it into reality, she felt a hand on her arm and looked up to see Steph standing there in her snug white tank top and beautifully sleeved arms. Susan felt her mouth fall open. Steph reached in with both arms and gave her one of her signature hugs, the type that made you feel truly loved. Some people gave one-armed hugs. Others gave you a quick squeeze. But Steph hugged you with her whole soul. Lost in the moment, she made Steph pull away first.

"It's so good to see you, Susan," Steph said, her blue eyes smiling. The thing with Steph was that you could always feel she meant what she said. She just had a way of making people feel special.

"You too. I *love* your new glasses!" Susan said, admiring the funky black frames that suited Steph so well. Instantly, she felt herself blush as it came out of her mouth. What an awkward alternative to simply asking how she was, like most people would have done.

"Thanks." Steph put her hand on Susan's upper arm. "It's been too long."

Susan felt chills run through her like she always did when she connected with Steph. She was vaguely aware that the skit was coming to a close and the MC was back on stage, covering the microphone with his hand and talking to someone in a hushed tone.

"But we're here now," Steph added. "I was over there with some friends, and I was just so happy when I spotted you. I had to come right over. I see that you're alone. I was hoping we could...well, you know, start spending time together."

Susan froze, unsure how to reply. She looked into Steph's eyes, seeking some clarity. She thought she knew Steph's energy well enough to understand what she meant, but she had been painfully wrong before. And she remembered that final look they'd exchanged last July in P-town. It wasn't nothing. And now, when Steph looked back at her in a way she never had before, Susan knew she wasn't wrong this time. But it didn't matter; she was in love with Tamika.

"Okay, so we are just going to step away from the programming for a quick minute, everybody. It's a beautiful day to share love stories, so I am going to give the microphone to my new friend, Tamika."

Hearing Tamika's name lifted her out of that place where she was living in Steph's eyes. She stared at the stage now to see that Tamika was, in fact, standing up there holding the microphone. She jutted her chin closer and squinted, unable to process why on Earth she would be on the stage. Her mouth hung open. She didn't even know she was pointing at Tamika across the lawn.

"Hi everyone. Thanks for sharing this moment with me." Tamika laughed softly and shifted her feet. "I am just so lucky to be here in Boston today, especially because I am here with a beautiful woman named Susan. A woman I love with all my heart. And even though we are still fighting for marriage equality, I want to ask Susan Sibley to be my wife today."

Susan felt the blood drain from her face as people cheered and clapped. This could not be really happening. Staring straight ahead, she felt Steph's eyes on her. She had to do something. She couldn't just stand here looking like a deer caught in the headlights, and she certainly couldn't look at Steph. Tamika had spotted her, looked out at her, and laughed at her expression.

"I know she's a little shy, but I see her nodding, so I'm going to go celebrate and kiss her now." Tamika handed the microphone back to the MC and walked off stage, zig-zagging across the lawn as the crowd cheered.

Susan didn't even know she had been nodding. What had happened was beginning to sink in. As Tamika ran through the crowd, Steph was still standing beside her. Instead of turning her head to see what Steph's expression was, she looked into the crowd as people moved aside, and Tamika reached her and kissed her on the mouth as everyone cheered again.

A part of Susan wanted to shrink into the ground as everyone stared, but something giddy bubbled up inside her, too.

"Are you saying yes?" A stranger from the crowd shouted.

Susan giggled, realizing she hadn't said it aloud yet. "Yes!"

Everyone clapped and cheered again.

Steph stood there, silent.

After a long embrace, they parted, and Tamika spotted Steph.

Steph was shaking her head from side to side in awe. "Congratulations."

Tamika put her hand out to shake, but Steph leaned in, grabbing her in a bear hug instead.

"Oh my gosh, I am just so happy for you both. This was...this was just awesome to witness. Awesome. It was really nice to see you again, Tamika, but I'm going to let you guys have this moment." She paused. "It was great to see you, Susan. We'll catch each other again another time."

Steph disappeared into the crowd. Tamika grabbed Susan and

held her in another long embrace as Susan watched Steph walk away. As she walked away, she reached back, unfastened her baseball cap from her jeans, and put it on her head. She'd confided in Susan long ago that she had a habit of putting her hat on when she was hurting as if it could contain the pain and keep it from spilling out of her.

*****

Tamika initiated sex every night for the first week after they got engaged, and it was starting to be too much for Susan, but she didn't know how to say it. She just wanted to cuddle. And she needed to sleep. After making love one evening, they lingered, wrapped up in one another as the last rays of summer sun streamed in their bedroom window.

"What about a wedding next June? Pride Month would be perfect, don't you think? And that would give us almost a year to plan and save," Tamika asked.

"That could be nice. We met in June. Got engaged in June."

"Aww, right. It's perfect, then. Maybe we can keep the tradition, and our first baby will be born the following June."

Susan wasn't quite ready for that discussion. "It's pretty ironic, though," Susan said, changing the subject.

"What is?" Tamika asked.

"A June wedding."

"Why is that ironic?" Tamika asked, confused.

"You know, it's just so typical. It's the traditional wedding month. I mean, it made sense why someone conventional like DJ would choose June, but...I don't know, it's just funny."

"You like to put things in boxes sometimes, Babe," Tamika replied.

The comment irritated Susan, but she was pretty sure it was because Tamika wasn't wrong.

Getting married had been all that Tamika could talk about since she proposed a week ago, and it wasn't that Susan wasn't excited, but it was overwhelming, too. Now, she was talking about babies. This was it; she could feel it. She was choosing to dive fully into a traditional life; she just needed a little time for her mind to adjust. Except for Fiona, she hadn't even told anyone she was engaged yet.

"Where are you tonight?" Tamika asked.

"Oh, I'm sorry. I'm...worried about work. Had two people quit this week. I'm behind on this week's order, and it's supposed to go out tomorrow," she lied. Two people *had* quit, including her latest Assistant Manager, but she wasn't concerned. The weekly order would go out on time. It always did.

"Look at my baby being all professional and serious," Tamika remarked.

This comment annoyed Susan, too, but then again, she'd been irritable all week for no good reason. How could Tamika be impressed that she'd just said she was stressing over work? Was that the measure of success Tamika was looking for? A life so focused on earning a living that you took your worries home? She didn't want to bring it up. She knew that she was probably just overthinking.

"No, but really, how amazing would a pride wedding be?" Tamika asked.

Susan smiled. "Would be pretty cool to have rainbows everywhere."

"I think it could be perfect. We'll keep it small, maybe a hundred people?"

"A hundred people?" Susan practically shouted. "Do we even know a hundred people? Or...do we really *like* a hundred people enough to have them there?"

Tamika laughed. "Okay, maybe seventy-five? That's still small, Babe."

"I don't know. Sounds like a lot. I don't want to be up there in front of all of those people."

"You're adorable," Tamika replied.

Even that annoyed Susan. It felt like Tamika wasn't listening. But she stayed calm.

"No, really...who on Earth would we invite that would add up to seventy-five or a hundred people?"

Tamika jumped up from bed and grabbed a pad of paper and a pen. She quickly started jotting down names, many of which Susan had never heard before.

"Who are these people?" Susan asked.

"Well, my family, so far. I could probably get fifty just from there, with aunts, uncles, and cousins. And there's Hazel and Rebecca, and Sasha from college..." she paused for a minute to think, then continued, "Elle and Drew." She jotted down the names as she rattled them off.

Susan couldn't help but roll her eyes. Suddenly, it felt like she was talking to Michael, who was convinced he was friends with everyone on Earth.

"I've literally never heard you mention most of these people. Of those you listed, I've only met Sasha, and that's just because we ran into her at the store," Susan said.

"Oh, I went to high school with Hazel and Rebecca, and the rest are college friends. Oh, and yes, yes...coworkers." She added more names to the list as Susan grew increasingly mortified at the prospect of the kind of event Tamika had in mind.

"This is going to be expensive with all those people." Maybe if she spoke in terms that Tamika could relate to, she could sway her.

"We can do it on a budget. It's just what people do. You want to show me off, don't you? I know I want everyone to see my beautiful bride. And a pride wedding...I mean, how cool is this going to be?"

Susan wasn't sold. Of course, it would be special to have her mother there, and she knew Michael would be there, even if they had grown apart, but she couldn't think of anyone else she was certain she'd want to invite except Fiona. She didn't want anyone there who wouldn't take it seriously. Ed was ignorant. DJ would want to be there, but Susan even had reservations about that. She could feel it in her gut. DJ saw Susan's relationship differently than she saw a straight relationship. She'd called DJ out on it a few times, and every time, DJ denied it, but Susan knew...maybe DJ didn't even know. Matt was the same...he was always making jokes about gay marriage. She couldn't stand how ignorant most of the people in her life were; why would she want them there thinking she was abnormal or that it wasn't a real wedding? But Tamika had already begun adding names to the list of Susan's people. Every friend of Susan's she had ever met was on the list by the time she was done. She supposed Tamika was right; this was just what people did. But she was never one to do something just because it was what everyone else did.

"I'm at around sixty, but you know they won't all show up, so it will just be small, I promise. It's going to be perfect," Tamika insisted.

"It doesn't bother you that a lot of these people won't take our marriage seriously?" Susan asked, irritated.

Tamika shrugged. "Who?"

"I can't for sure about your side, but...Ed, DJ, Matt..." She scanned the list. "Most of your distant family, I'm sure, from what you've told me."

"DJ?" Tamika asked and eyed her with surprise.

"Yeah, I'm pretty sure her holier-than-thou Christianity makes her think it's a sin, even if she believes in forgiveness," Susan replied.

"But she's like your best friend," Tamika argued.

"So. Doesn't mean it's not true." Susan wasn't going to back down. She refused to deny her truth, no matter who was concerned.

"It's really not my problem if they take us seriously. I mean, how can they not? They're going to be there to witness our love. If they don't take us seriously, they won't show up." Tamika shrugged.

"Mmm, I don't know. I don't think it's that simple," Susan replied.

"What do you mean?"

"I mean that people are fake. I think plenty of people will show up just because *that's what you do* for family. And then those same people will go home and pray for us or laugh about how ridiculous we are." She sighed. At least Michael would be there. Even if they hadn't talked much since that weekend in P-town, she knew she could count on him to be there. He would always be that gay friend who showed up to support her through things that only other gay people could understand. She just wished her fiancée was one of those people, too.

"You're overthinking," Tamika insisted.

"I think you're underthinking. And I don't think you're considering how uncomfortable I'm saying I am with it all."

"You're being ultra-shy and antisocial about all of this." She wasn't mad, but she still wasn't hearing Susan. Yes, she was shy, but this wasn't that. This was about energy. She didn't feel they should share such an intimate moment with anyone who didn't love them as they were...and she'd learned a long time ago how painfully short that list was.

"I think it's just so nice when it's intimate. When you have people there who...really support your love. Besides my mom, the person I want there the most will never be able to come because she's over a thousand miles away. And, ugh, we'll have to invite Ed."

"We're going to have to find a compromise." Tamika popped up from bed, waved a hand at her, and began getting ready for work. The conversation was clearly over, and Susan knew what compromises looked like with Tamika. It was more like she learned to accept Tamika's visions and forget her own.

Although it had been a wonderful spring with Tamika's graduation and their engagement, as the weeks went by, Susan could see that it would be another summer without adventure. She knew how serious Tamika was about her goals, but still, she hoped that with the pressure of Tamika's rotation behind her, she could let go a little and take some time for fun. Even a week's vacation to the beach would be a well-deserved getaway. But every free moment of Tamika's time was spent looking for her first nursing position because she refused to settle for the first thing she was offered. Before graduating, her supervisor had offered her a position at the nursing home, but she wouldn't budge. Tamika wanted something better. Susan admired the strength it took for her not to settle, yet it seemed funny that was what she'd done when Tamika talked her into taking the manager position. She couldn't help but recall how Tamika claimed she was excited to graduate so their real life could begin, but not much had changed. Instead of going between work and her rotation, she went between work, job fairs, and interviews in addition to the wedding planning. It still seemed to Susan that their real life was playing out before them every day, and Tamika consistently failed to take advantage of it.

*****

As Susan suspected, Tamika's idea of compromise about the wedding details wasn't quite the same as hers. It wasn't that Tamika didn't try. It was just the same unrelenting focus on what she wanted that made her difficult to talk to. She was just so determined to get everything to match the exact vision she had in her mind. The flowers, the food, where people would sit. Despite Susan's preference for a small wedding, the guest list had grown as Tamika met new coworkers. Susan couldn't help but feel embarrassed that most of the guests would be Tamika's family and friends, but she shrugged it off, wanting to give Tamika the wedding of her dreams.

Susan could admit that sometimes she was overly sensitive. Still, it was beginning to feel as though being a perfectiònist about the details was more important to Tamika than her bride.

The pride-themed wedding Tamika had gotten Susan so excited about right after they'd gotten engaged had transformed into something else entirely as their year-long engagement went on. Tamika had rethought it; with Susan reminding her that few people would take the marriage seriously, she felt that they shouldn't be in people's faces with the pride theme after all. Tamika's new vision was far more conservative and traditional, and Susan wasn't impressed but didn't want to fight.

Susan would have handled the issue quite the opposite. She would have enhanced the pride décor to the hilt, not only from a place of genuine pride and celebration but to stand their ground and express that people could fuck off if they didn't like it. Sometimes, it took a little provocative action to create change. But she was too tired to argue about the small details anymore.

Now, the wedding was exactly seven weeks away, and while she wanted to be married, she was ready for the wedding itself to be behind her.

But today, Susan had a Saturday to herself. She'd wasted half of it by sleeping until nearly noon, but she still had a few hours left before Tamika arrived home from the day shift. She just wanted to get lost in a good book and not think about the wedding. But as she sat there trying to take in the story, she ruminated about her own life instead.

Surprised that it was after one now, she abandoned all hope of being able to focus on her book. Her mind was simply too noisy. She'd watch a movie in bed instead; she didn't need the same focus for a movie, and it could still carry her away from her reality for a couple of hours. But first, she would have to run to the store for some Ben and Jerry's.

When she returned, she threw the pile of mail on the island and pressed the blinking button on the answering machine. DJ kept telling her she needed a cell, but she still preferred coming home to a message rather than giving people full access to her every moment. Besides, there was something special about coming home to a message from someone who loved you after being out in the scary world. This time, it was her mom.

"Hey, Suze, it's just your mother. Me and Ed and the girls were going to the drive-in, and we were hoping you would join us. Everything is better when my kid is there. If you get this before seven and want to go, give me a call. Love you."

She just didn't have it in her tonight. While she always loved spending time with her mom, she needed the comfort of her pajamas and her own home.

Just hearing her mother's voice was a comfort in and of itself, so she played the message a second time, then walked away feeling guilty about not going, though she could hear in Alice's voice how much she wanted Susan there.

Sorting through the mail, Susan was excited to find a letter from Fiona. Another comfort. She quickly changed into her shorts and tank top and snuggled under the covers; her bed had always been her safe place. As she unsealed the envelope and pulled the letter out, taking care to preserve it as she always did with Fiona's letters, something else came tumbling out with it: an intricate silver bracelet with rainbow gemstones woven in between wire folds.

April, 29, 1999

Hey Susan,

The big day is coming, eh? I wish I could be there, but there's just no way. I still have the invitation on my fridge, and see it every morning when I make my coffee. If only I could win the lottery, I would show up and surprise you. The lottery would be the only way at this point. Went out on "sick leave" from my latest job at the gas station, but I ain't going back. It was either that or kill a few people. The customers are bad enough, but I can handle them. But the manager is on a power trip to make up for his small dick, and I couldn't play nice anymore. Like I said, I was this close to having to kill him. I know I was not a good Witch in a past life, so when I feel that resurfacing, I get out. Minimum wage ain't worth it anyway.

Best decision ever. Now, I get to collect for a few months and craft and make art and hole myself up in the house and be the savage beast I was meant to be. Will ain't working either though, so he's always here. Always. Loves him, I do, but I just want an afternoon to myself sometimes.

Just know I will be at your wedding in spirit. Thinking of you as the date gets closer. Look hard (not with your eyes though) and you will see me in the front row with my rainbow tutu and rainbow sports bra. Wouldn't that be great to show the uptight guests you been telling me about? Warning you...if I win the lotto, I WILL show up like that. Will can come in a dress as a bonus...IF I feel like letting him come.

I even sent this letter early enough so you'd have it before the wedding. Made you this bracelet to wear on your special day. It will look perfect with what you're wearing.

Remember, don't settle. Know your value. Live in the moment. Love hard. Enjoy one another. Choose your battles.

I would tell you to enjoy your day, but I know that's not likely, so just remember that it's about the marriage. The family you are creating. And of course...the honeymoon sex.

Love, Fiona

Maybe Fiona's letter and her mother's voice message didn't change her exhaustion from the rest of her life, but for that night, it soothed her, even if she was still profoundly sad that Fiona wouldn't be there.

She and Tamika had quickly agreed on one thing from the beginning: they didn't want a traditional wedding party. Jocelyn and Alice would be the only ones standing up for them. Mothers were powerful; these women would offer a special kind of strength and protection to their new marriage. While Tamika didn't often use the word feminist to describe herself, as Susan did, she agreed that the notion of a father giving a woman away was archaic. Besides, her father wanted nothing to do with it. Jocelyn had informed him that he *would* attend his daughter's wedding, no matter what his beliefs, but he would never give Tamika away, not to another woman.

When the wedding was eleven days away, it hit her in a new way. This was really going to happen. Tamika still didn't understand how nervous she was about being up in front of nearly a hundred people.

Knowing she would have her mother at her side that day wasn't enough to relieve Susan's anxieties about the big day. She knew she could get through it; she always got through everything. But how?

Once they were back home, Tamika fell asleep on the couch, exhausted from the last-minute wedding errands, and all Susan could do was sit there like a lump, worrying about her wedding day. As the date came closer, she'd thought about it more and more, sometimes struggling not to give in to full-on panic, but tonight it was especially heavy.

She would be on display and in front of so many people who, she was sure, would sneer about the validity of a lesbian wedding. Maybe she had accepted that this was how Tamika wanted it, with family present, but she wasn't sure how she would get through it intact. She had to make sure she didn't disappear into the blackness as she had done during a few traumatic times in her life, not on her wedding day.

She could remember the first time it happened. She was nine, and she sat in the judge's chambers after her father's trial. He'd been found guilty of sexual abuse, and now, the judge wanted to talk to her. She supposed the judge had been saying something to comfort her. She was able to hear a few words here and there. Not your fault. Prison. Safe. But suddenly, the room and everything in it wasn't there. She was sure she was still staring straight ahead, but except for a blurry peripheral view of the sun shining in the tall windows, she could only see blackness as she disappeared into her head. Like it was yesterday, she could remember how it felt, worried that the blackness might consume her. But that sun kept shining in the window, and eventually, she was back in the room, and she could hear her mother's voice calling her name.

Even at that young age, she had already mastered the art of appearing as if everything was okay. She always knew how to hold herself and make her eyes look as though she were fully there and she was not a bit upset, but on that day, she almost hadn't been able to keep that act up. After her mother's voice had brought her back to the room, she nodded at the judge when she heard pauses in his speech and tried to follow. Finally, she could sense he was done and heard him ask if she had any questions. She didn't. Even if she had, she wouldn't have willingly sat there any longer than she had to; no, all she wanted was to go home and snuggle under the covers or disappear in a book.

It had only happened a few other times after that, but each time was equally terrifying. At her gramma's funeral when she was ten. A few times in high school, when she'd been bullied in front of an entire classroom or the lunchroom. And most recently, on her first day in public speaking class. She'd nearly dropped the class rather than face that it might happen during a speech. But knowing that she needed it to graduate, she was driven to tough it out. One of these times, she might not manage to hold it together. She might get lost in that blackness and be unable to keep herself in the room at all.

Once she remembered how she had gotten through the public speaking class, the answer came: she just needed to get her hands on some marijuana.

CHAPTER TEN

Susan wondered what Tamika would think if she knew Susan was smoking marijuana again. They'd smoked it together during the first year of their relationship, but as they got more serious about their careers, it stopped being a part of their lives. Rather sure that Tamika would have an issue with it, Susan decided it wasn't something she would share, especially since the wedding was so close.

After she got out of work, she drove around the city for a little while, trying to decide where she'd smoke for the first time. She pulled into the Price Chopper parking lot, where she was meeting Tara, her friend from college. Tara came into the store every now and then, and Susan was right; Tara was more than happy to sell her a half-dozen joints worth of her homegrown pot to her.

As Susan waited in her car, she pondered how, although she had been here for years, she never quite fit into the city. Sure, she'd found so many parts of herself here, but damn, it was too loud. When she'd been with Michael back in her college days, she felt fine. When she was with Tamika, she was fine. They were both city people, and she could cling to them when she needed to, but when she was alone, the city just swallowed her up.

Tara had other deliveries, so their transaction was friendly but quick. After she held the baggie with the six joints in her hand, she smiled, feeling like a bit of an outlaw. She opened the baggie just to take a sniff, still unsure where to smoke. She didn't want to go home. The scent itself was a relief. She held a single joint in her palm and decided that her car was as good a place as any. She retrieved the lighter that she'd bought from her backpack. No one was in the cars parked next to her, so she didn't waste any time. She flicked the metal wheel of the lighter and inhaled slowly, feeling an instant sense of ease wash over her. With a second puff, the bustle of the city no longer blared inside of her. Marijuana had always helped her focus on what existed in her rather than that which was outside of her.

"Thank you," She uttered to the universe as she exhaled her third puff.

She turned her keys and turned the volume up. *Breakdown*, the latest Melissa Etheridge CD was still in the player. She rarely turned the radio on when she was alone; even music was too loud for her most days. Made her feel too much. But with some help, she was ready to feel just a little. Melissa was always one of her favorites, not only because her music was there when Susan came out but because she could tell Melissa understood rage and pain. Susan had so much of both, and it helped to know she wasn't alone. Pot tamed the rage and made the pain bearable. But now, as she got quickly stoned and listened to *Angels Would Fall* with a new perspective, she drank in the profound meaning of existence. Like Melissa, there was another side to her; she wasn't just rage and pain, she was divine. She just hadn't yet comprehended to be both divine and human.

She stared at the brick wall of the grocery store as Melissa sang on.

"I like brick," she said aloud to nobody.

She started to question why she was in so much pain at all. She didn't have it all that bad. She thought about other women. She wasn't twenty with four children like her gramma had been. She wasn't in an abusive marriage like her mom had been. She was a college-educated woman with a job and a decent place to live, and, most importantly, she was about to be married to a woman she loved like crazy. Hadn't this been pretty much everything she had always wanted? All the details of her life started to swirl through her mind and confuse her. It was what she'd thought she wanted, so why didn't it make her feel the way she expected it to? After a few more puffs, she got out and leaned against the car for a minute, letting the dying evening sun seep into her. When the warmth hit her arms, she felt a current in her skin.

She needed to walk. She grabbed her backpack and then, after a few steps, looked back at the keys in the ignition but said fuck it, and left them there. She crossed the street to Elm Park, stopping to look at each sculpture for a moment. The first, a genderless figure made from thick metal, looked upward with one arm in the air. The other arm seemed to disappear behind the spine, which was made up of delicate, boomerang-shaped pieces. But when she moved to the back of the sculpture and then to the front again, she never could determine where the second arm was. She wasn't sure if it was because she was stoned or if this was, in fact, a one-armed being, but she decided that it was dancing. Her favorite, though, was a giant, unidentifiable creature. It could have just as easily been an elephant or a unicorn. She was at eye level with the creature's knee joints. She touched the colorful fabrics and decided it must be something like papier-mâché, although it had rained the previous night and wasn't wet. She stared for several minutes, wondering what type of glaze they might have used to keep it dry.

"Over here," a little boy yelled and waved as a woman ran toward him, dropping down to embrace him. She couldn't be sure what was happening between them, but she felt the emotion, which brought tears to her eyes. She looked away before they let go of one another.

She walked around the park's periphery, counting her laps at first but losing count after seven. She wasn't sure if the scruffy dog dragging her pink leash was leading or following her, but it comforted her that she wasn't the only stray wandering alone. She looked at her wrist as she saw the sky fading into an almost dusky gray, but she'd never worn a watch. Gazing up, she remembered the giant sundial in the park. She walked around again to find it and, when she did, sat on the edge of the grass nearby. How much things had changed if her ancestors could use sundials to tell time and the moss that grew on trees to determine direction while she managed to get lost going from one end of the city to the other sometimes. Fiona would know. She would write to her if she had paper with her, but she'd forgotten to restock her backpack with stationery.

She thought about how the roads crossed and became one-way streets and dead ends and eventually began to picture the street their townhouse was on. It was nice enough, she supposed. Tree-lined. Clean. What was Tamika doing now? Although she wasn't sure what time it was, it seemed logical that Tamika was home already or maybe pulling up that little tree-lined street at that very moment.

"I love her," she whispered aloud and saw the dog staring at her from the edge of the street.

It was really all she needed to know. She lay back on the grass and laughed at herself, thinking about how she'd been feeling lately. She already felt better, even though she'd still have to stand up in front of a bunch of people very soon. Nothing really mattered. Maybe Tamika should take her more seriously, but the flip side was true, too; she could learn to let some things go. Fiona was always telling her to let go and live in the moment.

Realizing it had gone from dusk to dark as she lay there, she was sure she was clear-headed enough to drive home now. It was only a ten-minute drive anyway. She lay there for a few more minutes and only got up when the dog came and sniffed at her.

"Hi," she said, reaching out her hand to let the dog sniff. "You seem sweet, but I bet you're hungry. Want something to eat? She thought about going into Price Chopper to get something for the dog to eat but remembered the half-eaten burger in her backpack and gave that to her instead. The burger was gone in seconds, and without a plan, she let the dog trail at her side as she made her way back to her car. She heard a man shouting but didn't think much of it until the voice got closer.

"Sally!"

Susan looked over her shoulder to see a man approaching her with a shopping cart. Did he think she was someone else? Did he think she was Sally?

"That's my dog you have there." He grumbled as he approached and stopped.

"Oh!" Susan laughed, handing him Sally's leash.

"Been looking for you, girl." He stooped down, and Sally jumped up and licked his face.

"She was in the park. I...I just didn't want her to get hurt."

The man nodded, looking down at the pavement. "We love the park."

"I fed her a burger. Hope that's okay. She seemed hungry." As soon as she'd uttered the last sentence, she regretted it. Clearly, the man was homeless; she hadn't needed to point out the obvious.

At that, he looked up a little but didn't meet her eyes. "Thank you for that, Dear."

She wasn't sure what to say to him. She just wasn't good with people.

"Can I...buy *you* a meal?" She was certain she wouldn't have gotten it out had it not been for the marijuana. There was an uncomfortable silence between them for a few moments, and she was worried she'd insulted him, but he nodded and humbly accepted the twenty dollars Susan handed him from her wallet.

His stark blue eyes met hers for the first time. "God bless you. And good luck...with your new life and that beautiful little daughter." And then, he turned around and pushed his cart away.

He kept speaking as he walked away, talking in quick bursts. Susan couldn't make much out but clearly heard the word raven come out of his mouth several times.

Susan waited for the goosebumps to fade away before she got in her car and drove home.

As she parked her car, it felt like she had just spent a few hours in another universe and was about to enter her own life again.

Susan was sure Tamika would be worried or, more likely, pissed that she was so late. But, when Tamika looked up from the island as Susan walked in the door, it was obvious that she had been so deep into her own thoughts that she hadn't even noticed Susan was late. While she hadn't been looking forward to angering Tamika, surely it would have been better than her soon-to-be wife not noticing that she'd been about five hours later than expected.

"You're right, we spent a lot." Tamika laughed as she said it, but Susan could see the creases in her forehead that told her the bills worried her. Susan shrugged it off and gave Tamika a kiss. They'd already spent the money, so what was the point in worrying? After the wedding, they would just have to focus on digging themselves out of the hole they'd made.

Although she was still worried about the big day, Susan found the final days leading up to the wedding more bearable when she smoked a little here and there. She made sure the joints Tara had given her would last, usually only taking a couple of puffs in the car before going upstairs after work. Sometimes, she'd make an excuse to run out before bed to sneak a few more puffs, always worried that Tamika would smell it on her. It was ridiculous, really. They'd smoked it on their first date. But Susan knew that Tamika was all about growing up now, so she would keep it to herself. Besides, a part of her reveled in the secrecy of it all.

Susan took the two days before the wedding off, and on Thursday, she had plans to treat her mom to lunch to thank her for all of the help she'd been with wedding preparations. Her mother hated errands but seemed genuinely thrilled to help with them anyway.

Alice was supposed to pick her up at noon, but Susan jumped and screamed a little when the doorbell rang at twenty of. Since she'd had the house all to herself and Alice was driving, she took a few indulgent afternoon tokes. It was the first time she'd smoked in the house, and she was sure that this was the building manager ringing her doorbell because he'd smelled the smoke. He probably had the cops with him, too.

Susan waved her hands through the kitchen and living room, trying to displace the smoke, and yelled, "One minute!"

"Hurry up, I have to pee," Alice called from the other side of the door with a little knock.

Susan sighed with relief when she heard her voice and opened the door.

"Hug you after I pee," Alice said, shoving Susan's wedding shirt at her and making a bee-line for the bathroom.

Susan looked at every detail of her wedding shirt. She'd always admired how neatly her mother could stitch a seam by hand. The detail of the rainbow embroidery was amazing: a wavy pattern wrapping all the way around the collar.

"Please tell me you love where I'm going with it. I was going to stitch the sleeves with that same pattern if you liked it," Alice said, coming up quietly behind her.

"I do. I fucking love it! Thank you so much, mom...for everything." She turned around and hugged Alice, unsure why she suddenly wanted to cry but adamantly refusing.

She ran her finger along the shirt's side seam, in awe of the work. It was so perfectly done you might have thought it was store-bought were it not for the artisan quality that set it apart as handmade.

"I'm glad you like it. The pattern I used for the shirt was Gramma's, you know."

"Aww, really?"

Alice nodded, "I don't even remember keeping any of that stuff. You know I don't keep stuff the way she did. The way you do. But I'm glad I did."

"You still have to teach me how to do this someday."

"To sew?"

Susan nodded.

"You're a busy girl, but someday... This style is called a poet's shirt. I thought it was perfect for my romantic daughter," she replied.

Susan smiled at the way her mother saw her.

"Are you burning sage in here? I really can't decide if I love the smell or hate it."

Susan giggled. Her mother was so innocent. And gullible. She could have easily lied to her, and Alice never would have thought about it again.

"What?" Alice asked. But Susan couldn't stop giggling, and eventually, the giggles turned into a full-on belly laugh. Alice joined her, and they both had to flop down on the couch to recover.

"What the fuck is so funny?" Alice asked, still half laughing.

"Mom, it's not sage. It's pot."

Alice smirked. "You nervous about being up in front of all those people Saturday?"

Susan nodded. She knew her mother understood. They were so similar; neither liked to be the center of attention.

"Where the hell do you even get it?" Alice asked.

"Tara."

"Who?"

"You know, that hippie chick I tutored in English," Susan answered.

"Ahh, you crazy college girls." Alice shook her head good-naturedly. "Well, I think it's pretty cool. I'm just surprised that Tamika is okay with it."

"Well, we used to smoke it together when we first met, but it's been a long time. She doesn't really know I've been doing it again," Susan explained.

"Yeah, she's...I don't know. You're the wild, romantic one. She's more serious."

"You really think I'm romantic, huh? That's the second time you've said that."

"Don't *you*?" Alice asked.

Susan shrugged. "I guess so. I mean, I think I used to be."

"No, you always have been, and you always will be. That's not something you lose. It's who you are," Alice said, leaning in to give Susan a pat on the arm.

"But I'm so boring," Susan insisted.

Alice laughed. "Join the club, Honey. Growing up will do that to you."

"Tell me about it." Susan rolled her eyes.

"So, where is it? Maybe I wanna try some."

"Where is what?" Susan asked.

"The pot."

"Really?" Susan was convinced she was joking.

"Why not?"

"We'll have to order lunch in."

"I want Chinese," Alice replied.

After ordering the food, Susan wasn't sure if she should actually get the joint and light it.

"You feel weird smoking pot with your old mother?" Alice asked as she settled down on the couch and retrieved her lighter from her pocket.

Susan laughed. "You're not old."

"Well, I'm not young."

Susan opened the front of her backpack and remembered the makeshift ashtray she'd hidden in the oven when the doorbell rang.

She still had half a joint in there.

Alice only took one hit, inhaling slowly. "God, you were just a baby the last time I smoked this shit. And now, you're getting married."

Susan took another hit, even though she was still pretty mellow.

Alice shook her head and smiled. "File this under things you never thought would happen. You always detested my cigarettes, and now you're smoking pot."

"It's different."

"Still. I never thought I'd smoke pot again, much less with my daughter." She paused and took a second hit.

Susan watched her mother's face change as she felt the effects.

"It's weird."

"Are you spinny like you were with the wine?" Susan teased.

"Umm, no. It's more like..." She motioned to her head and closed her eyes. "It's not physical."

"Yeah. I get it."

"I don't know if I like it."

"Makes you think differently, right?"

Alice opened her eyes and nodded but didn't say anything else.

"Are you okay?" Susan asked after a few minutes of silence.

"I'm okay," Alice answered. But Susan could see it on her face, the thoughts that swirled around in her head.

The silence was too hard, so Susan escaped to the bathroom for a few minutes. When she came back, Alice had tears in her eyes. She hated seeing her mother cry.

"Aww, what's wrong?" Susan asked, trying to be sweet but so uncomfortable that she just wanted to disappear.

Alice shrugged and sniffed. "I wish I could get you two a nice wedding gift. I mean something really nice..."

"Oh, Mom. Please don't worry about that. This shirt alone

is...*so* special to me."

"But I do. I would love to give you guys something really great. Other parents give their kids big checks to get them started or...I don't know. See...I can't even imagine what I'd get you, that's how fucking poor I am." She sniffed again.

"We don't need anything." She instantly regretted what she'd said. She hadn't meant it to sound like she and Tamika had more than Alice and Ed had, though they did.

"I'm just so proud of you, Susan. I look at you and can't believe what you came from. How you turned out like you did with me and your father as parents."

"Mom!" She wanted to crawl out of her skin when Alice mentioned her father and hated it when she put herself down.

"No, really, you came from a single mother on welfare, and look at you. College graduate, good job..."

"No more pot for you," Susan joked.

Alice laughed a little and wiped her eyes. "I just want you to know...I wish I could do more for you guys. And I'm sorry I can't."

"You're here. You're going to be my maid of honor. That's all I need."

"You were always such a good kid. I really don't know how I got such a good kid."

Susan put her hand on Alice's arm but held back from blurting out all the sappy stuff on her mind. She was relieved when the doorbell rang.

"Food!" Alice clapped her hands like a kid and opened the cupboards.

"Where are all of your plates?" Alice asked.

"In the dishwasher. They're clean," Susan replied over her shoulder as she grabbed her wallet and went to the door.

"Right. The dishwasher." Susan heard Alice say from across the room. Susan snickered; her mother had expressed it before;

she thought having a dryer and a dishwasher meant that she and Tamika were wealthy.

Even though she didn't reach out for support as often as she should, one of the many habits she'd formed as a trauma survivor, as always, an afternoon with her mother was always just what she needed to help her get through.

*****

Tamika had talked Susan into taking two separate cars to the lodge, although Susan still wasn't sure why. Personally, she felt it would have been nice to be together every minute on their wedding day, not to mention that it would be easier to have only one car later.

Tamika had already been gone when Susan had woken up that morning. She had slept pretty well, thanks to a couple tokes before bed. She'd stopped worrying about whether Tamika would smell it on her when she snuck out at night. Tamika would just have to deal with it.

She stood in the hall staring back into the living room one last time before she left, as if the room might tell her if she'd forgotten something. She dropped her backpack at the door and headed to her bedroom, opening the drawer of her nightstand and looking down at Cocoa. She picked the doll up and looked at her worn features, considering stuffing her in the backpack. Somehow, maybe that would feel like her gramma was with her that day, too. Instead, after she looked one last time at the doll's cracked, plastic face, she returned her to the nightstand. She would be a married woman when she returned.

Her mother was standing outside waiting for her when she pulled up the long driveway on the side of the lodge. There were already two dozen cars there and busy people everywhere, but she spotted Alice right away leaning against her little blue Taurus, watching the action.

"Good morning." Alice smiled, tugging at Susan's shirt with the other.

"Come on. Over here. We have a few minutes before we need to go in and get ready. I need one last cigarette."

"I need a few tokes before I go in, anyway."

"Here? Susan Rose." She teased.

"Trust me, I need it."

"Okay," Alice smirked and waved her to the edge of the woods on the side of the lodge.

Susan flicked her lighter, inhaled, and held the joint out to her mother.

"God, no," Alice said, and they both giggled.

Susan took another toke and looked up to see the spots of blue sky in between the trees.

"That's kind of trippy looking," Susan said, pointing up.

Alice smirked.

"What?"

"You're such a little hippie...just like your mamma used to be."

Susan just smiled. She'd never thought of her mother as a hippie, but she supposed she was. Or could have been if she hadn't become a mother.

"I always thought you'd get married outdoors. You always did like the woods."

"Tamika didn't want to," Susan replied simply.

"There's a lot you don't agree on, huh?"

Susan laughed. "You have no idea. I wanted a small wedding. I mean *small*. Like...just you guys and Fiona small." She couldn't bear to hurt her mother's feelings by leaving Ed out.

"What about DJ?" Alice asked.

Susan shrugged. "There are a lot of people who have to try to act like they think our marriage is real. That our relationship is...normal, I guess. And for most of those people, including DJ, that's because Christianity has taught them our love is a sin. How can love ever be a sin?"

"I hope you don't think I feel that way."

"Naw. You've always been a pretty cool mom. Hippies are cool." She winked.

"You know, I regret how I handled it when you came out to me," Alice confessed.

Susan could hear the catch in her throat.

"You weren't that bad. I know it had to be a surprise after I dated guys in high school and all. And I think you were just uncomfortable and had to get used to seeing me with my first couple of girlfriends, but you never made me feel unloved."

"When you were younger, I thought this might happen...you know, because of the shit that happened when you were a kid. But then, I admit, I guess I was relieved when you dated guys in high school. Not only because it meant you weren't so hurt that you couldn't have love. But also, because being gay isn't easy in this world."

"Mom, I'm not a lesbian because I was abused. I believe this is just how I was born. I mean, I can remember feeling really connected to girls way back. The way I felt when Carolyn would brush my hair...that butchy teacher's aide...the moment I met Linda in second grade...I never felt any of that starry-eyed stuff for guys."

"Linda? I thought you were just interested in her because she wasn't White. You always did like diversity."

"I'm sure that helped." Susan smirked.

"Wait, when you were older, were you guys...?"

"Oh, Goddess, no. I seriously had no idea I was gay until about a week before I told you, although looking back, it should have been so obvious. All my friends knew before me. Especially when I wanted to take Trista to prom so badly."

"And, you know, I never thought anything about that. She

wasn't in the same class as you and DJ, so I assumed you wanted to bring her so she'd be with you guys like she always was."

Susan shook her head but didn't elaborate on the details of the romantic evening she had pictured having with Trista at her prom.

"Anyway, I just want you to know I don't think you're abnormal or anything. I mean, not because you're gay, anyway." Alice laughed and playfully smacked her on the arm.

"Thanks, mom." Susan laughed. "I guess I should probably go in soon. Just a couple more puffs."

"Wait. I have something for you. I was going to give it to you inside when you were dressed, but I just can't wait. I know you wish Gramma could be here today, and I feel her with us right now." Alice put her palm to her chest.

"I wanted to give you something special, so...here." Alice reached into her purse and pulled out a small floral bag.

Susan had already guessed what was inside and wanted to cry. She uncinched the drawstrings gingerly and pulled out what had been her gramma's sapphire necklace. She and her mother never had a lot of material things, and neither of them minded much, but this was one of the few things that her mother had cherished. The sapphire was in a simple setting with three small diamonds framing it at the top, and it hung from a gold chain. Over the years, sometimes she and her mother would get it out just to look at it and hold it.

"Oh, Mom," was all that Susan could say.

"I know, I know. I always swore you wouldn't get this until I dropped dead, but I want you to have it. And it covers your something old *and* something blue. Your shirt is your something new and here, take one more hit. My lighter can be your something borrowed."

As Susan inhaled, she could feel her gramma standing there, too, just as clearly as she could feel the physical energy of Alice standing close to her. It was so strong that she looked for her gramma with her eyes for a few moments and was surprised when all she saw besides Alice were trees.

"Come on. We have to get you ready."

She walked slowly around the side of the building, taking in every detail of the day. This was the last time she would see the world as a single woman. The caterers and their clinking trays. The photographer scoping out the perfect spots for photos. And Marcus, standing beside his wife and son, looking solemn, like he would rather be anywhere else.

She watched her mother disappear inside, unaware that Susan hadn't entered with her. She needed just one more minute under the open sky. This was it. She was going inside. It was just a ceremony; arguably, her soul would still be the same, but she also knew she would be transformed. In that moment, she could better understand how she had felt at other times in her life. The Christmas when she was fourteen and didn't know why she was so sad. When she'd graduated from high school, even though she should have been ecstatic to get out of that town, she felt solemn. When she'd made love to a woman for the first time, and her mind ran so wild that she considered jumping from the third-story porch. This was simply how change felt for her. She let her gaze fall back to the wooded area and admired the trees and sky one last time before going inside; the real things would never change. They would always be there in their soulful, simplistic nature, no matter what other details were different.

White lilies and gold ribbons greeted her as she entered the main hall. Despite the fact that she had smoked, her gut was still a bit heavy. A frazzled woman was on her knees, attempting to rub a grayish shoe scuff from the white floor runner.

She saw two doors, one on each side of the runner; both had identical signs that read bride, which she and Tamika had brought so neither had to get ready in the groom's suite. She swallowed hard, realizing she didn't know which room was meant for her. Her heart sped up, and her head began to swish; the sounds around her felt louder and louder, and she wanted to run out the door.

"Hmm?" Susan asked, vaguely aware her mother was speaking to her.

"What are you doing, you goof?" Her mother poked her head out from the room on the left, waving her inside.

"Oh. Yeah. Coming," Susan replied, rejoining the present.

Like the rest of the place, the room was a little fancy for her taste, but she did like the floral room separator that sat kitty-corner. Colorful wildflowers adorned the slats and appeared to be hand-painted. It looked out of place with the rest of the room, which was decorated with delicate things.

"I know. It's beautiful, isn't it?" Alice ran her finger along one of the slats.

"It is, but..."

"Doesn't really...go, does it?" Alice asked, looking around?

"No! Exactly what I was thinking. But...."

"That's why it's beautiful."

"Really stands out with all of this...rich crap." She chuckled.

"I think someone hand-painted this. Look." One crooked finger pointed once at a time at each type of flower. "You're favorite. Tiger lilies. Purple clover. Cornflower...like the crayon." She locked eyes with Susan, and they both smiled. "Dandelions. And...I don't know what this one is..." she pointed at a tiny, cone-shaped, red flower.

"Honeysuckle," Susan replied, shocking herself as much as her mother.

"How did you know that?" Alice asked with one raised eyebrow.

"Susan shrugged. "I seriously have no idea." She laughed.

There was a quiet knock at the door.

"Come in," Susan called.

The frazzled woman from the hall poked her head in. "How is the bride doing? Do you need anything?"

"No, I don't think so. Thank you."

The woman fidgeted, hesitating. "We have thirty minutes." She looked at Susan uncomfortably.

"I think it's time for you to get dressed." Alice laughed.

"Oh! Right."

"Of course, we *can* start a tad late if you need time," the woman replied meekly.

"No, no. We don't need much time. We will be ready," Alice assured the woman, who nodded but still looked as if she may cry.

"Very good, then. I'll come back for you soon."

They both chuckled once the door shut. "You think we're stressing her out?" Alice asked.

Susan nodded. "I'm sure she's used to overly girly brides who need layers of make-up and shit. But I suppose I really *should* get dressed."

"Who is that, anyway?" Alice asked.

Alice and Susan both laughed.

Susan shrugged in reply. "Tamika hired some kind of wedding planner to help with last-minute details. I don't even know her name. I thought it was unnecessary, but it calmed Tamika down, so whatever."

With that, Susan grabbed her pants from the back of the door and disappeared behind the divider. Alice carefully hung the garment bag on one of the slats.

"Shit, Mom, can you hand me my backpack from the chair in the corner?" She asked, already having stripped off her shirt.

"You can't smoke pot *in here*, Susan Rose."

She chuckled, knowing that her mother meant business when

she felt the need to use her middle name. "I'm not smoking pot, Alice Mae. I just need my real bra."

"Why? Do you have a fake bra on now?" Alice teased as she handed the backpack over the side of the divider.

"Ha. Ha. Very funny. No, I have a sports bra on. Like always. I actually had to go out and get a pretty, pretty bra for today and realized I haven't owned anything but sports bras in years. Finding one was hell."

"You should have let me come with you to shop. I would have helped," Alice said.

"Why, so you could make me try it on in the middle of the store like you used to when I was in high school?"

Alice laughed. "I didn't do that with bras! Just shirts. You weren't an easy kid to shop with, so after spending hours in the store, I wanted to save time."

"Mmm hmm. Well, I'm no easier now, so be thankful I went alone," Susan replied as she struggled to hook her bra. She looked in the mirror hung on the back of the divider and couldn't help but grimace at the rolls hanging over the bra. She'd spent thirty bucks, and it still didn't fit.

She unzipped the garment bag; she gasped, and tears stung her eyes when she saw the finished product. The wavy, rainbow embroidering on the collar and sleeves was bold against the white linen. She could not have been prouder to wear something from the fanciest store in New York City, and she didn't know how to say that to Alice without crying.

"You really love it, don't you?" Alices asked.

She never needed to tell her mom anything. She always knew.

"I really do. Thank you," she barely managed through a single almost-sob.

She carefully slid the shirt on, and her gut was heavy, knowing it was just about time to face everyone. She gathered her hair in a low, loose ponytail and looked in the mirror, deciding that, after much debate about this, the style suited her wavy hair perfectly. After swiping on lip gloss, she was ready. Wasn't she supposed to be feeling excited? Not only was the fear outweighing the joy, but it hurt that their marriage wouldn't be legal, and she wanted the ceremony to be behind her. She sighed aloud.

"You okay?" Alice asked.

"Yup. I'm ready." She stepped out from behind the dressing screen, and when she met her mother's eyes, she found the tenderness she was expecting, even though it was not her own.

"You look perfect."

Susan just smirked.

"No, really. I'm so proud of the way you are always true to yourself. A dress and lots of make-up really isn't you, and I love the way you always know how to be yourself."

Tears stung her eyes, but another knock at the door demanded her attention.

"I think it's time," Alice said softly.

Susan knew her mom sensed her anxiety. While the way her mom knew her so well could be a comfort, it also made her feel exposed. But there was no time to focus on that now.

She stepped out into the hall and let the wedding planner talk at her as Alice went to take her place. She talked a lot. Susan blinked at her a few times, trying to take it all in. She looked away and stared down the aisle instead, focusing only on the white runner to keep her anxiety at bay. When she was halfway down the aisle, she looked up and found the comfort of Michael's face among the rest of the eyes staring back at her. He looked handsome as always in his pinstripe shirt, suitcoat, and fresh haircut. His eyes glistened, and as he smiled softly, his lip quivered. They'd worked side-by-side as activists during their college years. They'd fought for the legalization of gay marriage and commiserated about the state of the world, where some pretty awful things were considered acceptable, a loving marriage wasn't recognized. No one in the room understood that reality the way Michael did. No one else had shared that pain with her like he had. Not even the woman that she was about to *marry*. Today, on her big day, his presence comforted her in a way nothing else could.

She made it down the aisle and through the ceremony with only a few blurry edges as the faces stared at her. The marijuana had done its job. She stood through what felt like hundreds of pictures afterward, smiling next to her new wife, and only felt as if she'd come back to the present when she and Tamika were alone after the ceremony.

While everyone filtered down the stairs and got settled, they reveled in being alone.

Tamika backed her gently into the wall, put a hand on each cheek, and kissed her slowly.

"We're married, Babe." Tamika rubbed her face softly with the back of her thumb and looked into her eyes.

"I do feel different." Susan smiled. "I wasn't sure I would."

"This, right here. It's...the magic I always knew I would find with you."

Susan let herself tear up. "I love you so fucking much," she uttered through both tears and laughter.

As they waited to be led downstairs and announced as wives for the first time, Susan could not keep herself from smiling. From day one, Tamika knew how to make her heart flutter. She was in awe that the charming woman she had met at Barnes and Noble was now her wife. She'd dreamt of this moment since the day she realized she loved women. This was what it felt like for one of your biggest dreams to come true.

CHAPTER ELEVEN

July 23, 1999

Dear Fiona,

Can you believe I have been a married woman for over a month now? I'm still sad that you couldn't be there. It's pretty fucked up to me that one of the two closest people to me wasn't there, yet, I had to parade in front of so many people I didn't even know and people who thought it was all a joke. Life is weird.

I wanted to hyphenate our names, Sibley-Bradley or Bradley-Sibley, but Tamika said we should wait until our marriage is legal and do all the paperwork at once. I know that being legally recognized is just a formality, but it still sucks. In a way, it feels like it's not even real. Without a name change, the wedding ring is really the only thing I have to remind me. Mostly, it's just fucked up because it's almost the year 2000, and you can't marry who you love. It's just not right! I hate the Western world.

On a happy note, I think I am beginning to understand why they call it the honeymoon phase (and yes, the honeymoon sex was awesome). Our three days in the Bahamas was nice, with the warm ocean and all, but it's not a place I ever really want to go back to either. I just can't feel the soul of a place when it's so noisy and populated. But I honestly feel more of the honeymoon phase now that we are home. I mean, it's easy to be happy when you are on vacation. But things feel better at home. It seems so cliché. I don't know; I guess I can see the Tamika I first met again – that strong, charming chick who drew me in so easily. The drive she has - I mean, that was always there, but it just seems sexy as fuck again. For a while, it was...I don't know, scary in a way, maybe. It was like she wanted to be a grown up, and that freaked me out. Change always scared me. But this - I mean, life is just so exciting. Somehow, it seems like there are just so many possibilities when you stop being afraid of the changes and grow up...but just a little. Even sex has been more amazing since coming home if that's possible. Maybe this is what it feels like when "everything comes together."

It feels like life is all new and exciting again. I was reading at work the other day and learned that June's full moon is called the honey moon because honey was typically ready in June in ancient times, and honey is one of the sweetest foods, like love is one of the sweetest things we can have in life. Pagan handfastings were traditionally held in June (I would have preferred THAT to the ridiculously expensive and traditional wedding we had, but Tamika just isn't that witchy). Still, I was so stuck on the fact that I was being overly traditional by getting married in June, yet who knew there were actually some witchy roots to the tradition? Who knew I would ever do anything traditional? It's all kind of romantic.

How are you and Will doing? Anything new and exciting? I wish I could get a better picture of what life is like there. From some of the things you say, I get the sense that it's quite different than it is here.

I put a wedding picture in with this letter; we should send more pictures. Show me what it looks like when you step outside every day. I feel like all I ever do is talk about me. Tell me something. You know, SOMETHING, so I don't feel like a shit friend who is always just talking about myself all the time.

Love, Susan

It occurred to Susan that writing to Fiona felt a lot like writing in a journal. She shared her innermost thoughts with Fiona in a way she didn't with anyone else. Fiona also hadn't seen the ugliest parts of her the way her mother and DJ had. But whatever the reason that she was closer with a woman she had never seen face-to-face than those she saw often, if Fiona had taught her one thing, it was not to question it. So, she didn't. She smiled as she dropped the letter in the mailbox before work and thanked the universe for Fiona.

*****

While Susan was less than thrilled about another boring summer, Tamika was ecstatic when, in early July, all of her interviewing paid off, and she was offered a position on a post-surgery floor at UMASS hospital. She went on and on about how the teaching hospital even offered a master's in nursing, and she could see herself considering doing that someday with the intent of working in a pediatric doctor's office.

While her surgical rotation had not been her favorite, at least this was an in. She couldn't expect to start with her dream job; everyone wanted to work in peds. As Tamika settled into the new position, Susan felt as though she saw her even less than when she was balancing school and a part-time job. She had to pay her dues, she said. Work whatever shifts were offered to her. Kiss a little ass when necessary. Besides, she kept reminding Susan they were still paying down the credit card debt they had racked up from the wedding.

After not even three months on the post-surgery floor, Tamika came home bubbling with excitement after work. "I have an interview on Friday!"

"Where? I didn't even know you were applying anywhere else."

"It's still UMASS, but it's the pediatric unit. But everyone wants to work there, and I have practically no experience, so I just assumed I'd need to put in a lot more time before anyone even considered me. But Tyler has an in with the Director of Nursing, so I got an interview."

"Who's Tyler?" Susan asked.

Tamika sighed. "Does it matter? Aren't you excited for me?"

"No, no, I am, I am. I'm sorry. This is awesome. I just didn't know you had...connections." Susan winked.

"Tyler. You know. I've talked about Tyler before. I have lunch with him and Stacy sometimes."

"Ohhh, yeah, yeah. Tyler. I guess I didn't know you were really...friends. I thought he was just another coworker."

Tamika paused. "No, the three of us are pretty close."

Susan wasn't sure if she was jealous, but something didn't sit right with her as Tamika talked. A flutter swished through her gut. But she tried to push the feeling away and be happy for her wife.

"You know this is my dream job, Babe." Tamika oozed, shaking her fists with excitement.

"I know it is! I'm thrilled for you."

And she was. She wasn't sure what else she was feeling, but she knew she didn't like it.

Susan lay awake that night with a gnawing feeling in her gut that she could only describe as dread. At first, when Tamika mentioned the job, it was just flutter, but now, it was much heavier after she'd thought about it over and over. It made no sense. After two hours of lying in bed trying to analyze why this bothered her so much, she couldn't lay there anymore, so she got up and walked around the apartment aimlessly for a few minutes. She spotted her sweatshirt on the arm of the couch and put it over her bare shoulders. It was unusually cool in the house tonight. She wandered into the office; the moon peeked in at her from the only window in the tiny room.

It was a full moon; maybe that was another reason she couldn't sleep. Or maybe next week's Autumn Equinox was responsible for the buzzing she could feel throughout her body. She gazed at the golden Goddess for another minute and decided she wouldn't find anything profound or comforting within the confines of the walls and roof; she needed the infinite outdoors. She needed to go back to her picnic table on the side lawn.

She crept quietly to her altar to get a chime candle. She generally didn't overthink which color to choose, letting her intuition lead her, but tonight, she couldn't have, even if she wanted to, as she carefully felt around in the dark. She took the first one she felt and pocketed it, then tip-toed out of the bedroom, grabbed her backpack, and headed outside. She avoided the pavement, walking along the strip of lawn, remembering how much she needed the feeling of damp grass and earth on her feet. When she reached her picnic table, she set her backpack down and looked around. There didn't seem to be any angry villagers staring from the windows, and there was no light coming from the office. Maybe she'd be safe out here since it was three a.m.

Still, Tamika would be pissed if she knew she was out here. What would she say if Tamika was awake and waiting for her when she went back inside? That she felt trapped? Restless? Downright blah about life, sometimes? That she needed to feel dirt on her feet to remind her she was a part of this Earth and the expansive sky above her to remind her that she was connected to everything? That she needed the moonlight on her face and not through a window pane or even a screen?

An even worse image entered her head; what if Tamika came out here and caught her as she said a blessing over a lit candle? She couldn't worry about all the what-ifs. She needed this. She stuck her hand in her pocket and cupped the candle, but her heart thumped hard, so she released the candle and retrieved the joint from her backpack first. It was a funny world if she was less worried about getting caught with an illegal drug than with a candle speaking a blessing to the moon. Fuck the WASP culture of New England. The manager could kiss her ass.

She took a couple of hits and welcomed the calm. Her heart stopped thumping and found its normal rhythm again. It was one of those nights that felt warmer outside than it had been inside, even though summer was dying. She closed her eyes for a minute, aware of her breath; being out there in this moment was essential in the same way she needed air in her lungs.

How good it felt to be alone. She needed that more than most people did, she was pretty sure. A little buzz washed over her; she stuffed the joint in her backpack and retrieved the candle from her pocket, looking to see which color she'd grabbed. Green. The color of Gaia's soul; always an excellent choice for any blessing. Flicking the lighter, she watched the wick struggle to ignite, then finally, burn steadily.

She held it in front of her over the tabletop and spoke her words quietly.

"Gaia, thank you for always reminding me of who I am. A part of you. A part of everything." She paused. What did she want to ask for exactly? "Please bring me peace, but adventure too." It was really as simple as that tonight.

A rustle came from one of the trees. She didn't see anything when she glanced over, but she blew out the candle to be safe. She's given thanks and asked for what she'd needed anyway.

She spotted something at the other end of the table; it looked like a pamphlet. Her curiosity getting the better of her, as it usually did with anything that had words on it, she scooted to the other end of the bench to see what it was.

The front read, *Celtic/Gaelic Retreat,* and as Susan read those words, it felt as if the moon shone down just a little bit brighter on the pamphlet, emphasizing the ornate triquetra at the bottom. Since junior high, when she'd learned about ancient Egypt in social studies and about mythology in English, she had been obsessed with ancient cultures. But lately, there was something especially intriguing about Celtic culture. Maybe it was because of her Scottish heritage. She had no doubt that the pamphlet was meant to find its way to her. Maybe it was the pamphlet that had drawn her outside. And the green candle seemed even more fitting now.

She studied the cover carefully and discovered the retreat was in Nova Scotia in June during the week of the Summer Solstice. Carefully, she opened the pamphlet as if she was already embarking on the journey and about to discover treasure. As she read about the festivals honoring the Goddesses, Brigid and Rhiannon, the musical events, the poetry, and the spiritual healing elements, she felt both a longing to go and as if she were already there. She could hear the highland pipes and the harp, the poems recited in Gaelic brogue, and she feel the connection to everything she already loved as she embarked on a journey that included rituals of the divine feminine.

Maybe that was it; she just needed something to be excited about, too, and then she wouldn't feel whatever it was that she was feeling about Tamika's new career opportunities. Was that it? Was she jealous that something new was happening for her wife while she felt stagnant here? If that was it, she certainly didn't like that side of herself. Still, she couldn't wait to show her mother tomorrow.

Susan was actually coming to enjoy the weekends that Tamika worked. It was bliss for Tamika to finally have a chance to practice real nursing after so many years of being a nurse's aide. She always came home in a good mood, telling Susan she felt like she was finally a professional. Sure, a lot of what she did was give medication, but the post-surgical floor was an opportunity to creatively apply what she knew to help people heal.

But it wasn't just that Tamika was happier; Susan was learning to enjoy her time alone and her time with her other loved ones. In their first year together, Susan wanted to be with Tamika every possible moment, but it seemed to her that there was something even more wonderful about having reached this more mature stage of their relationship. The stage where they had figured out how to be individuals. While she and DJ tried to get together as often as possible, DJ worked so often that they were lucky to see one another every couple of months. But she could always count on the visits with her mom.

Over tea, Alice oohed and aahed as she looked through the pamphlet, asking questions as she went and expressing how she hoped Susan would go, even if it meant going alone. As always, her mother was excited for her as she listened to Susan dream about the Celtic retreat. Susan could tell when her mother was in awe of her. She'd remarked more than once over the years that she had such an adventurous daughter. Susan couldn't really understand it, though, for she saw herself as a rather dull, timid human being who'd probably never do something like go on a Celtic retreat alone.

When Monday came, Susan hadn't been so excited to go to work in a long time. She would get to work with Kevin, who'd started out as an employee but was quickly becoming a friend. While assistant managers kept quitting on her, and Susan never knew what kind of disarray she would return to after the weekends, at least she could count on Kevin to help. Even though he only worked about fifteen hours a week, he always managed to help her whip the place back into shape by mid-week.

Until now, she'd never really known what it felt like to be genuinely excited to come to work on Monday. Tuesdays were one of her busiest days, with inventory and ordering, so Kevin ran the store while she holed herself up in the back with paperwork. But on Mondays, she had more time to work with Kevin, and they had established a good rhythm, getting things done while still having fun.

With two extra desks in her spacious office, Susan had told him he could take one, at least until she got an assistant manager. She'd offered space to her other employees before, but mostly, they just left their bags and coats on one of the empty desks, which were always stacked with books, too. Although Kevin had begun bringing in a few personal effects, he rarely sat at the desk. The man could not keep still. He enjoyed working out on the floor and was far better with people than she was. In the few months he'd been working there, he'd already helped her grow. While he came to know more about the books from her, from him, she learned the finer points of how to talk to people. Early on, she noted how he always used someone's name when he spoke to them, whether on the phone or in person. If it was a customer, he'd specifically ask their names so he knew how to address them, and that small detail went a long way. She was working on doing more of that herself, although it made her uncomfortable.

She had always made it a habit of arriving at least a half hour earlier than the store opened so she could settle in before dealing with people, but lately, she found herself in earlier and earlier. She turned the key and walked inside; she loved being in the store all alone. The sun seemed to be shining in extra brightly today, and she forgot to flip the lights on before she headed directly to the travel section, where she plucked the Fodor's Guide to Nova Scotia. She circled the mythology section and then the new-age section, which she still insisted was a ridiculous thing to call ancient traditions. But it wasn't really information on myths or Goddesses and Gods she needed right now. It was more like... "History," she said aloud and headed toward that section instead. She was disappointed to find that the section had little to offer her, but not before removing her backpack, settling herself down on the floor, and looking through a dozen books, which eventually surrounded her on all sides.

"What *are* you doing?"

Her hand flew to her chest, and she let out a little yelp. She looked up to see Kevin standing over her, laughing with his cheeks all puffed out as if he was trying to hold it in but failing miserably.

"You scared me, asshole!" She said, shocked when it came out of her mouth.

"Hmm, I think that just might be considered employee harassment," Kevin said, trying to maintain a serious tone as he ran his hand through his neat goatee.

Her heart returning to its normal rhythm, she shrugged and replied, "Naw, I think it's more like that's how you know I'm your friend instead of just your boss." She smirked.

"But seriously, what are you doing, you wackadoodle?"

"Oh." She glanced at all the books strewn about, some half open. Admittedly, it was not how you'd expect to find your store manager. "I...well, it's hard to explain. I'm *trying* to look up some information about Celtic history, but nothing here is quite what I want. Apparently, management has no idea what to order," she joked.

He looked at her over his glasses, puzzled. "But why? Why are you researching Celtic history on a Monday morning?"

"Long story. Let's just say...I had an interesting weekend," Susan said.

"Of course you did," he joked.

"I need to plan an adventure."

"Oh, yeah?"

"Wait, please tell me you're early. It's not nine already, is it?"

"No." He laughed and glanced at his watch. "Eight-twenty."

"Thank Gaia. But why are you so early?"

He shrugged. "I could ask you the same thing. What time did *you* get here?"

"Umm...seven-thirty." She laughed. "Here, let me put most of these back, and we can, oh, I don't know, sit in the office...like real managers."

"Do you want me to put the lights on?" He asking with a laugh.

"Oh, I didn't even realize. Yeah, I guess you should."

"Need me to carry anything for you, or...help? You kind of have a lot going on there." He waved his hand theatrically at the books, teasing.

"Naw, I got it."

She brought two back to her office: the Fodor's Guide of Nova Scotia and History of the Celts, which looked a little basic but would have to do for now.

The lights snapped on, and the office was unlocked when she got there. Kevin was at his desk, maybe for the first time since she'd cleared the piles of books and the dust from it and let him know it was his. The first thing he set down was a pink-striped frame of two little girls.

"Aww, are those your daughters?" Susan asked.

"Yup," he replied, his blue eyes gleaming with pride. "Kayla and Bethany," Kevin replied, pointing at each of their faces as he spoke.

"They don't look like you *at all*," she joked.

Next, he adorned his desk with four Halloween bowls: a pumpkin, a vampire, a mummy, and a witch; he filled each to the top with candy, then leaned back and looked proud of himself.

"I *love* Halloween! Glad you're decorating in here. I always mean to...."

"Oh my God, me too. Halloween is the best! I kind of figured you might, too; you seem to like dark stuff."

She was surprised that she actually gave off that vibe; maybe he was just really good at reading people.

"So, why the research?" He pointed to the Celtic book on her desk.

She felt kind of dumb and hoped he didn't think to ask again. How could she explain? It still felt too early to let her freak flag fly with him just yet, although everything in her was dying to spill the excitement about not only the Celtic retreat but the experience of finding the pamphlet under the full moon.

"Oh. I...uhh...there's a trip I am looking into," Susan fumbled.

"Okay...?" he replied, motioning his hand to signal that he clearly wanted more.

"It's a Celtic retreat in Nova Scotia this summer."

"Oh, fun!"

She told him a little more about it, leaving out anything that might be too over-the-top witchy and scare him away.

During a lull in conversation, he glanced at his watch. "I bet Dawn is waiting out there; I suppose I'll go let her in. But only because I don't want to be on the main register." He liked to be a smartass, but she could tell he cared about people.

She could have let him go out alone, as she sometimes did on Mondays, but she decided to join him today instead.

"Have I told you how much I love coming in on Mondays?" Susan asked.

"Of course you do. You get to work with me." Kevin smirked, his ice-blue eyes dancing with childlike humor.

"Well, duh! But really. You manage to help me get this place running after Trish turns it into a disaster every weekend. By Tuesday, we always have everything going smoothly again."

He nodded, keeping an overly serious face. "I *am* awesome."

He was right; Dawn was waiting outside. They chatted about their weekends a little as Dawn opened her register. Kevin would jump in if it got busy, but that would be unusual for a Monday morning. For now, he busied himself by updating prices and rearranging some of the displays.

Susan retreated to the office again and pulled out the schedule to look it over. It was the only thing she didn't like about Mondays. Scheduling had taken her the longest to get the hang of; something about the type of organization it took always tied her brain in knots. Requests for days off changed the staff's normal availability, and threw her off. It took her a couple hours most weeks, but she did manage to get it done, and most weeks ran smoothly. But today, she couldn't focus; instead, as she stared off, the Fodor's Guide called to her. She slid the schedule away and flipped through the pages, in awe at the beauty of Nova Scotia.

"You want to order anything for lunch?" Kevin asked, poking his head in the office.

"Is it that time already?"

He nodded. Susan glanced at the clock on the wall anyway. It was quarter to twelve.

"But you're only here until twelve today," Susan said.

"Oh, I know...just thought it might be fun to have lunch with you before I left. I have nothing to do until I pick my girls up."

"Oh, sure. Sounds good. What were you thinking?" Susan asked.

"Oh, I don't care, really. It's more about the company. I mean, not sushi or something, but...Hey, we could go out. Denny's is right across the street. I could go for breakfast for lunch."

"Oh, I do love breakfast for lunch, but I don't know if I should leave."

Kevin laughed, "Isn't that one of the perks of being the manager?"

"I guess. I've just never really done it. But you're right. Who else is here with Dawn?"

"Sanjana," he replied.

"I guess I feel okay about it then."

"You'll just be right across the street anyway. If the place caught on fire or something, they could call you."

She looked at him funny. It wouldn't exactly be convenient for her staff to have to call her at Denny's. But then, she got his meaning. "Oh, I don't have a cell."

"No?"

She laughed, "Maybe it's time? Tamika's been telling me that for a while now."

"Yeah, maybe. Especially for things like this. As a manager, I mean."

"You're probably right."

"It's almost the twenty-first century," he joked.

Susan was relieved when they were seated quickly and the food came out fast. It still made her nervous to be away from the store.

"So, who's Tamika?" Kevin asked.

"Oh. My...fian... my wife." Susan laughed, shaking her head. It was so new that she almost forgot sometimes.

"Aww, newlyweds?"

Susan nodded. "We were married in June," she managed, around a bite of French toast.

"Oh, nice! Congratulations. You two should come for supper sometime. Renee and I would love that.

Susan squinted, trying to remember his daughters' names. Kayla and Bethany. Renee must be his wife. She'd assumed he was gay and hoped he couldn't read her mind. In a way, she was relieved. After her experience with Michael, she wasn't sure she was ready for another gay male friend; they were too dramatic.

"I mean, if you don't mind a couple of obnoxious kids," he added.

"Not at all. In fact, Tamika especially loves children. Sounds like fun."

"Wait, okay, so, this might sound...Tamika...I know there has to be more than one Tamika in the world, but...she doesn't happen to be a nurse, does she?"

"Yes! Do *you* know her?"

"I work with her at UMASS. Nursing is my full-time job."

"Seriously?" Susan asked in awe.

Kevin nodded. "I mean, we don't work together, together, but some of the patients who come to my floor get transferred from her floor. And I worked as a float on her floor a few times, so...yeah. I really wouldn't have even known her last name if she hadn't had to sign off on some of my people."

"Small world."

"Right?"

"How the hell do you do both, though? Do you ever get a day off?"

"I've been doing the thirty-two-hour week at the hospital since my girls were really little. Now that Bethany is in kindergarten and Kayla is in preschool, I have some free time, so I want to take the opportunity to make more money. Kids are expensive. I could have done the forty-hour week at the hospital, but I just needed something.... well, something that wasn't nursing. The days I'm here *are* like days off to me," Kevin explained.

"Wow, I can barely manage forty hours most weeks." Susan laughed.

"What a small world, though, that I work with both you and your wife. What are the odds? Does she like the post-surgery floor?"

"Actually, she's applying to move to the peds floor. It's like her dream job."

"Oh, wow. Good for her. It's not easy to get a position on that floor," Kevin replied.

"She has a friend who works there and knows the Director of Nursing. Tyler...something. He got her the interview."

"I know Tyler. We used to work on the same floor before he moved to primary care."

After paying the bill, Susan felt a tug at her gut. Would the store be okay? She must have been transparent because Kevin patted her on the back and joked as he craned his neck dramatically to look across the street.

"Doesn't look like it's on fire."

"Very funny."

"You're fine. We haven't even been gone an hour. Anyway, talk to Tamika. When I come in tomorrow, we can make plans for supper," Kevin said, getting into his truck.

"Sounds good."

It felt good that someone like Kevin saw something in her that made him reach out as a friend. But she knew she tended to come off overly affectionate, so she would be careful not to get to mushy with him or she might just scare him away.

*****

Despite her nerves, Susan was happy that the store survived just fine without her for an hour. A few customers were milling about, Sanjana was still on the register, and Dawn was tidying up the front merchandise. It was as if she had never even been gone.

She let them know she was back and headed for her office to finish the weekly schedule. She spotted Kevin's new creation: the Halloween display. Before, the books had been set up in a pretty standard way, but he'd managed to arrange them to look like a pumpkin. He'd stacked the books with orange, red, and yellow to form the outside and stood up two white books that looked like eyes while the black books formed the mouth. Clearly, he'd thought ahead and made sure a couple of the books were horror genre, too. She had always wanted to do something like this, but although she could picture it in her head and had tried to pull it off, she couldn't figure out how to place the books in a way that actually made an image. Her creations always looked more like abstract art or a mess a child had made. She would have to get Kevin to teach her how to do this.

"Susan, there is a phone call for you," Dawn called to her.

"I'll take it in the office."

"Hey, Babe."

When Susan heard Tamika's voice on the other end, Susan's

heart dropped. She'd assumed it was just a supplier, and Tamika never called her at work. Something had to be wrong.

"Are you okay?"

"Aww, yeah, no, I'm fine. I agreed to work a double with Tyler and Stacy tonight, and we were hoping that maybe you might be sweet to us and bring us some supper from Coney Island so we wouldn't have to eat this nasty hospital food."

"Coney Island?" Susan laughed.

"I know, right? Not my usual, but Stacy started talking about their chili dogs, and now that's all I can think about. I was hoping you'd stay and eat with us and meet my friends."

"Sure. What time is your break?" Susan asked.

"I think we should all be able to get a break together at six," Tamika replied.

"Okay. I'll just stay here and get some things done until I go grab the food and meet you guys in the cafeteria at six. Let me get a pen and write down your order."

Susan's mouth watered for a cheese dog and cheese fries as she jotted down their order. Sure, she was a little nervous about meeting Tamika's friends, but she would have food for them; they had to like her.

After rushing through the weekly schedule, Susan dove into her Celtic book again. When she ended her shift, she bought the two she'd been reading all day. So often, she told herself that she would just take advantage of the ability to read them at work but was unable to part with them. As she was checking out, she saw the Halloween display again. She was a terrible manager. How had anyone even believed in her enough to give her this position? Sure, they'd been desperate. She wasn't awful at it; she just wasn't great. Here she had been, holed up in her office for most of the day while Kevin was making the store better and interacting with people in ways she couldn't. She did what she had to without any big disasters, but every interaction was so difficult. Why was she like this? She hadn't even been a confident enough manager to feel good about going out to lunch. All the other managers here had done that and thought nothing of it. She had so far to go.

After leaving the store, Susan picked up the food from Coney Island and then drove back across the city to the hospital. At least the bustle had slowed down on the massive UMASS campus since it was after five, so she wouldn't have trouble finding a spot in the parking garage.

Already tired from the long walk from the parking garage, she fumbled with the food in her arms as she walked past reception. As a fat girl, she felt self-conscious carrying two trays of food down the maze of hallways. It might seem obvious that all that food wasn't for only her, but people were ignorant about fat people. While she tried to tell herself that she was a grown woman now, the weight of the stereotyping and cruelty she'd experienced in regard to her size was even heavier than what she carried on her frame.

She looked down as she walked, avoiding eye contact with people, but the colorful squares on the tile floor only brought her back to high school. She'd spent four years looking down at those ugly floors while people had mocked her. She hated those floors. It was time to look up. And when she did, no one seemed to even notice her.

When she finally rounded the corner into the nearly desolate cafeteria, Susan could see why Tamika and her friends had wanted her to bring them some hot food. Hardly anything was open. Metal grates were pulled down over whole sections of the serving area, with only small things like fruit cups, yogurt, and prewrapped sandwiches for sale next to the coffee station.

"There she is!" Tamika beamed when she spotted Susan.

She grabbed the boxes from Susan's arms, handed them to Tyler, and grabbed Susan into a long embrace.

After Tamika introduced Susan to her friends, the four of them sat to eat, Stacy and Tyler getting right to business, asking which hot dogs were whose and passing fries around.

"So, we really did want Coney Island, and I wanted you to meet these fools, but there's another reason I wanted you to come. I was going to wait until I got home, but when I agreed to work a double, I just couldn't wait until eleven thirty. I had to tell you. I got the job in peds!" Tamika said, drumming on the cafeteria table with both hands.

"Oh my Goddess, that's so great, Babe!" Susan blushed a little as it came out of her mouth, wondering what the others would think of her dorky saying, but they were already too deep in their food to notice.

"I'm just so thrilled. Like I said, I just couldn't wait to tell you," Tamika said.

"And don't forget to tell her that it was your man right here who was there for you to make this happen." Tyler sat up straight and pointed a finger to his chest, boasting through a mouth full of food.

The others laughed, and Susan knew that this was probably just how they got along, but personally, she found Tyler a little cocky, even if his freckles and light brown eyes made him rather endearing.

"Oh, hush, I told her all about how you helped me," Tamika said, waving him off.

"Okay. As long as you don't forget who's helping you move up," Tyler said.

"Okay, yes, we know. You're the man. But the man can be quiet now and eat his food." Stacy interjected. "We've heard so much about you, Susan. About time we meet you."

"You too." Susan smiled. She hadn't heard much about them, really. Aside from telling Susan that Tyler had helped her get the peds position, Tamika just kept saying it was nice to have some Black friends again.

Susan reached for something else to say. She always had to remind herself to ask others about themselves, but small talk didn't come easily to her.

"So, are you all working on the same floor tonight?"

"God, no. We never would have all gotten the same break if we were," Tyler replied.

"I'm a floater. I work all the floors at one point or another. But hardly ever peds. *That's* only for the elite." Stacy's curls bounced as she wagged her head at Tamika.

"I usually work days in primary care. I just needed the extra dough, so I'm working with Tamika on post-surg tonight. I don't do floor work often, but when I can work with one of these two, it's not bad," Tyler added.

"And we hear you got promoted to manager not long ago. Tamika tells us you just love your Barnes and Noble. She's always being sappy about how proud she is of you," Stacy said sweetly.

Susan smiled and looked at Tamika, who threw her a smirk.

"How'd you meet? Somewhere *gay*, I assume?" Tyler laughed and made air quotes as he said the word gay.

"We actually met *at* Barnes and Noble, jerk," Tamika replied with a laugh.

"Oh?" Stacy asked, arching her perfectly shaped eyebrows with interest.

"Oh yeah. Once I saw her that first time, I had to keep going back." Tamika paused and put a hand over her heart. "You might say I studied her. Not in like a stalker kind of way. But I had to see if I had a shot. Needed to figure out how to approach her. Took me long enough to figure out I could get to her through a book."

Susan looked down at her food, touched by the emotion with which Tamika told the story but shy, too.

"Well, you two are just so adorable together. But, I have to say it...I'm painfully jealous of what you have," Stacy said, looking at Susan and touching Tamika's arm with her French tips.

Susan wasn't sure how to respond. Had Stacy meant that she was jealous of their relationship, in general, or jealous that Susan had Tamika? Was Stacy even gay?

"Isn't it enough that I'm your work wife?" Tamika asked.

With that comment, Susan snapped her head over to assess Tamika's expression. Relieved to see Tamika wearing her sarcastic face, she quickly realized she was just being too sensitive, maybe even insecure. It was no wonder, though; with her athletic frame, Stacy was everything she wasn't.

Stacy shook Tamika's arm playfully. "Better than nothing, I guess." She laughed.

"Gee, thanks," Tamika replied.

"I'm just playing. I'm happy for you two," Stacy said.

"See what I have to deal with? I have to sit here and watch all this girly foolishness." Tyler rolled his eyes.

"Oh, shut up. You love us." Tamika laughed.

"That, I do." Tyler smiled, suddenly looking more sincere than arrogant.

"I have to go, though; Jean is in charge on my floor tonight, and if I'm a minute late...well, let's just say that last time it didn't go well. She suggested therapy." Stacy said, pulling out her chair and grabbing her trash.

"What? Why didn't you tell me about that?" Tamika asked.

Stacy shrugged. "Oh, she said it nicely. Meant well, I suppose. Just because I teared up when she scolded me in front of everyone, she pulled me aside later and said she thought I could benefit from having someone to talk to about *my issues*."

"Oh yeah, Jean does that. She's a shrink wannabe. Thinks everyone needs therapy," Tyler piped in.

Tamika shook her head. "As if therapy is a great option for our people, even if we do have *issues*."

"Right?" Stacy retorted.

Tyler nodded emphatically. "No, I know. She has no idea when she says something like that to us."

Susan was lost for a moment and tried not to let on, but the confusion must have shown on her face.

"Most Black people don't exactly embrace the idea of therapy and psychiatry and stuff. It's a whole thing..." Tamika reminded Susan.

"I mean, I guess it's getting better. But I certainly wasn't raised to think those were options," Stacy said.

"Nope. You kept it inside the family," Tyler added.

"Kept it *in* is more like it," Tamika corrected.

"It's still a very White system," Susan added sadly. After the words were out of her mouth, she was worried that she had no place to say anything in the matter, but everyone just nodded.

Although Susan was still a little sad sometimes that she couldn't understand everything Tamika went through, everyone needed someone to relate to them, so she was glad she had her work friends. Because the entire system had already criminalized them, it felt safer to suffer invisibly. Personally, Susan didn't hold the mental health system in high regard anyway; the arbitrary labels and forced treatment that were the hallmark of supposed mental health care in the West were no less than human rights violations. But still, it was awful that an entire group of people felt alienated from seeking support. Every time she was reminded of the things Tamika had to deal with that she never would, she loved Tamika a little more deeply. She was lucky to have such a strong wife who'd come out on the other side of the world she was born into.

Once back home with another few hours to kill, Susan returned to her Celtic book. She ordered a couple more she'd come across on the subject when searching the database, a perk she loved about her job. She lost herself in the one she did have, and after finishing chapter eight on the Celtic warriors, she'd managed to finish a little more than a third of it. She couldn't get enough; she was ready to dive in and read the chapter about the Celtic way of life. While Tamika had just landed her dream job, the retreat was the only thing she had to be excited about.

She snuggled into the couch and opened the book to where she'd left off, but after one paragraph, she hopped up, deciding to go outside with her book instead. It was a warm September day; why would she want to be cooped up inside? Since it was becoming a pretty regular thing for her to visit her spot, everything she needed was always in her backpack now. A chime candle in every color had a permanent spot in an oversized pencil case, and of course, she always had a joint and lighter.

When she reached her spot, there was no picnic table. Weird. She stared at the area. There wasn't even a mark in the grass from where a picnic table might have been. She looked around a little, but it was the right spot. She remembered the tree with the knot that looked like a face. She didn't know what to make of it. Had someone seen her out here again? Complained? Had management removed the table because of her?

She shrugged; the grass was as good a place to sit as any. She quickly ran back to grab the mail from the box, sure there was a letter from Fiona, then flopped down onto the warm grass to read it once her hunch was confirmed. The book would have to wait. Despite the missing picnic table, she was thrilled to be out here with her joint and letter. Without the table, the small, mostly enclosed area looked like a grove. That's what she would call it: Susan's Grove.

September 23, 1999

Hey Susan,

I hope when you get this letter, you still have that honeymoon phase feeling. Enjoy it while it lasts —life changes so fast. Will and I are fine. He's a pain in my ass and I'm a pain in his. That's love. Nothing really exciting here, as usual.

In your last letter you said I never talked about me and you wanted to know more about what it was like here. It's hard to tell someone about a place when you have lived there your whole life. I mean, we just see it through our own eyes, which is limiting. I mean, what is there to say? Newfies are a bunch of tough island folks. We're assholes. We tell it like it is and we don't give a shit what anyone thinks. It's beautiful here. I have never lived anywhere where I can't look out my window and see the ocean. Oh no, that's a lie – the last place me and Will lived, we had to go to the end of the street to see it. Hated that. That's why we moved. Honestly, if you really want to know what it is like, you will just have to come and find out. You're always telling me you need adventure, so c'mon already. I'll give you an adventure. I did include a few pictures I took. I labeled them. One is taken from the cliffs near my childhood home. The second is from where I live now. And the third is just a picture of a lupin. I thought it was pretty. When I see purple, I think of you.

Tell you something? Ok. You might be sorry you asked... I have been obsessed with everything relating to Celtic culture lately. I mean, it isn't really a recent interest, but I have attention issues –always something new keeping me busy, so I put one thing away, start another, then come back to the other things again...usually when I discover something buried at the bottom of a box or a drawer. A few weeks ago, I found my Claddagh ring which I thought I lost, and then I fell down a rabbit hole doing research. I really love this whole internet thing. I have been rereading about the Vikings and the Druids and stuff online, and I need an adventure too...to see the old castles in Scotland and Ireland. I know you will want to come with me and look for fae, like we did a few hundred years ago.

Interesting fact—it seems the Celts were fascinated with severed heads. I know they were warriors and all, but it seems like they liked the heads themselves, not so much to symbolize their triumphs, but as art. I also suspect that there was something religious about that, but that's just a hunch.

Have you heard of Queen Boudica? Research her. I think you will find her interesting. Pretty sure I was her in a past life.

Celtic music is soulful too. It calls to me.

Is that enough "something" for you for one day? I know you don't have the internet yet, so I can see you running to work and looking up Queen Boudica. Have fun. You're welcome.

Keep in touch. And remember all the things I have been telling you...something tells me you're going to need to remember real soon.

Love, Fiona

P.S. I see something coming your way....an opportunity for an adventure. Keep a lookout for it. Things could get really wild and crazy...IF YOU LET THEM.

After reading the letter, she sat there staring at it in awe for a few minutes. What were the odds that Fiona would write to her about Celtic stuff now? Wait, had she written the date on the letter? She had; it was dated September 23, which was right around the time she'd found the pamphlet.

Susan barely noticed the moon dimming and the lights coming on, and even when she acknowledged it, she just lay there on the grass.

Only when she noticed the moon peeking between the tall trees did she question the time.

"Shit." She gathered her things, nervous that Tamika was already upstairs waiting for her.

Sure enough, she was.

"Where were you?" Tamika asked, her hands on her hips.

Susan glanced at the clock on the wall. It was just nearly

eleven-thirty. Had Susan really been out there for over four hours?

"I was in the back yard."

"What were you even doing in the yard?" Tamika curled her lip, and Susan didn't like the attitude.

She shrugged. "I love my little spot, even if they did take my picnic table. I was reading until it got dark, and then I was just lying there enjoying the warm night."

Tamika gave her a sideways glance.

"Don't worry. I didn't light a candle," Susan said, intentionally being a smartass. It was true; she hadn't lit the candle, even if she'd brought it out. She lit a joint instead, which was every bit as magical in its own way. But she didn't mention that, nor did she mention the letter from Fiona.

"Since when do you go out there at night, though? I just think you need to be careful since..."

She didn't need to finish the sentence. Susan paused. She wanted to flip out and reply that she could do whatever the fuck she pleased but remembered Fiona telling her to choose her battles. She forced a smile and realized that keeping her cool might be a nice change. Make Tamika see her differently. Staying calm would have to be a superpower she would take time to master.

"And please, I know you're smoking pot again, and I don't really care, but just don't do it out there. We don't need any trouble."

Susan wondered how long Tamika had known she was smoking pot again and why she hadn't said anything. Relieved that Tamika didn't look angry and that she didn't have to hide her smoking anymore, Susan got closer and pulled Tamika into a passionate kiss. Like it usually did, the kiss softened Tamika.

"Let's not talk about that. I'm just so proud of my love. For landing her dream job." She talked slowly, with a kiss in between each sentence.

"Well, I didn't know you'd be *that* proud of me. Maybe we should celebrate," Tamika said, running her hands up the back of Susan's shirt.

As Tamika kissed her again, Susan felt herself stiffen just slightly. Of course, she wanted sex. She'd just been on the verge of being nasty and making her feel ridiculous for sitting in her own yard, but here she was, wanting to make love, if you could even call it that. She didn't want to ruin the special occasion, though, so she let it go.

Susan pushed away her hurt feelings and went about the motions, and the sex was great; it was intense, as it always seemed to be lately. But after it was over, she couldn't help but feel lonely. That wasn't how anyone should feel after making love. Once again, she knew she just had to put it all out of her head.

CHAPTER TWELVE

As Tamika prepared for the new position, Susan found she wasn't as happy for her wife as she should be. Of course, she wanted Tamika to do what she loved, and this was an amazing opportunity, especially for someone new to the field, but it wasn't as if the job was at least Monday through Friday, so they could have weekends together. Still, maybe something like that would come in time. She had to heed Fiona's urges to live in the moment.

Still, something gnawed at her. She was willing to live the every-other-weekend and every-other-holiday life with Tamika for a few more years if she had to, but something else was off; she just couldn't place what it was. Although she couldn't point to one thing specifically, Susan felt there was something very different about Tamika. And as much as Fiona told her that she overthought things, and she admitted that she could be dramatic, she was sure that whatever it was that was changing in Tamika wasn't a good thing. It wasn't as simple as the fact that they were growing up; Susan was convinced that whatever it was she could feel shifting in Tamika had the potential to change everything. But what could she do? Without anything she could name, she couldn't confront Tamika yet. Sometimes, being committed to someone meant waiting patiently while life unfolded and people changed.

Tamika woke her up Saturday morning, beaming like a kid. "I want to go shopping."

"Umm, okay," Susan said in her half-awake state.

"I couldn't sleep last night, and when I was laying there, I realized that I'll be on the peds unit for Halloween. I want to get some cute new scrubs and a Halloween costume," she prattled on.

"Okay." Susan smirked. How could she not be happy when her love was so excited?

"How about I make you some breakfast?" Tamika offered.

Susan nodded and rolled over. "Wake me up when it's done."

But twenty minutes later, the noises from the kitchen roused her instead. She scuffled to the bathroom and then made her way to the kitchen, where she found a breakfast that consisted mainly of things she wouldn't eat.

"Morning," Tamika said, flashing her dimpled smile.

She looked especially adorable today in her pink joggers and sweatshirt. But more importantly, she looked happy.

"Morning. Are you still cooking?"

"No. All done." Tamika replied with a confused look as she motioned to the spread of fresh fruit, Greek yogurt, and scrambled eggs.

"I'm going to starve without any meat or bread. I need more than just eggs. I'm going to make some toast."

Tamika sighed.

"I appreciate the fact that you made breakfast, but you know I won't eat most of that, Babe."

"It wouldn't kill you to eat healthier. To have some fruit once in a while. At least try the yogurt," Tamika said, wagging a finger at her.

Hand on her hip, she replied, "You know I don't like fruit and veggies. That's that. I don't want to argue about it. I switched to fucking whole wheat bread...don't push it."

She didn't want to ruin Tamika's cheerful mood, but if there was one thing she couldn't tolerate, it was a lecture about how she ate. She wanted them to have a great day together, and was grateful that Tamika didn't push further.

After Tamika picked out some colorful scrubs for her new position, Susan was stunned to see that the bill came to nearly three hundred dollars. But still, Tamika was so giddy that Susan couldn't say no when she insisted that they indulge and pick up some new home décor to freshen up their place. It wasn't like she was the epitome of self-control either; what could it hurt if they threw another couple hundred dollars on credit?

"See how fun it's going to be to own a home?" Tamika asked as she placed more stuff in the cart.

Susan didn't reply. It was all she could do to accept Tamika's new position; she certainly wasn't ready for a discussion about owning a home. Besides, the day was going too well; she didn't want any tension. It wouldn't go over well if she told Tamika that she only tended to think of the fun aspects of things but not of the disadvantages like a leaky roof or annual taxes or the complete time-suck that came with owning a home.

"Want to go to lunch?"

Mentally, Susan tallied up how much they'd spent that day but had no intention of saying no. If she was being completely honest with herself, she'd been trying to figure out how to bring up the Celtic retreat to Tamika all day, and she wanted to keep her in a good mood to improve her odds.

"We could go to Nancy Chang's." Tamika flashed her dimpled smile again, knowing she could always talk Susan into Nancy Chang's, not only because of the food but because it was sentimental to them.

As they waited for their food, Susan decided she couldn't wait any longer.

"I want to talk to you about something," she said, jumping right in.

"Oh, God," Tamika replied.

"Hey." Susan clicked her tongue.

"I'm sorry. Go ahead."

"No, why did you say that? That hurt my feelings. Like you always think, I don't know, I am going to bring up something..."

"Oh, stop. I don't think anything. What is it?" Tamika asked.

She wanted to drop it now but knew Tamika would accuse her

of being oversensitive.

"There's a trip I've been looking into. Something I *really* want to do," Susan explained, playing with her ponytail to ease her nerves.

"Oh yeah?"

Susan told her about the Celtic retreat, babbling on and on about all the details. When she finally stopped to breathe, Tamika looked back at her with a blank expression.

"How much does it cost?" Tamika asked.

"I honestly don't even know. I've been so excited about the other details that I haven't even called to ask about that."

"Well, I think that is a pretty important *detail*," Tamika replied.

"Well, yeah, sure," she said, irritated that Tamika hadn't seemed to worry that they'd spent about six hundred dollars on the things she wanted. "I've just been so busy daydreaming about the music and the poetry and the bonfires. The soul of it all. Plus, I wanted to talk to you first before I looked into it."

"Where did you even hear about this *retreat*?" Tamika asked.

Susan was careful how she answered, knowing that sharing the strange experience of finding the pamphlet on the picnic table that apparently didn't exist now wasn't in her best interest. Besides, she kind of liked keeping that magical moment to herself.

"I see all kinds of events come across my desk at work." It wasn't a lie, exactly.

"Well, it sounds expensive. Retreats usually are. And, like, what's the point of it anyway?"

She wasn't sure how to answer that. Somehow, the fact that she felt passionate about it didn't feel like a good enough argument. She couldn't really explain, and so often, when she'd tried in the past, Tamika had seemed downright judgmental about her interests. She'd have to answer carefully and try to speak Tamika's language.

"I mean, adventure, I guess. What's the point of any vacation?"

"Well, I wouldn't call that a vacation," Tamika replied, curling her lip.

"Trip. Vacation. Whatever," Susan replied.

"If it's called a retreat, isn't it more for...I don't even know. Religious leaders or professors, maybe?"

Susan shook her head. "It's *not* religious. It's spiritual. It's a chance to connect with nature and the folklore..."

"Ahh, so it's *a Witch thing*," Tamika said.

"Yeah. I guess it is." She knew that the admission would be the end of the discussion.

"I just think...like I said, what's the point, you know? Sounds like a lot of money...and for what? I mean, Nova Scotia? Sounds pretty boring to me. Besides, if you want an *adventure*, I'll take you on a real vacation. The Florida Keys or something."

Later that night, as they were winding down together in bed, Susan was still simmering about the fact that Tamika had shut her down about the retreat. As she lay there unable to sleep, she indulged in a fantasy about standing her ground and going on the retreat alone, although she knew she'd probably never do it.

Her ruminating kept her from sleep, so she sat up, turned the lamp on, and grabbed her spread of Celtic books. She'd take the risk that Tamika would continue on about how ridiculous her interests were, but she didn't care. If she couldn't go, at least she could read about it. As she flipped the pages, though, her anger just increased.

But Tamika didn't seem to notice her books; she was too busy on her phone. Susan hated it when Tamika brought the thing to bed with her, but she never said anything. Lately, she never put it down at night unless she was ready to sleep or wanted sex.

Just as she became immersed in the chapter about Celtic legends, she was interrupted as Tamika let out an uproarious laugh.

"What are you doing over there?" Susan smirked, despite her annoyance.

"Having one text conversation with Tyler and another one with Stacy. They're each telling me their own very different version of drama about this other woman we work with. It's pretty comical." She laughed and waved her hand at Susan. "It wouldn't be funny to you. You'd have to know her." Susan's gut dropped. There was that feeling again, the same one she had when Tamika had mentioned Tyler when he'd helped her get the interview.

"You *text*?" Susan asked.

"Yeah. It's almost the Millennium, Susan." Tamika laughed.

Admittedly, she was behind the times. Kind of prided herself on it, in fact. She had never been one of those people who hopped on board with new trends. But this was more than that; she didn't like the fact that Tamika was texting with them, and she had to question why. Tamika had called her controlling so many times that she was beginning to worry it might be true. She had to keep herself in check.

"I just didn't know you were that friendly with them."

Tamika huffed and put her phone down, shaking her head as she looked at Susan. "You're so insecure, Susan. So, I need my Black friends."

It wasn't the first time Tamika had accused her of that. Now, she had to keep herself in check about being controlling *and* insecure.

Susan tipped her head and studied the floral pattern on the comforter to avoid Tamika's stare. She really couldn't deny it; she *was* insecure about this. It seemed to her that a couple's bedroom should be a sacred space. A place where they only wanted to be with one another. She would never dream of sitting beside Tamika in bed and talking on the phone with DJ or writing to Fiona.

There wasn't much to say; even if Tamika had a point, the way she'd said it had hurt her feelings. Why would you throw someone's weakness in their face instead of trying to understand where it was coming from? Without a word, she rolled over and closed her eyes.

Even when she tried to back down, Tamika had to keep going. "I'm not sure how this is any different than you being friends with Kevin...or writing letters to Fiona, for that matter, but I guess I'm just not controlling or insecure."

She could hear Tamika click away at her phone again as she lay there and let out an occasional chuckle. Going to bed angry was never something she had handled well. It had been true when she was a teenager and she'd argued with her mom, it had been true with her dramatic friendship with Michael, and it was true now. The broken sleep she got on nights like this felt like insanity. Each time she woke up, fear came over her, and then, remembering their argument, she was unable to fall back to sleep for a long time.

She was sure she was dreaming or hallucinating the next morning when Tamika woke her up with an apology.

"I'm sorry, Babe."

Susan squinted up at her from the couch, trying to figure out what was going on. The details of last night came back to her again, and she wasn't sure what to say. Tamika rarely apologized.

"Really. I'm sorry. I didn't have to get so mean."

"I wasn't trying to be controlling. I just..." She could feel tears forming in her eyes.

"I know. Let's just let it go. We're okay." Tamika loved to say they should let things go despite the fact that Susan had made it clear she needed to talk things out, but she was too tired to do anything else.

As they finished their weekend of decorating and cleaning, Susan couldn't let it go. Although she never said another word to Tamika about it, something was off. She could feel it. The same as she'd been able to feel it when Tamika had taken the new position.

She just wished she could figure out what was sending up red flags.

*****

It was Monday again, and Susan was thrilled. Fiona's words came to mind; namely, *life changes so fast.* She never thought she would be someone who would look forward to Monday mornings for any reason. Not only did she love being surrounded by the books, but now, she looked forward to working with Kevin, too.

"Morning." Kevin popped his head into the office when he arrived.

"Good morning."

"I see you turned the lights on this morning. No research today?" He teased?

"No. No point," Susan replied, dejected.

"Uh oh. Want to talk about it?"

Susan shook her head no despite the explanation spilling out. "I was researching last week about a trip I wanted to go on, but Tamika doesn't think it's a good idea."

"Women," he joked.

She felt better already.

"Well, you knowww what might make you feel better? You guys should come to scarioke with us this Saturday," Kevin said, hopping a little as he spoke.

"Come to...what?" Susan asked.

"Scarioke. Scary karaoke. You know, for Halloween. After the kids are asleep."

"That sounds fun! I mean, I *do not* sing, but I bet people are hilarious."

"Oh, that's an understatement." He laughed.

"Tamika is working this weekend though."

"So, *you* come with us. Do you live here in Worcester?"

Susan nodded.

"We could even pick you up if you want, in case you want to have a few drinks. Or, you can come to our place for dinner first, and then we can ride together. Oh, and we're dressing up!" He waved his hands, excited like a kid.

"Your wife won't mind?" Susan asked.

"No, I already told her you were coming," he replied with a smirk. You love Halloween, and I'm a delight. I assumed you wouldn't be able to resist."

"Sounds fun."

"Hey, do you have to leave right at noon today, or you wanna grab some lunch with me?"

"Sure, where do you want to go?"

"I don't feel good about going too far, and I'm sure neither of us really want Denny's again, so you want to just order a pizza or something?" Had it been lame to suggest he hole himself up in the office to have lunch with her?

"That's fine."

"I think you're right, by the way. It's time for me to get a cell phone," Susan said.

"Oh, good! You going to get a family plan with the wife?"

"No, *she* already *has* a phone."

"Sore subject?" Kevin asked.

Susan nodded. "Kind of. I don't know; she has some friends from work who she's always texting with. It's bugging me, and I don't know why."

"Wait, are you talking about Tyler here?"

"Oh, yeah. Right, you know him. Duh. Yeah, it's him and some woman named Stacy. Like I said, I don't even know why it's bothering me."

"Yeahhh, well, I don't know Stacy, but I do not like Tyler. So maybe it's because he's a dick."

"Oh? How so?"

He shrugged. "Maybe I really shouldn't say he's a dick because it's nothing I can put my finger on. I just don't trust him."

"It's probably just me being insecure. Sorry about spilling my guts here." She didn't want to share too many personal details and scare Kevin away with her drama before they even hung out, and she certainly didn't want to make Tamika sound bad.

"Don't be sorry."

Desperate to change the subject, she refocused on work.

"Oh, hey, I didn't even notice the Halloween books display you made last week until I came back from our lunch last week. I love it! You've gotten tons of compliments. You have to show me how you do that," Susan said.

"Oh, I don't know *how* I do it. I mean, I can do another one and show you, but...you just sort of have to picture it," Kevin replied.

"That's really not my strong suit."

"I'd say we could do one for Thanksgiving, but I don't think I can pull off a turkey."

"What about something fall-themed?" Susan asked.

"What, like, oh, I don't know...a pumpkin?" Kevin teased.

"Technically, yours is a jack-o-lantern. That's for Halloween."

"We'll see what we can pull off in November. I'm sure we can come up with something."

"And what about Christmas? Do you think you will still be here, or am I going to have to create Santa all by myself? Because you do know, I can't go back to my old displays now? You've spoiled me," Susan said.

"I don't plan on going anywhere any time soon. I'll do Santa. Wait, that didn't sound right. Now, don't go writing me up for sexual harassment."

"I'll let it slide this time." Susan laughed. She liked that his humor gave her permission to be weird in return.

"I like being here on weekends. I love my girls, but I'm not overly fond of *my* wife lately, either. Might as well be here earning some extra money," Kevin said.

Susan was relieved that Kevin was planning on staying a while, unlike the last few assistant managers she'd hired, not only because he was good for the store but because he was good for her. Having a new friend was good for her.

As Kevin worked the floor that morning, and Susan thought about lunch and cell phone shopping, she sat in her office playing with the schedule and overthinking her life. Fiona told her she overthought everything, and maybe she did. Did people actually *not* do that? She had done it her whole life. She questioned whether she was being a hypocrite; she wasn't comfortable with Tamika's friendships from work, yet she was making plans to go out with Kevin? But more than anything, she replayed what Kevin had said: he hadn't been very fond of his wife lately either. And that was it; sometimes, couples weren't very happy. She knew that some people just saw that as a normal part of life, but she couldn't settle for that. Not for the rest of her life.

Not only did she have a blast with Kevin and Renee at scarioke, but since Tamika began her new job, she spent more and more time with Kevin outside of work. Tamika loved the new job so much that she offered to work whenever they'd let her. Her weekends off. Double shifts. She even offered to work all three of the major winter holidays. It became clear to Susan that this was a pattern Tamika had no intention of changing. Every time something changed for them, and Susan held out hope that they could begin a normal life together, the hope was squashed again.

Tamika kept saying how thrilled she was about all the extra income and talked about a house more and more. Still, it seemed to Susan that she was spending it as fast as it was coming in. She frequently bought new clothes and jewelry and even came home with a new leased Lexus one day without having talked to Susan about it. Susan tried hard to let her wife be happy, but even though she had other people in her life, she was lonelier than she had ever been in her life. Lonelier than when she was single.

Although Susan went to her mother's for Thanksgiving and Christmas, her heart wasn't in it. She lied, saying Tamika was working first shift on both holidays and would be too tired to join afterward. While she usually enjoyed the all-day party at her mom's on the big holidays, she left early, claiming that she was going home to be with Tamika. But really, she watched a couple of movies, then went to sleep early. Lately, she couldn't even focus her attention on a book.

At least Tamika would only be working the day shift on New Year's Eve. Susan tried to talk her into spending the night with Kevin and Renee, but she said she just wanted to come home and relax. Susan understood; Tamika was working so much that she must be exhausted. Besides, it would be nice just to have an evening with her at all.

Susan woke up early that day and in a great mood. Although she didn't do resolutions, she liked the fresh start energy that the new year always offered. 2000 was going to be a great year. Happier than she'd been in a long time, as she anticipated the evening with her wife and the new year ahead, she puttered around the house, cleaning and putting away the Christmas décor as it snowed outside. She made Tamika her favorite supper, eggplant lasagna. She hated the stuff, so she made a three-meat version for herself. They would ring in the new year together, and that was all she needed.

By the time three o'clock came, the snow had accumulated more than she had expected. It looked to be almost a foot if she had to guesstimate. She texted Tamika to be safe driving home, but Tamika never replied. After the paperwork and giving report to the next shift, she usually got home around four. When she still hadn't come home by five and still hadn't texted back, Susan began to worry. Even in this snow, it didn't take that long to get across the city. At five-thirty, she called Tamika's cellphone, but it went straight to voicemail. She distracted herself by putting the lasagnas in the oven to reheat and considered calling her mother in a panic but didn't.

Susan's mind raced about all the possibilities. Had she been in an accident? Finally, just after six, Tamika walked through the door covered with snow.

"Oh my God, I am so glad you're okay. What happened?" Susan grabbed her in a hug and didn't want to let go.

"It's awful out there! It's so dark, it's like a blackout on the road," Tamika said.

"You on the road this whole time? What happened? It's after six," Susan replied.

"No, no. I mean..." Tamika stiffened, broke away from Susan's embrace, and turned around, quickly stripping off her clothes and heading for the shower.

There was that flutter again.

"Were you at work later? I tried to call you."

"Yeah, yeah, my phone died. Sorry, Babe. The oncoming shift was all late. You know, the snow. So, yeah, I was there late, then the roads...ugh. I'm just glad to be home."

"I wish you'd called before you left. I was so worried," Susan said.

"I told you; my phone was dead."

"No, right, but you could've called from work just so I would know you were leaving late, but you were on your way," Susan continued.

"Well, I'm sorry. I'm really tired. I just want to go shower and get into some warm clothes."

Susan could tell that Tamika was getting irritated, so she

dropped it. She just wanted to have a nice night.

"Sure, yeah. You must be freezing. You get warm. I have supper in the oven."

They didn't talk much as they ate supper. In fact, she questioned whether it was all in her head, but there seemed to be a strange tension between them. Susan pondered the flutter feeling again. Was that what anxiety felt like? Was it just because she had been so nervous about Tamika being late? She couldn't be sure, but it was unsettling.

"Was it a rough shift? Are you tired? You seem...off."

"I told you. Everyone was late coming on, and it's just awful out there," Tamika snapped, then sighed. "I'm sorry, Babe. I'm sorry. Here, you made me my favorite supper, and I'm...." She didn't finish but put her face in her hands and stayed like that for several minutes.

Susan was concerned but resisted the urge to say or do anything.

Tamika looked up again, and Susan could have sworn she saw tears in her eyes, but she wasn't sure. She was definitely being weird. After finishing the last few bites of her lasagna, Tamika stood up and went over to Susan, hugging her from behind.

"I'm sorry. Supper was delicious. Maybe you're right. Maybe I'm just really, really tired. Would you hate me if I napped before we watch the ball drop?"

"Of course not. In fact, you go ahead, and after I clean up, I'll come and join you. You know I love snuggling."

"You're the best, Babe." Tamika teared up again.

Susan rarely saw her like this; she wished Tamika would open up to her if something was weighing on her mind.

Tamika was asleep when Susan went into the bedroom; Susan gently spooned her so as not to wake her. She didn't rouse. Susan lay there listening to the sound of her breathing and, she could swear she could even hear the snow falling outside. The last time she looked at the clock, it was seven-thirty. As she felt her eyes fluttering shut, knowing it was not even eight o'clock yet, she didn't care if they woke up to see the ball drop. But Tamika woke her up a couple of hours later with soft kisses.

"You feel better?" Susan asked with a smile.

Tamika nodded, running her hand up Susan's shirt, her kisses becoming more intense. Susan reciprocated, and they quickly shed their clothes. She wasn't sure what happened, but when they were making love, something washed over her. It was somewhat like the flutter, yet more of a sense of dread and a screaming in her head. For a few moments, she even felt nauseated.

She lay there wishing it was over but didn't know what to say. Was it just part of her PTSD from her childhood? When they lay in one another's arms afterward, Susan wanted to cry. Something in her never wanted to touch Tamika again. She was convinced she must surely be losing her mind because as her thoughts rolled on, all she could think about was going up to the roof and jumping off. She never wanted to feel this way again, whatever it was.

"Happy New Year, Babe," Tamika whispered.

CHAPTER THIRTEEN

The first week of the new millennium sucked. Something definitely hadn't been right between her and Tamika on New Year's Eve, and it was all Susan could think about. But at least the holidays were behind her.

Christmas and New Year's had fallen on Mondays, and on Tuesdays, Kevin was usually only there until noon, working out front while she did inventory and ordering. Since she hadn't worked with Kevin much for two weeks, she was especially excited to go back to work today. She was determined to adjust her attitude, and a fresh week and getting back to her regular work week was just what she needed. So, she'd had one crappy week. It didn't mean the whole year was ruined.

She arrived at work early again, this time hoarding an array of books that she'd had her eye on for weeks. She walked through the quiet rows and conservatively chose only five titles, knowing she usually went home with at least half of what landed on her desk.

Her office was looking better these days. Ever since Kevin had spruced up his area more and more, he'd inspired her to do the same. Nature pictures adorned the once-bare walls. She'd bought herself a throw rug, a lamp, and some colorful office supplies, including a giant blue paisley stationery box so she could sneak a letter to Fiona whenever she wanted. Her personal favorite touch was the grumpy fairy figurine that her mother had gotten her for Christmas. Tamika thought it was rather odd, and while Susan considered adding it to her cluttered altar, she decided it looked best here on her desk. While, for many years, she'd been reluctant to be too out at work, for the first time, she proudly displayed her and Tamika's wedding picture in the center of the photo collage she'd put together. It was pretty amazing how a little change and character could improve the energy of a space.

She walked in, flicking on the lamp and setting her books down. Her memories stared back at her from the photo collage: Emily's piercing green eyes, she and her mom at Christmas, the picture of the purple lupin from Fiona, and one of her and DJ at high school graduation. Her office was so cozy now. Some days, it felt as if it displayed her personality even more than her own home did.

She laid all four books out side-by-side, deciding which to crack open first. *Handbook for the Heart*, an inspiring book of spiritual essays, would most certainly come home with her so she could save that one for later. The one about tarot and oracle readings intrigued her. Although she wasn't sure what oracle was, when she was little, her mom, gramma, and even some of her Jesus-loving aunts had gone to many spiritual classes and were deep into tarot, and this seemed similar. Both the books on crystals and animal communication seemed interesting but were maybe deeper rabbit holes than she wanted to dive into. In the end, she indulged in the Llewellyn Guide to Kitchen Witchery until Kevin arrived. The herb guide intrigued her. Although she knew little about their healing properties, somehow, herbs felt familiar. But the colorful pages before the herb guide drew her in. Categorized by season, the recipes for cinnamon and clove cider, dandelion wine, and gingerbread cake alone might not have called to her, as she never had enough energy left to enjoy the kitchen the way her mom and gramma always had, but the pictures of the final product, each on an ornate altar decorated for the corresponding season made her swoon.

"What are you doing *this week*?" Kevin teased when he walked in.

"Thinking of cooking more," she replied, the half-truth coming out of her mouth before she thought about it. She turned the page back to the gingerbread cake, the least witchy-looking photo of all, and held it up to show Kevin. While it was a little safer to be out as a lesbian these days, at least in Massachusetts, it still wasn't always safe to come out of the broom closet.

"Yum."

"You have so many different interests," Kevin commented, pointing to the other books on the desk.

Susan had forgotten that the other books were there and wasn't quite sure how to respond.

"I think it's great to be scholarly. You're free-spirited but smart. You seem like someone who'd get a PhD in something unique just because. Teach something eccentric at some university or something."

"Wow," Susan replied, surprised. Kevin had to be one of the most sensible and grounded people she knew, so hearing that he saw her as scholarly was a compliment. You never really knew how others saw you. Sometimes, you needed an outside perspective to see yourself. Maybe she didn't have to hide her witchy nature with him as much as she thought; it seemed that, while she felt she kept it quiet, it must be written all over her. That was an even greater compliment than being called scholarly.

"Well, thanks. I think I'm more...I don't know, unconventional. I think I'm done with formal education. I don't belong in the professional world, so I don't see the point. Barnes and Noble is one thing, but a university...I don't think that's me."

"You really don't give yourself enough credit. You'd fit in great there."

Susan grunted. It wasn't so much that she felt she *couldn't* fit in; it was more that she didn't want to. Yes, she was called to something where she could engage with books and ideas on an even deeper level than she could ever hope to in retail, but academia was far too snobby for her taste. She preferred to hide in her bookstore over going into that world.

Maybe Kevin couldn't fully understand that about her, but the conversation had given her some insight. While she had once considered an advanced degree, until it had come out of her mouth just now, she hadn't fully known that it was no longer something she wanted. It felt like a weight lifted off her shoulders, as if she could move on in some way with the new realization.

Casting off all self-control, despite the massively growing library that had begun to fill every tidy corner of the townhouse, Susan bought all five of the books she'd plucked from the shelves before heading home to swim in their depths. Unable to get enough of her job, Tamika was working another double today, which meant that Susan had the whole night alone with her books.

Ironically, the realization that she had no interest in further formal education only invigorated her desire to learn. Without stuffy syllabi and rote tests, she was free to explore. Even if she didn't dive into crystal magic or animal communication anytime soon, she would have the books waiting for her in her library when she was ready.

Only when she stepped through the door of the townhouse, New Year's Eve, which she had put out of her mind for most of the day, came flooding back to her. It was as if the energy of it hung in the air. Maybe she should sage the whole place. But before she could get to her altar, the phone rang.

"Hi!" DJ chirped from the other end.

"Oh, hi," Susan replied, slightly annoyed to be taken away from the task at hand.

"How are you?" DJ asked.

"Not bad."

"How was your day?"

"Good. Just got home. Brought home five new books to spend the night with," she said, not including the new revelation about her future. With a master's degree and a professional job, DJ would never understand how she wanted to live her life. "How are you?"

"I'm...okay," DJ replied quietly. "But I miss you! The four of us need to get together for a late holiday celebration."

"I miss you too," she half lied. Of course, she missed that special connection she had only with DJ, but another part of her didn't want to see anyone. More and more, she was becoming a homebody.

"So, when can we get together? Let's put a date on the calendar right now."

"I have to talk to Tamika. She's always working."

"Well, let's do something just you and I, then. What about this weekend? Saturday?"

Susan thought about her weekend ahead; they had nothing planned, and it was likely that Tamika would pick up at least one shift, although it was her weekend off. Although she really wasn't feeling it, it *had* been a while. She had to socialize at some point.

"Yeah, sure." Susan quickly scanned the house. It was a mess again, and she doubted she'd find the energy to clean it before Saturday. "I'll drive out there."

"Great. What time?"

"I want to sleep late, so maybe we could do a late lunch? I could come to your place by one, and then we could go to Chili's or Applebee's or something."

DJ hesitated. "I think that should work. I'm just thinking about...yeah, I can go to the gym after breakfast. But lunch...hmm..."

"What?" Susan snapped. DJ always had to complicate things; it was one of the reasons she didn't get together with her more often.

"I'm just being more careful about what I eat, but if we can do Applebee's, I think there are some healthier options for me."

Oh great, another one. Maybe she and Tamika should just go

to lunch together; they could sit there and talk about health food all fucking day, and while they were at it, judge her for the way she ate.

"Okay." Susan rolled her eyes.

"Can't wait to see you!" DJ said.

"Me too. But I'm going to go, Deej; I'm just so exhausted today. I literally just got in the door from work."

"Oh, okay. I'm sorry. Isn't this kind of late for you to be getting in?"

Susan glanced at the clock. It was almost six already.

"Yeah, I guess it is. I stayed late at work and...." She wasn't about to say that she spent half an hour in the Burger King drive-through and then had run into the grocery store for Ben and Jerry's. "Yeah, I stayed late."

"You've been doing that a lot lately. Going in early. Staying late."

"So?" Susan asked with an attitude.

"Oh, no, I get it, trust me. Sometimes you have to, especially when you're a big manager."

Susan didn't appreciate the condescension. Maybe she wasn't a professional like DJ was, but she liked her job—most days.

"I just wonder if that's maybe why you're so tired. Maybe you've been working too much? But I know, I just keep talking...I'll let you go. I'm glad I caught you and can't wait to see you."

"I'm sorry if I'm kind of bitchy. I'm just..."

Susan felt tears stinging her eyes. This was why she stayed away from people sometimes. People like her mother and DJ anyway. Although she didn't always let them in, they could read her, and she didn't always like it. She didn't want them to see it on her face. To hear it in her voice. A part of her just wanted to blurt everything out, but what was there even to say? That something had felt off on New Year's Eve, although there was nothing specific she could name?

"Well, I love you.... I'm here if you need me, okay?"

"Thanks. I love you too." She was so ornery; sometimes, she didn't know how DJ had stuck by her side all these years.

After saging every room, she brought her new books to the bedroom and settled on the floor in front of her to-be-read shelf. Running her fingers over the spines of the titles that were already on the shelf, she pulled each out, looking at the cover art and reading the synopses. Sometimes, especially when her head was too noisy to focus on reading even a short story, she just liked to be with her books. After reading the synopses of a dozen books, she stared at *Eat, Pray, Love* for a minute. She remembered taking this one home the week it had hit the shelf, although she'd never made the time to read it since its homecoming. Now, she wasn't sure what that rich girl author could teach her. What she could possibly know about pain.

She left the rest of the books in a pile on the floor in front of the shelf, changed into shorts and a tank top, and eagerly jumped into bed with the kitchen witchery book and the one on tarot and oracles. As always with nonfiction, she grabbed a pen in case she found the need to underline. Where had she left off? She flipped through, practically being able to smell the food as she saw the recipes again and found the page where she'd left off. Summer. The recipe listed both intrigued her and made her wrinkle her nose. Lavender lemonade and lavender lemon scones. Lavender was one of her favorite scents, but wouldn't it taste perfumy? Still, there was something earthy about it; maybe she would try it someday.

After reaching the end of both the ice cream container and the recipe section, she drifted off. She woke with a start when Tamika came home a few hours later. Shit! She hadn't gotten rid of the Ben and Jerry's container like she usually did. She didn't need any lectures. She leaned over, found a sweatshirt balled up under the bed, hid the container inside, and then rolled back over again, pretending to be asleep. She would have to remember to throw it in the dumpster when she left in the morning.

When Susan got home from work on Friday night, Tamika met her at the door. "I have a surprise for you." She beamed.

"You do? Is it still Christmas?"

"I want to make it always feel like Christmas for you, Babe." Her dimple made Susan melt.

"Aww."

"I've been thinking...about how lucky I am to have you as my wife."

Susan didn't know how much she'd needed to hear that until it had come out of Tamika's mouth. She leaned into her, looking into her eyes.

Tamika was in her sweats, so Susan knew it wasn't about sex, and she savored the romance.

"Remember I told you that when I first saw you in Barnes and Noble, I knew I was going to marry you. Knew you were going to be the other mother to my babies?" Tamika asked.

"Yeah."

"I saw you five or six times before I talked to you, you know? Like I said, I kind of...studied you."

"So, how'd you know?" Susan asked.

"I just knew. I wanted you, so I was going to make it happen," Tamika replied.

Susan chuckled. "And what did you learn when you studied me?"

Tamika paused. "That you love hard. That you're deep. That's what I wanted in a wife. After I understood that, I was able to talk to you. But I realize I'm not always attentive or sweet. I'm not perfect, but I want to be a better wife. We have to keep learning about each other more deeply. And I'm finally understanding how much you want adventure. Need adventure. So, we're going away this weekend."

"We are?!"

Tamika nodded. "Bretton Woods. We leave tomorrow morning. I booked a luxury king room with a mountain view."

"Ooh, what is Bretton Woods?" Susan asked.

Tamika chuckled. "You're adorable. You know about far-away places, but you don't know what's practically in your own back yard. It's a ski resort, Babe."

She wanted to be excited and was grateful that Tamika had planned something adventurous for them, but skiing? She would rather die than strap skis to her feet. In fact, she probably *would* die if she tried to do that. Mostly, she was disappointed that Tamika didn't know her well enough to know that a trip to a ski resort wasn't exactly her thing. But she didn't want to let her disappointment show.

"A king suite? That sounds luxurious."

Tamika nodded, "Has a fireplace and a view of the mountain. Ski trips were my family's favorite vacation. Two weeks every year in Colorado. Those were some of my best childhood memories, so I wanted to share that with you."

"It sounds beautiful, Baby. Thank you." Susan got up and gave Tamika a hug. She decided she would wait to tell her she didn't plan to ski. She would just enjoy the moment.

* * * * *

They arrived at Omni Mount Washington a few minutes before check-in, but they let them check in early. The lobby was grand, with high ceilings and ornate columns. Susan had never seen anything quite like it and looked around the massive room in awe while Tamika checked them in.

"We have a tower room, so we have to use the stairs." Tamika smiled, pointing a suitcase in the direction of the stairwell.

But Susan didn't budge. It wasn't a place she would've chosen; it was a little too fancy for her taste, yet there was something about it. The atmosphere. It was almost like déjà vu, but that wasn't it either. She felt the same flutter in her gut that she'd been noticing more and more lately.

Tamika's dimple flashed as Susan looked around. "You like it, huh?"

It wasn't that she was impressed by the opulence of the place. She would have felt more at home in a one-room cabin. It was the air of the place; there was something special about it. She smiled back at Tamika; she couldn't even figure out what she felt herself, much less explain. Maybe she'd needed variety in her life more than she knew; besides, she felt everything so intensely that she tended to overdramatize when she journeyed beyond her everyday world.

As she climbed the stairs to their room, she felt it even more intensely, though. The air felt dense. She glanced up, figuring it was just the air in the towered stairwell.

Once they were in the suite, Susan wasn't sure what captivated her more, the feeling of the place itself or the mountain view. She squished down into the window seat and gazed out at the snowy landscape while Tamika checked out the rest of the suite and oohed and aahed over the marble tub.

"So, I did good, Babe?" Tamika asked, coming up from behind and wrapping her arms around her.

"It's beautiful." It wasn't as rustic as she'd expected for a ski resort, but the dark wood walls and airy ceilings almost gave it a mysterious air, so it was right up her alley.

She still hadn't talked to Tamika about skiing; she'd been worried about bringing it up since last night, but she would have to do it soon.

Susan lit the fireplace, then sat on the couch and got lost in the flames while Tamika unpacked.

"Do you want to grab some lunch at the café downstairs?" Tamika asked, sitting beside her.

"Sure, but...I have to tell you something." She gritted her teeth.

Tamika chuckled. "What's that?"

"I can't ski," Susan said.

"I can't ski either, Babe. Not really. You'll learn. There are bunny slopes."

"No. I mean...I can't do it. I'm too scared. I can't strap something to my feet; you know I'm not athletic like you are. I mean, I walk into the wall at home when I'm tired. I've never been what you would call coordinated, you know? I'm not going to ski," she said, making sure to finish softly but make herself clear.

Tamika stood up and asked, "You mean you're not going to ski at all?"

Susan shook her head.

Tamika didn't really look mad, just confused. Susan felt her heartbeat increase anyway, worried about what was going through Tamika's head.

"I just, I don't...why didn't you tell me until now? I guess I'm just confused. You are always saying you want an adventure."

"Oh, no. This is beautiful. It *is* an adventure. I don't need to risk an injury to have an adventure." She joked. But Tamika didn't smile. "And this place...I can't even tell you. It's...soulful or something. I didn't say anything until now because...I mean, I didn't want to ruin the trip you planned or make you..."

"You were *afraid* to tell me," Tamika said.

It felt like a trap. She didn't want to say that was the case and risk a fight.

"Well, I just didn't want to ruin it. I appreciate this so much," Susan replied.

Tamika sat down again and put her hand over Susan's. Susan

was pretty sure she could see tears in her eyes.

"I feel awful that I'm so difficult that you were afraid to tell me."

"It's not that. I just didn't want to disappoint you. I wanted it to be the perfect weekend," Susan lied.

Tamika nodded, and her voice was soft. "I mean, I *am* disappointed. Skiing was something I wanted to do together. To introduce you to. I just wish you could step outside of your comfort zone sometimes. Try new things."

"I think we all have our own idea of fun and adventure, you know? You know me, I love this anyway...the nature, the quiet room...I mean this room...there's something soulful about it. The whole place, really. I'm happy just reading in front of the fireplace."

Tamika nodded. Susan's heart dropped when Tamika got up and walked away. It was almost more uncomfortable than if this had been a full-blown fight. She sat and stared out at the mountains for a moment, then rose and went to Tamika, wrapping her arms around her from behind.

"And then, helping you warm up when you come back..." Susan whispered in her ear and kissed her neck.

She turned around, nodded, and held Susan sweetly. "Let's go get some lunch."

"I'm sorry." Susan apologized.

"I'm not mad. I guess I just wish I did better at planning an adventure for you."

"Noooo, I love this. You know it doesn't take much to make me happy. Just the fact that you did something special for me is everything. I brought books.

After lunch, Tamika was disappointed at the idea of hitting the slopes alone but finally gave in. It had been cloudy all day, and now, light flurries were coming down.

It was a tough choice between reading in the window seat with the mountain view or the couch in front of the fireplace. Since it was chilly in the room, the choice became apparent. Susan added some wood to the fire, grabbed her tarot and oracle book from her backpack, and settled in. Two pages into section one, she sensed a shift in the room and looked over her shoulder, fully expecting to find that Tamika had returned to the room. But she was alone.

She tried to get her attention back to the book, but the cold was distracting. Weird. The fire was going well. She sighed, reluctantly rose, retrieved a blanket from the closet, and snuggled back in. It took her several interrupted attempts to get through the section on symbolism.

She must have dozed off, and when she woke up again, it could have just as easily been five hours as it could have been five minutes, only it was still light outside. She untangled herself from the blanket and got up to stare out the window again. Thinking about her wife skiing down even a slight incline made her nervous, and she was glad that her view didn't allow her to see the slopes. Thoughts of broken limbs and head injuries raced through her head. Suddenly, out of nowhere, she felt her heart begin to race. Then, as quickly as the dark thoughts came to her, they were replaced with peaceful reassurance as she stared into the snowy sky.

"She will be just fine, Little Darlin'."

She turned around quickly. Of course, there was no one there. It had felt the same as when she had heard, *"choose wisely."* It was just like how she talked to herself in her head, only she certainly didn't call herself Little Darlin'. Though she hadn't exactly heard the words aloud, she couldn't shake the feeling that she wasn't in the room alone. As if someone were standing right next to her. The feeling was familiar, yet she couldn't place it. She stood motionless, but not due to fear. No, whatever this feeling was, it didn't scare her. It was only unsettling because she couldn't figure out what it was.

She closed her eyes and was brought back to the bedroom she

had shared with her mother while they lived with her grandparents after they left her father. That was it. That was the feeling. It was a knowing that she was not alone in the room, and it was profound.

She was pulled back into the room from the depths of herself with a knock at the door. Maybe Tamika had forgotten her key card. But when she opened the door, she was surprised to see a shaky young man wearing a uniform on the other side. Susan could see from his nametag that his name was Brian and he was the manager.

"Hello, miss. Are, are you...." He paused to look at a piece of paper in his hand. "...Susan? Susan Sibley?" He looked at the number on the door despite it being the only room in the private hallway.

"Yes," Susan replied in a panic.

"Medical has asked me to assure you that it looks like it's *just* a bad sprain, but your, your...umm...wife? She was injured on the slopes," Brian stammered.

"Tamika?!" Goosebumps covered her skin.

He referred to the piece of paper again and nodded. Pretty sure that he was actually less confident as a manager than she was, Susan actually felt a little bad for him.

"No, no, really, she's fine, but she would like you to go over to medical just to be with her. We have a golf cart waiting to bring you over. She's being cared for by one of our nurses...." Brian assured her.

Susan was already slipping her shoes and coat on and wasn't quite listening.

The short ride over felt as if it took an hour, despite the manager's assurance that Tamika was fine. The cart barely stopped on the walkway before she hopped off and flung open the door to the medical cabin. She spotted Tamika on one of the beds, looking both adorable and pathetic in her hot pink ski pants and jacket, one leg raised on several pillows but otherwise seeming fine. Susan leaned in and hugged her for a long time, only letting go when she finally felt as if she could breathe again.

"I guess you were right. You *don't* need an injury to have an adventure. But I got one anyway." Tamika smiled, flashing her dimple.

"Are you okay, Babe?" Susan held Tamika's face in her hands and stared into her eyes.

Tamika nodded.

"What happened?"

"I don't know. I know it's been years, but I was doing okay. I was wobbly and weaving a little, but I was upright. Until I wasn't. I guess the gym isn't sufficient to give me the kind of muscle I need for this." She shrugged.

"So, you just fell? Didn't hit a tree or anything, right?"

"No, I'm fine. Really. They said it's just a sprain," Tamika replied.

Susan could feel two nurses staring at them from across the large, airy medical cabin but didn't turn her head to look directly at them. When she turned to glance at them, the petite brunette pursed her lips and stared harder with a look of disdain in her eyes. Then, Susan distinctly heard her as she attempted to whisper in the blonde's ear.

"Too bad the dyke didn't break her neck out there," she said with a vicious laugh.

When Susan snapped her head to stare back at them, the petite nurse turned away, and the blonde searched for something to say.

"Just a sprain," the blond said.

Silent, Tamika looked down at her hands, but Susan stood up, swallowing hard as rage and fear clashed inside her.

"Seriously? Did you grow up in a religious sect or something? Have you actually never met real, live *lesbians*?" She asked, whispering the last word sarcastically.

Their eyes grew wide, and neither said a word. She had made her point. The brunette didn't seem ruffled and met Susan's stare, while the blond sat there uncomfortably, fidgeting with her shoe.

"Are you sure you're okay?" Susan asked.

Tamika nodded. "I want to get out of here. Now."

"Can you call the shuttle for us? We're going back to our room." Susan insisted.

The blonde fumbled with the phone and quietly put in the call.

Tamika carefully lowered her leg from the pillows, then swung both legs over the side. Susan stood up, offering her shoulder for support, and Tamika stood, leaning on her.

"I'm okay," she assured Susan.

"What about the stairs?" Susan asked Tamika quietly.

"Can we help?" Asked the blonde.

Susan suspected they were playing nice, hoping they wouldn't be reported to the manager.

"No, thank you," both Tamika and Susan said in unison, and with that, they walked outside to wait.

The shuttle was there within minutes; Brian was driving it himself this time. Susan helped Tamika situate herself on the back of the golf cart in the back, then sat up front with Brian, giving him an earful. She knew Tamika would have preferred to avoid the confrontation, but Susan couldn't stay silent.

"I have a complaint about those nurses, and I expect serious action to be taken. I didn't get their names because we rushed out of there after the tiny one used a homophobic slur," Susan started.

While trying to focus his on the path ahead, Brian turned his head momentarily, looking at Susan with confusion. "I don't understand."

Susan sighed, trying to keep nasty things that wanted to escape from her mouth. She wanted to ask if they were really in New Hampshire or if they'd been transported to some backwoods place that was still stuck in the mindset of a hundred years ago. But she could see that Brian was young and clearly not equipped to deal with these worldly matters. As much as she wanted to unleash her wrath on someone, he was probably just a sheltered kid.

"Brian, she used the word *dyke.* Specifically, she said she wished the dyke had broken her neck out there. Technically, she didn't deny my wife care, so it wasn't an act of discrimination, but it *was* hateful prejudice. The second nurse didn't say a word but didn't exactly put the other one in her place, either." Susan yelled to be heard over the hush of the snow and the hum of the golf cart motor.

"I'm so sorry. So, so sorry, ladies." He sputtered as they came to a stop at the back door of the hotel. "That is completely unacceptable, and I, I..."

"You're right. It's unacceptable. But I don't just want an apology. I want something to be done about it," Susan insisted.

It was apparent Brian wasn't sure what to do with this information. "Oh yes, this will be handled. And I'll see to it that your stay will be complimentary. If there is anything else that we can do...that *I* can do...I'm so sorry."

While Susan had to appreciate that Brian looked as if he might cry at any moment, her frustration got the better of her.

"I hope this will be *handled.* I will be reaching out to someone higher up to ensure that it does. And I have to add, it isn't just them," Susan continued.

"Ex...excuse me?" Brian asked.

"It was you, too." She softened her voice. While the nurses had been hateful, he'd just been ignorant and uncomfortable. "When you came to my room, you could barely bring yourself to say the word *wife.* My *wife* had been hurt, and you couldn't even..." She couldn't finish her sentence as she choked on her tears.

"I'm...I'm so sorry. Can I do anything at all? Can I offer you a complimentary stay here in the future to show you that this is not how we...."

Susan just shook her head; it was obvious that he didn't get it. If he did, he would have known that nothing he could say would make them ever return there.

"No, thank you," Tamika replied.

She stood up and grimaced, and Susan quickly went to her and helped her hobble inside.

"Can I be of any assistance, ladies?" Brian asked.

"No, thank you," Tamika repeated.

As much as Susan worried they wouldn't make it up the stairs alone, she wasn't about to argue here. They were both too proud. If there was one trait that she and Tamika were matched in, it was stubbornness. Even if her ankle had been broken instead of sprained, she knew Tamika wouldn't have accepted help.

They entered the stairwell, and Susan did her best to offer support, helping Tamika up one step at a time. She could hear Tamika wince with every hop and wanted to cry. As she helped Tamika up the last step, she pulled a muscle in her lower back but tried not to let it show as she helped Tamika in the door and across the room, knowing she was making her injury worse with every step as Tamika's weight added to her own.

They made their way to the couch in front of the fireplace, and both breathed a sigh of relief. Susan thought she broke down crying first but couldn't be certain. All she knew was that as she and Tamika were holding one another, crying together, somehow, it felt like one of the most beautiful moments they'd ever had.

"I'm so sorry this happened," Susan sniffled through snot.

"I'm sorry I brought us here. It's my own fault," Tamika replied.

"Don't you dare blame yourself," Susan replied, wincing as she sat up too straight and wrenching her back again.

"Oh, no, are *you* okay now?" Tamika asked.

"I pulled a muscle," Susan answered, reaching back to massage her tight muscle.

Tamika took over, massaging her back, both on the verge of tears again.

"It might sound dramatic, but things like this bring back the Matthew Shepard murder all over again. That mentality..." Susan couldn't finish, finally giving in to her tears.

Tamika hugged Susan more closely, letting her tears flow too.

"You know the worst part is?" Tamika asked when their tears had subsided a bit.

"What?"

"I was relieved when I heard that nurse say dyke. That's not the slur I expected. I thought they were treating me like that because I was Black. I've felt that feeling a hundred times in my life, so I was sure it was that. You should have seen the way they looked at me when I was lying on their stretcher, Susan. They were okay at first. I assumed they just didn't see many Black people at their ski resort, and whatever...but when I said I wanted them to go get you...my wife...the look on their faces. It was hatred. Pure hatred. I was honestly terrified they were going to leave me there to freeze to death," Tamika said, getting quieter as she spoke.

Susan burst into tears again. The world was too much for her with its division and hate. As much as she struggled herself, it broke her heart that her wife had to struggle in ways she couldn't even begin to imagine. Sure, she had seen it plenty of times in the last few years with her, but she knew she would never truly know the pain of living in Tamika's skin. She hated that they had to live in a world where a homophobic remark was the better alternative to a racist one.

"I just want to go home," Susan said, sobbing.

Tamika nodded, and they held each other in silence for a long time as they watched the snow fall. Some things would always remain simple and true.

"You know..." Tamika said quietly. "I want to go home too, but obviously, we aren't going anywhere tonight. So, I think we should order some room service. Even if they don't follow through with their promise to comp us, I don't care."

"Do you think they have a heating pad?" Susan chuckled.

"The medical center might. I know they have ice," Tamika replied.

"I'll ask for both. Chances are that they are going to want to kiss our butts. I'm sure they'll find one."

The hotel provided them with everything they asked for, and despite the heaviness of the day, they spent a tender night together. Helping one another apply heat and ice, making it to the bathroom through fits of hobbling and laughter, and finally, getting into bed, where they fell asleep in one another's arms.

"Everything will be just fine, Little Darlin'." Susan heard it again as she drifted off to sleep.

CHAPTER FOURTEEN

Reluctantly, Tamika took Monday off to give her ankle another day to heal, and when Susan got home from work, the smell of Tamika's signature garlic chicken wafted through the air.

"You were supposed to stay off your feet," Susan scolded. "But thank you. I think this is my favorite dish of yours." She wagged her finger first but then kissed Tamika on the cheek.

"It's quite a bit better." Tamika smiled, leaning into Susan's kiss and wrapping an arm around her. "I wasn't on my feet too much, I promise. I prepped right here and just had to hobble over to throw it in the oven." She tapped on the island as she spoke. "In fact, I've been sitting here most of the day."

"Doing what?" Susan asked.

"Bills, mostly."

Susan knew the serious expression. "Uh oh."

"It's not really *that* bad. We just need to focus on our credit so we can get a house. I'm already behind schedule. My scores are good, but I want them to be even higher so we can get a mortgage with a low interest rate. The high balances on my cards reduced them a little, and I want to get them back over that line into the 800's."

Over supper, Tamika brought her up to speed. It was no shock to Susan every one of their cards was nearly maxed out after the wedding, although she hadn't checked recently. Plus, Tamika had leased a Lexus to celebrate her peds job, which had increased their monthly bills by nearly five hundred dollars. Susan's credit scores were far lower than Tamika's, and her student loans didn't help. Tamika reasoned that it made the most sense to improve her already decent scores and try to get a mortgage in her name. It would take much longer if they waited to get Susan's scores in shape, too.

Although Tamika was disappointed that she was behind schedule on the timeline she'd mapped out so precisely, she made it clear to Susan that she was determined not to let her plan become delayed any further. At least they would have the house by the time she was thirty, she reasoned. She was just as adamant that now was the time to start trying for a baby, even if the baby would come after she was thirty. Getting pregnant would be an extra expense, too, so they had to take great care to balance it all out.

Susan had mixed emotions about Tamika's timeline. On one hand, Tamika's drive was what made her beautiful. It amazed Susan how Tamika could consider things that hadn't even become a problem yet and organize their finances around that. But still, she never understood why Tamika was in such a rush for everything. Why she had a formula for when things *had* to happen. They were young. Still, she supposed their age difference was a factor, and she needed to consider Tamika's perspective since she was nearly five years older than Susan. Since she had turned thirty in November, she had been talking about a baby nonstop. It wasn't as if she'd ever made her plans a secret; she'd been talking about a house and children from day one.

While there were plenty of things that Susan spent too much time worrying about, finances had never been one of them. That had always been Tamika's thing. She pondered everything Tamika was saying as she ate her chicken.

She shrugged. "Sounds like a plan. Just tell me exactly what we have to do. You know I'm not great at all this stuff, but I'll do whatever we need to. Make extra payments on your cards or whatever."

"Really? That simple?" Tamika asked.

"That simple." Susan chuckled. "You know me. If we have a place to live and food to eat, I really don't care. The only other thing I want is a cat and probably more books. Whoever made up this notion of credit scores, anyway? It's all a fucking capitalist game if you ask me."

After last weekend, Susan was prepared to do anything to make Tamika happy. She had never seen her so vulnerable, and while it brought them closer, it also ripped Susan's heart out. She never wanted Tamika to have to worry about anything ever again. She would give her the house and the baby she wanted.

Besides, she was far more concerned with the latest psychic incident that she'd experienced. She'd written to Fiona about it, knowing that she would understand. She eagerly awaited Fiona's reply, hoping that she would share some wisdom that would help her understand, too. If she had the same gift that so many in her family had, that was great, but she didn't know what to do with it.

* * * * *

By March, with a new, secured credit card in Tamika's name and extra payments on her already existing cards, Tamika's credit scores were slowly rising. Tamika tried to explain how it all worked, and Susan understood the basics, but frankly, the details overwhelmed her. She was happy to let Tamika handle it all. It was a relief that all she had to do was deposit her checks. Focusing on wanting Tamika to have everything she wanted in life pulled her through most days.

She was sure that Tamika must be glad that Susan had been spending more time with both DJ and Kevin. Clearly, they'd both realized how satisfying being a responsible adult was long before she had; maybe her friends were rubbing off on her. She was just lucky that Tamika had been patient and waited around while she caught up. Susan would never have guessed that growing up could make her feel so proud. Some days, all the talk of fertility specialists, sperm donors, babies, and mortgages still made her panic, but it was all kind of exciting, too.

The changes also brought her closer to DJ, for the first time since they'd graduated from high school. During times when they got busy, at least they'd managed to talk on the phone more, which was something that DJ had always needed more than Susan had. Susan hated the phone.

"I missed your face." DJ greeted Susan with a smile as she got out of the car.

"I know, I know. I'm an awful friend. I feel so bad," Susan replied.

DJ shook her head and gave her a long, tight hug. "You're here now."

"With work and everything, it's crazy how hard it is to find time to get together. We live, what, forty-five minutes away from one another? This is why I never wanted to be a grown-up." Susan laughed.

"I know we're both busy, but I would love to see you more. I need my bestie," DJ said sweetly.

"I mean, it's been since...when *was* the last time we saw one another?" Susan asked.

"Around Thanksgiving," DJ replied.

"Oh my gosh, has it been that long?"

DJ nodded; Susan could see tears in her eyes. DJ rarely cried so she didn't know what to say.

"What...?"

"Let's go inside. It's cold out here," DJ urged.

"Only one more week until spring!" Susan chimed in to make DJ feel better as she followed her inside. The increasing sunlight always made them both feel better.

"The reason I've been dying to see you is because you are going to be an auntie! I couldn't wait another minute to tell you," DJ practically shouted, her blond hair flying everywhere as she jumped up and down.

Susan's mouth fell open, and she stared at DJ for a minute

before uttering, "You're pregnant?"

With a wide smile, DJ nodded.

"Wh...?" Susan couldn't form a question as she grabbed DJ in a tight hug.

"I'm due on November seventh," DJ said.

DJ sat on the couch, but Susan could just stare at her in awe.

"You knew we were trying again," DJ said.

"I know, but...I don't know. It's just so real now," Susan replied. It had been twenty years since she'd met DJ. It was the first day of second grade. They'd known one another the majority of the time that they'd been alive and had seen one another change from children to women. She'd had the best of both worlds, being raised as an only child yet having DJ, who was so much like a part of their family that she was just like a sister. Now, they were about to embark on motherhood together.

"Sit." DJ laughed at Susan's expression and patted the couch next to her.

"So, if you're due in November, then you're not that far along," Susan said, counting out the months on her fingers.

"Nope. Just four weeks. We actually know exactly when we conceived. It was Valentine's Day." DJ smirked.

"How do you know that?" Susan asked.

"It's one of the advantages of getting the help of a fertility specialist," DJ replied.

"What kind of help, exactly?"

"Well, it turns out I have an oddly shaped uterus, which was making it harder to get pregnant. It was pretty surprising to the doctor that I even got pregnant naturally the first time. So, we went with a procedure called IUI. Intrauterine insemination. But you never know; we came home and gave ourselves an even better shot, too, like they suggested."

"But, is the problem with your uterus going to...cause any

problems?" Susan began to ask, trying to be cautious.

DJ shook her head. "The doctor said that the miscarriage was a separate issue. Not related. It was God's way of saying that baby wasn't meant to be. But we have to focus on the good. On the now."

"You're right. We have to focus on the good. So, how about this for good...it looks like we will get to raise our children together, just like we always dreamed about," Susan said, so excited that she could barely get it out.

"What?"

Susan nodded. "Yeah, Tamika has started seeing a fertility specialist, too, and we've picked out a donor and everything. I know all about IUI. We're about to start trying, too. In fact, we have our first appointment next month. As soon as Tamika ovulates."

"What?! I had no idea that you guys were even close to that," DJ said, clapping her hand to her mouth.

"I didn't either." Susan laughed. "Everything has just been happening so fast, and I just want Tamika to have everything she wants."

DJ opened her mouth, but only a breathy sound came out.

"You don't feel like I'm stealing your thunder, do you?" Susan winced.

"No, no! We can share the thunder! It would be amazing if we could raise our babies together. I just didn't know you two were in that place," DJ replied.

"Like I said, it all happened so fast. We've been working hard on Tamika's credit. You know how she is with her timeline; she is set on getting a house before the baby is born."

DJ nodded. "It's just so much at once."

"No shit." Susan laughed.

"And you're okay with it all? I mean, I know you get overwhelmed with change."

"Oh, some days I'm absolutely overwhelmed. But Deej, you should see Tamika's face when she talks about all this. I see that driven woman I fell in love with. It's just so fucking beautiful to see how she knows exactly how to create a life for us. Every step. Every detail. Especially when we sat down to choose the donor."

"What do you mean?" DJ asked.

"Well, we were sitting there with the sperm catalog. Sounds fucking ridiculous, I know. It felt kind of cold and scientific to me at first, but she really opened up to me, and it helped make it a bonding opportunity. First, we talked about race, which was harder than you'd think. I'd honestly never really thought about the race of the donor. I really didn't care about any of that because the baby will be part of Tamika. But she'd thought about it a lot. And it makes sense why. It's always been a part of who she is to be a strong Black woman with the drive to raise a strong Black child. So, she was firm about choosing a Black donor."

"But don't you want to feel like the baby is, I don't know...part of you, too?" DJ asked.

Susan couldn't help but click her tongue at DJ's narrow view but immediately tried to cover up her frustration and not be so defensive. "You know, biology is really nothing to me." She shrugged. "I don't think something like race or genes makes someone a part of you. Look at you and me; you're a part of me. We're family, and we don't share blood."

"Very true," DJ agreed.

"Maybe it's what I went through with my father that makes it so easy for me to cringe at the idea that blood is thicker than water. Or maybe, as a lesbian. I accepted long ago that I would never have a baby that was part of both me and the woman I love. But mostly, I think there's something more magical about connection than genetics can ever offer. I think that kind of true magic comes from the soul."

"That makes sense. It's a great way to look at it," DJ replied.

"But you know what? One thing did surprise me when Tamika and I were choosing a donor," Susan went on.

"What's that?"

"On each profile, the donor lists the usual things, right, like race and height, and family health history and career and hobbies and things like that. And after we ruled out some other donors, in the end, we were down to about three or four. And I had no idea how the hell we were going to choose from there, you know. They were all great in my eyes, healthy, creative, talented, you know, as far as you can tell from a profile. But in the end, Tamika singled out one of those four donors specifically because she felt he represented me in some small way."

"How so?" DJ asked.

Susan hesitated. She was pretty sure that, even though DJ loved her unconditionally, she was a little freaked out sometimes that Susan called herself a Witch. When she'd first come out of the broom closet, DJ had asked her if it was true that Witches had sacrificed children long ago. Susan had put DJ in her place, reminding her that the same exact scenario had come close to playing out in her precious Bible. Despite DJ's misgivings, Susan was never one to water herself down, and if she couldn't say these things to her oldest friend, all hope was lost that she could be herself anywhere in the world.

"Because under the section marked religion, he identified himself as *Pagan slash Witch*," Susan said, using air quotes as she spoke the final words. "Not that it's a religion, but still..."

"It's not?" DJ asked.

"No, it's a spirituality. Spirituality is very different from religion," Susan explained.

"Oh, okay. But that's sweet. That she chose that donor because he sort of represents that part of you. That's really special."

"Totally. I was really surprised since she gives me shit about the Witch thing sometimes," Susan added.

"She does? I didn't know that."

"I mean, not really. I don't know. Same as most of the other people in my life since the day I came out of the broom closet," Susan said, allowing a hint of a snarky tone to come through. "You know, she doesn't have a *problem* with my being a Witch; she's just made me feel like...I don't know, that it's immature or silly or something. Like it's a phase she expects me to outgrow or something, the same way many people treat gay people when they come out. Some people still hold the outdated belief that both things are a sin."

"Oh," DJ replied, clearly uncomfortable as she looked down at the floor.

There was a long pause between them, but finally, DJ broke the silence. "Well, this is a great change, then. Obviously, she's seeing things differently if she prioritized that detail."

"Yeah, the gesture was really special. This process has brought us closer in a way I never expected. Not only did she surprise me when she factored in the donor's spirituality, but it goes even deeper. It's like I got to know her more. Understand her. I always knew that family meant a lot to her, but as hard as she tries, she just can't maintain that closeness she wishes she had with her family. I've told you how they are. She used to be close with her brother, but more often, she feels like her parents and her brother have some sort of alliance, and she's on the outside. It's only gotten harder since her father hasn't been quiet about his disgust of us bringing a child into the world the way we are. So, anyway, as we were sitting there with the catalog, she told me how she feels like this is her chance to create a real family. She keeps using that term: real family. I think she just means that she wants to do things differently than her parents did so she can have that close, loving family she's always wanted."

"I think a lot of us feel that way when we start a family. That we just want to do things better," DJ piped in.

"Oh yeah. I feel the same way, even if it's for different reasons than Tamika has. I have my mom's unconditional love, but I want to give my child a world that allows her something more than the limits my mom or gramma knew or even the ones I've known in my own life."

"Right. Exactly. But you're really ready for all of this? I know Tamika is, but what about you?" DJ asked.

Susan shrugged. "I'm getting used to the idea of being a mom. I mean, maybe we can't always wait until we're ready. Maybe I have to stop being scared shitless of growing up and join the rest of you."

"But, a baby. I mean, you have to be *sure* about a baby. And I know that you and Tamika were having some problems." DJ said, wearing the disapproving expression that Susan had always hated.

Susan sighed; why did DJ always have to act more like a mother than a friend?

"Like I said, this has brought us closer," Susan said, trying not to make her voice snippy.

"Well, that's great, then. If this is what you really want, it's great. All of this is so exciting. For all of us." DJ switched to her Mary Poppins voice to cover the tension.

"I mean, we aren't even pregnant yet, though. But still, it's so cool that, even with how different we are, we are going through so many of the same things. Getting to do this together. I can't believe I will have a niece or a nephew by Christmas. This is crazy. DJ, we're like, *really* adults."

*****

It was the first Friday in April, and today was their first attempt at getting pregnant. As Susan spotted the delicate, white snowdrops poking up from the Earth as they entered the clinic, the energy of spring ran through her.

They were quiet as they were checked in and as Tamika changed, preparing for her first insemination.

"I can't believe we're really doing this," Tamika said, looking half giddy and half terrified.

Susan wasn't used to hearing anything like that come out of her mouth.

"It's just so real," Tamika said.

"It is. I know exactly what you mean. It's...what's the word? *Sur*real?" Susan asked.

Tamika nodded. "You think maybe it would have hit me when we chose the sperm donor. But no, putting this gown on was what it took to realize...we're going to be moms, Susan."

Susan smiled, realizing a part of her hoped Tamika *would* say she was having second thoughts. She just had to focus on the part of her that couldn't wait to look at that little human being with Tamika's features. The part of her that had always dreamed of she and DJ raising their babies together. Sure, she worried about how she could possibly be a mother when she felt so lost herself most of the time. Still, she hung onto Fiona's words of wisdom that reminded her all things come together exactly how they're supposed to and when they are meant to and that moms throughout the ages generally figured it all out as they went. It seemed easy for someone like Fiona or even DJ to say; they both were born to be moms like Tamika was. But she wasn't so sure that was true about her.

They'd been told that there was a good chance that it would take several tries at the procedure before Tamika got pregnant, but when they went home that afternoon, it felt to Susan as if some cosmic creation was taking place.

The doctor had instructed them to wait two weeks to take a

pregnancy test, and the first week felt painfully long. Susan tried to distract herself by reading about fertility, pregnancy, and parenting, but her poor attention span prevented her from taking much in. She didn't seem to be doing anything right at work this week either; she'd ordered too many books in one shipment and somehow seemed to mess up the schedule, which meant that she would have to work until closing the following Monday.

On Friday afternoon, one thing made her feel better: coming home to find a letter from Fiona in the mailbox. She pulled out the chair and dropped her things on the island, opening the letter feverishly. She didn't take as much care to keep the envelope in good shape as she usually did; she had to know what advice Fiona had to offer her about her latest psychic experience.

April 12, 2000

Hey Susan,

Lots of changes for you and Tamika huh? A house and a baby to look forward to? I could always see this happening for you two (YOU knew it too), but how exciting that the time is here? Remember when it felt like it would never happen? like it was only a dream? It's always like that when we are trying to be human – we forget that time is trippy.

As for the latest message you got during your ski trip, I can't say I'm surprised. What can I say? We're magical. You knew this. Dip your toe in, but be careful – it's a powerful gift, but we can go too far sometimes. Stay here on Earth too. Use the messages to help you be. Use the gift to help you live your life and be who you want to be.

Love, Fiona

She bubbled with irritation as she read the last words. What the fuck was that? She sat there with her jaw agape, staring at the one-page letter, looking it over as if another sentence might appear if she kept looking. One that would guide her in some solid way, as opposed to the vague bullshit Fiona had offered her. She'd expected something far more profound. Something that could give her answers. It was the first time she could remember being angry with Fiona. She reread the letter, then stuffed it carelessly in her backpack and lit a joint.

She spent the next week feeling irritated with Fiona. It was an uncomfortable feeling, as Fiona had always been pretty much the only one in her life who everything was right with, and now she'd let her down. These feelings only exacerbated the difficulty of waiting for the two-week mark to take the pregnancy test.

Finally, that day was here, and she and Tamika planned to be downright ceremonial about it. But despite the single chime candle on the bathroom sink and the fresh flowers Susan had brought home, there was no pink line. Tamika teared up a little as relief and genuine disappointment competed in Susan's chest. She hugged Tamika for a long time, and they recovered quickly, resolving to try again next month.

After no pink line in May, Susan's mixed feelings began to wane. The emotional roller coaster was already wearing on her, and it was only month two. She'd accepted that life was about to change. Was already changing. She knew the changes would mean she'd have to adjust. She'd have to grow up quickly, and she was okay with that, but the appointments, the waiting, and the wondering were overwhelming. On top of that, seeing Tamika stress about tracking her cycles and managing the intensifying emotions from the hormones as she struggled with heartbreak each time there was no pink line was killing her. She was surprised to learn that growing up and taking on new responsibilities didn't plague her nearly as much as exhaustion and just not knowing.

Susan felt bitter that, despite a miscarriage, DJ and Matt had already accomplished their goal. DJ was three months along now. When she had gone with her to see the baby's heartbeat for the first time, she found herself more jealous of DJ than ever, and she hated herself for feeling that way. Just a few months ago, she wasn't sure she even wanted to be a mom. Not really. Not sure, like Tamika was sure. Like DJ was sure. But now, here she was, jealous.

They tried again in June. A week after the insemination, Susan came home to find Tamika crying on the couch.

Susan dropped her backpack on the floor and held Tamika as she cried.

"Aww, what's wrong?" Susan asked.

Tamika shrugged, trying to talk in between sobs.

"You didn't take the test early, did you?"

Tamika shook her head no but began to cry harder, so Susan hugged her more tightly.

"I know. It's just all so much. But listen, in a week, you'll take the test, and then, if we need to, we'll try again. We knew this was going to be a process. You have to hang in there," Susan said, not letting go.

"I know. I just...I don't know how many more times I can try. I feel like...I'm not used to being this...I don't even know what *this* is. I hate it," Tamika gurgled through a half sob, pointing at herself.

"I think I get it. I'm pretty much this emotional all the time, and with the hormones running through you, it's just way more than you're used to. I know how badly you want this, though, so you just have to...."

"I know, Susan. I know I just have to hang in there." Tamika pulled away, got up from the couch, and walked away, beginning to cry harder as she walked down the hall.

"I didn't mean...I'm sorry." Susan sighed.

As upset as Tamika was, Susan couldn't just leave her alone, so she followed her into the bedroom, finding her doubled over into herself in tears.

"I'm sorry. I know that probably sounded...well, stupid. I mean, hang in there, no shit, right? You know you have to hang in there. I was just trying to...I hate seeing you like this," Susan said.

"I know, I know. I'm sorry. I'm just a pathetic mess," Tamika replied.

"You're not pathetic. Your body is going through a lot, and there are so many feelings to process. Trust me, I get it, Tam. I'm going through it too, you know, even though it's different for me. I know I don't have the hormonal piece."

Tamika stopped crying, sat up on the side of the bed, and gave her a serious look. Was she mad?

"You called me Tam." She stopped crying.

"I'm sorry." Susan sighed.

"No, no." She shook her head. "I liked the way it sounded. Tam. Tammy. I think I like it. Tammy."

"Oh. Umm...okay." It was an unexpected turn, but Susan was relieved she hadn't said something wrong.

"Someone at work called me Tammy once. I mean, they really thought that was my name. And I remember it felt like she looked at me differently than she would have if she knew my name was Tamika."

Susan was at a loss for words.

"I have to wonder why my parents ever gave me the name Tamika in the first place."

"I love your name. It's...it's you." Susan smiled tenderly.

"I know, but a name is a huge thing. It sets the tone for how people see you. It's obvious why Marcus Junior is Marcus Junior. But even so, Marcus is a pretty neutral name. So, when someone sees that name before they meet him, they don't have a preconceived notion...but Tamika..." She paused. "Maybe I'll go by Tammy from now on. It might be nice to have a fresh, new me as I become a mom, you know?"

Susan just nodded, knowing anything she could say might upset her. She was pretty sure that, if she was hearing Tamika correctly, she was saying that her name sounded too Black. Not only had Susan learned not to push the issue regarding anything related to race, but this was also sensitive and personal. Instead of risking saying the wrong thing, she just listened and let Tamika process. Tamika was so emotional right now that she probably needed to get all those feelings out of her head.

A week later, the pink line failed to appear for the third time. Susan wasn't even sure what she felt. She was too exhausted to feel much except wanting to sleep. But Tamika was surprisingly positive.

"It's okay. We just try again. We knew it could be like this, and I just need to stay calm and know it will happen eventually."

"I'm proud of you, Babe. I know this is hard, but it can take time. Look at DJ and Matt." Shit, maybe she shouldn't have pointed out that it had taken them over two years and a miscarriage to get to where they were, but luckily, Tamika was too focused on trying again to think much of it.

Tamika nodded. "You were right. I want this, so I have to deal with the process, even if it's hard. It's only been three months. We can try again in July."

Their finances were on Susan's mind as Tamika talked about trying again. Every time they tried, it cost them a little over a thousand dollars. But she didn't want Tamika to worry about money when she was already so emotional.

"And you know, I was thinking...I definitely want to start going by Tammy. I think people will see me differently."

Susan was surprised to hear this come up again; she'd assumed it was just something that had gone through Tamika's head when she was overly emotional. Those kinds of things happened to Susan all the time and then faded away as quickly as they came. She didn't know what to say.

"What do you think?" Tamika asked.

This time, Tamika was asking Susan directly, but Susan was still hesitant to say what was really on her mind. It seemed to her that Tamika was trying to replace a core part of who she was. She took a long pause, considering her words carefully. "I don't know. I mean, I love Tamika. To me, you're Tamika, you know? Your name is a big part of who you are. It's just hard to think of you as Tammy."

"Yeah. But people change, right? Maybe Tamika was the girl, and Tammy is...well, the mom. The woman," Tamika reasoned.

"Aww, like the maiden transforming into the mother," Susan replied, trying to put a supportive spin on it.

Tamika nodded. "Something like that, yeah."

"Change *can* be beautiful. I guess I can understand that." If being called Tammy instead of Tamika would help her through this, maybe it wasn't that big a deal. Besides, maybe it was a phase that would still pass.

"In fact, you know what? I knew a woman who legally changed her name. It was something hideous like Precious. Ugh, my God. Why would anyone do that to a child? Anyway, all she had to do was go to the courthouse, fill out some forms, and pay the fee. I think there was some waiting period, but yeah, it was that simple. I'm going to do that. I'm going to go to the courthouse on my next day off. I am going to be Tammy Bradley. I like the sound of that."

It wasn't a phase; Susan could see she was serious about this. There was nothing for Susan to say; it wasn't her choice to make. She just hoped her wife wouldn't regret it.

Following through with going to the courthouse later that week, Tamika was told that the change wouldn't be official until August, but she insisted on going by Tammy immediately. Susan was glad that she called her Babe most of the time because it was hard to get used to, and when she had forgotten and slipped, calling her Tamika, *Tammy* hadn't been impressed.

When June turned to July, Susan still hadn't raised her

concerns about the finances. Tammy was always on top of those things, anyway. Surely, she would have brought it up with Susan if she felt it was a serious problem, but still, with an extra thousand dollars going out every month, Susan couldn't imagine how they were managing.

One afternoon after work, Susan decided it was time she stopped being afraid to step foot in their home office and try to understand their finances better. With the hormonal upheaval Tammy was going through, it would feel good to take some of the strain of managing finances from her wife's shoulders, so she resolved to sit down and make sense of it all.

She looked around the office before she dove in, taking in just how dull the room was, even more so than the rest of the place. Tammy had hung a single picture on the wall, and a set of gold office supplies sat atop the desk, but overall, it was in stark contrast to her own colorful office at work.

As she looked over the bank statements, she found herself feeling bitter and sad. Sure, they could have gotten a joint checking account, but they always agreed that they might as well keep everything separate until they could be legally married and do joint taxes. Susan simply deposited money in Tammy's account when she needed to, and Tammy's credit continued to improve as the months went on.

It was all so much more complex than she'd imagined. How was it that she could manage to run a store and do that budget, yet this was all foreign to her? Maybe it was because she could detach herself from that emotionally, whereas this was personal.

She sorted through some of the other unopened mail that had been sitting there for weeks and found that her credit scores had dropped into the 600s. Since Tammy had said the goal was to get hers to 800, Susan could only assume that the low 600s was pretty bad. Even though she made the minimum payments on her cards every month, the balance wasn't decreasing by much. Tammy had taught her that it was because the interest was accruing so much that the minimum payment barely covered that. Like she'd told Tammy, it was all a game. A capitalist game.

Before she knew it, she'd been sitting there for two hours, having made no headway. Every time one thing seemed to make sense, something else took her a half hour to understand. It was like everything was written in a different language.

"Babe, are you home?"

"I'm in here," Susan replied with a sigh, disappointed at her lack of progress.

At least she'd discovered something good as she'd opened the mail. Excited to tell Tammy, Susan held the letter up with a smile as she heard Tammy getting closer.

Nearly walking past the office, Tammy stopped in her tracks. "What are you doing in *here*?" She chuckled, seeing Susan surrounded by paperwork and mail.

But Susan's jaw dropped; Tammy had replaced her dreadlocks with a bob.

"Do you like it?" She asked, smoothing her hair.

Why did she want to cry?

"No?" Tammy asked, pouting.

"No, no. It's cute! I'm just shocked, I think," Susan replied. She stood up and took in the change. "You're beautiful with any hairdo."

"Aww, really, Babe? I think I love it. I feel like a new woman. I had to secretly take the whole day off to do it. It's a whole thing to do Black people's hair." She laughed.

Susan circled Tammy, looking at her from all sides. "Yeah, it's really cute. The dreads were just the only hairstyle I've ever seen you with."

Tammy nodded. "It was time for a change." She paused. "But

hey, what are you doing in here? You look a little frazzled."

"I was just trying to surprise you and go through some of the bills. I want to help. Make things easier on you," Susan said.

"Oh, you don't have to do that, Babe. I know you hate this stuff. Besides, I have a system." Tammy grabbed her by the hand and pulled her into the hall.

"But look...." Susan said, holding out the letter that held Tammy's shiny, new credit scores. 795 and 801.

"Oh my God! This is amazing! This means we could get a mortgage with excellent terms and get a house. Soon."

Susan nodded.

But Susan had no idea just how soon Tammy had been thinking. When she woke up Saturday morning, she was excited, remembering that Tammy had the weekend off, and they'd talked about doing something fun. She rolled over in bed to snuggle, but Tammy was already up.

"I want to go to some open houses today," Tammy declared when Susan entered the living room, still half asleep.

"Morning," Susan replied through a yawn.

Tammy explained they didn't have to wait for an official pre-approval to go to open houses. Although they'd been working toward this for months, it still felt a little sudden to Susan, but she welcomed anything that would distract them from the hormones, the appointments, and the negative pregnancy tests.

"Oh my God, look at this one." Tammy held out the glossy real-estate magazine and pointed to a white rectangle of a house.

Susan leaned in over Tammy's shoulder to get a closer look.

"Isn't it amazing?" Tammy asked.

"It's okay, I guess. Nothing special, really," Susan replied.

"Nothing special? It's a brand-new Colonial."

Susan shrugged, "It's just not my style. It's...not very homey looking to me."

Tammy sighed. "I know, if you had your way, you'd have a shack."

Susan grimaced. "A cottage. A sweet little homey cottage."

"Same difference."

"Besides, moving is exhausting. It feels like we just moved," Susan argued.

"You're kidding, right? We've been here over two years!" Tammy said, exasperated. "You have such a hard time breaking out of old mindsets. Seeing how things could be. I think you're afraid to want anything better because you grew up in an apartment. This is just what people do, Babe. They better themselves. Why pay someone else's mortgage when we can build equity and have a house of our own to raise a baby in?"

"Hey, that's not true! I *do* want something better than the life I had growing up. That's why I went to college. That's why I'm working a dead-end job and paying things down. I want more for our child, too. I actually just happen not to like that house. I find it rather extravagant," Susan said, defending her position.

"Seriously? It's just simple colonial. It's really just a house that an average family might have," Tammy said.

"Right. I've never liked average. You know that. It's just not me. You know what, I'm not even awake," Susan replied and walked away, then returned a few minutes later with a glass of water and a bagel and cream cheese.

Tammy looked at Susan's plate, threw down the guide, and held her face in her hands.

"What?" Susan asked through a mouth full of food.

"I'm not trying to be a jerk. It's just that you can't keep eating like that forever, you know?" Tammy said softly.

"Jesus fucking Christ, Tammy! I'm not in the mood for the food police. I was looking forward to this weekend together, but I've been up all of fifteen minutes, and you've already insulted everything from my taste in homes to what I'm eating."

"I'm not trying to insult you, Babe. Really. If we're going to be mothers, we have to evolve. Focus on our own health. You could even start coming to the gym with me."

"Evolve?" She glared at Tammy.

"Well, yeah. I mean, we can't just stay the same people forever. Remember, change can be beautiful." Tammy smiled, throwing Susan's own words back at her.

But Susan didn't think it was cute and didn't respond.

"It's just...we can't raise a child to eat like you do. I know your mom raised you to eat that way, but it's unhealthy, and I want better for our child. That's why you've seen me eating differently in the last few years. And why I make time to exercise."

Susan hated it when Tammy brought up the way she ate. And when she referenced the way that Susan grew up, using it to explain one of her many shortcomings, Susan always lost her cool. She was already self-conscious enough all on her own. In the past few years, she'd put on an additional twenty-five pounds. She'd already been heavy and knew she needed to do something about her health. Still, if she wasn't allowed to share her thoughts about race, including Tammy's name change, then Tammy would have to mind her business about Susan being fat.

"Well, today, I really just want to eat my fucking bagel. Please. Just leave me alone about food. Maybe I need to make some changes, but I will do it when *I* am ready. I don't want to talk about it." She wanted to add that the child wasn't even conceived yet but knew it would be hurtful with all that Tammy had gone through in the last few months.

"Okay." Tammy nodded with a sigh and flipped through the house guide again while Susan finished her breakfast.

"Come on, this is a gorgeous house, Susan. It couldn't hurt to just look at it." Tammy held out the guide and pointed at the dull, white house again.

"Do you even want to raise a baby with *me*? Or do you just want to mold me into another you so there will be two of you to raise the kid?" Susan asked.

"Oh my God, what?" Tammy asked, taken aback.

"It has nothing to do with the way I grew up. I *don't* like it. I don't like that style at all. And it's too big. We don't need something that big, especially at that price. I can't even imagine what the mortgage would be on that kind of house. And I *hate* the neighborhood. You know I can't stand subdivisions. But it's like you don't care what I like. You are always so damn focused on what you want that...it's like I feel I'm just in the way of *your* dreams. I thought this was about *our* dreams. Us, together. But sometimes, I feel like I'm not even here in your vision. Or, if I'm lucky, my feelings about things are an afterthought," Susan rambled on.

Tammy was silent for a minute, then patted the couch. "Come here."

Susan felt tears stinging her eyes as she sat next to Tammy. Tammy put an arm around her and handed her the real-estate guide. "Show me what you *do* like."

She wasn't done being mad yet, but it seemed like Tammy was trying to find some sort of compromise. If she was trying, Susan could too. The tension dissipated slowly as they found a handful of houses they both liked enough to truly consider.

"So, what do you think about going to a few open houses this weekend? Just to get our feet wet, I promise. You're right. It's *our* dream. I want to make sure we find something that we both love."

"How do you expect me to say no when you show me those dimples?" Susan asked, cuddling into her. "And you want to know something? You're right too. I do have a hard time with change."

"Well, we just need to take it slowly. I know you get overwhelmed, but I know what I'm doing, and if we just take it one step at a time, it will all fall into place."

Shit, now she sounded like Fiona; how could she argue with the wisdom that Fiona had helped her find?

"Besides, you hate it here. You're always saying you want a private yard," Tammy continued.

"And a cat," Susan added.

"And a cat. See..." Tammy said, playfully nudging her with an elbow.

As they went to five open houses over the weekend, Tammy attempted to teach Susan about the different styles of homes. She would never remember the details; she just knew what she liked and didn't like. She liked cozy, and she didn't find colonials to be cozy in the least. In general, she liked ranches, but Tammy didn't. But there were a few other styles that Tammy suggested they could agree on; Susan would just have to trust her on that.

The process made Susan's head spin even more. Tammy would have to be approved for a mortgage first, but she assured Susan that wouldn't be a problem. Once they found a home they liked, they'd make an offer, hire an inspector to make sure everything was in good shape, and then wait to see if their offer was accepted. Although she tried not to get overwhelmed, it was a lot to take in.

Still, Tammy was right; it was exciting, too, especially when she considered having a private yard and a cat. She was beginning to truly see them raising a baby together and making a home out of one of those houses. Painting the nursery, decorating, and planting a flower garden all sounded fun. Maybe the financial part wouldn't be that bad after all. Sure, a mortgage sounded scary, but Tammy was good at managing the finances and laying out a plan to help them do what needed to be done.

Tammy went to the bank the following week to start the pre-approval process for a mortgage. As she suspected, she was pleased with the terms she qualified for. Susan still couldn't understand how Tammy wasn't just as overwhelmed as she was. Susan had to wonder if Tammy's focus on the house wasn't, at least partially, an attempt to keep her mind off the pregnancy test they had looming ahead of them the following week. But Tammy assured her that having financing in place gave her peace of mind.

But when July's pregnancy test was negative, Tammy broke down again. Each time, there was only one thing that Susan could do to console her. Words of encouragement never succeeded in helping Tammy to recover like making love to her did.

"I love you, Tammy," Susan said as she looked into her eyes after giving her another just-for-you night.

Susan knew that hearing her new name meant a lot to Tammy. And it might have taken Susan some time to adjust, but it was true; she loved Tammy just as much as she had loved Tamika, if not more.

CHAPTER FIFTEEN

Even the air conditioning at the store hadn't been able to compete with the August heat. Humidity always made her miserable, and combined with dealing with people all day, Susan was eager to get home to the quiet and coolness.

Heading straight to the bathroom for a cool shower, Susan saw the syringe from the fertility treatment in the trash can, reminding her that Tammy had started another round of hormones a few days ago. Her tears blended with the stream of the water. She stood there for an extra-long time, wondering how much more of this she could take. She'd always been emotional enough herself; now, there were two oversensitive women in the house, and it was getting to the point that she couldn't stand to be around Tammy some days.

After drying off and throwing on shorts and a tank top, she holed herself up in her favorite corner of the bedroom, lit a joint, and stared out the window. "I feel like I am taking the hormones myself this month," Susan muttered aloud, reaching out to pet a cat that didn't exist.

Although she always tried to be gentle and understanding when Tammy was emotional, she was beginning to feel so exhausted that she felt as if she might snap. She could never have a bad day because she was so intent on pampering Tammy and was sick of it. She hated all of it: house hunting, hormones, finances. She just wanted a simple, quiet life.

But when Tammy came home that night, her demeanor surprised Susan. She seemed to be on top of the world since the lender had told her she was pre-approved for a no-money-down mortgage, and apparently, even the hormone shot hadn't shaken her.

Still, she had seen it, though. Tammy's mood could change in an instant, and Susan could barely deal with herself, so she was relieved when Tammy said she'd signed up to work two doubles over the weekend, even though it was supposed to be her weekend off. Susan was beginning to understand that while home was an escape for her, work was Tammy's escape. It was probably the most significant difference between them, for while Tammy found a sense of purpose at work and could shut everything else out, Susan was convinced that, if she had the financial means, she'd quit her job and rarely ever leave home.

Although Susan thought about spending some time with DJ or her mom one afternoon while Tammy worked or seeing if Kevin wanted to go out Saturday night, she ended up spending the entire weekend between the bed and the couch with pizza, ice cream, and one joint after another. One part of her wanted to have fun and connect with someone other than her hormonal wife, but another part of her simply couldn't find the energy. She recharged best when she spent time alone, and she was drained. She dug out her Anne of Greene Gables VHS series and eased the first tape from the worn box. She sat through the entire series again every couple of years, enjoying it differently each time. As she grew, she could appreciate Anne in a new light, but always adored the enduring qualities of the series. Not only did the sassy, wordy girl inspire her, but the simple times and sheer beauty of Prince Edward Island mirrored the kind of life she imagined living. If she couldn't live oceanside in a tiny village, at the very least, she would have to take an adventure and visit the charming province. By the time Tammy got home, she'd already made it through tape two.

"Hi, Babe," Susan greeted her. She'd cleaned up all the evidence of her indulgences before Tammy was due back.

"Hey," Tammy replied but seemed far away.

"How was work?"

"What? Oh, it was...busy." She walked down the hall and into the bathroom and started the shower. Afterward, Susan heard the bedroom door close.

It wasn't like her. She usually needed some time to wind down before she could sleep. Worried, Susan turned off the television and joined her. When she walked into the room, Tammy looked up from her phone with an odd look.

"Is everything okay, Babe?" Susan asked, climbing into bed and wrapping an arm around Tammy.

"Oh. Yeah, yeah. I just forgot to do something at work." She held her thumb down on the power button, threw the phone in her bedside drawer, and closed the drawer hard.

Instantly, Susan's belly fluttered. Tammy had just lied to her. Susan was sure of it. But what could she say?

"Well, I'm glad you have Monday off. I think you need it."

"Oh, no, actually, I decided to work. Just the day shift, though."

"But we have your appointment."

"I'm going to do both. I changed the appointment to three-thirty. I can go right after work."

"But I was going to leave work and meet you there at eleven, then go back to work."

Tammy shrugged, not looking at her as she spoke. "You don't have to be there every time. I know it's been a lot. It's okay."

Something else was going on. Susan wasn't sure whether she was hurt or relieved. Mostly, she was confused. Why wouldn't Tammy need her? She wanted to be there with Tammy every time; it was the conception of their child, after all. But Tammy was right; it had been a lot to manage, leaving work every month for the appointments. Maybe she should just welcome the break.

On Monday, Tammy said that her insemination had gone fine but didn't have much more to say about it. Susan found her casual attitude odd, but maybe this was her new way of dealing with the waiting.

"I want to go look at houses again this weekend," Tammy

announced the following week.

Susan would have liked to take August off from everything, but she knew better than to say so. Instead of open houses, at least they'd be seeing specific homes this time. Ones they'd found together and decided they might both be able to love. Tammy had hired a realtor, and they had two appointments on Saturday and one on Sunday.

Although they were not set on buying a house in Worcester, it was one option. Neither wanted to be too far from work, and most of the towns that bordered Worcester were expensive. They both hated the first they saw on Saturday. It was too close to the other houses for Susan, and it was too old-fashioned for Tammy. They both liked the second one but didn't love it. Technically, it had everything they wanted but just didn't feel like the one. The realtor assured them that seeing homes they didn't like was important, too. It would help her filter out other houses as she learned what they liked and didn't like. For instance, while Tammy wasn't flexible about having two bathrooms, Susan saw that as just another thing to maintain. Another toilet to clean, more plumbing to potentially repair. Aside from privacy and a yard, Susan didn't have many specifications as long as it felt cozy.

"I love this house," Tammy said after they toured an adorable white cape on Sunday.

"Actually, I do, too," Susan agreed, surprised that Tammy could appreciate the modest home. It wasn't boxy and stuffy like many of the ones Tammy seemed to be so crazy about. It was homey and had more character. Susan especially liked the nooks and crannies like the bay window and the built-in bookcases, not to mention the skylight in the main bedroom, the one feature of the townhouse she'd hate to lose.

"Yeah, this would be a great starter home. It's got just enough space, and the updated appliances are great, even if the accents are a little outdated. I like that it has a dining room, too," Tammy added.

Susan refrained from rolling her eyes. It made more sense now why Tammy could get on board with the house that Susan could easily see herself living in forever; to Tammy, it was merely a stop along the way as she continued to reach for bigger and better. Still, they were on the same page for now, and Susan wasn't going to worry about the future.

"I'm noticing that you both seem to like capes," the realtor noted.

Tammy nodded. "I don't like ranches, and she says she hates colonials, although I think there are some that would surprise her."

"Well, there certainly are a lot of capes to look at in the city," the realtor added.

"No, this is the one," Susan said, not even aware it was going to come out of her mouth.

Tammy chuckled but quickly realized Susan was serious, and Susan saw her dimple emerge. "I like that enthusiasm. I totally agree."

Susan's head swirled with mild panic. They'd just begun looking; was it crazy to commit to one so soon?

"I *am* approved for up to two-hundred-fifty thousand, so it's within our budget," Tammy said.

"That's the top of our budget. Can we afford that mortgage? Maybe we should look more? At lower priced houses?"

"You're right. There *are* lower-priced options, but for this neighborhood, with the privacy factor, this really is an amazing opportunity. If you both like it as much as you say, you should probably put in an offer. I don't think it will be on the market long," the realtor interjected.

"It can't hurt. And you're already in love with it," Tammy replied.

"And, you *can* put in an offer what you're comfortable with, I mean, within reason. I wouldn't go *much* lower, but I do know the owners are motivated to sell," the realtor added.

"Let's do it. Let's put in an offer." Tammy smiled, shaking her fists with excitement.

Susan didn't reply but instead wandered off, feeling the house's energy one more time. They could figure it out financially. And Susan *did* love the house. Who was she kidding? The realtor had her when he'd reminded her of the privacy it offered. She could already picture herself lighting a candle in the back yard and planting her garden. Tammy and the realtor followed her and talked as Susan headed up the stairs one more time. She was drawn to the smallest bedroom at the end of the hall. It was cozy, and one of the windows looked out over the spot in the yard where Susan would plant her garden. She closed her eyes and could see herself rocking their baby girl in that room. Yes, this was the house they would raise their daughter in.

"So, what do you think?" Tammy asked quietly, standing behind her as the realtor waited in the hall.

"This is our house," Susan replied, acknowledging something inside her that felt a little like the flutter but different somehow, too.

After a quick hug, Tammy hurried into the hall. "We want to put in an offer."

Glued to the nursery window and smiling through tears, she was vaguely aware of the talk of inspection and closing costs. Having a house meant finally getting a cat, too.

The realtor told them they should know whether the offer was accepted within a few days, but Susan knew it was a formality. She could already see them in this house. No, she could feel them there; it was as if all the laughter and pain they would experience was already bubbling up inside her as she stood there.

Why was it that she could feel the future when sometimes

the present was enough to manage? She didn't quite know, but she put her hand over her belly as the flutter became more active than usual. It was different this time, though. It was light and airy this time, while some of the other flutters had been so heavy. She reveled in the light, airy knowing as she gazed into her garden-to-be and imagined herself running around after a little one in a diaper on a hot, sunny day like this one.

"This feels just like waiting to see if there is going to be a pink line," Tammy said with a huff as they went to bed that night.

But it didn't. Not to Susan. She hadn't been sure of many things in her life, but she was sure of this. And it wasn't just the house. Their attempts to get pregnant would be successful soon, too. In fact, maybe her wires were crossed because that light, airy feeling in her gut was trying to tell her that Tammy was already pregnant, even though she wasn't sure if she could trust herself enough to be convinced. Susan was sure she would come off as a complete lunatic if she tried to explain any of this to Tammy.

"Gaia has our backs."

Tammy giggled, which made Susan giggle, too, and for a few moments, Susan remembered how close they could be when their own human struggles didn't succeed in separating them. Thoughts about why it couldn't always feel this way began to creep in, but Susan resisted, remembering Fiona's advice to learn to live in the moment and allow herself to be happy.

The realtor called the following evening as they ate supper; she told them what Susan already knew. The joy of watching Tammy's face light up as she was on the phone made Susan happier than she'd been in a long time. She was already picturing the joy in her eyes when she discovered she was pregnant; it would be soon. It was all coming together for them.

"Susan, come in here," Tammy shouted to her from the bathroom one night in the last week of August.

Tammy stood up from sitting on the side of the bathtub; tears were streaming down her face, but she was smiling. "We're going to be moms. Look!" Tammy held up three pregnancy tests; all had pink lines.

"What?!" Goosebumps on her arms and tears in her eyes, the news slowly sank in. Maybe it was just the elation of the moment, but it felt as though every one of the fears she'd ever had about becoming a mother were suddenly insignificant. She'd always compared herself to the women who were so clearly born to be mothers, focused on her shortcomings. Maybe she wasn't soft and nurturing in a traditional sense like DJ or as wise and balanced as Fiona was, and she certainly wasn't responsible and driven like Tammy. But if there was one thing she could offer as a mother, it was unconditional love, and love always won out over any fears or shortcomings.

"I'm pregnant!" Tammy hopped up and down, repeating it over and over.

Susan grabbed Tammy and cried with her, hopping as all three pee-soaked sticks tumbled to the floor.

"And we're going to have a house for her, just like you wanted," Susan added.

"Her?" Tammy asked with a smirk.

Susan nodded. It was just another thing that Susan knew.

For weeks after Tammy told her she was pregnant, Susan couldn't stop staring at Tammy's belly. Their daughter was all she could think about. She daydreamed about the things she wanted to do with her daughter, all the magical things in the world that she wanted to show her. She even envisioned the cute clothes, the nursery, and the milestones, just like all of the other mushy moms she'd rolled her eyes at. Excited for Tammy to share in her certainty that the baby was a girl, Susan couldn't wait for the three-month mark. Witnessing Tammy's face when she found out what Susan already knew would be just like when she'd gotten the call telling her that the offer on the house had been accepted.

Since the first month she met Tammy, she'd known that they would have one daughter together. Only one daughter. She was relieved about that but was wracked with guilt for feeling that way when she knew Tammy wanted a big family.

Things she knew had been coming to her more readily lately, and with it, intense fear. The initial elation when she found out she and Tammy were going to become mothers was now overshadowed by these fears. Fear of some of the things she didn't know. Fear of the things she did know but made no sense. Although she knew that love overpowered fear, she couldn't quiet her mind.

If they were only going to have one daughter, what did that mean for Tammy's dream of having a house full of children? Could she make Tammy happy with just her and one daughter? Did it mean that something might go wrong during the baby's birth? Was Tammy going to die? Would Susan have to raise this baby on her own? It was the what-ifs that worried her. All the things that could go wrong. Having a child meant that she would have more to lose than ever.

Her knowings ran through her mind loudly, especially as she tried to fall asleep each night. They were so loud that most of her favorite forms of escape weren't working anymore. She couldn't concentrate long enough to read, and sleep was becoming a challenge. On sleepless nights, she lay awake trying to come up with solutions for some of the things that might happen, but she knew she had to push it all out of her mind, or she would go crazy. Hell, who was she kidding? She was *already* going crazy; lack of sleep was enough to send her into a spiral.

At least she had Fiona. Autumn had arrived, and though the nights were getting chillier, she felt drawn to her grove. Tonight, since the buzzing in her body kept her from sleep again, it felt like the perfect place to smoke and think. Crawling out of bed quietly so she wouldn't wake Tammy, she threw on a flannel, grabbed her backpack, and made her way to the grove.

She sat down and looked at the October trees, half-dead but still colorful. The seasons that she loved the most seemed so short sometimes. While the steamy dead of summer and the frigid height of winter always felt so long, she wished these perfect, balanced months could last forever.

After a couple of tugs from her joint, Susan opened her backpack and got out the stationery with spiders and bats.

October 5, 2000

Dear Fiona,

In a way, I think this might be the best autumn of my life. Certainly, the most powerful. I keep telling Tammy that we are having a girl. She doesn't get it, that I KNOW, but it's kind of fun having a little secret. I can picture Raven in her Halloween costume next year. I can see her, Fiona, like really see our daughter. I can see her dark hair and dark eyes. She even has Tammy's dimple. I see freckles, too, but those won't come until she's older. I think she will have really chubby cheeks when she's a baby.

We close on our new house in December, and I can clearly see her there for her first Christmas the following year. I'll teach her how to squint at the lights like my mom taught me. I can see her running around in the back yard in the summer in the little hippie sundresses that I'll buy her.

So, here is my question – why the fuck am I so terrified all the time now? I can't sleep. It's almost three o'clock in the morning right now, and I am outside in the grove writing to you. That is what I call my little hideaway in the yard now, ever since the picnic table disappeared. Sounds downright enchanted, doesn't it? And I just realized this will probably be my last time writing to you from the grove. We are supposed to close on the house in two weeks. It got pushed a couple of times, but I think it's really going to happen this time. I guess I'll have to create a new grove. I'll miss the grove, but that back yard calls to me. Even the house has me all worked up. So, how can I be so terrified when I am also so fucking happy? I mean, I really am. I know I was worried about being a mom, but it's not even that anymore. I'm excited about everything. 3AM feedings (maybe that is why I am always up at this hour – practice), shitty diapers, and all. I can't wait to move into the house and paint the nursery. I can't wait to see her walk and say mommy and mamma, and go off to kindergarten. So, what the fuck is wrong with me? Why can't I just be happy and excited? I know, I know – I try to tell myself to live in the moment, but I'm telling you, I can't figure out how. I'm just so fucked up.

I'm going to be an Auntie in just a few weeks. DJ and Matt are having a girl, too. Maybe being around my niece will help me somehow. Babies really can be magical – they're kind of otherworldy little creatures, aren't they?

Anyway, I suppose I should get back to bed and try to get SOME sleep before I have to go to work in a few hours, even though I feel wide awake. I really just want to dance around under the moon all night and sleep all day. I think I might be part owl or a gargoyle – did you know that, in some legends, gargoyles turn to stone in sunlight but come alive at night? Too bad there wasn't a midnight bookstore I could run. I could name it Gargoyle's. I think I might be just delirious now.

How's it going there? How's Will? What have you been up to? Tell me something!

Love, Susan

While purging her thoughts was cathartic enough sometimes, waiting for Fiona's reply was still hell. She needed some guidance, and no one knew her quite like Fiona did. Although Fiona's letter came far more quickly than usual, it wasn't at all what Susan had been hoping for.

October 10, 2000

Hey Susan,

How many times do I have to tell you to live in the moment, Bitch? I know you can see things. Feel things. I get it. It's hard to be a magical being, but you have to reign it in and come back to the now or you will get lost. Enjoy this season. Just let it happen. Let it be.

Love, Fiona

Susan sat there staring at the letter in disbelief for a long time. It was the second letter from Fiona that had infuriated her. One of the things that she'd relished the most about their friendship was how strange they could be with one another. How real they were. No one else understood that she was magical the way Fiona did. But how was she supposed to benefit from this advice at all, if you could even call it advice? Why was she being so vague when Susan had poured her heart out?

"What the fuck, Fiona?" Susan hissed aloud. She half crumpled up the paper in her fist before sticking it into the top drawer of her desk, only coming back to smooth it out before she got into bed later that night.

Susan had predicted that Fiona would remind her to live in the moment, and she was trying, but she was finding it more challenging to do that with all the unanswered questions. It was as if the gift of knowing some details about her future made her want more. She read the letter from Fiona over and over, trying desperately to take some small thread of wisdom from it, but only managed to feel more lost. She couldn't stay angry with Fiona for long, though; Fiona had a mysterious nature and wasn't very wordy.

DJ gave birth to Ashley on November fifth. After twenty-one hours of labor that had ended with an unplanned C-section, everyone was exhausted. Susan had been there with them the whole time but was happy to let DJ and Matt sleep while she stared at the mini version of DJ. The tiny face brought her back to her childhood; it was the same face she saw the first day they had met at the bus stop. Yet, at the same time, the existence of her niece made her feel as if she'd matured in some monumental way. If becoming an aunt to Ashley had changed her like this, she could only imagine the ways that becoming a mother would transform her.

At Tammy's three-month appointment, they officially found out what Susan already knew: they were having a girl. Though it wasn't new information to her, it still moved Susan; hell, everything moved her lately as if she was the one with new hormones coursing through her body.

"Now that we know it's a girl, we should talk about her name," Susan said as they rode down the elevator.

"We already know her name. You told me years ago, remember?" Tammy smirked.

In awe, Susan wasn't sure how to respond. Of course, she had told Tammy that their daughter would be named Raven, but she wasn't sure how seriously Tammy had taken her then and was surprised that she was still so definitive about it now.

"Well, what about her middle name?" Susan asked.

"I've been giving that a lot of thought, actually. Since we don't share a last name, and I suppose she'll have my last name, I want part of her name that shows she is a part of you, too," Tammy replied.

"Aww, that's really special, Tam. But...?"

"I was thinking Raven Grace. I know how important your gramma was to you," Tammy said with a soft smile.

Susan felt the sting of tears in her eyes. Not only was it beautiful that her daughter would carry her family's legacy in a small way, but Tammy's thoughtfulness was just as moving. She took a step closer to Tammy and touched her arm.

"Thank you. It's perfect. I love it."

Most days, it was like Tammy was an entirely new woman, and it still took Susan by surprise sometimes when Tammy went the extra mile to be considerate. In fact, Tammy's first trimester had gone quite smoothly; she was calmer and more agreeable than ever. So many of the traits that had rubbed Susan the wrong way seemed to have all but disappeared. In stark contrast to Tammy's approach at the townhouse, concerned with only what she wanted, they worked together to make the new house their own, a place they could both love. Not just a house but a home for their family.

Closing on the house in mid-December felt like good fortune to Susan. Maybe she was whimsical, always looking for signs and symbols, but sliding their new key into the lock for the first time on the day before the Winter Solstice felt simply perfect. She had envisioned the house blessing that she would carry out, and it couldn't get much more magical than doing it right on the Winter Solstice.

They wouldn't officially live there until after the new year. They'd paid for the entire month of December at the townhouse, so it made sense to move in slowly, with one final trip in January. But there was something quaint about having a couple of weeks with the house still being nearly empty; it felt as though she could learn its energy and infuse it with her own energy much more easily this way. They could go in and clean, and she could take a box or two of books every time she went.

She considered asking Tammy if she would take part in the house blessing ritual with her. After all, it was their house; Tammy's energy was an important element, too. But, in the end, remembering how Tammy had looked at her when she talked about magical things, she thought better of it. Besides, she was increasingly beginning to understand that she was meant to be a solitary Witch.

So, on the Winter Solstice, Susan told Tammy that she would

be late to arrive at the townhouse after work and snuck away to the new house. As she drove up Pierce Ave., Susan decided it was a cute enough area, especially for a city. She hadn't preferred such a traditional neighborhood, but the house had chosen them. With tall bushes on each side of the back yard, at least she'd have some privacy.

When she pulled up, the house looked even sweeter than she remembered it. The bare windows looked like welcoming eyes, and she spotted a bright red poinsettia on the front porch. She got out of her car, shoes crunching through the snow, and picked it up. Although she'd never been able to have them herself, as they were poisonous to cats, she'd picked up her grandmother's love for the majestic winter flower. She knew that sometimes people's realtors would leave a gift when their clients closed on a home, but there was no card attached. She carried the poinsettia inside and set it in the bay window, then looked around, taking in the details again.

Even though Tammy wasn't fond of the carpeted stairs or the old-fashioned wooden banister, saying it was dated, they made the living room look homey to Susan. With the bay window and the built-in bookshelves, she was in love with the room. She had never imagined that she could love a physical space so much.

She was far less impressed by the dining room, as the burgundy paint wasn't a shade she was fond of, and frankly, she preferred an eat-in kitchen. Still, the kitchen was almost as cute as the living room, with a tiny pantry and country cupboards that Tammy insisted they would change out as soon as they could afford it. While Tammy was focused on updating things, Susan loved the features that reminded her of homes she'd lived in with her mom and her gramma. And, even though she didn't want to admit it, she saw that Tammy had been right. Susan's vision for her life was based heavily on her past. She hadn't necessarily expected to ever own a home at all, and while she could understand that part was limiting, she still loved the old-fashioned features; there was something soulful about things that represented a simpler time.

Since the day they'd met, Tammy had made her stretch her thinking and go out of her comfort zone, and Susan had given her a lot of resistance without even knowing she was doing it. Now, here they were, homeowners. In a roundabout way, Tammy had helped her get closer to her aspiration to live a more fulfilling life than her mom or gramma had been able to. Before Tammy, her need to learn had sent her to college, something no one in her family had even considered, but she had struggled to bring herself much further. Surely, her mother and even her gramma had wanted more, too. But in addition to the time period they were both born into, they had something in common: becoming pregnant had been the deciding factor about their path, or more specifically, in halting any other dreams they may have imagined for themselves.

Now, a brand-new generation was about to start, and Susan knew it was time to outgrow some of her outdated ideas about herself so she could help her daughter find a path without the same restrictions. Having been so focused on magic and adventure, she'd never imagined that it could be a house that could offer the foundation she needed to do that. Building a home with intention meant that although she was about to join the generations of women who had to put another person before themselves, she also had a space to create magic.

After visiting the back yard and making a layout of her future garden, just beyond the flagstone patio, which was now covered with snow, she lit the lavender sage stick that she'd made special for this occasion. Slowly, she walked through each room, starting with her cozy little living room, silently infusing the fragrant smoke into every nook and cranny. She stood still in the center of each room before moving on, focused on her breathing and visualizing the room filled with a soft yellow light.

Saving the future nursery for last, Susan closed the door behind her. She wanted to contain as much good energy in Raven's room as possible. She walked the periphery of the room and watched the smoke dance lazily around the room, then looked out over the yard and spoke her blessing aloud.

"On this enchanted Winter Solstice Day, I want to thank you, Mother Gaia, and all the other powerful Goddesses and Gods out there who have my back. From the depths of my soul, thank you. This life I have been given is already so much more than I could have ever dreamed of. I promise to work hard to make this house a home. Please continue to bless my family, and most especially, please help me in my pursuit of creating a beautiful, safe, and magical life for my daughter, Raven. So mote it be."

Still, after all these years, she stepped away from each ritual with at least a hint of imposter syndrome, despite the fact that she could so clearly feel the magic running through her. But as she walked back to the front door, she was satisfied she'd done exactly what she'd come to do, for she could sense the energy in the home had changed in the house. As she descended from the front porch, she snuffed out the sage stick in the snowbank, feeling accomplished.

As much as she usually struggled with letting time pass, Susan welcomed the year 2001, convinced that the entire world was about to change as her daughter emerged into the world.

CHAPTER SIXTEEN

Tammy was determined to work as much as she could for as long as she could throughout her pregnancy. This allowed Susan to spend every free moment at DJ's house; she couldn't get enough of Ashley, and DJ appreciated the extra hand, especially since she'd returned work in February.

"Have you guys figured out what you guys will do after the baby is born? With work, I mean?" DJ asked.

"Tammy's going to take maternity leave for three months, and then I'm going to take one for three months. I'll tell you, after seeing how fast Ashley changes, I can't imagine how I'm going to go back at all. I'm going to be afraid to miss...even...one...moment," Susan said, changing her tone to baby talk and leaning in to make a goofy face at Ashley as Ashley babbled back.

DJ nodded and teared up. "It's hard. I hate it."

Susan cradled Ashley in the kitchen sink and poured the last cup of warm water over her head, watching her wrinkle up her little nose.

"Are you sure you'll be able to take maternity leave?" DJ asked.

"Yeah, why? Barnes and Noble is great with that stuff. And my district manager is always extra accommodating when I need something. Personally, I think it's because she's a closeted lesbian." Susan laughed, lifting her chubby, dripping niece from the sink.

"Here, let me take her." DJ offered, holding open the baby towel. "Well, I just don't know how it works. I was going to say if you aren't the one giving birth, but...I don't know how it works for your situation," DJ continued as she patted Ashley with the towel.

"People take maternity leave for adoption all the time."

"Right. I just mean, in normal...normally, both parents adopt the baby. So, you're going to legally adopt the baby? How does that work?" DJ asked.

She and Tammy hadn't even talked about that yet, but Susan didn't like DJ's implication that she would somehow be less than a real mom unless some court papers recognized her as such.

"A normal family?" Susan asked, putting her hands on her hips.

"I didn't say that...I said *normally*. Usually, both parents adopt, so it's just cut and dry," DJ replied.

"I know, two moms isn't *normal*. I get it," Susan said, trying not to raise her voice around her niece, despite the fact that she could feel the angry feminist in her ready to attack.

"No, I..."

"Just drop it. Barnes and Noble supports *alternative* families. My district manager already approved me for leave starting in August, so, yeah, our abnormal family will be all set. The money isn't as important to us; we want to work together to make sure she is not in daycare any earlier than she has to be." She hoped the last part of her comment hurt but didn't stop to look at DJ's face before she charged outside onto the porch. If she didn't get some air, it might get ugly.

As she stood there in her short sleeves for what felt like forever, she wished she had grabbed her sweatshirt but was too stubborn to go back inside and get it. Although spring had been trying to triumph over the last days of winter, this evening, it felt like it was losing its fight. The sight of her breath in the cold air, mixed with the anger she was still trying to quell, made her want a few puffs from a joint. She couldn't help but chuckle out loud as she thought about the way DJ would panic her ass off if she were to ever see Susan standing on her porch with a joint out in the open.

Just then, she heard the door squeak open. She wasn't done being mad, so she wiped all traces of the humor from her face and refused to look over at DJ. She wasn't ready to stop being mad just yet.

"It's cold out here," DJ said.

"Not too bad. Kind of refreshing," Susan replied, tucking her blue fingertips into the pocket of her jeans.

DJ let out a long sigh. "I didn't mean to piss you off."

DJ was trying, and Susan couldn't help but soften.

"You know, I know it might seem like I'm pissed off all the time. But you have to understand, it's easier to seem pissed off than...heartbroken." She managed to get out, swallowing hard to fight tears.

"But I didn't mean anything..." DJ said sincerely.

"I know you didn't. That's the thing, though. I'm not trying to be mean, but you're clueless sometimes. Not just you. But the whole fucking world. I feel like I have to live my whole life explaining who I am. Trying to be understood. About everything: being a Witch, being a lesbian, my feminist values. And I know no one's perfect, but it would be nice if I didn't have to explain myself to my oldest friend. If *you* don't understand me, how the hell do I have any hope of being understood by anyone? Any hope of being taken seriously?" She talked a mile a minute, holding back tears the entire time.

"I'm sorry. I know we're different, but that happens with family. I love you, and that's it. I don't know. I'm trying."

"I know," Susan replied, then scuffled her feet along the porch and moved toward DJ. "I love you, too. Obviously." She wagged her head playfully.

"You know, your niece is all cozy in her PJs and waiting for her Auntie to read her a bedtime story," DJ said, her huge brown eyes holding an even louder apology than her words had.

"I have a book for her in my backpack," Susan said, gratefully moving toward the door to escape from the cold.

"Big surprise."

Although they'd made peace, Susan lay awake that night, still ruminating about the conversation. She knew DJ hadn't meant anything wrong, but she also knew that a part of DJ constantly saw her as different. And now, she saw the family Susan was building as different, too. Just like DJ saw their marriage as different than her own, she saw her and Tammy as different kinds of parents. DJ could explain her words away all she wanted, but they'd been friends for twenty years, and Susan knew her. If it wasn't a man and a woman, a mother, and a father, it wasn't a real family to DJ; it was merely an attempt at trying to be one. The way Christianity was woven into the everyday culture brainwashed people, and it was just so exhausting trying to fight to be validated in that world.

And to add insult to injury, DJ had brought up another sore spot. Susan had already been worried about her place in the baby's life. Not only legally, but she'd begun to question things she never thought she would. Would she have a strong bond with the baby without the biological connection? Surely, Tammy would have the advantage. It wasn't as if it was a contest, but she wanted the baby to have two moms, not a mom and just another woman who was raising her with her real mother. Maybe giving their child a middle name after Susan's grandmother wasn't enough. Biology wasn't everything, but as she saw Tammy's belly grow, the connection was so much more apparent. She hadn't anticipated feeling a loss at not having that kind of connection to her child. And the hardest part was that she couldn't really talk to anyone about it. How could she when she didn't even want to admit it was true?

Susan's insecurities continued to grow as Tammy's pregnancy progressed. When the baby kicked for the first time. When Tammy received smiles at her growing middle. When Susan looked at pictures of Tammy with her gramma and mother and saw the features they all shared. She wasn't proud about it but was jealous that she would never share these things with her daughter. Her own hazel green eyes that she saw mirrored from her mother's face would never look back at her from her daughter.

How could she even feel this way when she was the first one to argue that DNA wasn't everything? In fact, it meant so little. But it was something she would never have, and that bothered her. She didn't want to burden Tammy with her pain, and she thought she was finally coming to terms with it all until one day in mid-April when DJ and Ashley came to visit.

"I wanted to tell you guys that we have a date for Ashley's Christening," DJ said.

"Oh, that's exciting," Tammy replied.

"We wanted to be sure it wasn't too close to when your little one will be here, so it will be the first Sunday in May."

"That was thoughtful," Tammy replied as she rocked Ashley.

"Oh wow, that's coming up quick." Susan was surprised that DJ hadn't mentioned it earlier. Asked her to help like she always had for significant events.

"Yeah, it all just fell into place. That's when Lisa is coming up." DJ couldn't look her in the eye when she said it.

Ahh, that was it. DJ's sister was coming up. Now she knew why DJ hadn't mentioned it earlier. She was choosing her sister as Ashley's godmother, the same way she'd chosen her as the maid of honor for her wedding. Susan remained silent. She wasn't going to make it easy for DJ; she would make DJ say it to her face.

"She and Dave are going to be Ashley's godparents," DJ said, looking down at the floor.

It was probably silly that she was still bitter about the maid of honor thing after all these years, but Susan never could make sense of it; they weren't even close. At least DJ had only been nineteen when she was married. She was a traditional girl and had listened to her mom, who'd assured her that her sister should be her maid of honor. But now, they were women. DJ was a mother. How could she choose someone to be her child's godmother when they talked a few times a year?

Now that the words were out there, Susan wished they weren't. What could she say? The cooing noises that Tammy directed at Ashley were the only thing breaking up the silent tension.

Susan nodded, pretending not to care, but she and DJ knew each other. She didn't need to say a word. But she wouldn't cry. She got up, grabbed her backpack, and retrieved her planner, scribbling down the date before DJ left.

"What time?" Susan asked.

"Nine o'clock," DJ replied.

"I'm sure I can get someone to cover for me if that's my weekend to work," Tammy said.

"Are you planning on working right up until the end?" DJ asked Tammy.

"Oh, yes. I know I'll have a lot of downtime afterward, so I've been determined to work as long as I can and not get off track with the gym." Tammy answered.

"I was the same way," DJ said.

Susan casually escaped to the bathroom, leaving the two mothers to discuss. She closed the door, leaned her forehead against it, and felt a catch in her throat. Did her presence in this world matter in the least to either child? Why did all of this hurt her so much? Was it really just jealousy? Was she being childish? She would never be like DJ or Tammy. The urge to tear at her own skin with something sharp washed over her. Shit! She hadn't felt this in years, certainly not since she'd rediscovered marijuana. She'd carried the habit from high school into her first few years of college. By the time she graduated, though, she had stopped cutting altogether with the help of a therapist and the sense of self she found through her work with the Women's Center and the Pride Alliance. The impulse had arisen every now and then, mostly when one of her relationships had ended or when she'd been afraid of change, but it hadn't been this strong in a long time, and that scared her.

She inhaled a long breath and willed herself not to cry. She couldn't hide it if she cried; her eyes stayed red for too long. She opened the bathroom window, retrieved the joint and lighter from the band-aid box in the medicine cabinet, and took three pulls on the joint before rejoining DJ and Tammy, who were now discussing labor. Taking Ashley from Tammy's arms, she snuggled into the couch with her, tuning out the conversation until Ashley began to cry. She got up and gazed out the sliding glass door, pointing up at the moon, which was already visible in the sky. It was so far away, but Ashley seemed to see it, or maybe it was just Susan's imagination. Sometimes, she still felt like Ashley was, like her, more part of another world than the one their bodies were in.

As DJ grabbed her purse to leave, she locked eyes with Susan.

"I hope you understand. About the godmother thing. I talked to the reverend, and he said that the Godparents should be, you know, Christian," DJ said.

She understood perfectly. It had always been apparent that her being a Witch, like being a lesbian, set her apart in DJ's eyes. Separated them. She was surprised that DJ even referred to her as Auntie. But sure, if she wanted a woman she wasn't close with to be her daughter's godmother, just because they both worshipped Jesus, it was her right. Susan nodded and smiled, but inside, she felt like a feral cat.

After Susan shut the door, she waited until she heard her footsteps fade but couldn't hold the tears back any longer.

"Oh my God, Babe, what's the matter?" Tammy asked, hurrying to her side.

"Everything. Just...everything." Susan buried her face in her hands.

"Is this about the godmother thing?" Tammy asked.

Susan nodded, choking on her sobs.

"I was worried that was going to really get to you. Come here," Tammy said.

Tammy pulled her into a hug, but Susan couldn't manage to leave the comfort of her own inner world. She didn't push Tammy away but didn't let her in either. Tammy held her for a few minutes but talked at her the whole time.

"You have to understand that DJ is just coming at this from a very different way than you are," Tammy said.

What did that mean? For some reason, it just made Susan sob harder.

"She isn't doing it to hurt you. It isn't about you at all," Tammy added.

She wished Tammy could just hold her and let her cry. She hated it when Tammy told her something wasn't about her, as if she was self-centered.

"She's doing what she thinks is best."

So, even Tammy thought that someone else would make a better godmother to Ashley?

"You don't understand," Susan managed and pulled away. "Next to her parents, I'm the closest person to Ashley. I was there when she was born. I've been there every moment I could. But DJ chose her fucking sister. Again. A woman who lives eight hours away and who hasn't even met her niece. Just because she worships *Jesus*."

"Well, that is an important part of being a godmother, Babe. That's what I mean; DJ is seeing this very differently. I know you didn't grow up with godparents, but my brother and I did. The point is to have someone to help your child understand their faith if you aren't there to do that. Sometimes, it isn't about any more than that. Not about who is closest or anything," Tammy explained.

Susan laughed and shook her head. "You're right." And she *was* right. The whole thing was ridiculous; why did she even want to be a part of it? If DJ wanted someone to brainwash Ashley into thinking a certain way, she certainly wasn't the one. So why did it still hurt so much?

"I've even been worrying about my place in Raven's life," Susan admitted.

"What?!" Tammy replied.

"I mean, legally, I am nothing to her. We haven't even talked about that. Adoption or whatever. I mean, if something were to happen to you...and I guess this godmother situation just..." She began to cry harder again but managed to finish her sentence, "It just made me realize I'm nothing. To anyone."

"Wow, Babe. I think you're getting out of control here," Tammy said with concern.

Susan pushed Tammy's hand away and walked across the room. "I can't believe I tell you how I'm feeling, and *that* is what you say to me."

"You have to stop for a minute. Breathe. Take control of your mind," Tammy said, speaking calmly.

The comment pissed Susan off even more, but she paused to appease Tammy.

"I'm not going to be our daughter's legal parent. I'm not even legally your wife," Susan said.

"Now, wait a minute. You're the first to tell me that the laws don't make something real. Love makes it real," Tammy replied.

She hated when Tammy used her own logic against her, but she could see the point she was making.

"You *are* my wife. You *are* Raven's mom. And you *are* Ashley's aunt, whether you're her godmother or not. We don't need papers to tell us that stuff, and you know it," Tammy said.

Susan shrugged and wiped snot on her sleeve.

"I'm just saying you need to slow down and take a breath here. You can't let your emotions control you, Babe. I mean, to say you are nothing to anyone...that's pretty heavy. It worries me when you get so carried away."

Susan closed her eyes, nodded, and sat down on the couch. She didn't know what to say to that. Maybe Tammy was right, but she didn't know *how* to do what Tammy was suggesting.

"But this *is* a little different...I need to know that I won't have to fight to prove I'm her mom if something happens to you. This time, I *do* need the papers. Just to help me sleep at night," Susan said.

Tammy sat next to her and touched her arm. "We'll have to talk to a lawyer, then."

"Really?" Susan asked.

Tammy nodded. It was a step in the right direction. At least she knew Tammy had heard her.

The next couple of weeks brought another resurgence of nightmares. When awake, churning thoughts troubled her even more than some of the disturbing images she saw in her dreams. Until something was legally in place, what would happen if something happened to Tammy? She was sure that Tammy's parents would take their daughter. Once again, she had to hold it together alone because Tammy was going through something of her own.

Now that she was about to be a mother, Tammy quickly discovered that working in peds had caused her to ache more deeply than she'd anticipated. Many days, she came home on the verge of tears, and others, stony, as if her heart hadn't really come home with her body, and she never wanted to talk about it, no matter what state she came home in. She'd vaguely mentioned that she had access to employee counselors at work. It was common, especially on the pediatric floor, for people to break down and need support with what they saw, but Tammy wanted no part of it. She was determined to power through.

And when she saw Tammy aching, Susan ached too; suffering seemed to have a ripple effect. But mostly, she was concerned about her wife. While she didn't expect Tammy to give up a position she loved, she also questioned the logic behind struggling through something that made her hurt so much. Struggling alone.

****

By mid-May, Tammy had reached the point in her pregnancy where she was too tired and uncomfortable to do anything outside of work. She was determined to work until the end of her pregnancy, but Susan saw how she struggled to do even everyday things, so she took over everything else to allow Tammy to rest and ensure they were ready to welcome Raven.

As Tammy's due date came closer, Susan began to feel more confident about being a mother to Raven. While moms like DJ and Tammy were grounded and organized, she had something special to give, too: magic.

With a clear vision for the nursery, it was the first bit of magic that Susan would offer her daughter. While she considered herself creative, she was no artist. Hannah's talent was exactly what she needed, so she and Hannah and Alice had been working on it little by little each weekend and, at the beginning of May, were finally nearing completion.

"Take a break with me," Alice said, laying her paintbrush down.

"And leave Hannah with all of this?" Susan asked, looking at the paint trays spread around the room.

"It's not that much. I can totally handle the finishing touches in plenty of time before Tammy comes home. Go relax, mamma," Hannah piped in.

"Okay. If you're sure. The smell is kind of getting to me, anyway," Susan replied. Hearing someone call her mamma made her heart flutter.

Hannah nodded and waved them away as she brushed her dark blond hair back with her painty hands and dabbed more purple onto the wisteria flower she was working on.

"I've been so overwhelmed with my baby to-do list that I really *could* use a smoke," Susan said as they headed down the stairs.

Alice laughed. "With how much you've always hated cigarettes, it's so weird to hear you say that."

"Well, these are magic smokes." Susan smirked. "They help me not to kill people."

Alice held her cigarette up. "And you don't think these do that? How do you think you made it to adulthood and Ed and the girls are still alive today?"

"How's that going anyway? Having Hannah at your house full time?" Susan asked.

"She's not bad," Alice replied.

Susan could sense she wanted to say more. They settled into the lawn chairs near the garden and took out their smokes. After a few puffs, Susan noticed her mother wiping tears from her face.

"Having Hannah with you full-time isn't going well, is it?" Susan pressed gently.

"No, it's not her. She's fine. She's quiet, like you were. But Ed thought it was a great idea to invite all four of them to stay the entire fucking summer. And he asked them right in front of me, so what was I supposed to do?" Alice asked with a catch in her throat.

"Oh, no! That's a lot of people in that little apartment. Did they all say yes?"

"Of course, they did. There's never any food at their mother's house, and even though Ed gets crabby a lot, they all know his bark is worse than his bite. He makes it seem like it will be one long slumber party all summer. Didn't even stop to think about me. Alice paused and began to cry harder.

Susan never knew what to do when her mom cried. It broke her heart to see her hurting; she wanted to fix everything. Despite her discomfort, she patted Alice's arm and let her cry.

"It just wasn't supposed to be like this. It was supposed to be just the two of us. I mean, except for every other weekend, obviously. But it's..." Alice sniffled. "He loves his girls so much, and that's why I love him, you know? But I just wasn't cut out for this bullshit. I knew that after I had you. That I wanted you to be an only child."

"I know." What else could she say? She wasn't sure what her mother thought life would be like when she married a man with four daughters.

"Anyway. I'm sorry. This is just life, I guess. Life sucks, and then you die."

"Don't be sorry. I can't imagine four. I can't even imagine two. Raven is going to be an only child." Susan didn't know it was going to come out of her mouth.

"Have you told Tammy that?" Alice asked.

"Naw. I'm just going to let us both enjoy Raven for now." She wanted to tell her mother that it was more than just that, it was something she knew to be true. But she held back.

"You're a lot like me. You just want a quiet life. We know the simple stuff is the best stuff in life. Takes some people a lifetime to understand that." Alice patted her on the back.

Susan smiled, taking the compliment. That was exactly it; she liked a quiet life. And when her mother said it, it didn't sound so bad. It was not like it sounded in her own head when she told herself she was lazy, inept, and selfish.

"I still feel bad that Hannah is up there finishing all the work," Susan said.

"Are you kidding? Hannah is happier than a pig in shit," Alice replied, blowing out a puff of smoke.

Susan burst out laughing. "What a disgusting saying."

"It is, isn't it?" Alice laughed and took another drag from her cigarette. "But really, Hannah has been resisting the urge to draw on the walls for years after her and Nicki's Sponge Bob incident, so just let her enjoy it."

Susan remembered how Hannah had stared at one wall after another, mentally drawing on each with her finger, eager to create.

"Ugh, I forget about all the things I have to look forward to. Drawing on walls and cutting their own hair and stuff," Susan said.

"Yeah, it's fun sometimes." Alice rolled her eyes.

"What's the worst part? Of being a mother?" Susan asked.

"With these four, or when you were young?"

"I don't know. Both," Susan replied.

"With you, the hardest part was not being able to protect you from things. With your stepsisters...there are just *so many* of them. Feels like someone always needs something. And they're so fucking loud. Don't they know I just want to read my damn book?"

Some things never changed. Some of her favorite memories from childhood were the bedtime stories and the quiet afternoons spent on the couch together, each immersed in their own books.

"I mean, you were needy in your own way sometimes. But mostly when we were out somewhere. You didn't like to leave my side. But when we were at home, you could always occupy yourself," Alice said.

"Only children are better at that," Susan added.

"So true. I mean, you think when the others go back to their mother's, the one that's left with us would be thrilled to have some time alone, but none of them ever know what to do with themselves except for Hannah."

Susan nodded.

"What part of being a mother are you most worried about?" Alice asked.

Susan sighed. "Depends on what day you ask me. Tammy is just so...amazing. She was born a mother. I'll never understand where she gets all her energy, working right up until the end. I guess sometimes I'm just afraid I won't have what it takes."

"I don't think you give yourself enough credit. I have seen you take on a lot more in the last few months. The way you make sure everything Tammy was doing is covered if she can't do it. And you're always there for DJ and Ashley. And all that while you're still running the store."

Susan shrugged.

"Fuck, I was proud enough when you went to college, and now, you're the manager at work. I could never juggle everything like you are," Alice said.

"Right now, I'm mostly worried I won't get everything done before she gets here," Susan explained.

"As long as the important stuff is done, you shouldn't worry."

"I know I *shouldn't*." Susan laughed.

"So, besides the nursery, what needs to be done?"

"That's the thing; I don't even know. I *know* there are a million little things to do, and I'm so busy at work with Mother's Day and graduation promotions that I get scattered, and half the time, I can't even remember what needs to get done." Susan shook her head, exasperated.

"I always told you to make a list. God knows you always have a pen and paper in that backpack of yours," Alice said.

"You're right." Susan nodded.

"What was that? Say that again, would ya?" Alice joked.

"You're right," Susan repeated with a laugh. "I guess most of the important stuff is done or will be. I just want it all to be perfect. We haven't gotten much furniture for the room. Just the changing table. The crib Tammy picked out has been on backorder and won't be in until the week after next. Cutting it kind of close. I just hope Raven doesn't come early."

They sat in the garden until Tammy got home from work. As they talked it out and Susan thought about how she would change when she became a mother, she wondered what Alice was like before she was born. Who would Alice have been if she had not been her mother? Susan would never really know.

"So, do I finally get to see it today as I was promised?" Tammy asked as she joined them in the yard

"I'll go check with Hannah," Susan said.

"No, I'll go. Give us a little while," Alice insisted.

Tammy put her hands on her hips and cocked her head. Susan looked her over; her scrubs barely fit over her bulging middle, her hair was in a frizz, and she wore an attitude on her face.

"I better get to see it; I've been waiting for weeks." Tammy smirked, softening.

"You know, I don't think you have ever looked more beautiful to me," Susan said.

"Aww. You're sweet, Babe. But you're crazy. I feel so...I don't know, inflated. Like I'm a pool float that needs to be popped." Tammy groaned.

Susan gave her a kiss. "You're a beautiful pool float."

"Come on, sit down, Honey. You must be so tired," Alice said, patting the chair she'd been sitting in.

Tammy nodded and lowered herself into the chair.

"I may not get up again." She laughed.

"I'll help you up." Susan winked.

Tammy told Susan about her emotional day on the peds floor. While working with sick children was never easy, some cases just broke her heart, and she was eager for maternity leave. Susan updated her about the home front; the furniture store had called, and the crib was in. She and Kevin planned to pick it up Monday after work, and he'd help her assemble both the crib and the changing table. Susan thought about how different their reality was from when they'd first met. The adventure of getting to know one another had turned into a real, adult relationship. A family. While she was sometimes nostalgic about those days, the depth they'd created with one another was more wonderful than even she could have imagined for them.

Finally, after nearly an hour, Alice opened the nursery window and poked her head out.

"Come on up, mommies," she called down.

They stood in the doorway of the nursery, and Susan gave a little knock.

"Come in," Hannah and Alice called through the door.

Susan turned the doorknob, and though she'd seen the room in its many stages, even she was in awe as they took it in.

Tammy looked around, taking in the details of each wall.

"Do you love it?" Susan asked.

Tammy nodded silently, tears in her eyes.

"What a beautiful color," Tammy said, rubbing a hand lovingly over the yellow base.

"It's called bumblebee," Susan said with a smile.

"I don't think that is bumblebee yellow at all," Alice analyzed.

"I agree. I think Crayola would have called it...." Susan gave it some thought.

"Canary!" Alice and Susan said in unison.

But now, Tammy was fixated on one single detail: Corduroy the bear.

"You remembered," she said softly.

"Of course, I remembered," Susan replied. "With a storybook theme, Corduroy had to be a part of Raven's world too, since he was your favorite as a kid."

"And Charlotte's Web was *your* favorite...." Tammy said, pointing to the tiny pink piglet and the giant, detailed spider web that stood in the corner over the rest of the barnyard animals, with a single spider looking like it was swaying in the breeze.

"And we both loved the secret garden," Susan added, pointing to the next wall. They'd painted morning glories and fuchsia and ivy vines creeping from the sides to the center, where they all converged at the window that looked over the back yard.

Only this time, she spotted a rocking chair by the window and, in the corner, a handmade trellis woven with colorful flowers, delicate butterflies, and ivy to match what they'd painted on the wall itself.

"Oh, my Goddess, Mom?"

Alice nodded. "The trellis is what I've been working on. That's *my* gift to my granddaughter. And the rocking chair is from Ed, the girls, and I."

"It's perfect," Susan said.

"It's absolutely amazing, you guys," Tammy uttered.

The Cheshire cat and the caterpillar stood guard, one on each side of the door, while a cow jumping over the moon and a dish and a spoon dancing around took up residence on the fourth.

Susan's vision of a storybook nursery had come to life.

CHAPTER SEVENTEEN

After Tammy had been in labor for seven hours, it was apparent to Susan that her wife's entire being was consumed by exhaustion. She was beginning to understand that exhaustion was one of the first feelings of motherhood. As Tammy struggled through each contraction, it looked as if she was being hit by a tidal wave. Susan had to hold back her own tears as she watched, helpless. In that moment, she understood what it was like to wish with all her soul that she could take on someone's pain. She'd scoffed when she had heard people say it before. It was just something people said. But she understood now. Bearing the pain herself would have been easier than witnessing the agony of her love having to endure it. But that, too, was selfish in a way. You couldn't truly save anyone; sometimes, love was just being there while someone suffered.

By hour nine, neither had the strength left to fight the tears. Although she vowed to be strong for Tammy, Susan let go first. Sitting on the side of the bed, holding Tammy's hand with a firm grip, she turned her head away, looking out the window, willing the tears to simply well up and fade, but once she spotted the moon, they came streaming down her face. She tried to manage quiet tears, but a slight heave took over her body, and Tammy pulled her hand closer.

"Babe?"

Susan shrugged and turned her head back, staring her wife in the eyes.

"I'm sorry. I'm okay. Really. I'm good. I'm so sorry," Susan rattled on frantically.

"No, don't be sorry. I know." Tammy nodded.

"I just hate seeing you in pain like this," Susan said.

"I'll be okay," Tammy replied.

Tammy joined in, tears spilling down her cheeks. Her face

changed, taking on a look of gentle strength, but something else, too. Maybe it was just the shared agony. Maybe there was nothing more powerful than that. Susan reached up and wiped the wetness from Tammy's face; she could feel her wife's every emotion as if they'd been infused in her tears.

After eleven hours, Tammy looked as if every ounce of energy she had in her cells had been expended, like a wave receding back to the sea. She didn't struggle anymore because she couldn't. Susan could see the contractions taking over her wife's body, but the wave was rolling in now. It felt nearly the same as when Susan's gramma was dying. But then again, it wasn't that different, really. While Tammy was about to bring a new life onto Earth, it was as if a part of her was dying, too. Susan could see the wild maiden fading away and being replaced with the stunning beauty of a mother. She was sure she had never truly known what love was until that moment, for Tammy was so much more to her than she'd been a lifetime ago when they were both maidens.

In the thirteenth hour, the doctor finally told Tammy she was ready to push, and yet again, Susan saw a new Tammy. A warrior. Face straining in anguish, doing what needed to be done. Going beyond the limits of her own body. Willing a life into the world, as much from the depth of her soul as with the muscles she used to push.

Susan stood in awe as her daughter's head crowned. The veil was thinner than Susan had felt, even on the darkest Samhain night.

"Go ahead, Mamma." This time, the doctor was speaking to Susan and took a step back, motioning for Susan to receive the baby as it emerged into the world. Raven Grace Bradley arrived on Wednesday, May 31, 2001, at 3:03 AM.

Susan stilled herself, just holding her little body. In the ten seconds that she held her baby, she had no fear. She was in the moment, yet letting it unfold. When the nurse asked if she wanted to cut the cord, Susan shook her head no. She knew it was necessary, but she couldn't be the one to separate her daughter from the mother who'd carried her. A nurse took the baby from Susan and lay her in Tammy's arms. Susan leaned into them, encircling them and wanting to stay that way forever. Once again, she was certain she'd never known love stronger than she did in that moment. It had been over thirteen hours, yet it had all rushed by so fast. Their daughter was here, and whether or not she had anything to do with it physically, she had every bit as much involvement in the creation of this child. Conception was not just a physical act but a type of magic in which she'd played a part.

Eventually, a nurse put an end to the perfect moment, taking Raven away to clean and bundle her up. Susan lay a hand on Tammy's face, wishing she could find words.

"I'm going to rest now," Tammy uttered with a smile as her head fell back with accomplished fatigue.

After the nurse brought Raven back, Susan talked to her daughter silently for a long time as she slept in her arms. She told her all about all the plans she had, especially with her aunt DJ and her cousin Ashley. *There are so many things I can't wait to show you in this world, my girl. We are going to have so many outdoor adventures. And I'm going to read you lots of books. I promise, promise, promise that I'm going to make sure you know magic.*

Raven wriggled in her arms and opened her eyes slightly for just a moment. Susan stared into her eyes and felt something she'd never felt before. She didn't know she could talk to someone the way she had just talked to her daughter, yet it was the same way she felt when she wrote to Fiona or read Fiona's letters.

"It's like they can hear your thoughts. Like they can actually understand you, right?" the nurse leaned over and whispered.

Susan nodded emphatically. That was it exactly; she was glad someone else understood.

"I'm sorry, but I need to take her back to the nursery for a little while."

Susan rubbed Raven's cheek with her thumb, made sure her blanket was tucked, and reluctantly handed her to the nurse.

After scratching out a message on the hospital room whiteboard that she would be back, Susan grabbed her backpack quietly and headed toward the cafeteria; she hadn't eaten all day. Walking down the maze of hallways, she was reminded why she hated hospitals: too many emotions swirling around. Although the noise and activity of public places, in general, overwhelmed her, there was something even more overpowering about hospitals. She hadn't had much experience with hospitals other than visiting her gramma before she died, but there was always something about being there. She felt like the filter in a swimming pool. All the emotions, good and bad, seemed to cling to her. The joy and wonder of birth, the simultaneous strain and relief of healing, the exhaustion of being ill, and, of course, the grief that came with death. She didn't even know these people, yet she absorbed every feeling. She had yet to find a means of clearing out that filter once it was filled with gunk. She wondered about others' stories as she walked the halls and futilely attempted to push them out of her mind so she could get on with her own life. Live in the moment. She just wanted to be home with her family and only their energy, where they could create their own little world. Home was like a reverse filter, keeping everything else out.

*****

Susan had never truly understood when people said how much a baby had changed them and their entire world, but she felt it the moment they stepped across the threshold of the door with Raven for the first time. She could literally feel the energy in the house shift, although she couldn't quite describe it. It just felt like an entirely different home.

Tammy dropped the diaper bag by the door and lowered herself onto the couch, pulling a blanket over her, despite the warm day. Susan started to open the curtains and windows, but Tammy told her it was too bright, so she closed them back up and headed directly to the back yard with the baby instead.

In the past two days, Susan was beginning to understand energy differently than she ever had before. Although logically, she knew the infant couldn't really see the beauty of the daffodils and irises or the statues of bunnies and fairies, Susan was certain that Raven could feel the energy that was infused there. She set the carrier on the flagstone, tucked the soft, teddy bear blanket snugly around the baby's chin, and pulled down the sun shade. Then, just sat there taking in birdsongs and the tinkling from the windchimes that hung from the tree, a baby gift from Fiona.

She just sat there, eyes closed, letting time pass. Time felt so strange now, as if she could not tell if five minutes or five hours had passed. The calm she felt since Raven had come felt like a different kind of high. It was not a peace that came from knowing everything was perfect, which was, perhaps, what she'd always been aiming for. This was a peace that came from knowing that everything was as it should be in that moment and that even if something was off, all would be okay. Now, she just needed to hold onto that feeling. The peace had always washed over her many times in the last few days, like a warm ocean breeze, but she'd found she couldn't sustain it. Tammy had been more exhausted than Susan had imagined she would be. Worrying about her wife kept pulling her out of that place, but she was in it now, so she would soak it in. Eventually, she decided they should go inside.

With a huge sigh, she looked at her sleeping daughter and whispered, "I promised I would show you magic, but I think you *are* magic."

The baby stirred but didn't wake.

Susan placed the carrier down softly on the floor by the couch and gazed at Tammy's form. Craning her head to see her face, Susan could see Tammy's eyes were open; Tammy just stared.

"You okay, Babe?" Susan asked.

Tammy nodded. "Just *so* tired."

"Do you want to go upstairs and nap?"

Tammy shook her head no and continued to stare, never even shifting her eyes to look at Susan. She understood that Tammy was exhausted but found it unsettling that Tammy wouldn't even talk to her.

"Okay."

Susan scanned the dining room table covered with mail, some things from the hospital, and the groceries that had never made it to the cupboard from two days ago, but Tammy needed quiet, so it would just have to wait. She wanted to snuggle into her wife, but there was so much to be done.

"I'm going to go upstairs and get a few things done. I'll bring Raven to you when it's time for her to eat," Susan said.

Tammy nodded, and her eyes fluttered shut.

She reached the top of the stairs, setting down the carrier with a sigh. The exhaustion was hitting her now. With the bump of setting the carrier down, Raven stirred. Susan waited; she might fall back to sleep. But instead, she began to whimper softly. There was laundry that needed folding, but it, too, would have to wait. She would have to learn to ignore things that didn't demand immediate attention. To prioritize. She moved the carrier to the nursery, closed the door so Raven wouldn't disturb Tammy, and pulled the shade halfway down. She lifted her squirming daughter from the carrier and settled into the rocking chair. In minutes, both were asleep.

Susan woke, startled, worried that it had been reckless to fall asleep with the baby in her arms; she could have dropped her.

"But you didn't. You're doing fine. Everything is okay, Little Darlin'."

There it was again: the voice. Just like what she'd heard at the hotel when Tammy had been hurt. It differed from a naturally flowing thought, like when she made a mental checklist of things to do. Although she'd determined it had come from inside herself, the difference between this and her own thoughts was in how she felt when the message had come to her. Her own thoughts were rarely that calm or reassuring. She replayed the words she'd heard. *"But you didn't. You're doing fine. Everything is okay, Little Darlin'."* That was it; someone was reassuring her.

She gazed down at Raven. Everything *was* okay. This, right here, was everything that mattered. She wondered how long she'd been asleep; was it time for Raven to eat? She'd have to pick up a clock for the nursery.

"She will tell you when it's time."

At the same time as she was getting used to it, she was in awe every time she heard the voice. This time, her gramma came to mind; maybe *she* had come to reassure her.

She watched the baby sleep, mesmerized by the rising and falling of her little form, the wrinkle of her nose, and the occasional puckering of her little mouth. Again, she acknowledged how time was different when holding Raven. When watching Raven. It almost didn't exist. If it hadn't been for the slow creep of the sun from the back of the house to the corner, she would have thought that maybe time wasn't passing at all.

Susan smiled when the baby's light cry turned into a full-on wail; Raven did, indeed, know when it was time to eat, and she had come programmed to let her needs be known. Maybe she didn't need to worry about a thing; she just needed to still herself and learn to flow with the baby's rhythms instead of being so anxious about every detail.

Tammy awoke as Susan brought the baby downstairs. She sat up, adjusted her nursing bra, and reached for Raven with a fatigued smile.

"You seem like you got a little rest," Susan said, noticing she looked a little brighter than she had earlier.

Tammy nodded.

In awe, Susan watched her nurse. She would never share that bond with Raven; they would be two very different kinds of moms, and that would have to be okay. But still, she felt jealous about it sometimes, the biological connection. Would Raven ever really see Susan as her mom, too, especially when she was Black like Tammy and Susan was White? Annoyed with herself at these thoughts when, just minutes ago, she was wrapped up in the magic of motherhood, Susan let them have the moment together, walked past the messy dining room table again, and retreated to her garden.

The first week of Raven's life was rushing by so fast. It had already been four days since they'd brought her home from the hospital. How could it be Friday already? How could it be June? In addition to the official maternity leave in August, Susan had arranged to take the first two weeks off, and part of her couldn't fathom how she could go back and miss all of these moments with Raven. In fact, although it made no sense, her gut told her that she wasn't going back.

Tammy still seemed to have no energy, and breastfeeding was proving to be difficult for her. Even with both of them, they were barely managing. Susan was trying to keep the house neat while Tammy slept, which still seemed to be as often as Raven was sleeping. Susan didn't mind doing all the housework and cooking; she was happy she could do something for her family. Even if

Tammy couldn't keep the house neat when Susan returned to work, it wouldn't be the end of the world. But what did concern her was the fact that even when Raven was sleeping right next to her in the bassinette in the bedroom or the carrier in the living room, Tammy didn't wake when she cried. Not even if Susan let her cry for five solid minutes. Susan always had to physically shake her to wake her up. Once awake, she would just sit there and cry when the baby wouldn't eat. Susan felt helpless. Useless. She could only hope that the few days they had left together would be enough time for Tammy to get the rest she needed because she was worried about how Tammy would care for the baby alone when Susan went back to work on Monday.

Things seemed to get worse over the weekend. On Saturday, Tammy went from crying only when Raven wouldn't eat, saying she was a failure, to crying nearly all the time. Susan had asked her what was wrong, but she never answered; she usually just shook her head and shrugged. No matter how much Susan tried to console her, it was like Tammy couldn't hear her.

On Sunday afternoon, when both Raven and Tammy were asleep, Susan called her district manager, Paula. She needed at least a couple more days. Both Raven and Tammy would see the doctor on Monday. She wasn't sure what two more days would do, especially if Tammy wouldn't even talk to her, but she knew she couldn't let Tammy manage both appointments alone. Tammy would get better. She had to. But right now, she needed extra support.

On Sunday evening, Tammy stopped crying just long enough to announce that she wasn't going to breastfeed anymore. Susan urged her not to make that decision until she saw the doctor, but Tammy's mind was made up. With the biggest burst of energy Susan had seen from her since Raven was born, Tammy sprung up from the couch, headed to the nursery closet, and reappeared with a breast pump and bottles, stating that they'd get formula if that didn't work.

If this was what she needed to do, Susan would support her, even though she worried Tammy would regret it later. She'd already beat herself up so much. While Tammy pumped, Susan sanitized the bottles, looking out at her garden as she stood at the sink. When she was done, she found Tammy crying again, this time expressing how relieved she was about the decision.

"Come on. Come with me. You need a little sunshine." Susan held out her hand, but Tammy didn't move.

"Come on. It's beautiful out." She managed to be a little firmer this time. She was desperate to help Tammy feel better, and this was her only idea.

She had to reach down, take Tammy's hands in her own, and pull a few times before Tammy finally gave in. She walked by Tammy's side as she reluctantly scuffled along toward the back door. Susan looked back; Raven was asleep in her swing. She took a few steps back, grabbing the baby monitor, and Tammy stopped, still in the same spot when Susan returned. With a gentle hand on Tammy's shoulder, she managed to get her out the door and to the garden. It concerned Susan that Tammy hadn't seemed to remember Raven. She hadn't appeared to know she was there at all. It was clear that she could barely manage to function.

Tammy had never appreciated nature quite the way she did, but Susan hoped she would find some comfort in the garden. Be able to feel the energy there. Knowing that a scientific explanation might reach her, Susan reminded her that just ten minutes in the sun every day can make a difference in mood. Tammy sat next to her on the loveseat swing, yet it felt as if she was sitting there alone.

This was not at all as she had pictured their first weeks as mothers. Sure, she knew that they'd be tired. That they'd be rookies at the mom thing. Even that they'd be a mess sometimes. She knew about the hormones Tammy was dealing with, and she hoped it was just a matter of time, but she had not expected a lack of joy from Tammy. She didn't expect Tammy to disappear. Fiona would tell her to sit in the discomfort, but she just wanted to fix it.

Susan was hopeful when Tammy woke up a little more herself on Monday morning and asked Susan to feed Raven while she took her first shower in days. While Susan didn't mind, Tammy hadn't fed the baby even once since they'd switched to bottles. In fact, she had barely held her at all in the last two days.

Raven's appointment was rather uneventful; the doctor assured them that Raven was doing great. But Tammy's appointment wasn't until three o'clock, and they had an hour to wait in between.

"Maybe we should go outside. It's warm," Susan suggested. "I hate just sitting in there for an hour with her. So many germs."

Tammy nodded but just stared at the elevator. Susan could see that she hadn't really heard her.

"You know, I think I might like to visit my floor," Tammy said.

"Great idea. Everyone can meet Raven," Susan said.

"No, I'm just going to go up and quickly say hello," Tammy replied.

"Oh, okay. I can take her outside for a little while. Take her for a walk. Just come get us out there when you're done."

Tammy had already begun to walk away, though. Susan could only hope that visiting her coworkers would be good for her.

But forty-five minutes later, Tammy hadn't come back. As three o'clock grew closer, Susan wracked her brain to remember just what suite Tammy's doctor's appointment was in. The place was a maze, and all the floors looked alike to her. She slung the diaper bag over her shoulder, picked up the carrier, and went to the directory. There were two separate OBGYN suites, and Susan was pretty sure Tammy's was the one on the third floor.

The elevator was slow, and there were so many people waiting that she had to wait for a full load of people to go in and catch the second one that came. When she finally entered the elevator, Raven began to cry. They hadn't planned the day well at all. They should have brought the stroller in. Raven was due to eat at the same time as Tammy's appointment, but how could they have known that when they made the appointment? She reached out to push the button for the third floor, but someone accidentally elbowed her, knocking the diaper bag to the ground.

How on Earth did anyone manage this alone? Clearly, neither of them had any idea what they were in for. People were right; every single thing was different now, right down to the fact that her backpack had suddenly been replaced by a diaper bag. Although she'd had to pee since they went outside, she didn't have that luxury.

Once on the third floor, she looked at the clock on the wall. It was now five past three. Shit. She debated whether to carry a still screaming Raven in the carrier or take her out. Everyone was looking at her. Was it awful to leave her in there screaming? Was it rude to just let her scream? Was she spoiling her if she took her out?

She was concerned about Tammy and wanted to be there for her, but Raven needed her too. Doctors tended to run late; maybe Tammy hadn't even been taken in yet. She placed the carrier on a bench and picked the baby up, only to realize she had no idea how she could carry everything. She wanted to cry, but she took a moment to bounce Raven a little, and it seemed to help some. Her wails turned to mere whimpers.

She was sure she could still make it over there and be there for Tammy, too. She considered placing the baby back in the carrier, but it didn't feel right since she wasn't fully settled down yet. Desperate, she left the carrier on the bench; she would just have to hope it would still be there when she got back.

She walked as fast as she could to the suite; Raven began to cry harder again. Susan glanced back at the carrier but kept walking. When she finally made it to the suite, she was relieved. There appeared to be a half dozen moms with babies, talking with one another and a couple of very pregnant women taking it all in. She was in good company; they were clearly more understanding about the screaming baby than the people in the elevator had been. Still, she hated being on display like this, fat and out of breath, and she was tempted to just turn around and leave.

Tammy wasn't among the waiting mothers, and suddenly, she was sure that a couple of them were looking at her strangely. She had to let it go.

"Can I help you?" The receptionist asked a second time.

"Oh, I'm sorry. Yeah, I..."

"It's okay, being a new mom is like that." The woman smiled. "Do you have an appointment?"

"Not me, my wife. It was for three o'clock. I think she is already in there," Susan explained.

"Oh, okay. Sorry about that. I assumed you were mom," the woman replied.

"I mean, I am. But the appointment isn't for me," Susan continued, feeling flustered.

The woman looked confused, and it felt as if everyone in the room stared at her.

"And what's your wife's name?" The receptionist asked.

"Tammy Bradley."

The woman clicked a few buttons, scanned her computer screen, and nodded. "They already took her in. Feel free to wait. I'm sure mom will appreciate this time to just breathe." She motioned to the seating area. Now, everyone's eyes were definitely on her.

Susan wanted to scream at the woman and tell her she was

Raven's mother, too. That she needed to be more educated if she was going to work with people. She wanted to scream at all of them and ask them if they'd never heard of lesbian mothers. Pausing for a moment, Fiona came to mind; she would've accused her of jumping to conclusions. And maybe she was.

"No, I mean, I was hoping to go in with her." Damn it, she should have been more insistent.

The woman pursed her lips. "Well, okay. You still need to have a seat until someone can come let you in and escort you to the room she's in."

Susan nodded and stood in a quiet corner, bouncing Raven. After five minutes, Raven hadn't calmed down, and she had no choice but to sit among the other moms. She wasn't thrilled about putting the diaper bag on the floor where people's shoes had been, but it was the only way she could reach the bottle.

The bottle quieted Raven, and Susan felt guilty that she'd made her wait as long as she had. She was developing a headache, still had to pee, and desperately wanted just to be back home. It was so much easier to care for Raven in their own home, where things were clean and quiet, and she could just count on everything being right where she needed it – mostly, anyway.

At quarter past three, no one had come back for her. Raven was almost done; at this point, it made more sense to wait until she was finished, then ask about going in again. But at twenty past, Tammy came walking through the door into the waiting room with a big smile on her face. She didn't spot Susan and Raven, and after she checked out at the desk, she started toward the door of the suite.

"Tammy," Susan called to her as Raven squirmed in her arms. From the look on her face, she assumed the appointment had gone well, that she had talked about her mood issues, as they agreed she should.

Tammy looked back and looked as if she was surprised to see

them.

"That was a quick appointment," Susan said. "I got here at five passed. I asked them to let me in with you...but no one ever came to get me."

"Yeah, they took me in a little early," Tammy replied.

"Early? Did you...forget about us?" Susan asked.

"What? No, I just figured I'd pop in real fast, then come get your guys," Tammy replied.

That hadn't been the plan they'd agreed upon, but Susan didn't want to argue.

"Well, can you take her? She just finished eating. It's been..."

"Where's the carrier?"

"I had to leave it on the bench."

"You what?"

"Can you just take her? I have to go pee, like *now*. Just burp her, and I'll grab the carrier on the way back from the bathroom and then come back for you."

Reluctantly, Tammy took Raven and, with a sigh, sat down and patted Raven's back. "I can't believe you left the carrier," she muttered.

As Susan walked away, she heard one of the women in the back whisper, "Oh, that makes more sense. *That's* the mom."

So much for jumping to conclusions. Susan stopped for a minute and looked back; she just had to know what someone who was so incredibly fucking ignorant even looked like. But she couldn't tell who'd said it. She glared in the direction of the entire row and walked away.

Fully feeling the tension in her neck and shoulders now, she walked down the hall and spotted the carrier still on the bench. She supposed if it had been there that long, it would still be there on the way back and continued to the bathroom.

She lingered an extra minute as she sat on the toilet and resisted the urge to cry. How was she going to do this? One trip out of the house with the baby, and she wanted to have a meltdown. After the second knock on the bathroom door, she got up, washed her hands, and told herself to buck up. She retrieved the carrier and headed back to the OBGYN suite.

When Tammy saw her, she stood up and began to hand the baby to her. Raven was crying again, and Tammy no longer had a smile on her face.

Susan shook her head. "I have to wipe down the carrier."

"I'll do it, I'll do it. Please, just take her." Tammy sounded almost angry. Desperate.

Susan took Raven into her arms, and Tammy stood there for a minute, watching as she quieted the baby.

"The disinfecting wipes are in the back pocket. Can you do the carrier and the bottom of the diaper bag?"

Tammy nodded but seemed robotic as she followed through. Raven was asleep by the time the carrier was wiped down and dried, and Susan was grateful. She buckled the baby in. Tammy had the diaper bag and was heading out the door. Why did it feel as if they were an afterthought to her?

Susan caught up with Tammy; she seemed so happy again when she'd come out of her appointment, and now she wasn't herself again. Susan was exhausted trying to keep up.

Tammy just stared out the window as they drove home.

"How did your appointment go?" Susan finally asked after they settled in at home.

"Fine, Susan. Clean bill of health. I don't know why you thought you needed to go in with me," Tammy replied.

"Aww, I just thought..." She knew she had to tread lightly. "You haven't been feeling yourself. I was just worried. I thought maybe there was something he could do to help. Did you talk to him about it like we agreed?" She knew the question was a risk, but she didn't see any way around it; she was worried about her wife. Hell, she was worried about all of them.

"Didn't have to." Tammy beamed.

"What do you mean?" Susan asked.

"I know the hormones have been kicking me in the butt, sure, but I figured it out," Tammy replied.

"Figured what out?" Susan asked.

"What I need to make me feel better," Tammy answered.

"That's great!" Susan replied, feeling hopeful yet confused. "You know I'll help any way I can."

"I'm glad you said that, actually, because I'm wondering what you think the chances would be of you taking maternity leave *now* instead of in August. I think I need to go back to work. If you take maternity leave now, Raven will be old enough to get into the hospital daycare by the time your leave is up."

Susan could see the tension fall from Tammy's face as she spoke, but personally, the thought of daycare made her want to panic. She was silent for a minute. It was the last thing she ever expected to hear Tammy say.

"Wow. I...I, well, I don't know," Susan faltered.

Tears started down Tammy's face, and she shook her head, looking lost. Because Susan could count the number of times she'd seen Tammy cry on one hand, it scared her to see her like this. She scooted over and rubbed Tammy's back. What the hell was she going to do? She felt panic rising in her chest. She was supposed to go back next week. But then, she heard it.

It's all going to work out. You have to trust.

It was becoming more and more frequent, and every time it happened, Susan still looked around the room as if she might see who'd spoken the words. This time, the voice gave her a sense of calm.

"I think I just need to go back to work, Babe," Tammy repeated.

"I just felt so...I don't know, being back on the floor...*that* made me feel better. Like myself. You know I've wanted children all my life. I've known that since I was little. And I've been feeling like such a failure. But when I got back on that floor at work, it hit me. I'm not a failure; I'm just meant to be a working mom."

"I can understand that." It made so much sense, and it was such a feminist issue. Tammy had a deep maternal instinct but was driven, too. How had either of them thought Tammy would be happy not working, even for a short time? Maybe it was because, even though the world had come a long way, women were taught that motherhood was supposed to look a certain way.

"You can?" Tammy asked.

Susan nodded. "Totally. And, honestly, I would *love* to stay home. As much as I love my store, home is my happy place. I know it's not permanent, but I'd be thrilled about having a few months here with Raven. And Paula has always been supportive of our family, but at such a late date, she might have to get approval from corporate, which may raise some questions. It might help if we had legal paperwork in place."

Tammy just nodded.

Her mind raced with thoughts of calling her district manager. There was no time to do anything about legal paperwork now, so she just had to put that out of her mind. But even the thought of leaving her beloved store in someone else's hands without any preparation in her wake was hard to swallow. She truly wanted to be with her daughter, but leaving the store was almost like leaving a child, too. She was proud of what she'd made of her store. Sure, it would have happened in a few months, anyway, but she would have had time to train whoever would take her place for those three months.

"What about your job? Can you go back early just like that? Not take your maternity leave now, when you were already approved for it?" Susan asked.

"I talked to my supervisor when I visited the floor. She said she'll talk to HR. It shouldn't be a problem; they really need me," Tammy replied.

"Okay," Susan replied, mind still racing about what she needed to do.

"But do *you* think you can get it to work on your end?" Tammy asked.

"I don't want you to worry about it; let me call Paula," Susan answered.

"Thank you for being...thank you." The look in Tammy's eyes said it all.

Susan had the opportunity to make everything okay for Tammy, and she wasn't about to let her down. Sometimes, family was about sacrifice, and if she could save Tammy from her pain, she could overcome her reservations about leaving her store in someone else's hands, even if it was sudden.

After spending nearly an hour planning out exactly what to say to Paula, Susan finally picked up the phone. But when she did, she found herself dialing Kevin's number instead. He'd be home by now after having picked up his girls. Although she hadn't even stopped to think about it before she dialed and wasn't sure what he could do to help, she needed to spill everything that was going on before she approached Paula.

It turned out her instincts to reach out to Kevin had been the perfect choice. It seemed he had some information that could help her. In the short time she'd been away, Paula had come into the store a few times and talked with Kevin and Sanjana. She'd mentioned Susan's upcoming leave and someone named Robert who, she said, might be a candidate for the assistant manager position. Paula had explained that she hadn't wanted to bother Susan with it when she had a new baby but that Robert was someone he had trained himself at another store, and it was likely that he could start almost immediately.

At first, Susan's heart fell. No matter how hard she'd tried, she hadn't been able to keep an assistant manager to save her life. While Paula had always given Susan the power to hire someone on her own, it looked like she was stepping in now. But Kevin assured her that this could be a good thing, considering her situation, and advised Susan that, when she talked to Paula, she could tell her that Kevin was willing to help acclimate Robert to the store if Paula approved her early leave. The last thing Kevin said to her before she hung up was to trust it would all work out, which left her in awe. He'd spoken nearly the same words she'd heard in her head not long ago.

Susan swallowed hard, called Paula, and explained her predicament. She spoke confidently, asking about Robert and explaining her strategy to let Kevin help Robert get used to the store. Paula was agreeable to all of it. While he had a few questions for Susan about logistics and told her she would have to come in to meet Robert herself at some point soon, Paula felt confident that the plan was feasible and that they could all work together to make it all come together smoothly.

When Susan hung up the phone, she broke down in sobs, a mixture of gratitude and relief flooding through her. All she'd had to do was trust.

CHAPTER EIGHTEEN

Since Tammy would be working the day shift, and Susan was already awake early every morning to feed Raven, she'd planned the perfect breakfast for Tammy's first day back. She'd made a special trip to the store to get all Tammy's favorite things, and now, happily puttered around in the kitchen while Raven slept in her carrier on the table.

As she balled melon, something she'd never done in her life, Susan decided that she intended to learn to love working in her new adorable kitchen. In fact, she decided that being home for the next three months gave her the perfect opportunity to make wiser choices with food, although she still had no intention of touching fruit or vegetables.

Although she'd never been very domestic, she remembered the moments spent cooking with her gramma and mom whenever she stepped foot in the room. Although those years had been spent making mainly sugary treats and fried food, she felt powerful knowing she could be the first generation to provide her family with healthy meals. She envisioned long afternoons spent cooking with her mother and chattering over tea in the garden afterward.

It was good to see Tammy happily bouncing down the stairs at five-thirty in her teddy bear scrubs. Showered and ready, Susan hadn't seen her look this cheerful in weeks.

"Morning. I made you a fruit salad and picked up some yogurt and cottage cheese." Susan pointed toward the fridge.

Tammy wrinkled her nose as she pulled out the fruit salad, then put it back. "I think I just want a bagel and cream cheese this morning."

As much as Tammy was constantly nagging at Susan about carbs, it ticked Susan off that she suddenly preferred a bagel over the healthy breakfast she'd prepared. No matter how hard she tried to please Tammy, it felt like she could never succeed. She hadn't even gotten a thank you for the meal, not to mention the grocery shopping, cleaning, and taking on nearly everything in the last few days. But she didn't say a word. She didn't need praise, but it would have been nice if Tammy had noticed and pitched in a little rather than spending her last few days laying out her scrubs and texting with Tyler and Stacy about work.

With a plan in place to eat healthier, Susan had only bought one last gigantic garlic bagel fresh from the bakery instead of a whole package. She thought about being sweet and letting Tammy have it but was too annoyed.

"We're all out," she lied, feeling a little spiteful as she thought about savoring the delicious cream cheese bagel combo after Tammy left.

Tammy clicked her tongue and sighed. "I'll just get one at Dunkin Donuts."

"I made you a lunch, too. It's on the bottom shelf in the fridge," Susan said, keeping her cool.

"Thanks." Tammy grabbed the salad and stuffed it in her lunch bag, rifled around the counter for her keys, then headed for the door to put her shoes on, but spent several minutes fluffing her shiny bob in the mirror first. While it was good to see her upbeat, Susan couldn't help but notice it was almost like Susan wasn't even there. She was pretty sure she hadn't even made eye contact with her since she'd come downstairs; it was as if she simply couldn't get out of the house fast enough.

"Okay, I'm going." Tammy had the door open and waved across the room.

"Hey!" Susan called.

"What?"

It was bad enough that Tammy was all but ignoring her; no kiss goodbye, no I love you. But, once again, she acted like she didn't even know Raven existed.

"You're not going to say goodbye to your daughter?" Susan asked.

"Well, I didn't want to wake her. She won't know the difference anyway." Tammy blew the baby a kiss across the room and shut the door behind her.

Susan was torn between feeling hurt that she'd been so distant and relieved that she was gone and hated herself for feeling both. She supposed she was being petty. Tammy was always telling her that she made everything about herself. And maybe she did sometimes. She couldn't truly understand what Tammy was going through, but they'd built a family together; this was about her, too. But she just had to get on with her day and focus on Raven.

When Raven slept, she slept solidly. This allowed Susan to do what she needed to around the house without worrying about waking her. She was determined to refresh not only the house but herself to give her whole family a boost.

Her first order of business was to invite some sun into the house. She slowly walked through each room with her steaming mug of tea, opening up each curtain and window as she went and taking in the way the sun illuminated each room in their sweet little house. The old her had always been more attracted to the darkness, rarely even thinking to open up curtains every day and happily hiding in her cave. But the house had changed her. She welcomed the rhythm of the day; waking up with the sun and watching it cast shadows across each room as it circled the house, until it eventually faded and went to sleep again, gave her a new sense of peace.

The staleness that had enveloped the house was replaced with the fresh smells of spring as she took genuine pleasure in cleaning the downstairs. Although Tammy kept saying that some of the house's features were outdated, they happened to be the details that Susan loved the most. The checkered country border was one of her favorite things about the room. The scalloped woodwork over the kitchen sink and the tiny pantry made her feel much more at home than the townhouse ever had.

After doing dishes and making the floors and countertops spotless, she emptied every cupboard, cleaning out all the unhealthy food as she went. Although she knew it meant wasted money, it gave her great satisfaction to empty half-eaten boxes of sugary cereals, chips, and cheese puffs into the trash. As an educated woman, she knew that most of the stuff she ate was terrible for her and understood what she should eat if she was going to avoid becoming the third generation with diabetes. She'd known for years but simply hadn't had the willpower to make the necessary changes. Raven gave her that willpower. She would do it this time.

She held some things in her hand, staring at them for a minute before deciding whether they really had to go. Surely, having tacos once a week was still okay, even if they were flour tortillas. She placed the taco shells and an unopened box of Thin Mints back in the cupboard. Everything in moderation.

After the last cupboard was done, there was still time to indulge in her bagel and cream cheese before Raven would need to eat again. She watched it closely as it browned, making sure that the garlic got perfectly crispy, yet not blackened, then sat down at the dining room table. Knowing it would be her last bagel made every bite more delicious. She watched the curtains blow in the breeze. Even a dining room had always felt too formal to her; she preferred a cozy eat-in kitchen, but with the sidewall of windows where she could watch the birds chatter away, she had to admit this was rather homey. She still wasn't sure if she liked the burgundy paint, but maybe it was growing on her. Putting up a few more pictures would help make it even sweeter.

With half of her bagel left, she jumped up, retrieving the magnetic list pad from the front of the fridge. She felt like such an adult as she scratched out a list of healthy foods to pick up from the grocery store: chicken and fresh garlic, fresh produce for Tammy, and an assortment of nuts to satisfy her snack cravings. Raven was running low on diapers, and there wasn't much left in the cupboards, so she'd have to make a trip soon. Fiona popped into her head the moment her pen hit the paper, so after writing out a dozen things to get her started on her journey to being healthier, she flipped over the page and started a letter. Fiona would be amused to receive a letter scrawled out on a grocery list adorned with spices along the border instead of their usual animal motif.

June 12, 2001

Dear Fiona,

How have you been? Anything new? Everything feels new here. Raven has already changed so much in just two weeks. I'm SO UTTERLY IN LOVE with this gremlin that I just want to cry sometimes. Tammy went back to work today instead of taking maternity leave, and I took mine early. I'm happy that it all worked out because it feels awesome to be here in our sweet little house, making a home for our new daughter. My return date is September 10.

I'm not an expert, but I'm pretty sure Tammy has postpartum depression. I'm trying to help her as best I can, but she's stubborn about getting help. I just wish that she would talk to me! But I honestly think that just being back to work will be what helps her most. This is a whole new chapter of my life, and it just feels so profound. I honestly don't even have the words... I'm going to make a fresh new start with everything. Be healthier, be a great mom, be a better wife. I included Raven's first picture in with this letter, but expect many, many more. She's just changing so fast; it's crazy!

Love, Susan

As she took her last bite of bagel, she questioned if she could succeed in giving up all the delicious things she had ever loved. She usually didn't even make it one full day when she had attempted to eat healthy. She'd just spoiled this day with the bagel, so she'd officially start eating better tomorrow. One day. Just one full day would be a start.

Her concerns were quickly replaced with joy and excitement when she heard Raven's tiny cry. Every time was still a reminder that she was a mom to an amazing little creature.

"You're timing is perfect. I don't even need a clock with you around," Susan babbled at Raven as she picked her up, still in awe about how compact she was in her arms.

It had been three hours since Raven had woken up. Already, her eyes were open so much wider this week; Susan could see that they were light brown, unlike Tammy's, which were much deeper brown. The doctors would say babies couldn't see or focus well early on, but the way Raven looked at her made Susan sure that they could connect in their own unique way, even communicate. It was funny; she'd been so worried about how Raven would bond with her, and now, her greatest fear was about the baby's bond with Tammy. She simply couldn't understand how Tammy wasn't just as excited as she was about every little thing Raven did.

She was satisfied with what she'd accomplished when she fell into bed that night. She'd gotten through her kitchen to-do list, tidied the dining room, and even found time to sweep and vacuum the floors, her least favorite household task. Tomorrow, she would tackle the bathrooms, bills, laundry, and maybe even get around to hanging more pictures in the dining room, although that sort of task wasn't exactly her strong suit.

As the week went on, Susan quickly learned that not only did she tend to get carried away when she made her to-do list for the next day, but that she hadn't factored in the possibility of Raven having a fussy day or the recurring things like laundry and dishes piling up. By the time her first week home came to an end, she'd given up on making lists altogether, using the notepad only to scrawl random thoughts to Fiona here and there, and, at the end of the week, finally mailed them all in one messy bundle. Maybe the house wasn't as neat as she would like, but she was just happy if there were clean bottles and clothes for Raven. All in all, she was proud of the rhythm she'd found around the house but was more exhausted than she could have fathomed was humanly possible.

"How was your first week back?" Susan asked Tammy when she walked through the door on Friday afternoon.

"Really good, but I'm *so* tired," Tammy replied as she sorted through the mail, then began to head upstairs.

"Hey, I really need a shower. Can you just sit with Raven for a while?"

"You can just bring the monitor up there with you. It's okay to do that, you know," Tammy replied.

Susan wasn't so sure Tammy was right about that. The thought of leaving Raven alone made her sick. But that wasn't really the point, anyway.

"But, I mean...don't you want to...you haven't seen her all day," Susan said, treading carefully.

"I just told you I'm tired," Tammy snapped.

Susan didn't want to argue, especially not around the baby, but this was ridiculous. She had to make some time to spend with her daughter.

"I am too, Tam. Exhausted. I deserve fifteen minutes to take a shower before I cook supper," she retorted, knowing Tammy would have no intention of cooking.

"Fine," Tammy replied, flopping onto the couch across the room from where Raven lay asleep in the swing. She didn't even look over at her, immediately getting out her phone instead. Susan was hating that phone more and more every day.

There was so much that needed saying, but instead, Susan escaped to the shower and cried. She shouldn't have snapped back, but this was a new level of exhaustion for her, and she already felt as if she might just break down and stop functioning if something didn't change. It wasn't only everything she had to do, but she was worried. She couldn't let this go on much longer before she confronted Tammy about how concerned she was, not only for Tammy but for all of them. When Tammy acknowledged that the baby existed, it was as if she didn't like her. Almost like a teenager might act toward a new sibling.

When Susan attempted to broach the subject, she did so strategically, focusing on the baby and asking Tammy if she wanted to take over simple things like bath time. Maybe Tammy would snap out of it and see what she was missing if she talked about the mushy baby things.

She never used the words postpartum depression. She knew Tammy's feelings about therapists and couldn't help but agree, so what was she supposed to do? Susan could understand if Tammy didn't want to see a professional who might treat her like she was crazy or try to medicate her, but why couldn't Tammy at least talk to her? She already had to walk on eggshells with Tammy as it was, though; it would be ugly if she pushed too hard. Surely, this would pass anyway. How long did postpartum depression even last? She could do some research if she could find time to go to the library or the store. In the meantime, she would have to ride it out and support Tammy as she struggled through this.

After cooking supper and cleaning up, feeding and changing Raven two more times, then giving her a bath, the feeling of accomplishment she'd had earlier was replaced with despair. Tammy had retreated to the bedroom right after supper, seemingly without a thought about whether or not Susan needed help with anything. She couldn't believe it was only week one and had no idea how she would do this for the next three months. Longer if Tammy couldn't find her way out of the hole she was in.

In her exhaustion, Susan couldn't bring herself to join Tammy in the bedroom. Being near her would just fuel more anger; she needed to smoke a joint first. She was trying with everything in her not to be angry, but wasn't succeeding. She took the monitor and a joint out to her garden and cried. Again. What if she couldn't do this? How was it humanly possible to go on being this exhausted much longer? The fact that Tammy was the one who'd wanted to be a mother so desperately kept running through her mind. She knew she was a terrible person to even think that way. Of course, she wanted Raven, too, but she'd never signed up to be a single mother.

She calmed down a little more with each puff and reminded herself that, as hard as things had ever gotten, she'd always gotten through. The marijuana allowed her to relax enough to finally go into the bedroom, and slept solidly for three hours before the baby woke her up the first time. Then, she managed to get two more hours before she was up again at five, this time for the day.

Since Tammy had the weekend off, Susan had planned to catch up on some solid, uninterrupted sleep. The broken sleep she was getting now still wasn't cutting it. But her vision didn't quite match the reality. Trying to understand that Tammy needed rest, too, Susan set up camp with Raven downstairs while Tammy slept. She needed to be more patient and give her wife time to adjust.

By week three of being at home, guilt plagued Susan. She was actually coming to hate it when Tammy had a day off. What kind of person was relieved when their wife left the house? Not only was she able to accomplish household tasks more easily when Tammy was at work, but she was quickly finding the energy in the house was less heavy. She was no stranger to depression herself, but she wasn't sure how many more times she could handle finding Tammy in bed crying, refusing to get up and even try. No matter what Susan said, she was always inconsolable.

Aside from the marijuana, her garden was one of her greatest comforts. Unreturned messages from her mother and DJ had filled her voicemail, first on her home phone, then her cell. Although she hadn't found the time to give her garden as much attention as it needed, and some of the spring flowers had wilted to nothing, many of the wildflowers were just beginning to pop up, giving her hope that she could make another go of it. While she'd never considered herself a morning person before, she loved her new routine. Waking up before Raven, she was often out there before dawn, which was a gorgeous time of day now that Summer was here.

This morning, instead of her usual cup of tea, she brought the mail from Fiona to the garden with her. She'd received it yesterday but had never found time to open it. This wasn't just a letter but a padded yellow envelope. Susan slid her finger under the seal and, although she felt something else inside, pulled out Fiona's letter first.

June 21, 2001

Hey Susan,

Congratulations on your beautiful daughter. She's every bit as magical as her mudder; I can feel it when I hold her picture. Magic can come with some serious scaries, but you will both be ok. You will find what you've been looking for in her if you look hard enough. Enjoy every single minute of this season. Pay attention to EVERYTHING. Don't take anything for granted. You're right. It all changes so fast. Do make sure you are protecting yourself in whatever ways you need to, but don't worry about petty things. For instance, you don't want to be your niece's godmother anyway, and you know it. That's not you. You're way more enchanted than that – you're more like her fairy godmother. Try to focus less on how you thought it was supposed to be and use all your powers to make the most of how it is. I made you and Raven each a little gift to manage the scaries.

Love, Fiona

Susan reached into the envelope again. Everything Fiona shared with her left her in awe, and while she wasn't materialistic, she was sentimental, so the little trinkets Fiona had sent over the years were among her most cherished items. She gazed at the two dreamcatchers that she held in her hand and smiled. A tiny, silver fairy dangled from each. One in earth tones and one full of color, it was obvious which would go above her daughter's crib and which would go above her own bed. Fiona knew her so well; although they were only sporadic, Susan's nightmares always left her struggling when they resurfaced. As she sat listening to the windchimes tinkle, she was startled by Tammy's voice.

"Good morning."

Susan turned quickly to see Tammy standing on the flagstone in her fluffy, white robe with a mug of tea in one hand and a mug of coffee in the other.

"Peace offering?" Tammy asked, extending the mug of tea with a smile, exposing the dimple that Susan hadn't seen in weeks.

Susan arched her eyebrows in confusion.

"I know I haven't really been..." Tammy paused, looking into the garden for a moment. "...here," she finished with a sad shrug.

Susan reached for the mug and met Tammy's eyes. "Thanks for the tea. That was really sweet."

Tammy sat beside her in silence and turned the patio chair to face Susan.

"I'm sorry. I honestly don't know where I am," Tammy said quietly, looking into her coffee.

Susan could hear the tears in her voice and reached her free hand over to touch Tammy's arm.

"I know what it's like...to be somewhere else. It can be hard to come back, especially when you don't know where you even are. Sometimes, we don't even really know what's wrong."

Tammy looked at her again, something like relief in her eyes, nodding, silent tears streaming down her face.

"I never thought anyone could understand that, Susan. Never. I certainly don't understand it."

"I've kind of known that feeling my whole life. That...not really being here sometimes. Always trying to get back to be with the people you love," Susan confessed.

"Seriously?" Tammy asked.

Susan nodded silently. It was funny what you assumed people knew about you, especially the most important people in your life.

"You've never told me that," Tammy said, with sadness in her eyes.

Susan shrugged. "It's almost impossible to explain to someone who's never been there." Tammy had opened up to her just enough to remind her that she wasn't a villain; she was just struggling. And, in turn, Susan had the opportunity to let Tammy see inside her own heart in a way she'd never been able to. She hadn't been aware how much she'd needed that until her truth had hit the air. Isolating herself had been heavier than she'd realized.

"I don't know how anyone...how you can...I'm so lost." She let out a quiet sob and paused. "I've always been so put together. If I wanted something, I did whatever it took to get things done. And now..."

Susan gave her time, but Tammy never finished the sentence. It was apparent that Tammy was trying to pull herself out of a dark place.

"I know. Trust me, I know," Susan assured her.

"I'm going to do better. I mean, I'm going to try to do better. I can't be...this. This poor excuse for a mother and wife. I refuse to be a failure," Tammy said, sniffling and wiping her nose on the sleeve of her robe.

"Hey. Don't be so hard on yourself, Babe. Raven is only a month old. You're *not* a failure. You can't forget how much you've been through. Hormones alone are nuts. This is all new. We're adjusting. Not to mention the screaming gremlin." She smirked, surprised as the gentle words came from her mouth. Her anger was replaced with something far softer when she saw Tammy this vulnerable.

"Looking at you, you wouldn't know that. The way you take care of everything around here," Tammy replied.

"Are you kidding me? Have you not seen the pile of dishes in the sink? Or the dining room table? This place is a fucking disaster."

"Still. Just the way that you take care of Raven. You would never know it was new for you at all. I was supposed to have it all together the way you do," Tammy said, shaking her head.

"This isn't a competition, though. We're *partners*. We're both exhausted; we just have to figure it out together so neither of us gets so lost that..." Susan started.

Tammy nodded. "You're right. So, let's do something as a family this weekend. Anything. I have the weekend off. Let's just take Raven for a quick walk in the park or something."

"Have your parents already left for Martha's Vineyard? It might be nice to visit them before the go," Susan suggested.

"I think they leave for the summer house on Sunday. It's probably better this way, though."

"What do you mean? I know you want Raven to know her grandparents and uncle," Susan insisted.

Tammy shook her head. "I'm done trying."

Susan knew how much Tammy's strained relationship with her father hurt her, but it worried her that Tammy was just ready to give up all of a sudden when family meant so much to her.

"It's too hard. My father makes it impossible for me to try with any of them."

"Maybe we should take them up on their offer to spend a weekend with them at the summer house," Susan replied.

"Don't push this, Susan, okay? *They* didn't invite us; my mom invited us. You saw how he was when they came to meet Raven. I don't think I even have a family anymore. *This* is my family."

Maybe Tammy just needed some space to grieve the loss of the idyllic family she'd always dreamed about, but Susan remembered something when Tammy brought up her parents' visit. It wasn't her father who seemed different the day that they'd come to meet Raven; his judgmental air had been the same as it always was. But Tammy had pulled herself out of her hole, gotten out of her sweats, and put on an act for them just long enough for their visit, then had crashed right back down into the dreary place she'd been in before they'd arrived. Now, it seemed pretty clear; Tammy was done trying because it was too much work to hide the fact that she was depressed from them.

As they spent the weekend together, Susan even found the courage to bring up the topic of legal paperwork again. She was compassionate about the fact that Tammy was already dealing with a lot in her own mind, but it simply didn't feel fair that Susan should be left sitting with this fear any longer than necessary. She deserved the peace of mind that being recognized as Raven's legal adoptive mother would bring to her. Although Tammy swore they would see a lawyer as soon as she felt better, that answer didn't sit well in Susan's gut. She couldn't keep putting her own needs aside for Tammy, no matter how much Tammy was struggling.

Susan thought she could feel a subtle shift in Tammy some days, even if there was no romance between them. They'd attempted to make love once since Raven had been born, but it was clear that they both sensed something was missing. Although Tammy's disinterest in sex was another red flag that something was seriously wrong, the lack of sex bothered Susan far less than some of the other things. Sometimes, it was like there were two Tammys.

There was the Tammy that Susan could see was working to be

a stronger mother and wife, making an effort to pick up groceries on the way home or feed Raven, even after a long day at work, instead of just coming straight home and shutting herself in the bedroom and sleeping for twelve hours straight. The Tammy who remembered to kiss her goodnight and sing to the baby. But sometimes, it was hard not to let the bad outweigh the good because the other Tammy was downright intolerable.

It was pronounced when Tammy had a difficult day at work. On those days, Susan felt as if she had to walk on eggshells, never knowing what would set Tammy off. Not only did she snap at Susan over the least little thing, but she didn't even want to look at Raven. Sometimes, it was exactly like Tammy had explained it; it was as if Tammy wasn't even there. Even worse, sometimes it was like Susan wished she wasn't.

It felt like precious chunks of time were being wasted with these ups and downs. She knew they'd both regret it later if these milestone months were overshadowed by their struggle when they should be joyous times. Still, Susan was the first to admit she'd never been the most patient woman. So, on the bad days, she had to just grit her teeth and remind herself that Tammy was probably just doing the best she could, just like she was.

CHAPTER NINETEEN

Although the intense heat had kept Susan from taking Raven into the garden throughout July, the first of August brought the relief of cooler weather. People often regarded August as the hottest, deepest month of summer, but this was when Susan always felt the first hints of autumn creeping in, and she intended to share the summer garden with Raven as much as she could before the flowers started to fade away. After strapping Raven into her carrier, Susan grabbed a joint and headed to the patio. She placed the carrier far enough away that the smoke wouldn't reach the baby and sat in her chair, proudly admiring her thriving patch of wildflowers. Tammy thought they looked messy, preferring the rings of spring daffodils and tulips around the trees, but the colorful, untamed blend of coneflowers, milkweed, and zinnias was just perfect as far as Susan was concerned.

Although Tammy had started taking double shifts again despite her exhaustion, she was only working first shift today, and Susan expected her home in about a half hour. As worried as Susan was, it never went well when she expressed her concern to Tammy. Instead, she welcomed the long days alone with Raven. She took a few tokes to help herself prepare herself for Tammy's arrival home. Which Tammy would she get today?

"How was your day?" Susan asked when Tammy walked through the door.

"It was work," Tammy replied flatly, passing Raven without a glance and walking to the kitchen.

Susan tried to read her as she followed her. "Hard day?"

Tammy tossed her lunch bag and keys onto the counter. "Just tired, I guess. Working with sick children is a lot."

Her expression told Susan that she was mildly annoyed, but Susan wanted to help. "I can imagine. Maybe the doubles are too much for you," she suggested, treading lightly.

"I don't think it's that. I'm fine when I'm there. But once I step away...I don't know. I think too much." Tammy shook her head as if in a fog.

"If you cut back, you could return to the gym like you wanted. Take that time for something that makes you feel better," Susan suggested, pushing a little further.

Tammy shrugged. "I guess."

Tammy's blatant retreat from her family had caused Susan some concern. She questioned whether it was just the inevitable progression of their complex family dynamics, Tammy's depression, or a combination of the two. But Tammy's apathy about returning to the gym made it evident that Tammy wasn't herself.

Tammy didn't seem too upset as Susan tested the waters. Since her wife seemed to hear what she was saying today, maybe pushing even further could help.

"Do you think...maybe working with children is too much for you? Now that you're a mom, I mean? Maybe it would be easier on you if you went back to the post-surgical floor." She could easily imagine that witnessing the worst possibilities, especially when Tammy was already struggling with mood issues, could overwhelm a new mother.

Instantly, Susan saw one Tammy vanish, and the other one appear as Tammy looked at her wild-eyed.

"I'm just worried about you..." Susan tried to extinguish the fire that she had clearly started.

But Tammy cut her off, holding up one hand to stop her. "First, you get on me about the gym when let's be honest, you're no one to talk, and now you're telling me I can't do my job?" Tammy asked with a steely tone.

She'd become familiar enough with Tammy's moods to know

she needed to stop talking immediately. Too often, she'd tried to explain herself but only managed to further upset Tammy. She was relieved when Tammy merely mumbled under her breath and walked away, letting it end there. Even though it wasn't even supper time, Tammy retreated to bed for the evening as she often did.

Susan was still wondering how long postpartum depression lasted. If only she was at the store, she could find a book about it. Raven was only two months old, but it had felt like an eternity already. Maybe she was selfish, but she didn't know how long she could handle Tammy's mood swings. She didn't expect the three of them to go frolic in her wildflowers, but she didn't think it was too much to expect some sweet moments as they built a family.

After putting Raven down for a nap the next day, Susan took a few hits from a joint, watered her garden, and tidied the house to get herself out of her funk before DJ and Ashley came after lunch.

While she liked to tell herself keeping everything inside was easier, a part of her knew she could only bottle things up for so long. It wasn't, however, obvious to her how badly she needed the company until she saw DJ's smiling face at her front door. She fought tears as DJ hugged her hello. Just the thought of having another adult to talk to was comforting.

Since DJ had the summer off, she'd been visiting every Friday, and seeing Ashley and Raven together, future friends, always made Susan smile. Each week, Susan rehearsed what she might share before DJ's arrival. But since there were so many things she refused to admit, there was no point in opening up at all if she could only utter half-truths. She knew DJ and Matt had struggled to adapt to family life, too, but somehow, it felt like admitting these things meant failure, and she had to maintain the hope that there was still a chance that she and Tammy could turn things around. She'd always noticed that something changed once a truth hit the air, as if saying it aloud made it true. So, she thought it best not to speak these particular things into existence.

As usual, the visit started off great. With the knowledge that her maternity leave would soon be coming to an end, Susan could hear the relatable emotion in DJ's voice as she talked about going back to work in September. For a moment, she thought maybe she could open up after all but lost her courage, and when the topic changed, she grew irritated by the same stale conversations they had every week. Even if Raven was the center of her world, she didn't want to discuss diapers and teething and feeding schedules.

Did it make her heartless that she was already sick of the stock phrases that you could always count on hearing? *"She's gotten so big. She looks just like so and so. Is she sleeping through the night? Is she a good baby?"* Susan always rolled her eyes at that one. It was impossible for a baby to be bad. At Raven's check-ups, she hadn't really given a shit that she'd gained 1.8 pounds and a half inch. Of course, she cared that her daughter was healthy, but was something wrong with her because she didn't squeal with delight every time the child so much as farted? She played the part, chattering on about all the things that good mothers talked about: the different types of crying she'd identified, how Raven could hold her head up now, and how Raven was doing well with the bottle.

But, when DJ and Ashley left that day, Susan felt lonelier than ever. That's how it had been for most of her life; she'd felt just as lonely around others, even those most important to her.

The following week, Raven's check-up allowed Susan to see that she wasn't heartless after all. It was a relief when she broke down sobbing after getting the baby settled into the car. At her one-month appointment, Raven had received just one vaccine. *That*, Susan had been able to handle. She soothed Raven quickly after just one poke, but today had been different. Susan had counted; the nurse had stuck her daughter six times. After the third, Susan was convinced she could rip the nurse's throat out with her bare hands had she not been using them to hold Raven. She imagined herself a much darker Witch when it came to protecting her daughter. Raven was crying so hard that she'd gone silent, and Susan had been convinced for a moment or two that she'd stopped breathing. She had tried to ask the nurse to stop, or at least wait, but the nurse finished anyway with three more needles. When the nurse said she was done, Susan turned the baby around to snuggle her and wanted to cry, too, but she didn't cry in front of others; she just didn't. Instead, she glared at the nurse as she told Susan that they could check out whenever they were ready.

It took her over a half hour to regain her composure enough to drive. Knowing that Raven would sleep pretty solidly after all the shots, Susan had planned a visit to the store, but now, all she wanted was to get her girl home. She'd been visiting the store occasionally, usually when Kevin was working, and her visits always brought mixed feelings. On the one hand, seeing the displays and the shiny new titles made her miss her job like crazy. Yet, as the end of her maternity leave grew closer, she already grieved staying home with Raven, too. Mostly, an odd feeling washed over her every time she thought about her return to work. Maybe it was merely that she couldn't imagine being away from Raven and hated the idea of putting a three-month-old in daycare, but something told her that she wouldn't return to work on September tenth.

Holding Fiona's sage advice close to her heart to stay in the moment, Susan promised herself she would try to push it all out of her mind and enjoy Raven. With six rolls of film ready to go, Susan was also determined to capture as many moments as possible. September tenth didn't exist yet, but she always had today.

Quickly using the first four rolls of film in as many weeks, Susan had to laugh at herself. If she was this intent on getting so many pictures now, when the baby barely moved, how much film would she need later on? Still, she couldn't resist capturing every adorable outfit, every new expression, and every posed position. When they weren't in the garden, they spent most of their days in the cozy living room. Although she did her best to stay present, she couldn't imagine how she'd pull herself away from the haven she'd created. Everything she needed was there. She'd been adding more and more titles to the built-in bookshelf since they'd moved into the house. And despite the housework that needed to be done, she indulged in long afternoons of reading with the natural light of the bay window shining on her pages while Raven napped in her swing. Together, with the comfort of soft blankets and pillows and some of Raven's toys, this was her happy place.

Today, she'd nodded off herself for a few minutes as she read and couldn't help but smile when she was awakened to Raven's soft whimper. After a bottle and a diaper change, Susan decided it was time for more pictures. Raven had been getting stronger and stronger, and although she hadn't quite mastered it yet, she'd been getting better and better at holding her head up, and Susan hadn't captured it on film yet. After laying out the blanket with the forest animals that Fiona had sent, Susan lay Raven on her tummy, then dropped down on the floor in front of her, propping herself up on her elbows, on a mission to get some perfect pictures to send to Fiona. She looked especially sweet today in her grass-green onesie with the bunnies, and Susan couldn't help but chuckle to herself that the theme matched the blanket.

With the camera pointed at Raven, Susan scooted forward slightly and began to make silly noises to get the baby's attention. Raven began to wobble her head toward the sound, trying with all her might to find that newfound muscle strength in her neck, with a determined look in her light brown eyes. When she finally stopped wobbling, holding her head fully upright, she wore an expression that Susan would have sworn was pride or, at the very least, awe. Susan snapped away as Raven held strong and locked eyes with her. She couldn't believe how many moments like this that Tammy was missing.

She tried to be understanding, knowing what Tammy was going through, but it was difficult for Susan to understand. She herself wanted to be with her daughter every moment she possibly could, but sometimes, when Tammy came home, it was apparent that she had to make an effort to pay attention to Raven. Tammy seemed to be trying, but every interaction between her and the baby appeared more routine than joyful. Maybe Susan could understand that diapers and bottles were more mundane, but she rarely even saw a spark of tenderness when Raven babbled away, something Susan couldn't get enough of.

Being present with Raven eased the feeling that gnawed away at her gut every time she thought of returning to work and even helped her to move past the growing concerns about Raven's adoption. In awe about how much she enjoyed her daughter's existence, there was a part of her that wished she could remain a stay-at-home mom forever and see every little change that the gremlin went through. At the same time, she knew deep down that she could never be fulfilled without books and ideas to fill her mind. But still, if they had the money to allow it, maybe she could be happy staying home until Raven went to preschool. It didn't matter, though; there was no use indulging in that idea since they couldn't afford to have her stay home.

When she flipped the calendar from August to September, the date of her return, circled in red on the calendar, glared at her. She must have walked past the calendar twenty times on September first, each time trying not to look at the red circle.

That night, her nightmare actually woke her from sleep. Although it was much more vivid because she could clearly remember how she'd felt in the dream, it was hazy, too. What was weird was that the instant she woke up, all she could picture was the circled date on the calendar. She welcomed the glow of the moonlight, which illuminated the dreamcatcher from Fiona, closed her eyes, and begged it to do its job, but she couldn't get back to sleep.

She rose from bed, checked on Raven, and fished a joint out of her backpack. Giving the calendar a side glance as she walked into the kitchen, she stepped out into her garden despite the summer heat. As she sat there drawing in some calm, she desperately tried to remember more about her dream but didn't come up with much. She could never quite remember them, not exactly. What she could remember the most clearly was massive amounts of fire. One of the only images she carried from her sleep to her waking reality was the flames and the black, billowing smoke making its way up into the sky. Instead of images, she was left with a feeling. Almost as if she was witnessing a natural disaster, but from a distance. The only logical conclusion she could reach was that the dreams were merely the manifestation of her anxiety about returning to work.

But the next night, the dreams grew worse. She woke up in what she could only call a panic attack, although that had never been something she'd experienced. She'd been jolted awake, rousing Tammy, too. She downplayed the severity of it and urged Tammy back to sleep so she could resume her panic on her own. Except for the sounds of screaming, she could never remember any more specific details, but she could feel that as she watched whatever was happening, Raven was in her arms, safe.

She knew there was no way she was going back to work on the date she was supposed to. First thing in the morning, she would have to call Paula to buy as much time as possible to sort through whatever this was. She would need Fiona's help to do that, for if there was one person in her world she could turn to for help with otherworldly matters, it was her. And this felt otherworldly, as if there was a part of her that was living an experience that she wasn't really in. Fiona would know what the dreams meant.

The next morning, after Tammy went to work, Susan pulled her employee paperwork out of the office. She wouldn't tell Tammy about this until it was all worked out. She would need to know what her options were. While she was sure her issues could fall under mental health if she wanted to be open about them, she had no intentions of going that route. Employee regulations had forced her to use all the earned time she had accumulated before her paid maternity leave kicked in, so she had nothing left. Not only was she about to call her boss and ask for an extension on her maternity leave just eight days before she was due to return, but even if she was approved, her only option would be unpaid time off. But she didn't care; she knew she needed more time. Tammy's overtime pay should be enough to carry them through, anyway.

Paula was surprisingly easygoing, stating that two extra weeks was no problem. She assured Susan that the acting manager, Robert, would happily take on the role for a couple more weeks. In fact, he would be taking on the assistant manager position upon her return. While Susan wasn't altogether thrilled about having an assistant manager that she'd met twice, she couldn't worry about any of that right now. Her new return date was September twenty-fifth, which meant she had about three weeks to figure out why she was, apparently, losing her mind.

Susan never wrote to Fiona about the dreams. At first, she didn't find the time, immersed with Raven every possible waking moment, but it felt pointless, even when she got out the paper. Fiona would never even get the letter in time to be able to help her. She needed to figure this out quickly because it was already the eleventh, which meant she now had two weeks. She had already wracked her mind about what to do, had ruled out consulting a therapist, and was seriously considering visiting a psychic. She tried to remember the name of the woman that everyone in her family had counted on, but every time she thought about doing anything, something told her over and over to just remain still and wait.

One of the things that Susan loved about this stage with Raven was that she was awake far more often. Awake and content, that was. Yes, three months was a wonderful age. Getting Raven to sleep through the night was an accomplishment that Susan felt especially proud of; she'd never dreamed she could pull off what it took to put that routine in place, but she had. She'd even moved the first feeding every day from five to six-thirty by pushing it fifteen minutes at a time. Six thirty would be much more reasonable for her schedule when she returned to work. The baby even slept through the night most of the time now. Her broken sleep had been one of her most significant concerns about returning to work. However, it all seemed to be coming together just like Fiona said it would, even if she still had reservations about Raven being in daycare. How she fucking hated it that the bitch was always right.

While her attempts at healthier eating had fallen by the wayside a few times since the start of her maternity leave, yesterday, she'd begun another go at it and even made it through the entire day successfully. How many Mondays had she made that attempt in her life? If she could get through today, she would have two days of success. And if she could make it for two full weeks, that would give her two weeks to establish new habits she could carry with her when she returned to work. It didn't matter how many times she'd tried before; it mattered that she kept trying. A fresh start was always possible, and if she had managed to get Raven on a schedule the way she had, surely, she could do this for herself.

To secure her new habits, Susan was trying not to eat in front of the television anymore, so she opened the dining room window and had her breakfast there. She loved the new configuration; dropping the leaf and moving the dining room table against the windows had really changed the vibe of the room, and she was sure that making this her new morning routine could set the tone for her days. She had a small stack of books in a basket on the table next to her seat but hadn't gotten too deeply into any of them. She was too enthralled with watching Raven, who, from her blanket on the living room floor, had a firm grip on Rosie, the tiny, stuffed skunk that Granny had bought her. As Raven cooed away at the skunk, Susan teared up, knowing her time as a stay-at-home mom was really going to come to an end.

Clearly, the nightmares that she had been having weren't a premonition at all. She had obviously been paranoid and giving her supposed psychic powers out to be a little more than they were because all felt right with the world. She took her last sip of tea, grabbed her water bottle from the kitchen, scooped up her happy baby girl, and switched on the television.

Raven snuggled into her lap, and they locked eyes. Today, she was sure that was her favorite part about the three-month stage: she could tell Raven could definitely see her now. Recognized her. While the baby had clearly sensed her before, through scent mostly, the books said, there was something powerful about sharing a gaze. It wasn't just cliché that the eyes were the windows to the soul; it was exactly how she'd fallen in love with Tammy. But she didn't want to think about that now. In this moment, her whole world was right there in that gaze; nothing else existed.

Susan glanced at the clock; it was a few minutes before nine.

"Maybe we'll go for a walk today, baby girl. Yes, I think we will," she said to Raven. Empowered, she figured, why not add exercise to her new health routine?

She glanced up at the television screen; what darkness was the news covering now? She was beginning to despise the news. Not that she'd ever been a big fan, but Tammy had been, so she'd gotten used to it. All it seemed to do was make her feel down, and today was no exception because they appeared to be covering some massive disaster. She couldn't quite figure it out; smoke poured out of a very tall building in what looked like New York City. It looked terrible. Apparently, a plane had flown into it. People were fleeing for their lives. She glanced around for the remote. She didn't want to see this shit. It wasn't that she didn't care; to the contrary, seeing others suffering hurt too much. The remote was all the way across the room, and she and Raven had the perfect cuddle going. She could wait a few more minutes.

She kept shifting in and out. One moment, cooing with the baby and Rosie, then back to the television. Ugh! This right here. She had to focus on this moment that literally lay in her lap, not that. But, of course, it kept grabbing her attention. The news reporter's serious tones, the headline banners, it all kept drawing her away from her reality with her daughter and throwing her back into the rather unpleasant reality that there was, indeed, a larger world that they lived within. Honestly, it was a shame that they couldn't just live isolated from that supposed reality. That it couldn't be as simple as she and her daughter and nothing else. That was one thing Fiona was wrong about; one could not exist independently of this broken world.

What was the banner saying now? Suspected terrorism? She listened more intently; although she was relatively ignorant about political affairs, she could only assume that talk of terrorism could be substantial for everyone. The reporter was suggesting that someone had flown the plane into the building. One of the Twin Towers. *On purpose. Terrorism.* Something didn't sit right in her gut about those so-called facts, but she couldn't place what felt off.

It was only when she watched live as another plane flew into the second tower that her dreams came back to her. Fire. Smoke. Her whole body was taken over by a gasp, which startled Raven but not enough to make her cry. Susan held the baby more closely, maybe more for her own comfort than Raven's. She closed her eyes for a moment and let the baby's energy meld with her own, remembering the feeling from the dream now. Watching a disaster as her daughter lay safely in her arms. Goosebumps covered her skin. The dreams hadn't been just anxiety after all; she was living her nightmare, and she felt sick to her stomach about it. She didn't want that kind of knowing.

While she made every attempt to stay in the moment with her daughter, she could not deny the catastrophe taking place. Whatever this was that was going on in the world, the world that had felt nearly perfect just ten minutes ago required her attention, whether she wanted to see it or not. She had to be informed to keep her daughter safe, so she opened her eyes once again and tried to let the events sink into her mind. But it was truly unreal, even though the smoke wafting into the blue sky and the vague fearful sounds in the distance behind the reporter were precisely the details she'd been dreaming about for the last few weeks.

She couldn't stop the tears, and in fact, it took several minutes before she even knew that she was crying. Once she did, she couldn't even place the emotions behind the tears, maybe because there were just so many. At the forefront, though, it was the knowing. The dreams were almost all she could think of right now, for the realization of her knowing was too heavy. She couldn't wrap her head around the real-life details as the reporter spoke, but the knowing made her feel as though the weight of the world was on her shoulders. She needed marijuana; just a few puffs.

After she indulged, she returned to the television feverishly. She stared momentarily, took a deep breath to get back into her mind, and muted the television. Of course, Raven could not understand what she was seeing and couldn't read, but those sounds...Susan didn't want any of it taking root in her three-month-old brain. Never had she felt so strongly the will to protect her child as she did in that moment when it seemed the world was falling apart, or at least, the little portion of the world that she had always known as home.

But *she* needed someone, too. Fiona came to mind, but suddenly, the time it took for a letter to arrive was far too limiting. She needed someone now. A sadness fluttered in her chest when she realized only her mother and Fiona were on her mind when she thought of comfort and connection, not her wife.

Frozen to her spot on the couch, she couldn't reach out to anyone. She couldn't keep herself from watching it all unfold as a third plane crashed into the Pentagon. For once, the news was not overdramatizing; the country was in danger. She held Raven and watched until Raven fussed to be fed, trying to fathom what this meant for the world. Her world. Her daughter's world. She had never been more aware of how swiftly one's entire world could be altered.

Still stationed in front of the television, she fed Raven, who fell asleep soon after. Susan put her in her carrier to sleep. She couldn't bring herself to let the baby out of her sight, so she toted the carrier to the kitchen when the phone rang. Relief set in when she saw her mother's number flash across the screen.

"Hi, Mom," Susan answered, feeling as if she were about three years old.

"Are you watching television?" Alice asked with a somber voice.

"Uh-huh."

"Can you believe this shit?"

"I...no, I..., hey, wait, why aren't you at work?" Susan asked. In that moment, she realized that even though they were probably a couple hundred miles from New York City, she felt relieved that her mother was safe at home.

"Ed and I played hooky today. I woke up with a feeling...the thought of going made me feel freaked out. Glad we did. You just want to be home when..." She paused. "Do you remember when you were younger, I used to tell you that we were moving to Canada if we ever went to war here?"

"Of course." Susan could remember it very clearly.

"Still stands. This is just terrifying, Suze," Alice said.

Susan couldn't help but smirk as she heard Alice take a drag from her cigarette. Of course, she had a cigarette. She always had during the worst moments in Susan's memory, and Susan had no doubt that Alice would never give the things up. Hell, they would probably be what sent her to her grave. Like a chip off the old block, she grabbed a joint. She stepped out of the house and into the garden, putting the carrier on the ground and wishing her mother was there to smoke with her.

"I mean it, you know. I'm not going to just stay here if this is war," Alice insisted.

Hearing her mother's words, she had a new knowing, every bit as strong as the premonition from her most recent dreams.

"We can go live near Fiona." It felt almost whimsical and lighthearted when it came out of her mouth. As illogical as it was, that didn't make it feel any less true. War or not, Susan knew that she would someday go to live in Canada near Fiona.

"I know you think I'm being funny, but you call her. Talk to her. At least we would know someone. I can tell she's special to you. Like family," Alice continued.

Susan was unsure how to reply to any of it, so she didn't. Just like when she was a Freshman and Alice had been spooked by the Persian Gulf War, Susan didn't know what to say to her rather unadventurous mother when she talked so seriously about moving to Canada. The woman had never even been out of New England and was talking about fleeing to another country. Even then, hearing Alice talk about it had given her chills. But she knew now that it wasn't the kind of chills you get from fear; it was the sensation she had in her body when she had one of her knowings.

"I'm telling you. You might think your old mother is nuts, but I have lived through that. War. In another life. And I know what they do to women in wars," Alice went on. A tenderness came over her as her mother spoke; they weren't like this with one another very often. Raw. More often, they were dark, sarcastic, and silly, like long-time best friends or sisters.

"I don't think you're crazy at all. I know I was burned to death. You know, as a Witch in Europe. Gramma had this...whatever you want to call it...power. Ability to see things. I know you and I both have it, too, in a different way. I've known I was a hereditary Witch for a long time now," Susan replied. Opening up about the family gift they so rarely talked about was a relief.

"Right," Alice replied simply.

"It probably won't come to anything. I mean, it's America. I'm sure our guys will have it under control, but still, can't hurt to think about this. I mean it; you should call Fiona," Alice repeated again.

It all sounded ridiculous. Neither of them had passports or any money to speak of, and they certainly didn't have connections.

As if her mother had read her mind, Alice said, "I'm talking if it were to get really bad. If we had to go as refugees, I doubt passports or whatever would be an issue."

Her mother was rarely so solemn and was even less worldly than she was, so Susan had to take her seriously, despite how absurd it all was.

"We don't talk on the phone. I mean, never. Not even once. But we did share our numbers in letters a long time ago," Susan said.

"See. There was a reason for that, even if you do hate the phone like your mother does," Alice replied.

"When I hang up, I'll dig the letters out and find her number."

"*Promise* you'll call her?" Alice asked.

Long ago, her mother had taught her that the word promise

was sacred. It wasn't just a word. You didn't use the word promise unless you intended to follow through.

"I promise," she replied, making sure the tone of her voice let her mother know that she meant what she said.

"Thank you." Her mother's voice sounded humble and, much like Susan herself felt right now, vulnerable, like she was a child.

"But don't go. Not yet." How many times she had wanted to say something that simple to her mother and hadn't done it. *Don't leave me. Hug me tighter. I need you.* It felt good to express how much she needed her to be on that line with her mother, even though they didn't say much more until they hung up. If the world did end today, at least she would be glad she said it and held onto her mother a little more tightly. They just smoked and uttered the things that came into their minds as Ed mumbled similar sentiments in the background. *Awful. Those poor, poor people. How could anyone do anything like that? We lived in a scary world.*

The moment they hung up, Susan went to her bedroom, set Raven's carrier on the floor, and gutted the closet as quietly as possible to get to the back where she had put the tie-dye box with Fiona's letters. Grateful that the baby was asleep, she settled back onto the couch, watching the television and looking through the letters. She remembered just which letter it was in, too. It was a few autumns ago now that she had thought to include her own number in a letter, and Fiona had done the same in return. She remembered because Fiona had done leaf rubbings on the outside of the envelope that the letter was in.

Although her own number had changed since then, and she'd even updated it with a cell number, Fiona's was still the same. Much like her mother, Fiona had been a consistent presence since the day they'd met. Still, despite the connection, she started to feel flutters in her belly as she thought about calling Fiona. Now. Like this. What the fuck would she even say? Oh, hey, I know we don't call each other, like ever, never have, but yeah, the stupid fucking United States of America seems to be under attack, and my mom's inner Witch is coming out, and she is telling me to make sure we have a plan in case we need to escape. Yeah, she says we'd go to Canada, specifically, and that I should call you. Sure, *that* sounded sane. The thing was, being sane was never a requirement with Fiona.

Still, she swallowed hard as she dialed. She didn't let herself think about what she would say. Fiona might not even answer.

But Fiona answered, and although her prominent accent was a bit of a surprise, it was also not at all like Susan was hearing her voice for the first time.

"Somehow, I knew you was gonna call. America gone and fucked up again, eh?"

"Hi," was all that came out in reply. Despite their bond, she felt silly that she had called.

"Hi. You okay?" Fiona replied.

"Yeah." She had to think of something halfway lucid to say now. "My mom told me to call." She put a hand over her face and shook her head at herself. Seriously, her mother had told her to call? That was seriously what she had just said to Fiona?

"Always listen to Mudder," Fiona said with a laugh, putting Susan instantly at ease.

"Okay, so this is going to sound fucking crazy," Susan admitted.

"What odds?"

"Huh?"

"I forget. You don't know Newfie. I'm trying to ask...what else is new?" Fiona said.

Susan was no longer sorry she called. Deep down, she knew she was safe with Fiona. All she had to do was get over herself. So, she proceeded to blather on for what had to be ten minutes straight about her morning, her dreams and her knowing, and the details of her mother's strange request.

"I'm always here. You can come home whenever you needs to," Fiona assured her.

And somehow, as crazy as it was, although it did not make a bit of sense how it could possibly ever unfold, should it come to that, she fully trusted that Fiona meant what she said.

"Thanks, Fiona."

"No need to thank me by' Just remember, focus on the moment. Focus on your own little world as much as you can."

"Right."

It was not as if the call accomplished anything tangible. She had no answers. No solutions. But she was glad she called. Somehow, just heating Fiona's voice made Susan feel a little better.

She glued herself to the television again. She couldn't *not* know what was going on. Alice was right; they could very well be at war. However, none of it felt real as she watched. It was far easier for her to get lost in a novel, feeling with every bit of her soul as if she were in that story with the characters in that place than it was to feel as if this was real life. It couldn't be. She had not seen people jumping out of the thirtieth story of the building on fire and screaming. Someone had not done this intentionally. No, she could not live in a world like that.

She fed Raven in the same trancelike state. While the baby usually settled down quickly after eating, she was fussy this afternoon. No matter how much Susan rocked her, bounced her, or talked to her, there was just no comforting her. Deciding that Raven must feel her own icky energy, she knew it was time to walk away from the television. But in the back of her mind, she knew she'd be back to watch again as soon as possible. She couldn't help herself.

She hurried to the back door with the baby; she couldn't get to her garden quickly enough. She pushed the door open; the warm, sunny day was no indication of the darkness that hung over the world. But that is where she stood. She and her daughter were safe. She had to hold onto that.

Spotting a ruby-throated hummingbird, she smiled and ever-so-slowly shifted Raven so she could see it, too. It fluttered above the honeysuckle flowers. Raven seemed to follow it for a moment and quieted before it disappeared out of their yard.

When the magic of that hummingbird had been here, she'd been able to forget. How she wished she could hold onto the reality of that magic rather than succumb to the one that existed after the departure of the tiny bird. But it *was* gone; she couldn't just deny what was taking place. She held her daughter to her chest and let a few tears slide down her cheeks. Just a few.

Feeling a touch on her shoulder, she turned around to see Tammy standing there. She had been so wrapped up in the magic that she hadn't even heard the car pull in. She quickly reached up to wipe her eyes, but Tammy's hand reached her cheek first, and with a soft touch, she dried the tears away, then took Susan into a hug with more feeling behind it than they'd shared in weeks. They both broke into sobs, and Raven cried along with them.

When they finally pulled apart, Tammy reached for the baby, which made Susan cry even harder. As she witnessed her wife comforting their daughter, Susan leaned into them, smoothing Raven's fuzzy hair. It was one of the few joyous moments they'd shared as a family.

The baby started to cry, and through her drying tears, Susan giggled.

"This kid is like clockwork," Susan said.

Tammy arched her eyebrows in question.

"She needs a diaper change. She poops almost exactly an hour after she eats," Susan explained.

"Oh," Tammy replied, looking at the ground.

Susan reached for Raven, "Here, let me change her."

"I'll do it," Tammy replied with a sad smile and a single nod of the chin. She patted Susan's shoulder, which made Susan look her right in the eye. The touch was almost foreign, yet familiar too, like something resurfacing from the distant past.

Susan started to follow Tammy inside but decided it might be good to give Tammy some time alone with her daughter, so she held back for a moment, then leaned into the kitchen doorway and retrieved a sleeve of mint Milano's, munching away mindlessly as she hoped for the return of the hummingbird. It hadn't returned by the time she reached the bottom of the cookie jar, so she lit a joint.

While she didn't exactly hide the fact that she still smoked pot, she was always intentional about doing it when Tammy was occupied with something else. But today, it didn't even cross her mind. Still, she was a bit startled when Tammy popped her head back out the door. Her hand jerked; for a split second, she thought about hiding the joint but refrained.

Tammy touched her on the shoulder again, the same way she had just minutes ago.

"It's okay. I know we all have...our shit." Tammy shrugged and smiled. Even her smile was different.

"I...I don't know where you keep the diapers." Tammy's eyes filled with tears. "I should know where my daughter's diapers are."

Susan took one last puff and put the joint out.

"Come on." She motioned inside. "I'll show you."

"Seriously...I should know." It sounded like a sob was stuck in her throat. It was not that she'd ever heard that from Tammy, but she'd felt it enough times herself to know where it came from. That place, as if half underwater, drowning, wanting to reach out to someone who loved you. Instead, stubbornly letting the weight pull you deeper into a watery abyss, half-willingly sinking more and more, eyes open, watching yourself become lost. Even since their last deep talk, it had never occurred to her that Tammy had continued holding in just as much pain as she always had herself. She'd just assumed that Tammy had stopped trying and was merely going through the motions by helping out a little here and there but still not attempting to connect with her. With her own experience, she should have known better; sometimes, even when someone needed desperately to connect, they simply didn't know how.

"Hey," she said firmly, cupping Tammy's cheek in her hand. "Like you just told me...we all have our shit. Don't be too hard on yourself. You've been doing the best you can." Susan could feel Tammy's remorse through her skin as she nodded.

After Tammy changed Raven, she bounced the baby on her hip and paced between the kitchen and dining room.

"I just can't believe what's happening out there, Susan."

"I know. I mean, I have no words," Susan added.

"It's that lost feeling again, right?"

"Yup. And it's surreal because even though it is happening out there, it's happening to all of us, really. Like, what is this going to mean for all of us?" Susan asked.

Tammy nodded as she moved into the living room. "Right."

"I mean, I just haven't been able to pull myself away from it," Susan confessed.

"Well, I think you need to." And with that, Tammy clicked the television off.

They ordered a pizza for supper, and Susan popped in her oldest, most played cassette tape: The Wizard of Oz. When she was younger, she had asked her mom to play it every time bad memories came back to her, and later, as a teen, it was the same title she turned to when the bullying became so bad that she needed an escape from the thoughts of taking her own life. Every time she pushed the tape into the VCR, she wondered if this would be the time that she'd find out the tape was so worn out that it just wouldn't play. But tonight, it played, and even if Raven couldn't appreciate one of the best films ever made, there was something special about the evening. This was what Fiona had meant when she'd urged her to focus on her own little world. As they watched Dorothy find her power, clicking her ruby red shoes to return home, they were shutting out the rest of the darkness of the world and choosing magic instead. It felt almost wrong that all felt so right with her world.

After the movie, she and Tammy stayed on the couch, talking in a way they hadn't in weeks, vulnerable with one another, and all because the world was imploding. In whispers, they discussed not only the terrorist attacks and what the events could mean for everyone but also shared their fears about their human existence.

Then, they brought Raven upstairs to her crib together; they hadn't seemed to want to leave one another's side for even a moment since Tammy had come home. Tammy lowered the baby into the crib, and Susan smiled as she let out the same tiny, little sigh she always did, usually after Susan had read her a story and tucked her in.

"Aww, she's..."

Susan started to speak, intending to tell Tammy about the sigh she was so familiar with. But after Tammy had become so emotional about not knowing where the diapers were, she thought better of it.

"She's just so fucking amazing," Susan said, instead.

"She is. And you are too," Tammy replied softly, with a familiar look on her face. The look of passion, longing for touch. It aroused something in Susan, too, something she had worried might be dead. She could forgive Tammy for barely being here for the last few months, but could she be vulnerable enough to let her back in this quickly? This intimately?

"I'm serious," Tammy continued. "From the moment I first laid eyes on you, I knew you were magical. And I think it intimidates me sometimes just how amazing you are. Amazing beyond anything I could even conceptualize." She took a deep breath and held up one finger in pause, her bottom lip quivering. When she regained her composure, she continued. "I could not have asked for a better partner. A better mother for Raven. And I want you to know I owe you everything, Susan. I constantly ask myself what a magical woman like you is doing with an ordinary woman like me."

Susan had cried so many times that day that she didn't know how she was producing tears anymore, but somehow, she joined Tammy in crying once more. How could she see her wife this vulnerable and not let her in? She could almost hear Fiona telling her to live in the moment.

"Shh. Don't. You don't owe me anything, Tammy. That is what it means to be *partners*; that you fill in when the other needs some time to figure shit out. That you hold them up. The only thing left in the world I want is legal paperwork for Raven."

Tammy led her by the arm into the hallway, then quickly took her into her arms, kissing her deeply, both still crying a little as they kissed. There was something almost feral about kissing in the presence of such raw emotion. In body, Susan had never wanted anyone so badly before, and while sexually, her norm was somewhat submissive, she couldn't help but push Tammy against the wall and begin making love to her right there. Wildly, her hand reached into Tammy's pants; it had been too long since she had felt her. Since she had made love to the woman she had loved so deeply for so long. She let her hand explore Tammy's flesh, becoming more and more breathy as Tammy let out soft moans of pleasure.

"Come here, Babe. This'll be so much better without clothes," Tammy implored, leading her to the bedroom.

They stripped one another down feverishly, stopping for only a moment here and there to lavish one another with all-over kisses as they went, and eventually falling into bed, still wrapped up in one another.

Their lovemaking was different tonight. Despite the familiar touch, it was like they were making love for the first time. It seemed that neither was really taking the lead, but instead, they had found a perfect rhythm for making love to one another simultaneously.

"This has to be the hottest fucking thing I have ever known," Susan uttered. As they rediscovered one another, Susan felt like she was in a new realm of existence. Although she had loved Tammy for so many years, she was certain they'd never connected to this level before. It had been tender, yet intense, in a way she'd never known their lovemaking to be, and falling asleep, sweaty in one another's arms afterward, was every bit as blissful as the sex itself.

Susan woke a couple of hours later to find Tammy still asleep in the same position in the crook of her arm. Not yet willing to let the moment shift from present reality to a mere memory, she lay there, arm numb, and listened to Tammy sleep as long as she could, thinking about the day. About their marriage. And about the terrifying world they lived in.

Sometimes, it took something catastrophic to bring people together. It was what she had seen on the news all day: people coming together *because of* disaster. People who had been strangers were holding pressure to one another's wounds and comforting one another. If strangers could find one another as a result of such utter doom, surely, she and Tammy could come together in the same spirit. Still, guilt surged through her as she drifted off to sleep. What did it say about her that she benefitted from one of the worst days in American history?

CHAPTER TWENTY

When she awoke the next morning, Susan's gut ached when she remembered what had happened. She couldn't believe that Tammy had to go back to work today when everything in her wanted to keep her family close for eternity. She lay there looking through the skylight, wondering how the world went on after something so devastating. How did the sun still shine through that skylight? How did people pack lunches and go off to work like it was a typical day instead of instantly committing themselves to being eternally homebound hermits? Maybe, just maybe, she could talk Tammy into that, or, if not, at least talk her into calling in sick just for one day.

But then, Raven let out the same signature squeak she did every morning; the one eventually turned into a full-on cry. It was just as Alice had told her after her gramma had died: life goes on. Alice hadn't said it heartlessly. It had been her way of telling Susan that they could be sad and still live. And now, her own daughter's cry reminded her of that; life goes on. You had to live your life, no matter how scary the world was.

She felt Tammy stir after Raven emitted a second squeak, and although Susan had been trying not to rush right to Raven the moment she fussed, as the books had suggested, today came with a different set of rules. Today, she wouldn't let the squeaks turn into a full-on cry. Today, she would hold her baby more closely.

She lifted Raven from the crib, gave her a snuggle, then went back to the bedroom. Crawling back into bed, she lay Raven between her and Tammy, leaned over, and softly took Tammy's hand. Tammy squeezed Susan's hand, and her eyes fluttered open. They were silent for a few moments, but Susan was relieved as she looked into Tammy's sleepy eyes; the energy between them told her the closeness from last night was still alive.

Her hand still in Tammy's, she shook it a little and smiled. "Come on. It's still early. Let's all go sit in the garden before you go to work."

Tammy nodded with a smile, and after lifting Raven from her crib, the three of them headed downstairs. When Susan reached the foot of the stairs, the television haunted her. Despite the blank screen, it was as if yesterday's images were burned into it permanently. As he passed it with a sideways glance, she wondered if she could ever go back to how she felt before. The world had always been a scary place for her, but this was a new level of horror.

Tammy made coffee and tea while Susan prepared Raven's bottle and popped a couple pieces of bread into the toaster. They worked silently side by side as if they did this every morning.

"*I* want to feed her," Tammy said when they reached the flagstone patio. Susan nodded and brushed a fine layer of mist from the side table so Tammy could put the mugs down.

As she nibbled away at her toast, listening to Raven sucking away at her bottle, she spotted that goldenrod was growing between the slats in the back fence. She hadn't noticed it there yesterday. Fiona was right; change was constant.

They didn't say much to one another while they sat there, but in the silence, Susan learned something. Although she'd been begging Tammy to talk to her, sometimes even more could be gained from sitting together quietly. As much as she loved words, they could be quite inadequate for sharing yourself with someone as deeply as you wanted. While she'd spent the last three-and-a-half months pushing Tammy to tell her what the fuck was going on, she could have been more patient. She understood now that the words probably just weren't possible for Tammy. It was likely to be why Tammy had always been so drawn to sex, too. From day one, Tammy's touch had always communicated so much. It was like they spoke two different languages.

Susan appreciated how Tammy took the time for a long, lingering goodbye that morning, though it would make her late for work. Holding Raven between them, Tammy gave them both gentle kisses that told Susan it hurt her to leave them. But life went on.

In the weeks that followed the terrorist attacks, Susan was torn about going back to work, more concerned than ever about putting Raven in daycare when all she wanted to do was keep her safe in a way only a mamma could. But it wasn't like she had a choice, and besides, a big part of her wanted to go back, too.

Sitting in front of her altar one evening while Tammy fed Raven, Susan thanked the universe that her loved ones were safe and healthy and simply asked for guidance and peace. As the white flame candle burned down to a stump, she alternated between closing her eyes and staring at the flame from a place of calm and stillness. Each time she closed her eyes, she saw an image – the same hummingbird she'd seen with Raven as the Twin Towers fell. She wasn't sure what it meant, but the image brought her new comfort and strength, reassuring her that everyone would be fine as she returned to work.

And even as she mourned the season of her life that was ending, her season as a stay-at-home mom, the moment she walked through the doors of Barnes and Noble, she knew in an instant that this was where she needed to be. New insights about herself came rather rapidly after her return to work. As she got her head back into work mode, it occurred to her that she was far more insecure than she realized. If she was honest with herself, she could see that her concern about returning to work wasn't merely about keeping Raven safe. Now, their daughter was in the hospital daycare, closer to Tammy. Not only did Tammy get to drive there and back with Raven every day, but she could spend her lunch break with her. Susan realized that her insecurity as Raven's mother had never gone away, despite their closeness over the first four months of her daughter's life. While Tammy forming a deeper bond with their daughter was exactly what she had wanted all these months, now she was worried that Tammy would replace her. The thought that she was less of a mother to Raven than Tammy still weighed heavily on her soul, no matter how hard she tried to fight it. Maybe it was, at the very least, time to press Tammy again about legal paperwork.

At the same time, Susan found a new sense of purpose in her job in ways she had never expected. Upon her return, Kevin filled her in about what had gone on at the store during her time away and why the store was without an assistant manager once again. The situation helped her understand how powerful management could be.

The place was a disaster when she returned. It wouldn't necessarily be obvious to an everyday person who walked in the door, but it was immediately obvious to her. The back-to-school displays were nowhere to be found, although she and Kevin had talked about it at length, and he'd assured her that he would guide Robert in carrying out the plan. It looked like some displays had been started, but she couldn't tell what their themes were; they were a total mess. The concept she and Kevin had discussed included non-fiction college-level reading, new releases in hardcover, and, of course, lots of displays of various levels of children's books. But the only thing that she could make out were two stands. The first included secondary and college study guides: PSAT, SAT, GRE, and GMAT. Immediately, she noticed that even that display was incomplete, lacking the TOEFL and the IELTS. The second was simply a display of the series many people used for elementary homeschooling: *What Your First Grader Needs to Know*, *What Your Second Grader Needs to Know*, and so on. Everything else in the store looked like a pile of rubble.

She was utterly ashamed of the shape her store was in. Sure, the back-to-school season would soon be replaced by fall and Halloween, but still, what was all of this? She would have to get to the bottom of it quickly and replace it all with something better, not that it would be difficult to accomplish compared to what was here now.

She walked around the store, making a mental checklist of what needed to be done, prioritizing what to tackle first, then, defeated, finally retreated to her office. Except for a fine layer of dust, her desk was exactly as she left it. Susan eyed the wedding picture of her and Tamika. Tammy. She still forgot sometimes. To be fair, she had still been Tamika in this particular photo. It felt like that picture had been taken so long ago, like she didn't even know those girls anymore. Maybe when Tamika had become Tammy, it had just taken some time for her to recreate herself. Maybe the woman she'd made love to on the night of the terror attacks and every night since was Tammy. They needed to get a family picture to celebrate their new beginning; they hadn't taken one of the three of them since the day that Raven was born. A new addition to her photo collage was exactly what she needed.

"Susan!" Kevin squealed, rushing into the office and giving her a loving pat on the arm.

She smiled and replied, "I missed you. I missed this place."

"We missed you too. Trust me," Kevin said with a big sigh.

"What the hell happened here?" Susan asked, sweeping her arm in the direction of the store outside of the office door, unable to hold back another minute.

Kevin let out a long sigh and nodded. "Yeaahh, umm...

"The front...it's..."

"Horribly, unbelievably awful?" He asked.

"Yeah, I mean, what is that? Two stands? Where is everything else? What the hell did that guy, Robert, *do* here?" Susan asked.

"It's been crazy. Robert just disappeared. Paula has been in a few times to deal with this disaster. Let me tell you, *this* is better than it was," Kevin said.

"Still, the displays should have been done weeks ago," Susan replied.

Kevin held up his hand. "Wait. It gets worse. The displays *were* done. In mid-August, just like you said. But then, after nine-eleven, you got a memo from corporate." Kevin reached over to his desk and retrieved a letter. "I had no idea. It was addressed to you, but Robert got his hands on it." He tracked his finger under the print and read from the letter. "We request that each store manager prioritize new displays that *exhibit the American spirit in light of the recent national* events."

"Hmm, okay," Susan replied, still confused.

"Robert only disappeared after he took the memo in a completely wacko direction. Last week, he was walking around here boasting about how he was ex-military and intended to remind people how to be good Americans. He was being utterly nasty to Sanjana. I think he took Bush's War on Terror a little too personally. Honestly, I think he snapped. He had some pretty awful displays started. It was like something that might resemble the home library of those loons from Waco, Texas," Kevin said, shaking his head, clearly still in disbelief.

Susan could feel the blood draining from her face as he spoke. Susan couldn't believe this had happened in her store. To her people.

"What was he doing to Sanjana?" Susan asked.

"Mumbling under his breath that the Indians were all terrorists just like the rest of them. Whoever *the rest of them* are. He was just racing around the floor, losing his mind, so I grabbed her purse and keys from the back and had her go home. Robert didn't even notice. He was too busy gathering what looked like every book in this store that celebrated the White American man, which would have been fine, I guess. But apparently, when he'd gotten the memo, he went and special ordered about a dozen titles that we don't carry regularly. And probably for a good reason. Not that I ever thought about it, but I never really knew that anything like these books even existed. And the fact that he just found them so easily tells me he knew very well that they existed. I'm talking almost like *Mein Kampf*, Susan. Beyond conservative ideas, with, I don't know...a wacko, religious feel, I guess. Like taking over the country kind of stuff. Those books came on the day I'm talking about, and when they did, he put those titles on a giant display with all the other books he'd gathered about presidents and colonists. I think he even had a bunch of books about Columbus in there. It was just bizarre because it was obviously not what the memo had in mind." Kevin was quiet and subdued now as he continued the story.

"Holy shit!" Susan shook her head and felt tears stinging her eyes. "Is Sanjana...okay? I mean..."

"Yeah, she's okay. I called her later that evening, and she actually seemed pretty collected about it all. Paula told her not to come in until they could make sure she was safe. After Sanjana left, I went back to call Paula, but she wasn't in. But later that day, she came in anyway, and when she saw it, she locked the doors and called the police. Robert had left suddenly by the time she got here. Didn't say one word to any of us; we just saw him walk out the door in a hurry. She thought the cops might want to take a look. But after they were gone, we took it all down as fast as we could," Kevin said.

"How long was it up before she came in and saw it?" Susan asked.

"A few hours. It was pretty scary, actually. The whole thing. But mostly the fact that he just disappeared. We were all kind of wondering if he was going to come back with a gun or something crazy. I was just about shitting myself until Paula locked those doors."

"You said he was ex-military?" Susan asked.

"Yeah, I guess. Marines," Kevin replied.

"Ahh, that explains a lot," Susan sneered.

"I'm ex-military." Kevin laughed.

"You are?"

He nodded. "I mean, just the National Guard, but yeah."

"Yeah, but you're not all...you know, a redneck flying the flag from his big Bubba truck," Susan said.

"Well, that's the extreme. He's the extreme. Not all ex-miliary are like that."

"Oh, of course not..." She felt mortified about what she'd said now.

"I never would have thought *he* was one of those types either," Kevin said.

Susan tried to wrap her head around it. There was so much running through her mind. Everyone was already terrified. It was somber everywhere you went. Even if the display had only been up a few hours, no one needed to witness anything else that instilled more fear in them, especially people like Sanjana, who were already being targeted.

"And I thought that the incomplete display of college study guides that was missing the TOEFL and the IELPS was bad," Susan said, trying to lighten the mood.

"Why, what did I forget?" He laughed.

"I'm sorry. I didn't mean... You didn't know." She kept putting her foot in her mouth.

"Oh, no, it's fine. I want to know. What else should I have included?" Kevin asked.

"Two study guides come to mind: one for speakers of foreign languages and one for international students wanting to study here in the U.S."

"Sorry about that. I just knew the basics: the PSAT, SAT, and GRE. I did a little research and found out about...whatever the ones are for business and law, but I had no idea about the ones you just mentioned."

"Ugh, I didn't mean to..." Susan winced. She'd put her foot in her mouth again.

"No, no, seriously, stop apologizing. That's why they hire educated people like you."

"You're educated!" Susan retorted.

"You know what I mean. We all know that you have a lot to teach us about...I don't know, diversity, I guess. This is a great example," Kevin explained.

Once again, Kevin had given her the opportunity to understand how people might see her, which was obviously with higher regard than she sometimes saw herself.

"After my comment about military people, I think we all have a lot to teach each other," Susan replied, humbled.

"I guess that's true. But trust me, though, we all wished you were here during all this. It would have been a very different thing to go through with you here, and we all knew it. Obviously, you would have gotten the memo instead of *him*, and none of it would have even happened, but if he pulled anything when you were in charge, you wouldn't have taken it. We've all seen your fierce side come out when any sort of injustice has been involved."

Every now and then, she still needed a reminder of why she chose to do what she did. She might argue that she didn't choose it, exactly, that books had chosen her. But still, suddenly, she saw that this was bigger than she'd realized. Managing people mattered. There was a lot to be said about the critical role libraries and bookstores played in society. Books represented ideas and the power of learning, but maybe, most profoundly, freedom. A freedom that not everyone in the world had. As much as she pushed back about so many American ideals, diversity and freedom of speech were nothing to blink an eye at. She was here to uphold those things and had the power to do so through the ways she supported her staff. Instead of telling herself that managing didn't matter, she could focus on doing just that and finding an assistant manager willing to do the same. Suddenly, it didn't matter what shape the store was in, and her checklist seemed unimportant. She had to call Sanjana right away.

By the time Susan had been back to work for a month, it was her favorite time of year: autumn. While she'd held her breath a little right after 9/11, struggling to trust that things would stay so good between her and Tammy, now, she felt she could finally exhale. She held as tightly as she could to her newfound understanding of Tammy. Although she still wished that Tammy would share more sometimes, she was trying hard to give her wife a little more grace. Everyone had dark times, and it wasn't unusual to need time to figure out who you were again afterward. It felt as if this might really be a new beginning, something even better than when they'd fallen in love. Susan could see the joy in Tammy's eyes when Tammy took care of Raven most days now, and it had been weeks since she'd found Tammy in bed crying for no apparent reason. She still didn't know enough about postpartum depression to say for sure, but Susan was glad that seemed to be behind Tammy because Raven needed both of her moms.

It might have sounded silly to most people, but the fact that Tammy had finally given in to her appeals to get a kitten signaled the change between them just as much as Tammy's attentiveness to Susan and Raven.

Sanjana's cat had given birth to another litter of kittens, and Susan was thrilled when Sanjana told her they would be ready to go to their new homes right around Halloween.

"A black kitten for the Witch on Halloween. How perfectly

cliché," Tammy had said when Susan had told her. But she didn't seem to say it spitefully, as she had in the past. Instead, Tammy seemed to look at Susan through new eyes, as if she understood her more and loved her because of those cliché details.

Today, three days before Halloween, Susan's lunch hour couldn't come quickly enough; she needed supplies for the kitten.

After she made sure Dawn and Kevin had the store under control, she hurried out the door and strolled across the parking lot, dreaming of her little black kitten and home. She loved their house, and the kitten was the last thing she needed to make it feel like home. Though her childhood had been painful, there had never once been a time that home hadn't felt like home, at least not after her mother had left her father and gone to live with Susan's grandparents. Home had always felt like a comfy blanket, or sometimes, maybe even a fairytale. With her mother and gramma, she'd always been able to find the sense of safety that home was supposed to provide. A place that offered her the space she needed to fold into herself whenever she needed to, whether it be coloring under a table or reading a book in her bed. And, from the time her first cat, Miss Kitty, had come into her life, there had been one final detail that made a place feel like home: sharing her space with a cat.

While Petco was her ultimate destination, she couldn't help but wander into the Halloween outlet first. She knew it would be busy this close to Halloween, but she didn't care. She was purely in her element once surrounded by the dark fairies, vampires, and witches. While her personal brand of witchiness was, admittedly, more about simple Earth magic, the pull of otherworldly creatures was real, too. She walked through the aisles, enjoying the strange décor with amusement, imagining a grand theme for their front lawn next year if only Tammy would let her. It wouldn't require such commercial items as much as elements of nature. She envisioned grand arches made from grapevines, lots of lights illuminating handmade creatures of all kinds, a pentagram made from sticks, and a great, big spiral in the yard made from rocks. In the meantime, she settled for a few kitschy items. A broom for the front door was a given, and once she spotted the giant mechanical cauldron, she knew she had to have that too. With a dim light and a blower that sent gray streamers floating above it, making it look like a bubbling witch's brew, it was perfectly witchy but not so over-the-top that Tammy would have to warn her about freaking out the neighbors.

After making her second pass through each of the aisles, she spotted it: Raven's Halloween costume. It was the perfect size for her, and it was a Raven. It was simply a jacket with layers of black feathers and a hood with a soft beak paired with thick black leggings. Wide-eyed, she snatched the last one off the hook as if a hundred crazed moms were competing for it. She had to laugh at herself; she was the only crazed mom there.

While she managed not to spend too much at the Halloween Outlet, she couldn't say the same about Petco. She knew dropping nearly a hundred-twenty dollars was an indulgence, especially since she'd recently had some unpaid time off. All she truly needed were the basics like food bowls, a litter box, and maybe a few toys. But she couldn't resist the overpriced cat bed once she spotted it: a soft, orange cushion was nestled inside a purple felt witch's hat. She walked out of the store, smugly proud to be a cliché.

While Tammy was disheartened that she had to work a double on Raven's first Halloween, Susan agreed to bring Raven by the hospital before bringing her to see Granny and then enjoy the Halloween parade with DJ and Ashley. Like she was a kid herself, the workday seemed to drag on forever as she anticipated the evening they had planned.

Although it was only a few miles, the drive from the store to the hospital felt endless, too. Once she arrived, Susan used the bathroom at daycare to change Raven into her costume. Despite the beak and feathers, it was her big, brown eyes that made her the most adorable little Raven on the planet. The eyes that made her look more like a person every day.

The elevator bell dinged as they reached Tammy's floor. She scanned the nurse's station, but Tammy wasn't there. She glanced down the right hall, then the left, but still didn't spot her.

"Can I help you?" Asked the man behind the desk without fully looking up.

"I'm looking for Tammy," Susan replied, pondering why his face looked familiar.

"Oh, hi!" The man stood up and seemed tongue-tied for a moment. "Yeah, yeah, yeah, right," he stammered.

Susan shifted Raven in her arms, unsure why the man seemed so uncomfortable.

"Oh...Tyler!"

He nodded, his eyes locked on the baby.

"I'm sorry. I didn't recognize you," Susan said. She'd only met him a couple of times, and she was pretty sure his hair was different somehow, but his freckles made him memorable.

"It's okay. My bad. Tammy told me you'd be coming. It's just been a little crazy here, and I forgot. I just cannot get over how sweet and perfect she is! Can I...?" He asked, reaching for Raven. It felt strange since she barely knew him, and both times she'd interacted with him, he'd seemed a little too arrogant for her taste. But still, he *was* Tammy's friend, and she didn't want to be rude. Reluctantly, she handed the baby to him.

He gazed at the baby with adoration and told her what a pretty Raven she was, which put Susan a little more at ease.

"Tammy should be done soon; she's in the back. I'll go let her know you're here. You can sit in there if you like." He pointed to the small waiting room across from the nurse's station.

When he started walking away with Raven, it roused Susan's discomfort again, and she stepped forward quickly with outstretched arms. "She'll wait with me."

Tyler deferred, but Susan could tell he didn't want to hand the baby back. There was something about the look on his face that Susan didn't like. She couldn't place it, but he had some nerve to think he could walk away with her daughter, even if he was Tammy's friend.

Tammy emerged a few minutes later, and Susan bounced up, meeting her in the waiting room doorway with a smile and giving her an awkward peck on the cheek.

"Thanks for bringing her. Everyone is dying to see her all dressed up. I'll just be a few minutes." Tammy reached for Raven, making it clear that she expected Susan to wait there again.

She stood in the doorway and watched through the window on the office door. The woman sitting at the desk was instantly charmed with Raven. She, Tammy, and Tyler talked and fawned over Raven for a few minutes. Tyler held her and spoke to her in a cooing voice again. On the one hand, if this big, buff guy could be so tender with Raven, she had to assume that her inclination about him must have been wrong; maybe he wasn't such a macho jerk. But that thought only lasted a moment because when Tammy turned to walk out of the office, there was something about the way that Tyler kissed Raven on the cheek that made Susan's gut flutter. Would she have felt the same way if it hadn't been a man? She wasn't sure why Tyler was so off-putting to her, but she couldn't deny it.

Tyler looked up, saw Susan watching them, and leaned into Tammy, whispering something to her as he put Raven back in Tammy's arms.

"They just adore her," Tammy bubbled when she returned.

Susan smiled, deciding that she must have been overthinking

again.

"What time is the parade, anyway?" Tammy asked.

"I think it starts at 6:00," Susan replied.

"Not bad. She'll probably just sleep in the car on the way home."

"Hey, I know it sucks that you have to work, but let's at least get a picture of the three of us on her first Halloween," Susan said, retrieving her camera from the diaper bag.

Tammy nodded and turned to flag Tyler over to them again. But this time, she felt something else, too: the tension in Tammy's body was undeniable. She didn't care how much both Fiona and Tammy said she tended to overthink things; there was something about this guy she didn't like.

After a quiet supper at her mom's, Susan headed to DJ's. While crowds were definitely not her thing, it was sweet to bundle Ashley and Raven into the wagon together, and spending the night with DJ like the old times turned out to be a blast. It was strange how they were both moms now, yet sometimes, when they were together like this, they were like kids again, too, giggling and indulging in too much chocolate. While her relationship with DJ wasn't perfect, there was something powerful about a friendship that lasted this long. With their struggles, they were more like real sisters, and that was pretty beautiful.

The following day, she was sleepy but wired as she tried to trudge through her workday. Although Halloween had been a long day, her excitement about taking the kitten home today had kept her awake last night. One of her cashiers had called in sick today, which meant that she had to hover around the front of the store this morning in case Dawn and the newer cashier, Ben, needed a hand or a customer needed some help. Working the floor was nearly as bad as working the register when she was tired. She flipped through a baby name book, making an unsuccessful attempt to conjure up the perfect name for the little girl. She wasn't convinced she wanted a regular girl's name for the kitten, though. She was hoping for something a little more magical but wasn't sure where to look.

By the time three o'clock came, she'd obsessed about it all day. At least she could retreat to her office after reshelving one more stack of books. She flitted from section to section, putting one book after another back in their homes, but when she spotted Sanjana walking through the front doors, carrier in hand, Susan waved her back to the office.

She put the last of the books down on her desk, welcomed Sanjana in, and delighted in the tiny mews coming from the carrier.

"Thank you *so* much!" Susan said, peering into the carrier as Sanjana set it down on her desk, sending the books tumbling hard to the floor.

Sanjana winced as she picked up the last book. "Yikes, sorry about that," she said, trying to bend the cover back into shape.

"Don't even worry about it; just leave it there," Susan replied, glancing to see that it was a book about Goddesses of Greek Mythology. "You know me; I'll just buy it and bring it home. I've had my eye on that one anyway." She chuckled.

"I can't stay long; my husband is waiting in the car for me. But, listen, he messed up."

"Messed up what?" Susan asked.

Sanjana unzipped the carrier and pulled the kitten out.

"Apparently, he doesn't know the difference between a black kitten and a tortie kitten. He gave the black one away to another family this morning," Sanjana explained.

Susan was too enamored with the squirming ball of fur to process anything.

"I hope you still want her," Sanjana said.

"She's perfect. Of course, I want her," Susan replied as she held her out, noting her markings. She was primarily black with patches of orange, but definitely not a calico. "Tortie?"

Sanjana nodded. "Yeah, like tortoiseshell."

"I've never heard of that. But she's gorgeous. She looks like autumn." Susan laughed.

"Aww, I'm so glad. I know you really wanted the black one."

"Nooo! That's how magic happens; it's not always what you think it's going to be. She's the one that was meant for me. These kitty vibes are everything," Susan said, losing some of the inhibition she had with her employees and snuggling the kitten into her chest as she began to purr.

After Sanjana left, Susan decided that even though the name Autumn had become so commonplace for both cats and children, it would suit the kitten perfectly if she didn't come up with something else.

With the kitten now asleep in the carrier, she retrieved the book with the bent cover, taking notice of the page it lay open to. The bold heading to the chapter was a single word: Thea. She read the subheading beneath. *Perhaps the strongest of the divine female names, since the name itself means Goddess, Thea was the Greek Goddess of profound vision, often thought to be the eldest daughter of Gaia herself.*

She'd spent the day wracking her brain about the perfect magical name, and here it was, lying right in front of her on the page.

CHAPTER TWENTY-ONE

While it made no sense to Susan since Tammy had given Susan her blessing about getting a kitten, something changed in Tammy after Thea came into the household. Maybe it wasn't the kitten at all, and the timing was just coincidental, but it was clear that Tammy was moving away from her again. Suddenly, just days after Thea came home, Tammy blindsided Susan, moving out of their bedroom and into the spare room with no previous discussion about the matter. Tammy simply said she needed more space, and from all that Susan had grown to understand about her wife since Raven's birth, she wanted to honor the space Tammy needed. Still, she felt she deserved some answers. But when she asked Tammy why, Tammy couldn't elaborate at all, which infuriated Susan.

Tired of basing her entire life on Tammy's fluctuations, Susan immediately embraced the benefits of the situation. Not only did she welcome the fact that her additional alone time gave her more time for her books, but she happily leaned into the crazy cat lady role. With a new cat condo by the window and climbing shelves all over Tammy's pristine, boring walls, her bedroom became a veritable cat playground.

While Tammy's parents had invited all of them for Thanksgiving, Tammy declined, agreeing to work a double shift instead so she could get Raven's first Christmas off.

They weren't necessarily ugly to one another, but the tension between them grew as they lived much like roommates, communicating almost solely to care for Raven. Every now and then, Susan would ask Tammy again why she wanted separate bedrooms and even where they were headed, but Tammy never had any answers. Susan questioned if Tammy's depression was resurfacing but didn't dare approach the subject. At least Tammy was still bonding with Raven.

Over the next few months, Susan's feelings about the separate bedrooms went back and forth. After the shock, a part of her was somewhat relieved. It meant she could have some space, too, and didn't have to worry about giving in to Tammy's sexual advances, even when they weren't connecting in other ways. It was nice to have Thea in bed with her every night; that never would have happened if she and Tammy were sharing a bed, and there was nothing quite like cuddling a kitten to soothe her soul.

She was angry and disgusted with herself on the nights she felt lonely, missing Tammy's arms around her. The loneliness worsened as Thanksgiving came and went, and the Winter Solstice and Christmas season arrived. She wasn't sure if it was the cold weather, the holidays, or just that every day they stayed apart, all hope was slipping away for her little family. With everything in her, she was trying to heed Fiona's consistent advice to let it be. All of it. But most days, she was failing. Unable to fully admit the truth to herself, she'd scribbled out a generic holiday card to Fiona instead of sharing how miserable things had become.

When she woke up on Christmas morning, the house was quiet. It was Raven's first Christmas; looking forward to this day had been all she had been all the kept her going. Still, grief filled her chest. It was like her mother had said; this was not how it was supposed to be. She and Tammy were supposed to give one another sweet kisses on the nose and spend the entire day in the glow of their love for one another and Raven.

Like so many other mornings, she lay there wondering if she might open the bedroom door to find the rest of her family gone, leaving just her and Thea. She simply didn't know what to expect from Tammy anymore since the decision to move out of the bedroom had seemed to come out of nowhere, so she couldn't put it past Tammy to up and leave with Raven one day.

Although she'd vowed to consult a lawyer after Tammy had

suddenly decided on separate bedrooms, she hadn't followed through and was disgusted with herself. She'd done some research and had zeroed in on a couple that might be a good fit for her, but every time she went to call, she couldn't bring herself to do it. After the legal issues she'd gone through as a child, she was still terrified of the system. Although she'd been the victim, cops, lawyers, and judges always left her feeling as if she were a criminal instead.

As if she needed another thing to make her feel like a criminal, the world was still a scary place for a nonbiological gay parent. She simply couldn't face how a lawyer might treat her, at least not alone. She was too proud to ask anyone to go with her, for it would mean admitting that things were getting dire with her marriage. She simply wasn't ready to admit that she'd failed at her entire life.

But instead of focusing on that, today, she had to focus on the opportunity she had in front of her; it was another thing Fiona reminded her of often. She would consult a lawyer after the new year. Maybe it wouldn't be the kind of Christmas she wanted, but she'd been living in fear for months now that she wouldn't get to be a part of Raven's first Christmas at all, and now the day was here. Perfect or not, the day was a gift.

She rolled out of bed as quietly as she could and tiptoed into the nursery. She paused in the doorway, smiling sadly as she saw Raven in her purple footsy pajamas. She and Tammy had picked them out together in October when things were good. When Susan had spotted them in the store, she'd commented that with the shade they were, Raven would be the most beautiful sugar plum fairy. She remembered it well because Tammy had given her the softest look of adoration, the same look she saw that first day at the bookstore when they talked about *Ain't I A Woman*, and the same way she had looked at her in the first few months that they were getting to know one another.

"I love the way you think, Babe. You're soulful," Tammy had

said as she'd plucked a pair from the rack and told Susan that these would be what Raven woke up in on Christmas morning. Tammy had been the one to bathe Raven the previous night. Had she remembered? Chosen these pajamas purposely because it was still sentimental for her, too?

Since Raven had been growing so fast, they had to make their best guess about size, and now, Susan could see that they'd missed the mark by about two sizes. She laughed out loud when she saw the feet and legs of the pajamas dangling empty beneath where the baby's little body was curled up inside as if it were a potato sack. Susan heard the door to the office open behind her and turned around to see Tammy standing there, half awake.

"I'm sorry if I woke you," Susan whispered.

Tammy smiled. "It's okay. What's so funny, though?"

"The pajamas." Susan pointed.

Tammy nodded. "I think they're a little big, those sugarplum pajamas."

Susan looked up, silent, but met Tammy's eyes.

"I remember. I *am* still trying, you know," Tammy said.

She hadn't known at all. She'd spent the last few months with assumptions racing through her head. Assumptions that had become her truth. She was convinced that Tammy was biding her time before saying it was over. She hated Susan, or maybe she just wasn't in love with her anymore; Susan wasn't sure which was worse. Not once had Susan entertained the idea that Tammy was trying to make things work.

She wasn't sure what to say and was surprised when she felt herself reaching out to touch Tammy's arm. They hadn't touched in weeks. But Tammy didn't pull away as Susan rested her hand on her arm.

"Should we wake her up since she's usually up by now anyway?" Tammy asked.

"She could be grumpy if we do that. I was thinking the same thing, though."

"Yeah. Maybe we should wait." Tammy dramatized a pout.

Susan stood there awkwardly, unsure of what to do next. Raven would have been a buffer. Sure, they were talking, but still. Were they supposed to go downstairs together and act like a family now?

"I'm going to go make coffee," Tammy said, yawning.

"Okay," Susan replied, still not moving.

Tammy scuffled away in her slippers, then turned around. "You coming? Aren't you going to make your cinnamon rolls?"

Susan nodded and followed her, but as they reached the foot of the stairs, she heard Raven cry.

"I'll get her," Susan said, relieved. She climbed back up the stairs and scooped Raven from her crib. After freeing her from the fairy plum potato sack and changing her diaper, Susan dressed her in the candy cane dress she and Tammy had picked out together.

When they got downstairs, Tammy was wrapped in a blanket on the couch with her coffee mug. All the shades were still drawn, so it was dark enough in the living room.

"Come here," Susan said, waving Tammy over to the tree.

Tammy looked up confused, paused a moment, then put her mug down and joined them.

"We have to look at the lights. Together," Susan said, feeling herself choke up.

Tammy took a step closer, and they both turned toward the tree.

"Too bad we can't teach her how to squint," Tammy said.

They stood there silently for a moment, and Tammy wrapped her arms around them.

"I'll go put the rolls in the oven," Susan said when Raven began to whimper, and they stepped away.

She handed Raven to Tammy and wiped the tears from her eyes

as she made her way to the kitchen. She found Thea licking water out of the sink. It was a good thing Tammy hadn't been the one to find her there. Snuggling the kitten's wet little body into her chest, for a moment, she placed Thea on the floor and gave her some food, amused as she inhaled every bite.

She peered out the back door, hoping to see that it had snowed or, even better, if it was snowing now. No luck; it was a gray day, but it felt like spring. She sighed as she walked onto the flagstone but smiled as she spotted a single red cardinal in her favorite oak tree. Whimsically, she embraced the idea that her gramma had come to wish her Merry Christmas.

Once inside, she opened all the curtains and returned to the living room, the smell of the rolls filling every room.

"I think she wants you," Tammy said from the couch, holding Raven out to Susan as she shrieked. Shrieking from frustration was her newest thing and wasn't nearly as adorable as the babbling.

"What?" Susan tried to be silly and put her face up to Raven's, but it irritated her even more.

The baby reached behind Susan's back, getting louder.

"Ahh, I bet I know what you want, Gremlin." She turned to face the tree, and Raven grabbed for the lights, babbling at them.

"What a great age for a first Christmas. She's just in love with the lights. The only problem is that she likes to grab at them."

"At least she's not crawling yet. She just kind of rocks her body back and forth and can't figure out how to move those knees." Tammy laughed.

"True. I'll just put her here; maybe if she can see the lights, that'll buy us a good half hour before she gets so mad that she starts shrieking again," Susan said, setting Raven down.

Thea came racing through the living room and promptly leaped into the tree. Startled at first, Raven toppled a little but managed to hold herself in the sitting position after some effort, then let out the best giggle ever as Thea poked her head out from the tree like a wild creature. Even Tammy, who was usually put off by Thea, couldn't help but laugh.

After eating cinnamon rolls and helping Raven open gifts, they enjoyed a quiet day with naps, Christmas specials, and a delicious lasagna for supper. Susan even found time to dive into a new book while Tammy and Raven played with some new toys.

Susan decided that the Christmas spirit had to be a real thing because she could feel a warmth between her and Tammy that she hadn't felt since Tammy had moved into a separate bedroom. There were several moments when they'd both looked at Raven, then at one another and clearly felt connected.

As Tammy put Raven down to sleep that evening, Susan scooped Thea up and headed upstairs.

"She fell asleep hugging the little snow girl," Tammy said as she quietly shut the door to the nursery.

"She loves that thing," Susan replied.

They stood in silence for a moment, then, as she and Tammy went toward their separate rooms, Tammy stopped and looked back over her shoulder with a familiar look of desire.

Susan didn't want to hurt Tammy, but she needed to protect her own heart.

"Night. It was a good day," Susan said genuinely, giving Tammy a soft smile. It had been better than any day they'd had in months, and she could be nice, but whether Tammy was trying or not, Susan still couldn't bring herself to let her back in.

*****

As if winter wasn't always long enough, the bitter weather insisted on keeping its hold right into the first week of April. After Susan failed to give in to Tammy's subtle advances on Christmas night, things went from bad to worse between them, and Susan desperately needed the sprouts of spring to provide her with some joy.

Unless they didn't talk at all, they were generally snippy and spiteful to one another. Disgusted with herself for living the way she was, Susan questioned if she could even call herself a feminist anymore. Not only had she begun to settle for being treated like shit, but she was giving it right back to Tammy. She'd never dreamed she would be this mean to any woman, much less the mother of her daughter, a woman she still loved, whether she liked her or not.

The weekend had felt as if it had stretched out forever. It was Tammy's weekend off, and the foot-high snowdrifts kept them trapped in the house together. Usually, they observed their newly established normal, although it was unspoken. Each made an obvious attempt at being on whichever floor of the house that the other one wasn't on as often as possible unless they needed to communicate about Raven. But this weekend, the house seemed smaller, and it felt like they couldn't steer clear of one another.

Susan decided to retreat to the nursery with Raven after lunch as Tammy did laundry and played the radio a little too loudly for her taste, which Susan suspected wasn't coincidental. Tammy knew how she hated noise; lately, she seemed intent on making as much of it as possible.

She opened the nursery door and stood near the window, Raven in her arms, pointing to the heavy snow on the tree.

"Snow. Snow," Susan said, pointing.

Susan had been reveling in trying to help Raven add more words to her vocabulary, but so far, she'd only said three words. Both bubba and Mamma were pretty clear, though Susan had been trying to get Raven to differentiate between Mamma and Mommy. The third was a little more garbled, but Susan was convinced that Raven was saying cookie, and the fact that she licked her lips every time she said it made it undeniable, as far as she was concerned.

"Snow," Susan repeated.

Raven just giggled at her, then took hold of Susan's ponytail with one hand and grabbed at one of her own puffs with the other.

"Hair," Susan said, touching her own hair, then Raven's.

With one hand, Susan lifted the window just enough to scoop up a little snow. She held the snow in her palm and showed it to Raven. Letting go of Susan's ponytail but still grasping her own puff, she poked a chubby finger from her free hand into the snow, then pulled it right back again, looking at Susan in shock.

"Snow," Susan enunciated.

Raven giggled again. Susan shook her head with a smile and let the rest of the melting snow fall onto the carpet. Raven began to wiggle out of her arms, so Susan lowered her to the floor, letting her land with an ungraceful thump onto her diapered bottom.

"Silly girl," Susan said, pointing at her.

Raven pointed back.

Making another attempt, Susan stood near the wall bearing the Charlotte's Web characters and pointed.

"Pig."

Raven shook her head slowly, ignoring Susan, and caught a glimpse of her favorite bedtime book, *Goodnight Moon.*

Susan grabbed the book and pointed at the moon on the cover. "Moon." That would certainly be an enchanted choice for a Witch's daughter's next word.

Raven grumbled and shook her hand toward the book, making it clear that she didn't want to talk; she wanted a story.

"Okay, you win. I'll read you a story," Susan conceded.

But Susan could hear Tammy marching up the stairs, and she entered the room before Susan could join the baby on the floor.

"What is this?" Tammy asked, holding the lidless cookie jar out to Susan with one hand, her other hand on her hip.

Susan looked at her with confusion. "What?" If there was one good thing about the fact that she and Tammy couldn't stand one another, it was that Tammy wasn't always on her about what she ate.

"You think this is okay?" Tammy asked, tipping the jar forward to remind Susan of its contents.

She'd forgotten that the country cookie jar had been the latest place she'd been storing them since Tammy had become morally opposed to both marijuana and cookies.

"Yes, I do, actually. What's the big deal? It's not like Raven can reach the counter." Susan snapped.

"What's the big deal?" Tammy asked, placing the cookie jar on the changing table.

"My daughter eats food from that kitchen. And I'm sure she eats cookies from this jar when I'm not here," Tammy said, wagging her head dramatically.

"Yes, you're right; I put her cookies right in there next to the joints. In fact, no, I make her edibles every chance I get," Susan retorted.

"You're funny. Do you even know what it looks like if someone finds out there are illegal drugs in the house with a minor? I'm talking social service involvement."

"Illegal drugs? It's pot, not heroin," Susan said, clicking her tongue.

Tammy let out a long, dramatic sigh and shook her head. "I thought you understood how careful we have to be that Raven and I don't become a Black stereotype. I would have thought you at least had enough sense to keep this stuff in your car."

"And I thought you didn't want to become your mother, but it sounds like she just came out of your mouth. You're being ridiculous, Tammy." Susan said.

Tammy froze, and Susan could see the rage building in her eyes.

She'd succeeded in hitting Tammy where it hurt.

"What are we even doing here?" Tammy said, motioning to all three of them, not quite yelling, but with a definitively raised voice. "I don't think you need your *crystal ball* to tell you what's happening with us," she spat, her voice thick with condescension.

Raven squirmed and whined, and Susan kneeled down, rubbed her back, and handed her a doll to comfort her.

"I'm just telling you right now, Susan, I am going to do whatever it takes to make the kinds of family my Black daughter deserves. No matter what that means." Tammy said, lowering her voice. After an extended pause, she continued, "I hope you're hearing me."

It wasn't lost on Susan that Tammy kept calling Raven *her* daughter. As bad as things had gotten, that was new. She was sure that Tammy's next move was to pick Raven up and leave the room with her, even if she couldn't leave the house, just to follow the threat up with some action, but she didn't.

Raven reached up toward the cookie jar and shrieked her version of the word, "Coo!"

Knowing how adamant Tammy was about not letting Raven have sweets, Susan couldn't have been happier if *her* daughter had just told Tammy to fuck off.

"I should smash this piece of junk," Tammy spat, looking at the cookie jar with disdain as she turned to walk away.

Despite everything else that Tammy had said to her, it was only this that made the tears sting Susan's eyes. Tammy knew the story of the cookie jar, and that's exactly why she'd said what she did. Alice hadn't been able to get them the kind of housewarming present she wished she could. Instead, she'd gone to the thrift store and picked up some unique, sentimental things that she knew Susan would love. Even though the cookie jar was still in a box, and Susan assured Tammy that ceramic could be washed, Tammy had turned her nose up at it. Alice didn't have a lot of money, but her gifts were always thoughtful, and she'd chosen the cookie jar with the country birdhouses specifically because it was the same one that Susan's gramma had in her kitchen.

"You didn't seem to be too worried about the kind of family we were building during the first few months of her life," Susan said smugly as Tammy walked away, thinking she would be proud but feeling only heartbroken and ashamed at what she'd become.

Next week couldn't come soon enough; she and Raven would have four days alone.

* * * * *

Snuggling under her blanket cocoon, moments of her relationship with Tammy replayed in Susan's mind. Moments that added up to nearly five years of her life. The first time they met. Their trip that summer, and then later that year, their first Christmas together. Tammy's proposal. Their wedding. Raven's birth. Maybe if she could pinpoint the moment when things had turned to shit, she could figure out how to go back in time and fix it all.

As many sweet memories as she had of them, the smaller, ugly details were much louder again tonight. She tried to focus Thea's purr against her chest and block out the panic from the prospect of her life falling apart, but suddenly, there seemed to be no air left in her cocoon. Flailing, she threw the comforter off her head and gulped in a breath. Thea squirmed, found her hand, and gave it a firm nudge. Her breathing eased, and she knew what she needed, at least in that moment. She grabbed the notebook that sat on her nightstand and scrawled out her thoughts. Although Fiona had made it clear that she could call her whenever she wanted, even if they both hated the phone, she hadn't bothered to add an international data package to her cell plan. Besides, she could always express herself so much better in writing.

April 9, 2002

Dear Fiona,

How the fuck did I get here? How did I manage to become the third generation of women in my family to be stuck in a shitty marriage? The third generation of women to be raising a child in a poisonous family? I feel so pathetic that I'm staying at all anymore. I've felt that way for longer than I want to admit, but I'm desperate. How the hell am I going to find a reason to go on if Tammy takes Raven away from me? Making things work with her is the only way I can hold onto Raven. So don't tell me to let it be. I refuse to let go of my daughter.

I have absolutely no legal rights to Raven. I didn't want to believe Tammy would do this to me. But now, here I am, trying to figure out how I can make it right with Tammy even though I can feel it - we are so close to our breaking point. I know she's cheating on me. She's away right now. Says it's a nursing conference, but in my gut, I know what's going on. It's that same gut feeling I had when you told me to get legal paperwork for Raven.

I think I'm finally going crazy! Like, literally crazy, Fiona. I honestly don't think I would be functioning at all if I didn't have to take care of Raven and Thea. Thank Gaia for them.

It still doesn't make sense to me how love can NOT be enough because we did have love. We were soooo good together in the beginning. But now, some days, it feels like there's less than nothing, if that's even possible. Like she dug inside me and took out everything. Can someone do that? Can someone steal your soul? Because I feel like she hollowed me out like an ugly, rotting jack-o-lantern.

I know we both love Raven. It might be the only thing I'm sure of anymore. I'm so confused because I do still have times when I love her, but I hate her too, like really, really hate her, could almost fucking murder her, Fiona. I mean, how can I NOT love her on some level? Do other people really just stop loving people? I don't think I ever have.

Sometimes, I wish I could. I think it would be easier if I could just not care anymore. But if I still care for people from my past, people I never even dated, people who crushed me, I'm sure I'll never stop loving my daughter's mother.

I'm sorry for dumping all of this on you again. I just need...I don't know what I need...I need help. I need things to stop feeling so out of control. I need the pain to stop. I just don't want to beat my head against a wall anymore. Something needs to change.

Thank you for being here for me. I always feel a little better after I get this all out. Even before I mail it, it always feels like you've already heard me the moment the words hit the page.

Love, Susan

A whimper from Raven's room pulled her away. She'd only been asleep for an hour. Although her exhaustion had lifted some since Tammy had been away, she was still soul-tired. She'd hoped to nap while Raven did but had mainly just laid there and let her mind race instead.

Turning her head toward the door, she didn't hear the baby again. As she was finally drifting off, Tammy's ringtone woke her.

"Fuck!" She considered not answering but gave in. "Hello?"

"Hey. I just wanted to call to check on Raven. Haven't heard from you," Tammy replied.

"She's asleep now. It's been a rough day with the gremlin," Susan said.

"Now? You let her nap *now*? It's like four o'clock there. That's going to mess up her schedule, and then I'm going to get to come home and make it right again. I go away for a three-day weekend and..."

She would have to come home and make it all right again? She held back all the mean and nasty things she wanted to say about Tammy's apathy for their daughter for nearly the first four months of her life.

"So happy I picked up the phone," Susan muttered.

"Did you at least use the cream from the doctor on her rash?" Tammy asked.

"What the fuck, Tammy? Of course, I did. No, I just let her loose in the yard to fend for herself since Friday. I may not do everything exactly like you do, but I know how to care for her. I'll have her schedule back to normal by the time you return, don't worry. *I* won't put it all on *you*." She hoped that Tammy would receive the dig right in her heart.

Susan could hear Tammy hushing someone in the background; more than likely, it was that bitch, Stacy. Susan wanted to rip her bouncy curls right out of her head when she remembered how Stacy had touched Tammy's arm that day at the hospital and said she was jealous. And now, they were at a nursing conference together? From the first time Tammy had mentioned the trip, something hadn't felt right, but Susan simply had no energy to care. Her stomach dropped. Although it wasn't exactly a shock that Tammy was doing something she shouldn't be doing, feeling it with such certainty now was awful. It was the same feeling she'd had so many times in their relationship but had willfully chosen to ignore.

"How's the conference?" Susan almost gagged on her words.

"It's fine," Tammy replied.

Susan could hear the wavering in Tammy's voice. She didn't have the energy to play the game. Whatever Tammy was doing, it was already done.

"I'm going to try to get a few minutes rest before our daughter wakes up," Susan said.

"Okay," Tammy replied.

"I love you." Susan hadn't even known she wasn't going to say it. Although she rarely said it to Tammy in person these days, her wife was halfway across the country, and life offered no guarantees that someone would return home. She couldn't *not* say it. Whether

Tammy returned the sentiment or not, she wasn't sorry.

After a long pause, Tammy whispered, "L...love you too."

Susan fell back into the same broken sleep she had become accustomed to. When she stirred again, she couldn't be sure if it had been minutes or hours. Thea mewed at her as Susan rolled over to see what time it was. She was surprised to find that it was just past one.

Why hadn't Raven woken up? Tangled in the comforter, she managed to get one foot out onto the floor but dragged the comforter with her, nearly falling face-first onto the floor. In a huff, she ripped the comforter from her leg and threw it on the floor, worried that she'd crushed the kitten in the midst of it all. But Thea scurried out a moment later with a sideways jump, diving back into the heap to play.

Susan found the baby still sound asleep and breathing, just like every other time she'd worried for nothing. Susan felt her shoulders relax and her eyes fill with tears. Motherhood was so hard. Raven must have been just as exhausted as she was if she was still sleeping; teething hadn't been easy on either of them. Should she wake her? Was she wet? Did she need more Tylenol? In the end, she had to remind herself of the one thing she'd learned in the last nine months of motherhood. She had to trust that her daughter's body had the wisdom to know what it needed. And, in this moment, it seemed she just needed rest.

She scooped Thea up and went downstairs. She needed some cold pizza and a joint.

The kitchen table was messy, covered with the pizza box from supper, dried-up baby bottles, toys, and groceries that had yet to make it to the cupboards. She'd have to clean up a little, but she needed food first. She trudged back upstairs, grabbing a joint from the cookie jar, which she'd kept in the bedroom since Tammy had threatened to smash it. Once back downstairs, she pulled out a chair to sit at the dining room table, but the mess was too much.

Plopping onto the couch instead, she slid her backpack over and retrieved a lighter from the front pocket. She was too lazy to choose a CD, so she switched the radio on. After some chatter from the DJ, she shook her head at the lyrics of *It's Too Late*. She'd heard the seventies song a million times, but this time she really listened. It was as if Carole King had a window directly into her little life.

Usually, when she was alone with Raven, she only allowed herself three or four tokes from a joint, but as the music played on, her emotions rose closer and closer to the surface until she could feel them like barbed wire on her skin. She'd be okay. Always had been. Always would be. But before she knew it, she'd smoked three-quarters of the joint and had begun sobbing. In this moment, she wasn't okay. DJ called twice that night; both times, she watched the phone ring and wrapped herself up in her isolation.

She remembered her and Tammy's first date, back when Tammy was still Tamika. The psychic CD player. The universe always found a way to communicate. How could she still love Tammy when she undeniably hated her, too? It was eating her up to feel so conflicted all the time about the woman she had built a life with. At least once a day, it crossed her mind that she was so exhausted she just wished she'd die in her sleep to escape. She knew it was dramatic, but her mind had stirred up the same extreme thought since she'd been very young.

She decided she wouldn't bother to confront Tammy about her so-called conference. There was no use asking a question you already had the answers to, and she certainly didn't want the details.

CHAPTER TWENTY-TWO

Although she'd spent the last several weeks unsure if she would follow through with going, now that Tammy was back from Boston, Susan was happy she was going out tonight. She'd almost decided against buying the ticket when she'd seen the e-mail from the Iron Horse arrive in her e-mail inbox last month. But it was rare for a big name like the Indigo Girls to play at such a small venue, even in a small lesbian community, so she couldn't pass it up. She'd even hesitated for a second when she had reached the step with the drop-down box to select how many tickets she wanted. It hadn't been an emotional pause but a habitual one. She had grown so accustomed to choosing two of everything that the one looked foreign. She'd even considered inviting Michael, but deep down, she wanted to go alone, even if she was anxious about it. She needed to do something just for herself.

She'd taken the day off from work. She needed the entire day to psych herself up about her adventure. The show didn't start until seven, but of course, she would be one of the first ones to arrive so she could get a great seat. The drive to Northampton would take nearly an hour, so it felt sensible when she started to get ready at three.

As she spent over an hour getting ready, she smirked, remembering that Thursdays had always been her night out back in her wild club days with Michael. It felt exciting to revive that part of herself a little bit. Maybe the Indigo Girls weren't exactly wild, but still, they had the lesbian vibe, which was wild enough. She wasn't fond of dancing, and the music at clubs quickly became too loud for her, but that sapphic energy always pulled her back in. It wasn't that she missed those days or wanted them back; it was the lesbian side of her she wanted back, one that she felt no longer existed since she and Tammy had grown apart. The Indigo Girls could always give her a good dose of that.

She'd become such a homebody book nerd that this felt unfamiliar. Wasn't it just weird to go out alone? Wouldn't it make her seem like she was looking? She certainly wasn't looking for anything other than something to bring her back to a part of herself that felt nearly lost. Was she? Fuck; why did she have to overthink everything? People went out alone all the time, even if she never really had.

She simply told Tammy that she would be home late and asked her to take care of Raven the next morning, finding herself surprisingly disappointed when Tammy didn't even ask why. Why did she even care that Tammy didn't ask? Would these little flutters of heartbreak ever stop? Would she ever just not care? Because, at this point, she truly hoped that day would come. Caring even a little bit was just too exhausting.

Tammy had often come home late herself recently, and Susan hadn't questioned her either, but still, it wasn't the same. Since Tammy always had Raven with her, Susan had to assume that she'd been visiting her parents more again. Maybe it would be good for both of them.

After spending two solid hours deciding what to wear, she ended up with simple jeans and a flannel over her old black tee with brightly colored music notes. She and Micheal had each bought one years ago and worn them to every concert. Keys in hand, she opened the front door to leave and patted her back pocket to make sure she had her wallet, proud that she hadn't bailed on herself. She had to laugh at herself, though. She wasn't traveling the world solo; she was just going to a show by herself.

She arrived well before the doors opened at 6:30, knowing she would need to psych herself up again once she reached Northampton and saw the Iron Horse. Still, it was too dorky to be the first in line, too. She could hear Fiona telling her to cut the shit with her overthinking, and she flipped her middle finger into the ether.

She could see a couple of people lined up, which was her cue. She looked in the rearview mirror to make sure her ponytail didn't need smoothing, grabbed her ticket from the console, and forced herself out of the car and into line. The woman in front of her turned around and flashed a smile at her. Susan had always been grateful for her red cheeks, for even when she could feel herself blush, no one else could see it. The woman was a soft butch and was probably in her mid-fifties. She was a little round and looked utterly powerful yet gentle. Maybe what stood out about her most was that she didn't look afraid. Susan imagined she might look a little like this woman in about thirty years if only she could work on her fear of the world.

Maybe she hadn't been friendly enough. She should have said hello. She just didn't know how to talk to people. At work, she was different; she could talk about books to anyone, but in the rest of the world, it was a different story. And places like this were even worse. She knew it was ridiculous, but as much as she was invigorated by the energy of places frequented by lesbians, being amongst other gay women made her anxious, too.

She didn't know what to do with herself when they smiled at her, and when they talked to her, she tended to freeze first, then panic, which usually ended up making her say something weird. For a long time, she was aware that people assumed she was a snob because she didn't say much, but it was really that she knew saying less was better for preserving her dignity.

Within a few minutes, Susan could hear people rustling about inside as they readied themselves to open the doors and more people lining up behind her. If the social aspect alone hadn't been enough, noise and action added to her anxiety. The real world was just too stimulating; it was why she was such a homebody.

Finally, right at 6:30, the door swung open. She could see the glow from inside and knew that she'd be glad she came once she got a seat. The woman at the door took her ticket and greeted her, explaining to her and the next few people behind her that there was open seating at the tables and no wait service, but the bar was open. She wanted a drink. Now. But she wasn't much for bar seating. Too loud. Too close.

Although she spotted the perfect two-seater table in the corner, she'd have to risk losing it to get her drink. Only one person was waiting there now, so she'd probably succeed in getting her table. The bartender held a finger up to her from the other end of the bar, then dumped two buckets of ice into a metal cooler. Susan wasn't much of an ass woman, but this chick truly did have a cute butt, which was framed in dark Lee jeans. She didn't think she had ever owned a pair of Lee jeans in her life; when you were chubby, you were lucky to find jeans that weren't so obviously stretchy that it just screamed out that you were too fat for real jeans. The woman tossed the buckets in the back, then walked toward her.

"What can I get you?" The bartender asked, brushing her black curly hair from her face.

Susan stuttered nervously for a moment but then laughed. "Shit. I'm sorry. I don't even know."

The woman put a knuckle to her chin and narrowed her wild, green eyes. "Let me see if I can guess. I'm known as the psychic bartender around here."

"Okay." Susan smiled. That was right up her alley.

"I can tell you one thing. You're not a beer person. But not wine, either," the bartender postulated.

Susan couldn't help but show her shock, although it could have been a good guess.

"Am I right?" The bartender asked.

Susan nodded.

"I want to say... Damn, you're hard to read. I know it's not beer or wine, but I don't know what your go-to is." She paused. "Is it because you don't *have* a go-to?"

Susan thought about it, then shrugged. "Hmm, I guess not. I mean, I just don't drink much anymore." She didn't add that she preferred pot.

The bartender nodded. "Still, still. My ego is bruised here. Usually, I'd even be able to tell you what you used to drink. Can't even do that. You're a closed book, Honey."

"You know, I think I might want to try something new, but I never know what to try," Susan said.

"Now *that* I can help you with." The bartender poked one finger at Susan. "I'm just going to go ahead and let my ego be bruised and have you tell me outright what you usually like best."

"Mostly spicy screwdrivers," Susan replied.

"What?" The bartender burst out laughing. "Been a bartender for a decade now, and I've never heard of that one."

"You know. Orange juice and Captain Morgan spiced rum," Susan explained.

"Oh, oh, sure." The bartender chuckled. "Never heard it called that. I like it. So, you *do* like a little kick, and you *do* like citrus."

Susan nodded.

"I think I know what to give you. You like margaritas?" The bartender asked.

"Not sure I ever tried one," Susan replied.

"I don't get the sense that you're exactly a lightweight, am I right?" The bartender continued her line of questioning.

"No. Not at all. I mean, I guess I could be now since I haven't had a drink in a while..." Susan said.

"Naw, if you can handle your liquor, I think you'd love a top-shelf margarita. It's not exotic or anything; it's classic. With shitty tequila, they can be rough, but with Patron, they're smooooth as fuck." The bartender squinted her eyes shut as if she was savoring the flavor as she stood there. "And if you don't like it, I'll make you something else." She turned around and began to work her magic.

"No salt," Susan said.

"No?" The woman asked but tipped her head thoughtfully. "Yeah, I guess I can see that. What about sugar?"

"Sure. I'll try that," Susan replied.

The bartender laid a napkin on the counter a minute later and set the margarita on top. "Give her a try."

She wasn't thrilled to be on display, and she would have preferred to just try it at her table, but she indulged the bartender. Even cupping it carefully, Susan let a few drops escape over the side but tried to ignore it cooly as the woman watched her sip slowly once, then twice to really let it wash over her pallet.

"Ooh. Yeah, that's really good," Susan said.

"Smooth, right?"

Susan nodded and took another sip. "I can't believe I've never had one before. Good call."

"It's what I do." The bartender smiled.

Susan reached for her wallet and retrieved a twenty.

"Twelve bucks," the bartender said.

"Thank you." A simple thank you wasn't quite what Susan had hoped to express; she wanted to thank the bartender for working so hard to connect and make sure she got what she wanted, even if it was just a drink. But she couldn't say all that. The tip would have to show her appreciation instead. She smiled and began to walk away, looking at the little corner table to find that, luckily, it was still free.

"Thank *you*. Enjoy the show." The bartender smiled.

"You too," Susan called back over her shoulder. Was that stupid? The bartender wasn't here to enjoy the show; she was here to work.

Susan sat down, sipping her margarita a little too quickly as she had always done with drinks. A comfortable buzz settled in as she watched people filter in and fill the seats. When the glass was half empty, she went up to get a second one before the bar got too saturated with people, leaving her flannel shirt on her chair to save her spot. It looked strange to have two drinks going, but then again, no one knew she was alone.

She slurped down the last few drops of the first margarita. The room was almost full now. The sounds of tuning instruments carried over the talk and laughter. Shifting in her seat, she felt her flannel slide off the chair and onto the floor. She leaned over to pick it up, and when she sat up to put it on the chair opposite her, a gorgeous face smiled at her from across the table.

"Oh, my gosh, hi!" Susan said excitedly once it registered that it was Steph standing there. Even in her plain black sweatshirt and olive cargo pants, she looked like a Goddess.

"I saw you from line and had to come over. It's *so* good to see you." It was one of the things that Susan had always loved about Steph. Some people just said that sort of thing when they ran into you, but you could tell it was a line. Something people had been trained to say. But not with Steph; with her, it was always genuine.

"You too. How have you been?" Susan asked.

With that question, Steph seemed to shrink into herself a little, and she ran her hand through her blond spikes. "You know. Hanging in there." She shrugged her shoulders and nodded as if she was trying to convince herself.

Susan knew that kind of hanging in there too well.

"How about you? How have you been?" Steph asked.

Susan let out a sigh and a little laugh. "Hanging in there about covers it."

"So sorry to hear that." Steph moved around the table and patted Susan on the shoulder.

"That's life." Susan shrugged and took a sip from her second drink.

"Anyway, I just had to come say hello. It's just so good to see you," Steph said. But she didn't walk away.

"You too. It's always good to see you." Susan said. The tequila must be helping; she almost forgot to worry that she was being too sentimental again.

"It's packed in here," Steph said, scanning the room.

Susan nodded, throwing back another gulp.

"Are you...with anyone? If not, do you mind if I join you?" Steph asked, motioning to the seat that held Susan's flannel.

"Oh my gosh, I'm sorry. Of course. I didn't even..."

"Thanks. I'm so excited now; this is so much better than seeing the show alone. Why *are* you here alone, though? No Tamika?" Steph asked.

"I can't believe you remember her name." Susan smiled, not correcting Steph about Tammy's name change. She shook her head. "No. She...we...no." Susan sighed.

"I'm so sorry, Susan. You guys looked so happy that day at Pride," Steph said softly, her blue eyes full of compassion.

"That feels like so long ago," Susan said.

"I can understand that," Steph replied.

"Sorry. I don't mean to be a downer." Susan lowered her head.

"Stop apologizing. You always did that. You don't need to be sorry. Not with me," Steph said.

Susan smiled. "I forgot that was the last time we saw one another. Feels like a lifetime ago." She reached into her back pocket for her wallet. "I have a daughter. Her name is Raven," she said, handing a photo to Steph.

"Oh my gosh," Steph squealed.

Susan had always adored the fact that, every now and then, Steph let out the most girly sound even though she was rather butch.

"She's just...awesome. I can't believe you're a mom," Steph said.

"I can't either." Susan laughed. I really need to update the picture I carry around with me, though. She's only like six months in that picture. She'll be turning a year old next month."

"So, how is that working out? I'm assuming you had her with Tamika." Steph asked.

"Yeah. It's...not. If I'm being honest, it's not working at all. It's fucking awful living with her like this," Susan replied.

"Are you two...? You know what, I'm sorry. You don't have to talk about it if you don't want to. It must be unimaginably hard," Steph said.

Susan nodded, appreciating Steph's thoughtfulness. "It is, but yeah, you know what, let's enjoy the music. Let's enjoy each other."

"This moment, right? There's nothing else but this moment," Steph said.

"That's it." Susan smiled, meeting Steph's eyes for a moment.

"In AA, they teach us that whole, *one day at a time*, thing, but it's not even that; it's really just this moment. That's it. I think September eleventh taught us that." Steph shook her head slowly as she spoke.

"Well said," Susan replied.

Susan could hear an attempted note being strummed on a guitar. The opening act must be close to starting.

"You want another drink? I'm going up," Steph asked.

"Yes, please. Here..." Susan reached for her wallet, but Steph put her hand over Susan's to stop her.

"I got it, I got it. What are you drinking?" Steph asked.

Susan wished Steph hadn't touched her. Everything she'd ever felt for Steph had always been held precariously behind the wall that only fell when she touched her. She met Steph's eyes and resisted the urge to pull her hand away. Steph smiled; she'd always been such an intense energy, and Susan had rarely known anyone with her genuine warmth, before her or since.

"A mar...margarita," Susan stuttered.

She watched Steph go to the bar, appreciating her solid, butchy frame and the way that she seemed to talk to the bartender effortlessly. Steph returned a few minutes later and set her drink down.

"Top shelf, huh?" Steph smiled.

"Oh, I'm sorry. I know it's pretty pricey," Susan replied.

"No, I was thinking that you deserved top shelf," Steph said.

"Aww." Susan wouldn't have let that come out if she hadn't been buzzed.

"Can I ask you a question?" Steph asked as she sat back down.

"Sure," Susan replied.

"Why *do* you always feel like you have to apologize? For taking up space?"

"I don't know. I mean...the drink was, what, twelve bucks? I never want it to seem like I'm taking advantage of someone or...I don't know, I don't want to be a..." She stopped.

"You were going to say a burden, right?" Steph asked.

Susan nodded.

"I thought so. You're not. And as far as taking advantage of people, I don't think anyone could ever think that of you. You're always trying to give; I think sometimes you need to let others give back. To take care of you," Steph said.

Susan took a sip of her drink and was thankful when she heard the opening act begin to play because she had no idea how to respond to Steph.

Although she had heard of the opening band, The Butchies, their music was unfamiliar to Susan. She'd discovered some great music this way, though. Punk rock had never really been her go-to. Still, she loved the girl power vibe that only gay girls could deliver.

Their set list seemed short, but based on what she heard of them, Susan decided she should probably buy one of their CDs to add to her lesbian music library.

As Kaia, one of The Butchies, welcomed the Indigo Girls to the stage, Steph turned around with a double thumbs up and a giant smile. "That was awesome!"

Sipping a fourth margarita, which Steph had brought her without even asking, Susan let the nostalgia of the Indigo Girls' older songs wash over her. By intermission, she was drunk, and everything felt bittersweet. None of the songs she'd held up on a pedestal so long ago as an example of what she thought living her life would be had been entirely accurate, yet, at the same time, each held a seed of truth, too.

"I want another drink. You want another drink?" Steph asked. She didn't slur her words, but her voice was slightly deeper. Susan remembered that meant she had a good buzz going.

Susan nodded.

"You going to let me take care of you?" She asked, patting her back pocket.

Susan smiled and nodded.

"Looks like you're deep in thought," Steph said when she returned.

Susan giggled. "Actually, I was sitting here thinking how surprised I am that you like the Indigo Girls."

"Why does everyone say that to me?" Steph laughed.

"They're softer and more poetic than the groups I think you'd like."

Steph moved her chair closer and leaned in playfully. "You know, you're not wrong. I like them, I do, but I admit I really came to see The Butchies."

"Okay, *that* makes more sense," Susan replied.

"I had no idea you could read me like that," Steph said.

"Seriously?" Susan slapped her palm to her forehead and shook her head. Steph still had no idea after all these years. Susan had been able to read her to an extent from the first time she'd laid eyes on her. Until she met Steph, she'd never believed in love at first sight; she'd assumed it was a notion based solely on appearance, which wasn't what love was about at all. But the connection she'd felt with Steph had made her understand it; it was a soul thing.

"I remember it was your birthday a few weeks ago, too. So, happy belated birthday. I should be buying *you* a drink," Susan added.

The music started again, and Susan couldn't help but think how fitting the lyrics to *Galileo* were for her at this time in her life. She was eternally certain that she'd never get it right, this thing called being human. After three more songs and another drink each, Susan couldn't be sure if feeling Steph's hand against her leg was purposeful or just the consequence of her being drunk and floppy.

"Can I buy you one more drink before we have to go?" Steph asked after the band had played its last song and exited.

"I mean...if they'll let us. I think they're closing up," Susan replied.

"Well, let me try." Steph went to the bar as most of the other people, minus the stage crew, exited the building.

Steph came back, beaming with two drinks in her hand.

"So, what about you? You came to see The Indigo Girls more than you did The Butchies?" Steph asked.

Susan nodded. "I've actually never heard The Butchies before. I've heard *of* them but never heard anything *by* them."

"Really? Steph dramatized a dreamy inhale. "They're just..." Steph let out a sigh and held her chest.

"I was surprised to see a punk band opening for the Indigo Girls. But I was in awe when they played a song together. Music kind of amazes me," Susan said.

"It's like a different language," Steph added.

Those were the kinds of things that Steph had always said that made Susan want to just get up and kiss her without saying a word. Susan nodded and sipped her drink, trying to get the thought out of her head. She could never pull that off anyway, at least not in the way she imagined it.

"The Goddess of music speaks." Susan smirked.

"I miss that. The quirky stuff that comes out of your mouth," Steph said and paused. "Do you have to be...home?" Steph asked as Susan finished her last sip.

Susan shook her head. "Honestly doesn't fucking matter. I don't have a *home*. Not really. Besides, I'm too drunk."

"So, do you want to get coffee or something? I'll stay with you until you can drive," Steph offered.

"I'm not going to be able to leave Northampton tonight. And you shouldn't drive either," Susan said, shaking her finger at Steph.

Steph hung her head. "Yeah."

"I'm either going to have to walk to a hotel or sleep in my car." Susan stood up and stumbled just a little. Steph held Susan's arm as she steadied herself.

"You okay?" Steph asked.

Susan nodded.

"I'm not sure walking too far is a good idea." Steph laughed.

"No, I'm really okay, now that I'm moving..." Susan giggled and put both her arms up, feeling silly. She'd been far more drunk than this but still felt as if she could fly.

"Susan..."

Susan put her hand up to pause Steph; she was pretty sure she knew what Steph was about to say, but she'd read her wrong before and needed a minute to prepare herself for the possibility that she was wrong again. She looked up and locked eyes with Steph, and

Steph took a step closer.

"What?" She asked Steph, feeling brave and hopeful but terrified.

"I mean, I just fucking adore you. I don't want to overstep. I know you're technically still with Tamika, but I'd love to spend the night with you. So, are you going to let me take care of you?"

Susan exhaled a breath she didn't know she'd been holding in.

"But, I mean, I can just make sure *you* get to a hotel if..."

"Steph, I've been waiting for you to *take care of me* for, oh, I don't know, what, seven years? Not that I've been counting. Do you know how many times I used to play, *Damn I Wish I Was Your Lover* over and over and think of you?" She laughed, feeling free as she said it aloud.

"Come on." Steph took Susan by the hand and led her down the street. Susan didn't know where they were going and really didn't care. When she fell in love with Steph, she knew she would follow her anywhere.

"The Hotel Northampton is close," Steph said.

Susan burst into laughter, and Steph joined in until they laughed so hard that they had to stop walking.

"Why is that so funny?" Steph asked.

"The Hotel Northampton is where I had my junior prom. I think it's pretty cool that there I was, some ten or twelve years ago, in a dress, feeling like I was in drag, both my date and I as gay as they come. So, it feels kind of full circle to go there again and actually get to do it right this time," Susan explained.

Steph giggled. "Glad I can be a part of that."

Although they giggled together for the rest of the walk, they managed to compose themselves long enough so they wouldn't be denied a room for seeming too drunk and rowdy. It wasn't just any hotel; it was too classy a place to rent to two drunk, obnoxious people in the middle of the night.

"This is gorgeous," Susan said when Steph opened the door to the room.

"Very Victorian," Steph added.

"Very bed and breakfast feel, without the socializing. Fuck bed and breakfasts." Susan laughed.

Steph emptied her pockets, kicked off her shoes, and sank into one of the grand armchairs by the window that overlooking the patio.

"Look." Steph pointed out the window.

A lone woman sat at the garden bar beneath the string of lights covering the wooden gazebo. You could see the woman's breath rising into the night air.

"Was it that cold out there?" Susan asked, unsure what she was supposed to be looking at.

Steph shrugged. "What do you think her story is?"

Susan smiled and looked at Steph, who seemed different here. Steph didn't look up at her but continued to gaze out the window, which allowed Susan to study her a little longer. The difference was that she looked tired now. Not tired, like she needed to sleep, but soul tired, like she needed peace. While all Susan had ever wanted for Steph was happiness, somehow, seeing her look this worn made her feel even more for her.

"I don't know. What do *you* think her story is?" Susan asked. These were the kinds of conversations she loved but didn't get to have nearly often enough.

"I don't know, exactly. Just seems like she can't be happy if she's out there drinking alone. I know that people will say some people can be happy alone, but I'm not so sure about that," Steph said.

"I agree. Seems sad to drink alone. I've always just wanted...you know, that someone. To share special moments with," Susan said.

Steph nodded and stood up. Susan could see her face change from serious to more playful; she loved all of Steph's sides.

"So, you'd never heard The Butchies music before, huh?" Steph asked.

Susan shook her head. "Am I out of the club?" Susan laughed.

Steph chuckled. "Naw. But you know, I wish they'd played *She's So Lovely* tonight. If there is one song by them that you need to hear, it's that one?"

"*She's So Lovely*? Like, the same one that Stevie Wonder sings?" Susan asked, surprised. "That's one of my songs for Raven."

Steph let out a loud belly laugh. "No. I think that's, *Isn't She Lovely*. This one is just so lesbian. I wish I could play it for you. It's the essence of how utterly amazing it is to be in total adoration of a female being. No feeling like it, you know?"

"I think I might just know that feeling." Susan smirked and looked away.

"Still?" Steph asked, sounding surprised.

"Always, Steph." She looked back and answered. "That's just how I am. If I love you, I love you for life."

Steph stood and came to her, touching her face softly. Susan tried to speak but couldn't.

"What?" Susan asked.

"I don't know. You just amaze me. The way you love..." Steph replied.

"What do you mean?" Susan asked.

"I don't know, I mean, why me? How? How can you feel all that for me when I'm...a mess?" Steph asked.

"All of us are a mess. That has nothing to do with your soul. I love you at a soul level. I just see past all that mess," Susan explained.

"I wish I could see past it. With myself, I mean. But I know what you're saying...it's easier to do that with someone else," Steph said.

"It is," Susan agreed.

Steph paused and took a long look at her. "Can I kiss you?"

"Seven years, Steph. Seven years," Susan said, leaning into her and meeting her lips. She'd waited for this moment for so long.

"You're adorable," Steph said when they came up for air. Lots of women had called her that before, and she'd never cared for it. Sexy. Passionate. Those were the ways she hoped someone might see her. But obviously, adorable wasn't so bad if Steph wanted to be with her.

"You do know why I never allowed myself to be, you know, into you, right?" Steph asked.

"What? No, I know. I mean, you told me. I was reserved and didn't have an edge," Susan replied.

"Well, yea, you were reserved. That was part of it. And now I know that it wasn't that you didn't have an edge. I just couldn't see that edge yet. But honestly, those things were only half-truths. You know how I told you earlier that you deserved top shelf?" Steph asked.

"Yeah," Susan answered.

"Well, I'm not top shelf. I just knew what you wanted. You wanted the whole thing, and I wanted you to have that with someone who was top shelf," Steph explained, adjusting her glasses with one finger and looking down at the floor.

"I hate that you see yourself that way," Susan replied.

Steph shrugged. "I have to get something else out before we... I mean, I want to be here with you tonight, whether we do or not. Just *be* with you. And it probably sounds awful, but I don't care that you're married. You're in a shit place, and if you really want this, too, it's like I said before...all we can focus on is this moment. And I know I want to spend this moment with you, even in the circumstances you're in, if that's what you really want, too. But I don't want you to do anything you don't want to," Steph said.

Susan nodded. "It's true. There *is* only this moment. I appreciate you making sure, but I do. I definitely do want to be with you."

"I have a question for you," Steph said.

"Oh, Goddess, what's that?" Susan laughed.

"Can I see the tattoo again?" Steph asked, her eyes serious.

"Ugh...my Goddess. You know, if there was just *one* thing I wished you didn't remember about me, *that* would be it," Susan said, hiding her head in her hands.

"What? That's silly. It was one of the things about you that wasn't reserved. I loved that you could wear your heart on your sleeve with me like that. Or, should I say, on your chest?" She grinned. "Can I...?" Steph put her hand on Susan's shirt.

"Yeah, but..." She didn't finish. Instead, she let Steph peel off her tee shirt, exposing the ink on her chest. "I had to get it covered up, but you can still kind of see your name under the sun's rays if you look," Susan said, pointing.

Steph traced the sun's rays with her finger. "Had to get it covered when you met Tamika?" Steph asked.

Susan shook her head. "No, I had to do it for me. To move forward. Let you go."

"I never felt like I deserved that place on you. In you," Steph replied.

"Love isn't something someone can deserve, Steph. You don't earn love. It just is," Susan said.

"See, that. *That* right there is what I always adored about you. The depth. When you actually let it out, that is," Steph said.

Susan smiled and leaned in, hungry to meet Steph's lips again, and Steph didn't disappoint her.

"I want this to be...nice. Sweet," Steph said, pulling away and taking down the bedspread.

Susan stood still, unsure if her trembling was from excitement or the fear that still lingered in her. Steph was about to see her naked; maybe they should turn out the lights. But she didn't make a move. Steph held out one hand, and when Susan came closer, she removed her own shirt, exposing the sleeved arms that had always turned Susan on so easily, and held Susan wordlessly for what felt like forever. Just to feel their skin touching was bliss.

Susan reached up and ran her fingers through Steph's spiky hair, and Steph lowered them both onto the bed. They kissed feverishly for a few minutes, then both lost their bras and, finally, everything else. Susan wasn't drunk anymore, and she was grateful that she could experience every moment fully. The fact that Steph was a gentle lover didn't surprise Susan, but Steph's primary focus on pleasuring her did.

Steph moved slowly down Susan's body, kissing every inch of skin as she went. When Steph pulled away from Susan's belly, moving lower, Susan stopped moving her hips.

Steph stopped and sat up. "Are you okay?"

Susan nodded. Steph put her hand on Susan's naked thigh. "No, what's wrong?"

"I just have a hard time letting go. Like *really* letting go," Susan answered.

"Let me take care of you," Steph whispered, enunciating every word.

Susan nodded and lay back, allowing her hips to move with Steph's rhythm. As if immersed in water, she felt nearly weightless as Steph held her ass up with her hands. And when she reached orgasm, she didn't stifle her scream. As she let the sound escape her throat, it felt like madness and bliss all at once, for there was so much held in the ether of the scream: longing and ache and the pure delight of being fully in the moment, something she wasn't accustomed to.

After making love twice, Steph crawled behind her and held her until they fell asleep. And when Susan woke up still in her arms the next morning and figured out she wasn't dreaming, she smiled in awe. She wasn't even a bit sorry; it had been one of the most special nights of her life. Now, she just had to accept that it would come to an end. But she could at least make it last a little longer; she lay still and watched the sun dance on the floral walls until Steph stirred, woke, and finally rose, ending their oneness.

"Good morning," Steph said with a warm smile.

"Morning," Susan replied, looking at the clock. "Shit, I have to call the store and tell them I'm not coming in," she said, grabbing her phone.

"Want to get some breakfast?" Steph asked after Susan hung up.

"Love to." Susan could feel tears forming in her eyes, knowing they would have to part soon.

Steph must have noticed because she touched her arm and said, "Remember, just live in *this* moment."

Susan nodded, thinking of Fiona. "People are always telling me that."

"Hey, I think I might have left my keys at the Iron Horse," Susan said, emerging from the bathroom after freshening up and getting dressed.

"I'm not sure if anyone is there, but we can swing by to see when I bring you to your car," Steph said.

Susan's gut fell; this *would* end.

"Wait, where's *your* car?" Susan asked.

"I honestly don't remember," Steph replied.

Susan looked at her, confused.

"I drank a lot yesterday. Before I drove in," Steph said.

"We'll find it after breakfast," Susan said, trying not to wince at what Steph had just told her.

Steph nodded.

When they entered the diner, there were only counter seats left. It wasn't Susan's first choice, but it would have to do.

"You know what's weird?" Steph asked after they'd ordered, and the waitress had disappeared into the kitchen.

"What?" Susan asked.

"That we can have such an amazing night and then have to go back to our lives like it never happened. Figure out our lives. Fix our lives. We can live in *that* moment, but then all the shit that was there is just still there, waiting for us," Steph answered.

"Yeah. It sucks. That all of life can't be that magical," Susan replied.

She liked how they weren't talking about the specifics. The ugly things they had to do to fix their lives. But one question burned in her mind: would they stay in touch? She couldn't imagine walking away from the connection they had to just go back to losing touch again.

"I don't think life gets much better than bacon," Susan said as she ate.

"Right? So awful for you but so delicious," Steph replied.

"I'll probably think of you every time I eat bacon from now on," Susan said shyly.

"*She's* so lovely." Steph's eyes shined, and she pointed a finger at Susan.

"I seriously need to hear that song. I'll have to buy their album," Susan said, feeling a blush on her cheeks.

"If we ever find my car, we can listen before we go," Steph said.

"I'm going to pay for this," Susan insisted when the check came.

"Nope," Steph said simply.

"But you've paid for everything," Susan said.

"You're going to let me take care of you. Just a little longer. It's okay if it's uncomfortable. You're just not used to it." Steph smiled and paused, looking around as if she was lost. "Hmm. I'm assuming I either parked in the garage or the lot that's back behind Thorne's Marketplace."

"Let's try the lot," Susan said, and they started walking back toward the Iron Horse.

"Do you think we should see if anyone is at the Iron Horse yet? See if they have your keys?" Steph asked.

"I'd honestly be surprised if anyone was there right now. Besides, I'm not in any hurry for this to end," Susan replied.

They crossed Main Street and passed by Thorne's Marketplace and Raven used Books, which made Susan think of the baby. Finally, they turned onto Crafts Ave.

"We should probably go into Pride and Joy while we're here," Steph said as they approached the store.

"Sure. Gosh, I remember my first time here. Northampton Pride. My *first* Pride. I think I spent about two hundred bucks in this store," Susan said as they entered.

They browsed, and Steph didn't buy anything, but Susan needed something to remember this day with, so she bought a second copy of Fried Green Tomatoes. There were some books that you just needed two copies of.

"I could have bet good money that you'd buy a book." Steph grinned.

They walked a little further, and it began to drizzle and then rain a little harder.

"It's really raining now. Better put this on," Steph said, tugging at the collar of the flannel Susan had draped over her arm.

Susan nodded and pulled it on, her keys falling out of the pocket as she did.

They both laughed, but Susan knew what this meant.

As they turned the corner, Steph pointed at her car. "Oh, good, there it is. Come on, let's stay dry together for a few minutes; it's raw out here."

Once inside, Steph started the car and turned on the heat. "You have to hear that song. Number five," she said, pushing the buttons on the CD player and turning up the volume.

Steph's hand was on the center console, and Susan hesitated for a minute but finally put her hand over Steph's. She needed to touch her one more time.

"What do you think?" Steph asked.

"I wish they'd played it last night. I see what you mean." Susan nodded. "It's sexy."

Steph ejected the CD and reached past Susan, getting the jewel case out of the glove compartment. "Here, *you* take it. Every lesbian needs a copy." She winked.

"Only if you take this. An even exchange. Besides, every lesbian should have a copy." She smiled, handing Steph the copy of *Fried Green Tomatoes* she'd just bought.

"Thanks."

They were silent for a solid minute before Steph spoke again.

"Let me drive you to your car."

Susan nodded, but didn't look over at Steph, who began to drive through the rain-soaked Main Street.

Their time together had been so perfect, and it had to end sometime, so maybe sooner was better than later. But when they reached the Iron Horse parking lot, she felt like she could cry.

"I had an amazing time, Susan. I'm so glad we had this time together," Steph said softly.

Susan teared up and didn't try to hide it, but didn't let the tears spill over either.

"I was hoping that we could maybe stay in touch. Just...I mean not like..."

"I'm not good at it, but we can try. I mean, I can at least text you my address. That's one thing that is pretty permanent, even if I do change my cell number a few times a year after I fuck things up."

"Okay," Susan replied, waiting to hear her phone ding.

"Take care of yourself, okay? I mean it. You deserve top shelf;

never forget that," Steph said, giving Susan a playful punch to the upper arm.

They'd had a brief stint as lovers and were reverting back to being buddies again; it was bittersweet.

"You take care of yourself too. Please? No driving when you're drunk. I just couldn't handle it if you weren't in this world anymore," Susan replied.

Steph nodded. "I won't make promises I can't keep, but I *will* try. Thank you for caring."

Susan opened the car door, feeling the rain mixing with her tears, and took one final look back.

"I love you," Susan said, not trying to hide the tears.

"Love ya," Steph replied and paused. "Remember, *she's* so lovely," she added, then put the car in reverse and pulled away.

Susan knew it was time to walk away from this moment, but it hurt. She sobbed the whole way home. Part of her wished she hadn't had to walk away from Steph at all. That Steph would tell her to come home with her, and they'd build a brand-new life together. She had known what the night was about; Steph had told her several times; it was just about that moment. No commitments and no further promises other than to be there with one another fully in that moment. Still, the fantasy of being taken home and loved was nice. At least she'd succeeded in doing something just for herself, even if it wasn't what she'd imagined.

As she drove through her tears, it crossed her mind that she could simply end her life right now and not have to move on from that moment at all. She could choose to die in the beautiful afterglow of this reality and never have to face anything else. She wasn't sure what else there could be beyond the moment in time she had spent with Steph, but there must have been something because deep down, she knew that wrapping her car around a tree wasn't the answer.

She pulled into the driveway, knowing that she'd made her choice to be there. Everything had changed. If there was one thing she wasn't, it was a cheater, yet here she was. But she wasn't sorry either, not in the least. Still, it told her so much. Maybe Tammy had really been trying, but there was nothing left. No hope. She never could have opened herself up to Steph in the ways she had if there'd been even a shred of hope that she could reconnect with Tammy. So why, then, was she too weak to walk away? As she entered the empty house and then stood in the hot shower, she realized she knew the answer; even if life with Tammy was terrible, she couldn't imagine that any force of nature could lead her to willingly leave Raven.

The empty house made the day stretch on like it was a week. Days like this reminded her of when she was in high school and had played hooky and watched game shows all day to escape the bullies. Now, there was something depressing about daytime television, so she turned it off, grabbed a joint, and retreated to her garden, where she spent the entire day staring.

When Tammy and Raven arrived home, Tammy simply handed the baby to Susan as if nothing unusual had happened. She'd dreaded the fight that she expected, but the calm terrified her far more. A panic rose in her chest as Tammy ascended the stairs. She could be packing her things and planning to leave with Raven. Or maybe she was going to pack Susan's things. Susan envisioned Tammy screaming at her as her clothes and books flew down the stairs. But she couldn't give in to any of that. She squeezed Raven a little more tightly, burying her nose in the baby's soft hair.

CHAPTER TWENTY-THREE

Just as Susan hadn't bothered to confront Tammy about her so-called conference, Tammy never did say one word about Susan's evening out. On one hand, Susan was relieved, but she couldn't live like this forever, either. Constantly wondering when the ax would fall might kill her before the ax itself would. Were they both just waiting for the other one to end the relationship? If she wasn't at work or asleep, she could no longer stop herself from ruminating about the possible ways that it could end, and still, she couldn't bring herself to make an appointment for a consultation with a lawyer.

Only the essentials were getting done at work, and Susan felt her performance slipping more and more each day. How could she focus on meaningless tasks when all she cared about was getting home and soaking up every moment of her daughter?

Right around the holidays last year, she'd hired a new Assistant Manager, Sherry, who was already proving to be an asset. Much like Susan, Sherry prioritized diversity in the workplace and on the shelf, which was one of the main reasons that Susan had chosen her in the first place. She was always willing to find new ways to support and accommodate the rest of the staff and was eager to learn more about management. But Susan had dropped the ball on teaching her. Sherry was patient and acted as a team player, always willing to help however Susan asked her to, even if she wasn't gaining the management skills that Susan had promised her. But Susan was disappointed in herself. Finally, she had someone she could take under her wing, and she didn't have the energy to do it.

Even worse, Kevin was starting to notice she was off and was beginning to suspect that things were more serious than she was letting on. She missed the days when she loved to come to work on Mondays; now, she just wished Kevin wasn't there to see through her.

Sitting at her desk, she massaged her tight neck with one hand while trying to make sense of the inventory order she'd just finalized. Why did it seem to be in a different language? She'd done inventory a thousand times, but now, it looked like everything was blending together, and she couldn't even calculate the simple math.

"Want a second set of eyes?" Kevin asked.

She hadn't even known he'd stepped into the office. With Sherry off on Mondays, she took every opportunity to let him run the floor and hide in her office. But now, it seemed, she couldn't even complete the paperwork that went along with the job.

"That would be great, thanks. I don't know what's wrong with me today," Susan lied, dropping her head.

"We all have days like that." After a long pause, he added, "Sometimes, we have weeks or months like that."

Susan could tell he was giving her the opportunity to open up, but she didn't budge.

Kevin scanned the inventory sheets, then lowered them to look at her. "I see a few things that are off. I can fix it if you like, then send it out; that's no problem, but is there anything else I can do to help?"

"I don't think so, but thanks," she answered, shaking her head.

He paused again, obviously choosing his words carefully. "Listen...you don't have to get into anything. I'm not asking. Like I said, we all have bad weeks. Bad months. But we can't let ourselves accept a bad life. Life can mean hard choices. We largely get to decide how things turn out," he continued, pushing a little more.

Although he had a good heart, she and Kevin weren't emotional with one another as a rule. When they weren't focused on work, they were more like a couple of teenagers together, silly and sarcastic. The depth in his voice caught her off guard.

She looked up, meeting his ice-blue eyes, which were full of something different than she'd seen before, although she wasn't sure what it was exactly.

"I'm no stranger to things falling apart. And I know those hard choices I'm talking about aren't easy when a child is involved. But you know what...after things fall apart, we always put something back together. Trust me, I have to remind myself that almost every day."

Now she understood why he was able to see right through her. She never would have known it, but he'd made it clear that looking at her was like looking in a mirror.

"I'll get these out before I leave," he said, waving the inventory sheets in the air as he walked out of the office, "but just remember...you know where I live."

"Thanks." The single throaty word was all she could manage. The last place she wanted to open the floodgate was at work.

It wasn't just Kevin she was shutting out, though. In true Susan fashion, she had chosen to suffer alone. She hadn't even written to Fiona in weeks. Some days, she couldn't even focus well enough to read as a means of escape, although she kept trying to dive back in, and she'd developed constant headaches and muscle spasms on top of the exhaustion. Some days, she wasn't sure how her body kept going. She told herself she was holding out to celebrate Raven's first birthday with her, just as she had told herself about Raven's first Christmas. Susan often found herself bargaining with whichever Goddess would listen to her, continually begging for more time with her baby.

One Sunday in early May, Susan finally spotted the tip of a daffodil poking out from under the Earth as she peered down from the nursery window. Raven was still asleep, but she couldn't wait, so she tucked the monitor under her arm and trotted down the stairs. On her way to the garden, she noticed the rapid red blink on the answering machine, which meant it was full again. She really should call her mom. Alice had been trying to get together with her for a couple of weekends, and since Tammy was working, it would be the perfect spring day to get together. Besides, if she continued to avoided her mother, it would become apparent that something was wrong. She was running out of excuses, so she called and invited her mom to brunch.

Alice arrived at Rise N Shine Diner before Susan did, and when Susan pulled up, Raven already had kicked both shoes off. Susan noted that Tammy was more patient and energetic than she was; every little thing exhausted her. The bottles that Raven threw on the floor five times in a row. The screaming that followed. Playing in the litter box now that she could crawl. Susan loved her daughter; seeing Raven grow and explore the world were the simple parts of motherhood she'd always dreamed of. Seeing Raven's face when she saw a bird. Watching the recognition in Raven's eyes when she understood a new concept. Despite the love she had for her daughter, some days were too much. It was only eleven o'clock, and she was already tired.

Raven struggled against Susan and kicked as Susan tried to put her shoes back on. Susan had gained another twenty-five pounds, and leaning into the car put additional strain on her already overtaxed back.

Her mom came up behind her. "She being crabby?" Her mom laughed, tapping the window and making a funny face at Raven.

"A little," Susan replied.

Eventually, Susan gave up, letting Raven sit there for another minute, happily kicking her socked feet around. Susan stood to meet her mother's smile, and the feeling of home settled in her heart.

"It's so nice to see you, Honey," Alice said, leaning in for a hug. "And Granny has missed you, too, Baby." She added, leaning into the car and planting a kiss on Raven's cheek.

Susan wanted to tell her mother how much she needed her right now, but instead, she simply replied, "You too."

"She tiring you out, Mamma Bear?" Alice asked.

Susan nodded but forced a smile. "It's great though. *She's* great. We've had a nice weekend watching Disney movies in the blanket fort."

"Sounds like fun. Not much has changed since you were little. Now, let's go get some food. I'm hungry."

As Alice grabbed the diaper bag from the front seat, Susan hauled Raven onto her hip, grateful that Raven had stopped crying. She wasn't sure she had it in her to be trapped in a diner of staring people with a crying baby.

"I didn't even know there was a diner here," Alice remarked as they walked toward the door.

"Only been open maybe a month, I think," Susan replied.

"I always loved the Brookfields. I'm going to live around here someday," Alice said.

"It is a nice area. Quiet. I wouldn't mind living here, either, but Tammy would hate it," Susan replied as they were seated.

Susan had ordered bacon, scrambled eggs, and French toast like she always did. Her mother got eggs benedict. That felt so fancy to Susan. As she had become a mother herself, Susan had begun to think more and more about the person Alice was aside from being her mother. Susan saw an inner fancy woman, obsessed with Princess Diana and the Royal Family, crossed with a strong, potty-mouthed country woman. The contradictions were what made Susan love her mom so much.

She wondered who her mom might have been if she had not become her mother. She thought about it a lot since Raven was born because *she'd* certainly become a different person. Surely, her mom could have been someone completely different, too, if she had lived more of her life before becoming a mother. It felt too intimate to ask Alice outright. And if Alice did share, Susan knew that she herself might break wide open.

"Can I have the salt and pepper?" Susan asked.

Alice handed her the shakers and smiled. "I love that I raised such a weird kid." She motioned to the buttery French toast with salt and pepper floating on top.

Susan laughed. "Tammy thinks it's disgusting. I don't understand people. It's delicious. How's yours?"

"So fucking good." Alice rolled her eyes. "So, hey, how are things at home?"

Susan shrugged as she chewed and didn't look up to meet her mother's eyes. She could feel the sting of tears but breathed them in and steadied herself. She wanted to tell her mom that she felt like a failure. That she was a waste of space as a human being. That her world was about to fall apart any day now. She even wanted to tell her mother about her night with Steph.

"Okay. I've actually been kind of enjoying the weekends that Raven and I have alone," Susan replied, keeping it light.

"We all need that sometimes." Although Alice smiled at her, Susan could see the sadness in her mother's eyes. It was obvious that Alice knew more than she said but didn't want to push.

Raven picked at pieces of French toast that Susan had given her, then, when she was done, began smooshing the food in between her hands instead. At least that was quiet. She could be cleaned up when she was done, Susan reasoned. As Susan and Alice talked, Raven began to utter a sound that Susan had never heard from her before.

"Kee-ee," Raven repeated over and over, smacking her messy hands against the window with some might.

Susan and Alice turned to hear Raven repeat herself one more time, seeing her eyes locked onto something in the parking lot.

"Kee-ee." This time, she nearly screamed it as she smacked the window again.

Susan leaned in even more, spotting a tiger cat strolling by.

"Oh! Kitty?" Susan asked Raven.

"Kee-ee!" Raven exclaimed again.

"Kit-ty," Susan enunciated. "Goddess knows I say that enough."

"Kitty," Alice piped in with a smile.

"She's never said that before!" Susan said in awe.

"I can tell," Alice said with a laugh. "Those moments make the exhaustion worth it, right?"

Susan nodded and listened to her daughter attempt to say kitty a few more times before she realized that she should probably clean Raven's hand and wipe the food from the window. Grateful that Raven had busied herself with toys after the waitress took the food away, Susan sat there talking to Alice for so long that they got hungry again.

"Order another tea, and we can split a muffin." Alice beamed.

"Don't have to ask me twice."

"And I don't want to hear any shit. I'm paying," Alice added.

"Mom, *I* invited *you*," Susan argued.

"Yeah, well, I'm your mother, so I win." Alice wagged her finger at Susan.

"Fine, but next time, we're bringing you for Chinese. And I'm paying," Susan insisted.

"Deal, and we should check out that little second-hand store on the end, too."

Her mother's company was everything Susan had needed for weeks. As she drove home, she looked in the rearview mirror and saw Raven bobbing her head and swinging her arms to Pink's latest album, and her soul was refreshed just a little more.

When Susan got home, she found a postcard from Fiona in the mail. Although the pencil sketch of two bears was beautiful, she only glanced at it, eager to see what Fiona had to say.

May 5, 2022

Hey Susan,

Will and I went to that marketplace last week, the one with the artsy native vibe I've told you about. Had hardly any money to our name, but something was calling me there. So, when we got there, I just "listened" and followed what I "heard." When I saw this postcard, I knew it was what had called me there. Something tells me that you are keeping yourself stuck in the mindset of the maiden these days and that you need to remember that you're a Mamma Bear. Remember how to listen. You've done this before.

Love, Fiona

Goosebumps formed as she read the term Mamma Bear; how strange that her mother had used that very same term earlier today. Susan flipped the postcard over again, this time studying the detail in the sketch. How could an artist get across such emotion? Thousands of lines added up to a mother bear and cub. The strength and nurturing came across in the mother's eyes as much as it did through her protective stance. In contrast, the cub's defenselessness and innocence were represented just as well through the way it looked out into the world, nestled into the security of her mother's form.

Briefly, she indulged in frustration. She wasn't sure what Fiona meant, exactly, about being stuck in the mindset of the maiden. But she didn't doubt that Fiona was right about one thing; she'd done this before. She believed in past lives, and something about the way that she was willing to sacrifice anything for Raven told her that the motherhood role wasn't new to her at all. She pushed aside her frustration as she looked at the postcard again and assured Fiona through the ether that she was doing the best she could every day.

But as she lay in bed that night, reflecting on her day, she could see that she hadn't been listening at all. When she thought about it, it had been months since she'd had one of her seemingly supernatural occurrences. When she thought back, the last time she'd heard it was just after Raven was born. When she'd fallen asleep, then woken up terrified that she'd been reckless to do so. The message that had reminded her she doing fine and that everything was okay. The voice that had called her Little Darlin again.

That meant she hadn't heard anything in almost a year. Was it simply that she hadn't been listening? After all, her mind had been so full of noise.

Some Witch she was. Maybe she hadn't exactly known what to make of the messages when she was still receiving them, but she was beyond disappointed now that they'd stopped coming. She'd been so hopeful that maybe the power had been passed down to her from her magical gramma. How long had she known she had a gift some might call a sixth sense?

While Fiona had called it listening, wasn't it far deeper than that? The ghost child she'd become acquainted with when she and her mom had lived with her gramma was the earliest thing that came to mind. Neither her gramma nor her mother had been surprised when Susan had told them about the little girl, and when she'd listened to them talking from the stairwell after they thought she'd fallen asleep, she'd heard them say that they'd seen her, too. They told the story of how the little girl had died in the pond in the back yard. It had been winter, so the girl's braids had frozen out straight and had still been like that when her parents had found her. The ghost's appearance made perfect sense to her after she heard that. Susan hadn't thought much of the strange braids when she'd seen the ghost; images of Pippy Longstocking had come to mind.

Thinking back, she could clearly remember how, over the years, even after she'd stopped seeing things with her eyes, she'd still been able to hear things. People arguing, followed by a gunshot in the apartment where one of her aunts lived, although her aunt had assured her no one else was there. After a while, these things had become so commonplace for her that she stopped thinking much of it. And as a teenager, she no longer saw things with her eyes or heard them with her ears, but she knew things. Like the time she was on the phone with DJ, having one of their marathon chats about nothing, and something told her to hang up immediately. The receiver was still in her hand when the phone rang. A family member was calling to say that her aunt Ruthie needed Alice to meet her at the ER, for Ruthie's husband had a massive heart attack.

As Susan recounted each memory, chills ran through her the same way they'd run through her during each of the experiences. It wasn't fear she felt, though; the majority of the experiences she had never scared her. No, she was certain that the chills she felt each time were simply the tinglings of magic.

So, now she had to wonder, when had she stopped listening? When had she stopped looking? And why did the knowings only come to her sometimes and not others?

With Raven fast asleep, Susan decided that, instead of feeling sorry for herself and accepting a magic that had gone quiet, she should take action. Other than the new house blessing she'd done on Winter Solstice, she hadn't utilized the private back yard for anything witchy. She'd been wrapped up in the magic of motherhood instead.

Susan wracked her brain for the name of the specific Goddess she wanted, nearly certain that the name began with an S. She rarely called on specific Goddesses or Gods in her rituals, other than Gaia or Persephone, mostly because she couldn't always remember each of their areas of strength. But she could clearly remember reading about the Hindu Goddess whose emergence was said to come with the vibration responsible for creating the universe, the sound known as om. Planting herself at the foot of her bookshelf, she looked through each of her books on Goddess lore until she found what she was looking for in *The Woman's Encyclopedia of Myths and Secrets.*

"Yes!" Susan said out loud, stabbing her finger onto page 894. "That's her: Sarasvati!"

Susan was reminded that Sarasvati was known not only to represent all things associated with all sound, including music and language but also personified wisdom and learning. Susan had to chuckle as she thought of the psychic CD player and psychic radio yet again.

"The Goddess of music speaks," she uttered aloud sadly. It was such a sweet memory, even if they couldn't stand one another now.

Shaking off her sadness, she rose, taking the monitor with her. Now that she knew Sarasvati's name, she was ready for her ritual. Leaving the books in a pile at her feet, she located the small, gold sound bowl on her altar and dusted it off. Since the focus of the ritual would be on sound and listening, the bowl felt necessary. Next, she took a lighter, a white chime candle, and the silver heart-shaped candle holder and practically ran down the stairs.

After settling into her chair in the garden, she struggled to pull the stone tea table in front of her chair, then had to laugh at herself for not having simply turned her chair instead. It was one of the many things that Alice had surprised her with since they'd moved into their house, and she couldn't believe she'd never considered how perfect it was for a ritual. Ed had carried it into the back yard for her, and it hadn't moved since. Now she could see why; it was far heavier than she'd expected for such a small table.

She set down her items, placing the candle in the holder and lighting the wick, and even remembering to mentally cast a circle this time. Taking the small, wooden striking stick in her hand, she closed her eyes for a moment and gathered her thoughts before she gently struck the side of the bowl. She opened her eyes again, letting the sound reverberate and dissipate. The flame flickered just a little as a soft breeze drifted through, bringing with it the scent of lilac. It surprised her, as she and Tammy had no lilac bushes in their own yard, and the next yard over was too far to carry a scent that way.

"Sarasvati, I call humbly on you today. Thank you for the sounds from the spirit world that you've already brought to help me on my journey. I am honored to have received these messages. I have faith that they are all around me, but I come to you today in the hopes that you might please increase my strength and wisdom in the area of listening more deeply for these messages. I am committed to improving if you'll offer me some support."

Now, she would wait. She knew that being dedicated to listening would mean she would have to quiet the noise in her own mind. That would be the hard part.

From that night on, her nightmares resurfaced. For the most part, they were vague. She usually couldn't remember much except for a sense of being immersed in some sort of chaos, but they all shared a common detail: the chaos always resulted in her falling a great distance. She was started each night as her body jolted her awake, leaving her even less rested when she woke up each day.

After a couple of weeks like this, time felt fuzzy. Unreal. One day blended into the next in strange ways, as if she were sleepwalking through her life. Except for her time spent with Raven, she was sure this must be what it felt like to lose touch with reality.

One night in early May, Susan had snuggled under the covers with a book of her own after she'd read Raven a bedtime story, and Raven had fallen asleep in her bed.

"Come in," Susan called when she heard a gentle knock at the door.

Tammy opened the door slightly and peeked only head inside.

"Hey. I was hoping we could talk..." Tammy whispered, noticing Raven in the bed.

"Sure," Susan replied, but she didn't budge from the doorway.

"You can come in." Susan laughed.

Tammy looked around, wide-eyed. It hadn't occurred to Susan that Tammy hadn't stepped foot in the room since she'd moved her things out. Although Tammy eyed the climbing shelves that Susan had installed for Thea, she didn't say a word. After fidgeting for a minute, her hands in her pocket, Tammy finally sat down in the chair across the room from the bed.

"What's up?" Susan asked.

"Uhh..." Tammy eyed Raven again and swallowed hard. "Raven's birthday is coming. What do you think about having a birthday party here for Raven?" Tammy asked.

"Yeah, of course," Susan replied.

"I was thinking Sunday, June second. Her birthday is on a Friday, and my parents are away the following day," Tammy said.

"Sure," Susan agreed.

"Just something small. Our families, DJ, Ashley, and Matt. There's a baby Raven plays with at daycare, Jasmine. I talk to Jasmine's mom every day when we drop off; I thought we could invite them. You could invite Kevin and his girls if you want. And I know Stacy and Tyler will probably want to come," Tammy added.

Susan snickered, shaking her head.

"What?" Tammy asked defensively, putting her hands on her hips.

"Oh, nothing. I just remember the old days. When *Tamika* said she didn't do drama." Maybe she had no proof that something was going on between Tammy and Stacy, but her gut didn't lie, and she wasn't going to sit there and let Tammy think she was stupid.

Susan could see the anger settle into Tammy's eyes.

"Let's just get through her birthday, okay?" Tammy asked. She turned to leave, then looked back over her shoulder, motioning to the book in Susan's hands.

"What are you reading?" Tammy asked, narrowing her eyes.

Susan was taken aback by the question and the changes in Tammy's energy. "*The Temple of my Familiar.* Alice Walker. It's a sequel to *The Color Purple*, and I never even knew it existed. There's a third one in the series, too," she babbled on excitedly, not realizing that Tammy had an ulterior motive and wasn't genuinely interested.

"You are just dying to be Black, aren't you?" Tammy sneered.

"What?" She asked, utterly dumbfounded.

Tammy inched closer. "You'll never be Black enough to be her mother, Susan. No matter how many books you read about Black women," she hissed. And with that, Tammy yanked Raven from the bed and left the room.

Susan froze. It felt like someone had knocked the wind out of her. There weren't even any tears as the dread reverberated through her with knowing. She'd explicitly asked Sarasvati to help her listen, and now she might be sorry she'd asked, for suddenly, she could hear Tammy loud and clear. She couldn't help but listen, whether or not she wanted to hear what Tammy was saying. Not only was she suddenly becoming casual about having Stacy in their home after Tammy's so-called conference, but now, she was telling Susan outright that she would never be Raven's mother. It was the beginning of their final end.

CHAPTER TWENTY-FOUR

Surprisingly, Raven's birthday party went smoothly. Stacy hadn't shown up after all, so Susan managed to relax and enjoy the day with her family and friends. Watching her daughter with the icing from her Winnie the Pooh cake all over her face was the moment that stood out in Susan's mind. The sweetness had made her wide-eyed, and it had been adorable to see her on a sugar high as she licked her fingers clean.

But now, as Susan cleaned up, she felt as if she could crawl out of her own skin. With the party behind them, there was only one direction for her and Tammy to go in.

As she cleared paper plates from the dining room table, Raven came toward her with a squeal, arms outstretched. She'd taken her first steps a few weeks ago and was on her wobbly feet every chance she got.

"Hi, hi!" Raven babbled as she approached, her tiny braids wiggling as she wobbled closer. She couldn't get enough of repeating this and "bye-bye" since she'd mastered them. Her party had given her the perfect opportunity. After greeting her guests, she'd spent the entire day looking at one of her moms with a question in her eyes every time someone approached a doorway, wondering if it was finally time to use "bye-bye."

As Raven got toddled closer, Susan felt goosebumps form on her arms. That yellow sundress. Tammy had dressed Raven in something else this morning, but after Raven had worn her chocolate cake, Susan had taken her upstairs and dressed her in this, not thinking much of it at the time. But now, she recognized the dress. It was the same one she'd seen in her vision years ago when she'd entertained the idea of leaving Tammy and had heard the mysterious message that urged her to choose wisely. She had chosen wisely, indeed, for if she'd left back then, she never would have had the opportunity to get to know this little gremlin, the love of her life.

Raven bumped into Susan's legs, knocking herself onto the floor with a giggle, and Susan bent down to pick her up.

"Come on. Let's go hang out in the garden, Baby Girl. The mess can wait."

She strolled through the garden and onto a patch of lawn, plopping them both down under the warm spring sun. While listening to Raven babble as she grabbed a handful of grass, Susan adored her every move. Raven quickly brought her hand to her mouth, scrunching up her face when she tasted the grass and dribbling as she spit it out.

"Susan?" She heard Tammy yell frantically.

A minute later, Tammy came out the back door, looking terrified, then relieved once she spotted them. Susan knew that look because she'd felt it so many times herself in the last few months; Tammy had been worried that Susan had taken Raven and left.

"I think she should probably go down for a nap," Tammy said as she approached them.

Susan leaned in and kissed Raven on the head, handed her to Tammy, and moved to her favorite chair on the patio. Staring off into the distance, she wondered if she could make reality disappear if she sat in her safe space for eternity. As if in reply to her thought, the sky grew dark and unleashed pouring rain. Quickly, she dashed into the kitchen and wiped the drops from her face. Where the hell had that come from? It had been sunny all day. She surveyed the messy dining room but didn't feel like cleaning. Instead, she let the couch swallow her.

"She's asleep," Tammy said, sitting down in the chair next to her a few minutes later.

They sat in silence for a long time until Tammy broke the

silence. "We should talk."

With those three words, Susan knew her life was about to change. "I know," Susan replied.

"I don't want to hurt you more; I honestly don't," Tammy said.

"I think the important thing is that we don't hurt Raven," Susan said quietly.

"I agree."

"So?" Susan asked, finally looking up to meet Tammy's eyes.

"I mean, we both know that we're...that this is over. I think we need to move on," Tammy said.

"I need you to tell me why," Susan replied. She wanted to ask what she had done wrong. What she hadn't done right. Why she wasn't enough.

Even as Susan sat there, thinking she had accepted that the end had come, her mind raced with possibilities. Stacy hadn't shown up to the party, right? It had to mean something. Maybe Tammy had broken it off with her. If Tammy could confess, and if she and Stacy weren't still involved and Tammy was sorry, maybe, just maybe, they could salvage this. Rebuild their family. Of course, it would mean she would have to confess about cheating on Tammy, too. But, wasn't it possible that they could get through this if only they could both admit how they'd each played a part in breaking the promises they'd made to one another?

"I'm pretty sure you already know," Tammy said.

"No, I need to hear you say it. I need you to tell me everything," Susan replied.

"Susan."

"You can't just leave me feeling like I'm imagining things. I think I deserve that much respect," Susan said.

Tammy nodded. "I know I messed up. Bad. It started after the fourth month that I didn't get pregnant. With the hormones, I swear I was unable to think straight. I was desperate."

"And?" Susan asked, confused.

"I...needed someone to comfort me. Plus, it gave me hope that..." Tammy started.

"Wait a minute," Susan interrupted, raising her voice. "You needed someone to *comfort* you? Are you honestly telling me that you think *I* wasn't there to comfort you through that? That I didn't hold you when the hormones made you a mess? When your heart broke each time there was no pink line? My heart was breaking, too, you know. But I *was* there for you."

"No, I'm not saying you weren't. You know what that's like, though. You can't always get everything you need from one person." Tammy paused. "Wait, that's not what I mean. This is getting... I'm trying to be honest here. I admitted I messed up. I know what I did was awful. Unforgivable. Especially with Raven to think about. I'm not just making excuses. I'm trying to tell you how I was seeing it then. He reached out to comfort me, and that felt good. But, as distorted as I can see it was now, in my desperation, I also thought it was another chance for a baby, too. And then, I was pregnant and didn't know what to do," Tammy explained.

Susan shook her head in a fog. Tammy wasn't making any sense. What the fuck was she talking about? *Who* was she talking about? She sat there trying to understand. Then, it hit her. She could picture Tyler's face, and she knew. Raven had the same face. Standing up suddenly, one hand over her chest and the other resting on the couch to keep her shaking body upright, Susan felt as if her heart would explode. It was racing so fast; she gasped a few times. Was she actually dying? She closed her eyes and willed herself to live, waiting for her breath to regulate.

"Susan..." Tammy reached toward her as Susan opened her eyes.

Susan tried to take a step away, but her feet wouldn't move. Tammy put her hand on Susan, as if to hold her steady, but Susan yanked her arm away from the touch.

"But you're... Are you telling me that Tyler is Raven's father?" Susan asked, sobbing on her words.

"I'm so sorry. So, so sorry..." Tammy said, also in tears now. "I thought you already knew that, though. You seemed to know. You said..."

But Susan wasn't able to grasp anything Tammy was saying anymore. All she could hear was the messenger she hadn't heard in so long. The one that she'd summoned to return to her. It repeated over and over, both gently and with conviction.

"It's time for you to go. It's time for you to go."

She must have listened to it a dozen times before she could will her feet to carry her away from the living room and up the stairs.

She reached the top of the stairs, and Tammy was right at her heels. Quietly, Susan opened the door to the nursery, took two steps inside, and looked down at Raven sleeping, taking in every detail. Her yellow sundress. Her stiff little braids going every which way. Her slow, peaceful breathing. And it was then that she felt her core begin to collapse like the beginnings of a black hole.

She heard the voice again, only it was a little more insistent this time.

"It's time for you to go."

She looked up to find a mixture of terror and ferocity on Tammy's face, as if she wouldn't hesitate to attack Susan if she felt she needed to.

Susan shook her head and whispered, "We already said the important thing is that we don't hurt Raven. I'm not going to..." She paused. "It's time for me to go." And with that, she walked out of the nursery, closed the door, then closed herself up in her bedroom.

As quickly and quietly as she could, she gathered the essentials first. After she took Cocoa out of the nightstand and put her in the backpack, she dragged the cat carrier and a large duffle bag from the closet and began to throw some things in, although she wasn't very thoughtful about what she included. When the bag was full, she slung it and her backpack over one shoulder and grabbed the carrier in her other hand. Looking around, she tried to determine if she needed anything else but knew that nothing she could put in the bag would make a bit of difference.

When she stepped into the hall, Tammy was still in front of the nursery door and watched her as she went into the upstairs bathroom. Taking a trash bag from under the sink, she dumped the entire litter box, litter and all, into the bag. Tammy continued to watch her every move as her shaky legs brought her downstairs. She set her belongings at the foot of the stairs, retrieved Thea's food from the kitchen, then scooped the sleeping kitten from the couch and put her inside the carrier.

"What are we going to do...?" Susan asked, pointing up the stairs toward the nursery.

Tammy shrugged. "Tyler wants to be a real father. Wants to be a real family. A real, Black family. A normal family. Without the drama. You *said* you didn't want to hurt Raven."

"I'm her mother, too. I have the right to..." Susan started.

Tammy interrupted her, a cold look on her face. "Actually, no, you don't. You have *no* rights."

"Tammy!"

"You have to go," Tammy pointed out the door, stone-faced.

"It's time for you to go." Susan heard it again and could have sworn she felt a gentle hand on her shoulder.

But she had to get one last thing out before she left. "You know...we both said we didn't want to become our mothers, but I never saw it coming. Looks like you turned into your father instead."

She savored the pained look that spread across Tammy's face before she descended the stairs and loaded Thea and her bags into the car as Tammy watched from the porch. For a brief moment, she envisioned herself going back and charging full-force at Tammy, knocking her down the front steps. Maybe she'd break her neck. Or maybe Susan could do that herself with her bare hands. But no, she had to remind herself she wasn't that kind of Witch.

Shaking, she started the car. *That* was why she had to go. Thoughts like that. She could see the same thoughts in Tammy's eyes when she'd been standing in the nursery. Things could easily get ugly, and after her own childhood experiences, she just wouldn't put Raven through any form of terror. She remembered leaving her father in the middle of the night and all of the times before that when they should have left. The screaming and the cops. The hiding and the fear. She didn't want Raven ever to know a moment even close to that, even if she couldn't understand how her heart would keep beating if she walked away from her daughter.

She felt as if she was in a trance as she drove. The streetlights reflecting from the rain-soaked roads made this all feel even more unreal. She avoided the highway at first, simply weaving her way around the city with no destination in mind.

She had to think. Where should she go? Driving probably wasn't her best option, seeing as she couldn't stop the incessant thought that she had another opportunity to wrap herself around a tree. Of course, she wasn't actually going to do that; she just needed a plan.

Barnes and Noble. She just had to focus on getting herself to work tomorrow morning. But where would she go until then? She had to get through the next twelve hours, but it felt like an eternity. The city had plenty of hotels, but could she find one that she could sneak the kitten into? The fancy hotels downtown would suck her money dry quickly, and she wasn't sure how much she had in her bank account since she usually put at least half of her paycheck in Tammy's account.

There was no question that she could always go to her mother's, even though they had a full house. The same went for DJ; if she showed up on her doorstep at any hour, there was no doubt she wouldn't turn them away, despite DJ's allergy to cats. Hell, even Kevin had told her that his door was open to her. But she wasn't ready to let anyone know that she'd failed as a wife and a mother by the age of twenty-seven. Holding onto what little dignity she had wasn't negotiable.

Finally, she settled on the Worcester City Motel. It was known to be a little sleazy, but it wasn't in the worst area and would be cheap. She could easily sneak Thea inside with the setup.

She gingerly pulled into the parking lot, trying to avoid the massive pothole filled with rain. Only when she parked did she realize that Thea was mewing incessantly from her cage and rattling the metal gate.

She leaned into the back seat, stuck her fingers into the cage, and rubbed Thea's head.

"Just a few more minutes, Baby," she crooned.

Mustering the energy, she walked into the motel office. The bell on the door dinged, and she almost had to laugh at the cliché when a greasy old man wearing a tight Hawaiian shirt greeted her from behind the front desk. But there was a vacancy, and it was only sixty dollars per night. Besides, she was too exhausted to think of an alternative.

After filling out the paperwork, Susan let herself into room 44. She was relieved that, although it was still light out, there didn't seem to be anyone around to see the pet carrier. She locked the door behind her and took Thea out, snuggling into her fur and absorbing her purrs. Thank Gaia for those kitty vibes.

She was thankful that the room wasn't as bad as she expected. Everything was worn out and old, but the prominent smell of bleach put her at ease. After a few minutes, Thea began to wiggle in Susan's arms, so she reluctantly set her down. Thea immediately dashed around the room, wiggling her butt as she went, then tried to get under the bed. To Susan's relief, the bed was enclosed at the bottom, which prevented the kitten from disappearing underneath.

After another trip to the car, Susan set out the litter box, fed Thea, pulled down the covers, and fell onto the mattress. Once she lay down, everything still intact inside of her collapsed; the black hole became infinite. Would she never see her daughter again? Was it too late to go to a lawyer now? Picturing Raven in her crib, she couldn't breathe. She sat up in panic, her chest so tight that, once again, she was sure she was dying. She wouldn't make it if she could never hold her baby again. Though a part of her welcomed death, she considered calling 911. Clearly, her will to live was still present. She gasped in a few dozen breaths until she no longer felt she was in immediate danger. Fiona always reminded her that she tended to get into trouble when she convinced herself she needed to solve everything at once. At that moment, Raven was safely asleep in her bed. At least Tammy was no longer in such a dark place that she couldn't care for Raven. For tonight, that had to be enough.

Complete exhaustion took over, and she was able to get a few hours of sleep. When she woke up, it was dark outside, and she could feel the obnoxious bass from the next room throughout her body. It took her a minute to remember where she was, and once she did, the panic threatened to take over again.

Thea was asleep on her chest. Focused on the kitty vibes to help her stay grounded, she was able to regulate her breathing. Turning her head to look at the ancient clock on the nightstand, she couldn't determine exactly what time it was since only the first two digits still flipped as time passed. It was eleven something; she knew that much. Easing Thea off of her, she retrieved her phone from her backpack. She considered texting Tammy to beg her not to take Raven away. To bargain with her however she had to. But it was nearly midnight.

Feeling the rumble in her belly, she wished she'd stopped somewhere to get something to eat. She would have to wait until morning now because she wasn't venturing out at this hour. Not from this place.

As she walked to the bathroom, pain shot through her feet. The moonlight poked in through the slats of the broken, yellowed blinds, and she could see that Thea had scattered litter everywhere. When she returned, she flipped the television on and mindlessly watched The Twilight Zone, hoping it would offset the bass. Through broken sleep, she woke to strange black and white images on the television, each time having to remind herself where she was again. When she finally saw the first hints of light in the sky, she rose from the bed and fed Thea again.

While she wasn't thrilled about leaving Thea at the motel all day, she knew she didn't have much choice. Aside from Thea, her job was all she had left. Before she left, she stopped by the office and paid for a second night, then hung the do not disturb sign on the door. She just hoped that housekeeping didn't ignore the sign and she didn't return to find Thea squashed dead on Route Nine.

After a quick shower, she picked up some breakfast and drove through the ATM to check her balance, then finally arrived at work feeling like a zombie. She sat at her desk, questioning how far $2155 would go. At least she could look forward to payday on Friday. Still, it wasn't much money to build a new life with. When Kevin asked what was up, she made up a story about Raven being up all night. What she wouldn't give to have been up all night with her daughter. At least there would be a decent reason to feel like death. She had to keep herself from crying each time Raven crossed her mind.

She opened up her backpack and flipped through the notepad

where she'd written down the numbers of the attorneys who might be able to help her. She had so much to think about.

While Kevin was on the floor, she spent the morning searching Craigslist and rental sites for apartments instead of doing her work, hiding her screen each time he ventured back into the office. The apartments seemed to be at one end of the extreme or the other, run-down or downright filthy in unsafe neighborhoods or simply unaffordable. It seemed there was nothing in between. As she searched and jotted down phone numbers and notes, she did the math to see how much she would need to rent even a shitty place. Had rents really gone up so much since she'd last rented alone? Some of these places were almost as much as their mortgage.

By the end of the workday, she wasn't even close to finishing anything that she'd attempted to do. Even if she didn't have so many personal things to attend to, she would never have been able to focus. She would just have to make some excuse about why everything would be late.

As she relived her last conversation with Tammy, pieces of the puzzle that had been their life came together. Thinking back, she remembered the signs she'd been getting ever since the day Tyler had helped Tammy get the peds position. The feeling in her gut when Tammy used to text him from their bed. Then, she remembered a specific night: Millenium New Year's Eve when she and Tammy had sex after Tammy had come home late and acted so strangely. The same feeling of nausea she'd had when Tammy had touched her that night washed through her body now. Tammy had lied to her yesterday; she had cheated on her with Tyler that New Year's Eve night. How many times over the years had she ignored her gut when she knew something wasn't right? She remembered Halloween, too, when she brought Raven to the hospital in her costume. The way Tyler had looked at Raven and Tammy had acted so awkwardly. She'd been a fool for so long, but the details of how Tammy had ruined their relationship didn't matter. All that mattered was Raven now. Finding a way to keep Raven in her life.

There was another thing, too. Suddenly, she saw Tammy's ever-present loathing for bisexual women in a new light. She'd never once considered it might be an internalized thing.

After barely getting through the day, Susan decided that there was no way she could work again the following day. Physical pain consumed her as she thought about Raven. She had nothing left and couldn't try to act human when she needed some time to gather herself, not to mention build a new life.

She called Paula before she left for the day, trying to make her voice sound even more wretched than she already felt. She needed a few days to get her shit together. As always, Paula was supportive, telling her to take whatever time she needed to recover.

She returned to the motel with a bag of groceries and more litter for Thea, relieved that she'd decided to take a couple of sick days. It took a little pressure off and bought her some time. Although she was eager to snuggle with Thea, one thing had been on her mind all day: the one thing that might help her get through another night without tucking her baby in. Not wanting to set the smoke detectors off, she poked her head outside the door. No one was around in the parking lot, so she took a joint from her backpack and lit it up. Besides, she highly doubted that pot smoking was the worst thing happening at the Worcester City Motel.

With the first puff, she felt less tense, and by the time she finished half the joint, she found a peaceful reprieve from her own mind. She sat there for a long time, new, slower thoughts in her head, but mostly, how grateful she was for the effects of the marijuana. It was funny; some people used the phrase, *out of your mind* as if it was a bad thing, but that was exactly her goal when she smoked a joint: to get out of her mind and into her soul.

Once inside, Susan stole a quick snuggle with Thea, then spent several hours crying, eating, and looking at the picture of Raven that she carried in her backpack. Although she would have to pull herself together first thing in the morning, wallowing in her pain felt like a necessary stage of grief. It had only been one day, and she felt like she was dying.

Desperate, she texted Tammy.

Please, even though you and I won't work, I'm just asking you to let me stay in Raven's life. Please text me or call me so we can talk.

She stared at the phone screen for hours, but as she expected, a reply never came. Eventually, sleep found her. Without worrying about waking up in time for work, Susan slept for eleven hours straight, unsure how she could still feel tired. Focusing on finding a new place would keep her mind off the baby. The notepad with the lawyer's numbers stared at her all day, but she couldn't bring herself to make the calls. Besides, she wouldn't have a case at all unless she had a place to live.

She spent the entire morning on the phone about apartments, feeling like she had made no progress whatsoever when noon came. Most landlords wouldn't accept pets. Some apartments had already been spoken for, and one would be ready for showing until July first. She left messages for several others. Every night at the grimy motel would mean her money would continue to dwindle a little more. She made a mental list of the things she would need to start over again, but it occurred to her that she still had the keys to the house, and Tammy was at work.

Since the post-lunch hour rush had passed, it was a quick drive. Too quick. When she pulled up, her stomach churned. After how extreme Tammy had been, she was almost surprised when her key turned in the lock. She stepped inside, looking around. Somehow, the house already looked different to her. It was so quiet that she could hear her own breathing as she stood there, afraid to move.

While she was almost certain that she had some legal right to be there, another part of her feared the cops might come at any moment. Tammy had always made it clear that she would do whatever she needed to get what she wanted, and Susan wasn't sure what she was capable of now that she was determined to build a *real family*. She didn't want to be here any longer than she had to.

Since Tammy hadn't replied to last night's text, the first order of business was leaving a note for her. Even if it turned out to be useless, she had to know she tried to fight for her daughter. She pulled a blank sheet of paper from the kitchen drawer, placed it on the counter, and stood over it with a pen for several minutes, trying to conjure the perfect words.

Dear Tammy,

Despite our human imperfections and the mistakes we've made, I know that neither of us wants to hurt Raven. I'm asking you to remember the feeling you had when you knew I would be your daughter's second mom. Remember the magic you believed I could help her find in the world. It might not look the way we thought it would, but you and I are her whole world. Let's come together and find a way to give her a life where she knows more magic than pain.

Love, Susan

It felt inadequate and far more poetic than she'd intended, but it would have to do. This wasn't a spell. No matter how clearly she set her intention, she couldn't control how Tammy would respond to her appeal. She put the note on the refrigerator, intentionally choosing the photo magnet of the three of them to hold it up and hoping Tammy still had a heart.

She walked through the living room and dining room and back to the kitchen. Not much she spotted seemed worth taking. There were a hundred sentimental things she considered, but most of them were things that she and Tammy had acquired together. She didn't want to remember. Surveying the contents of the cupboards, she removed a few boxes of cereal and a single mug that had been hers when she and Tammy had moved in together. She would need a bowl for cereal, too, but taking a part of the set didn't feel right, so she settled on a plastic storage bowl.

After hauling Big Blue out of the closet, she found a couple of smaller totes in the basement and brought them upstairs, filling them with as many books as she could fit, her Little House on the Prairie box set, and her favorite items from her altar. But when she tried to lift the tote of books, she couldn't manage and had to take several trips to the car with armloads of books until she could carry what remained in the tote. She filled a few garbage bags with blankets, pillows, and clothes and added the bags and a few more of Thea's things into the car.

On her last trip inside, she considered taking the television from the bedroom but simply didn't have the energy. Remembering that she'd hidden the cookie jar underneath her bed after Tammy had threatened to smash it, she returned to the bedroom, getting down on all fours. As she reached for the cookie jar, she spotted *Goodnight Moon* and pulled that out, too. Raven had liked the story so much that Susan had brought home a second copy for the nights that Raven fell asleep in her bed.

She had to see the nursery one more time before she left. She looked around the little yellow room, taking in the characters. She might never see Raven babbling away from her crib at the Cheshire Cat or rock her to sleep beneath the trellis of flowers again.

She turned the lock, shutting the door; there was nothing else she wanted. With the cookie jar in one hand and the book tucked under her other arm, she said her final goodbye to the little white cape before she drove away. She drove back to the hotel, her backseat full of her belongings, but didn't cry. It seemed there were just no tears left inside of her. Maybe she was actually dead.

On Wednesday, she woke up feeling even worse. She'd never

smoked as much pot in her life as she had the previous night, and her head felt heavy. Still, it had been worth it. It was already past ten o'clock. She hoped maybe she had slept through a message from Tammy, but when she looked, nothing had come through. She had no plan and a fading sense of hope.

After scarfing down an entire box of froot loops, she stared at her phone for hours as the television droned on in the background. Before she knew it, it was one o'clock. Raven would probably be napping at daycare by now, and Tammy would be busy on the floor. Again, she tried to think of the perfect words to reach Tammy. Another heartfelt plea. An apology. Whatever it took. Unsure if another failure to reply or an outright refusal to let her be in Raven's life was worse, she resorted to total surrender of her ego.

Please, Tammy, I'm begging you! I'm literally begging you to consider me and Raven. Call me or text me. We have to be able to find a solution that works for everyone.

When her phone rang later that afternoon, she felt a flurry of hope; maybe Tammy was reaching out to her. Instead, it was one of the landlords she'd left a message for, wanting to know if she was still interested in seeing the apartment on May Street. The landlord said he would be showing it tomorrow afternoon. He sounded every bit as greasy as the motel manager, and that end of May Street was just about the last place she wanted to live. But she couldn't turn any option away, so she jotted down the address and agreed to meet him at one o'clock.

An hour later, she'd dozed off and dreamt that Tammy had called her to reconcile and that after returning home, the four of them, Thea too, spent the evening watching the sunset from the garden. Her phone rang again, jolting her from her slumber. Once again, it wasn't Tammy. Waking up to discover that the happy scenario had been only a dream was far worse than waking up from even the worst nightmare.

Instead, it was another landlord asking if she was still interested in the basement studio apartment they had listed, this time on Camp Street. The woman stated that Susan was the first person she'd called about it and could see it this evening after supper if she was available. She tried to remember where Camp Street was, but it didn't matter at this point. She had to follow up on every lead, and chances were that wherever it was, it had to be better than May Street.

She left the motel at four to give herself plenty of time to get lost since she was awful with directions. The woman on the phone told her it was off Cambridge Street, but that still left a lot of room for error.

As she drove through the city and neared the area of Cambridge Street, she was whisked back to her life before Tammy. It turned out Camp Street was close to where she, Michael, and Steph used to hang out at Steph's apartment on Canterbury Street. The area was busy and loud enough to make her uncomfortable, but it still wasn't one of the worst areas either. She parked her car on the dead-end street, double-checked that she'd gotten the house number correct, and knocked on the door.

A raspy-sounding woman answered, and Susan introduced herself. She said her name was Iris, and she looked about eighty. Susan couldn't place the smell that wafted from Iris as she spoke.

After they talked about the details of the apartment, Iris brought her to the side hall and motioned to the flight of stairs.

"I'm too fucking old to do stairs, dear, but you go ahead and check it out. Like I told you on the phone, it's nothing special but livable," Iris said.

As Susan descended the stairs, she hoped someone wasn't downstairs waiting to kill her. But the only thing she saw once she reached the bottom was walls covered with the kind of tacky brown paneling that had been popular around the time she was born.

There was a tiny galley kitchen and a bathroom with a stand-up shower that she was pretty sure she could squeeze into if she angled herself just right. The whole place had only two windows and needed some bleach, but she decided she could make it work.

She hiked herself back up the stairs to find Iris sitting on the front steps with a giant glass of amber liquid in her shaking hand. She didn't seem to hear Susan there, so Susan cleared her throat. Still nothing.

"Did you say it's available right away?" Susan asked.

"Oh, you nearly killed me, for fuck's sake," Iris stood up quickly and nearly fell backward onto the sidewalk. "I think I dozed off." She laughed.

Susan was pretty sure she was, in fact, drunk.

"Yeah, it's available now. Is it just the kind of palace you were hoping for?" Iris asked with a snicker. "You seem ordinary, like me, so if you don't need anything fancy, just a place to lay your head, you can have it. You seem like a nice enough girl."

Iris was definitely a character, but she seemed harmless enough. Rent was seven hundred dollars, with electricity included, and Iris only wanted first and last. She wouldn't do a credit check and was offering it immediately. Most importantly, she allowed cats.

"I'd love to take it. I have the money for first and last with me now," Susan explained.

"Dear Lord, girl, you shouldn't walk around with that kind of money in your pocket. Come on." Iris waved her inside and handed her sign a gin-soaked rental agreement.

While her bleak new existence wasn't exactly a dream come true, she fell into the hotel bed with some relief that night. It was a step. Besides, Iris had been right. She *was* just ordinary. How had she ever believed she could end up anywhere but where she was now? She was a cliché. A once small-town girl who thought she could rise up, but instead, had crashed back down to the reality that she wasn't any better than living in a dingy apartment in a mean city, with only a cat and a decent job. And she'd reached a couple more conclusions: she would never call an attorney, and Tammy would never respond to her messages. She was a coward, and Tammy wouldn't settle for any less than her vision of a *real family*, which didn't include a White mom on the side.

As she thought about it more and more, she couldn't fathom how they could make any sort of arrangement work out with Tyler in the picture. She had meant what she said; the most important thing was that Raven not get hurt. Maybe it was best for Raven this way. She deserved better than chaos and confusion, even if she would hurt for a little while as a result of losing one of her moms.

Besides, she'd had enough opportunities to take legal action since Raven had been born. Losing Raven was the universe's punishment for her fear and inaction. Her punishment for cheating. She had made her choices and just had to live with the unimaginable pain of losing her daughter. At least she had Thea and her books. Besides, Raven wasn't the first precious thing the universe had ripped from her, and Susan was sure she wouldn't be the last.

She counted her money; after the motel and groceries and, now, first and last month's rent, she had less than five hundred dollars left to her name until Friday.

As Susan moved in the following day, she noticed something she had missed when she'd gone to see the apartment before: a cemetery entrance at the end of the dead-end street. It comforted her, for she could relate to the dead far better than the living.

Her first night there was much quieter than she thought. All day, she'd heard every slipper scuffle along the floor upstairs and then the springs of Iris's mattress when she went to bed. In a few more hours, she was left alone with the silence when the traffic slowed and the music stopped. She lay under her blankets on the air mattress she'd bought from Wal-Mart, and Thea lay beside her.

First, her mind began to race, and then her heart followed suit. She couldn't be here. This wasn't her life. Not that she was planning on staying here long, but she had to wonder what the likelihood was that she might wake up one morning and find that Iris had pickled herself, then dropped dead in her sleep.

She flipped the blanket off and shot up, rousing Thea. One thing was certain. No matter how little money she had, she would have to invest in a new television and a VCR. She would never make it with this kind of quiet, and she had to make it. She wasn't sure what there was left to live for, but she knew she wasn't done. Thoughts of suicide had been a part of her reality since she was seven, so she was used to it most of the time, but some nights, they were harder to fight. At least if she had something to watch, some noise, she might make it. She could pop in her Little House on the Prairie tapes and lose herself in that world.

But what could she do now? Right now, to keep herself alive? She took the lid off Big Blue and rifled around, pulling out a pen and a sheet of crinkled stationery with pastel moths she couldn't remember buying.

June 6, 2002

Dear Fiona,

It finally happened. I lost Raven. I'm to blame, too. For a million reasons. I knew Tammy was cheating, so I cheated, too, but she and I were over long before that happened. I just don't know how I will get through this, so I had to write to you to try to stay sane because whenever I write to you, it's as though you can already hear me, and I feel a little less alone. The good news is I am living near a cemetery again. Goddess knows the darkness keeps calling me back, no matter how hard I try to find the light. I have nothing left, though. I'm not even sure I am real anymore. Or if I ever was. I'm soul tired, Fiona. I just want someone to give me a pass to go – out of this world for once and for all.

She couldn't finish the letter. How icy and hardened she felt as she'd written it terrified her. If she didn't get some fresh air, this might be the moment she finally gave in to the voice that had been in her head for the last twenty years. She tiptoed up the stairs and out the door, finding solace among the gravestones. After walking endlessly under the moonlight, she thought maybe she was tired enough to sleep now and went back to her new basement home.

When she reached the foot of the stairs, she saw something lying in the middle of the floor. She stepped closer to see what it was. She felt her jaw drop when she saw the same picture of her gramma that had emerged as she was moving out of her old apartment. The one she was still certain she'd never seen before that day. She picked it up and noticed how the energy in her body shifted as she held it. Once again, it felt as if her gramma was trying to send her a message. But what? She couldn't reach a conclusion, so she put the picture back into Big Blue and snapped the lid on.

She snuggled in with Thea again, trying to quiet her mind. The walk in the cemetery had helped some, but now, the picture had her mind racing. Could a message from her gramma save her? If only Fiona lived close, she wouldn't be so utterly alone. Susan had no doubt that Fiona would have stayed up talking to her all night if she needed her to. Or maybe, if Steph was closer, she could take care of her again. Surely, there was someone out there who could save her. She'd once thought Tammy could save her, but instead, she'd become increasingly lost as she fell more deeply in love. Still, even now, other than spending four years of her life without kitty vibes, she could honestly say that she didn't regret her relationship with Tammy. How could she? It had given her Raven. Just like Fiona had told her, she'd begun to find everything she'd ever been looking for in her daughter. But what was she supposed to do with herself now that Raven had been ripped away from her? Now that she was no longer a mother?

In her gut, Susan knew that there was just one answer: she had to save herself. It was just that she hadn't the faintest idea how.

Author's Note

I'm very open about the fact that my main character, Susan, represents me and my journey. Although fictionalized, the books in the Spirit Warrior series hold so many true details. Since I was fifteen, I've known that I want to tell my story, and I've spent the last 30-plus years trying to figure out how to find a balance between truth and fiction. Truth is not only an individual thing, but it's everchanging. The truths told here are a perspective, a snapshot in time.

Spirit Warrior is not just a fiction series that depicts my journey but a movement to encourage others to choose healing. We all have a story to tell, and storytelling is a part of healing. The moment you choose healing, you become a Spirit Warrior.

Spirit Warriors are those resilient souls who do more than just survive as they resist the forces that threaten to destroy their divine energy. They transform their pain into something beautiful, healing not only themselves but the world around them.

While Susan's realization that she must save herself is a big step in her spiritual evolution, that was only the beginning for her. She has much more wisdom and growth ahead, which will be represented later in the series. I invite you to follow Susan throughout the Spirit Warrior Series as she journeys through the stages of the Maiden, the Mother, and the Crone. You will also meet Susan's ancestors and those who journey alongside her as they learn what it means to be souls in human form.

Author photo by Sam Smalley

I'm Tracey Love, author, poet, and book coach. I live in Massachusetts with my wife, Michelle, and cat, Storm. As a scholar, I studied Psychology, Women's Studies, and Education and worked in various careers that weren't a fit for me before returning to my true passion, writing. I completed my MA in English and Creative Writing at SNHU in 2016.

I'm a hippie-soul who honors my divinity and a woman haunted by the pain of my humanity. I've been a Spirit Warrior all my life – battling those things that threaten to destroy my spirit. As a Witch, the words and the energy I put out into the world are my most potent forms of magic. With a passion for improving the world, I work to foster community, peace, freedom, love (especially self-love), and the expression of differing realities. Through my work, I encourage folks to discover the inner wisdom that comes through strengthening mind, body, and spirit.

My future goals are simple - I will continue to master my craft and share my writing with the world. By taking in positive energy from a variety of spiritual sources, I will seek deeper wisdom to become the best version of myself. I will build community, have adventures, enjoy nature, and spoil my cats as I transition into a crone alongside my wife and the rest of my soul family.

I invite my fellow Spirit Warriors to connect with me:
Website: https://traceyloveauthor.com/
https://www.facebook.com/traceyloveauthor
https://www.instagram.com/traceyloveauthor/
https://linktr.ee/traceylove

www.ingramcontent.com/pod-product-compliance
Lightning Source LLC
LaVergne TN
LVHW091248110826
845146LV00002BA/469

* 9 7 9 8 9 8 9 3 6 9 3 0 0 *